A Paranormal Anthology

SHIFTERS

Stories by

Robin Bayne
Jennifer Dunne
Myra Nour
Jane Toombs

Paranormal

New Concepts   Georgia

Be sure to check out our website for the very best in fiction at fantastic prices!

When you visit our webpage, you can:

* Read excerpts of currently available books
* View cover art of upcoming books and current releases
* Find out more about the talented artists who capture the magic of the writer's imagination on the covers
* Order books from our backlist
* Find out the latest NCP and author news--including any upcoming booksignings by your favorite NCP author
* Read author bios and reviews of our books
* Get NCP submission guidelines
* And so much more!

We also have contests and sales regularly, so be sure to visit our webpage to find the best deals in ebooks and paperbacks!

Visit our webpage at:
www.newconceptspublishing.com

New Concepts Publishing
4729 Humphreys Rd.
Lake Park, GA 31636

ISBN 1-58608-552-2
Midnight's Door, copyright© April 2002, Jane Toombs
Demon Killer, copyright© April 2002, Mary Nour
The Tower, copyright© April 2002, Jennifer Dunne
Honor Bound, copyright© April 2002, Robin Bayne

Cover art by Eliza Black, copyright © April 2002

NCP books are available at special quantity discounts for bulk purchases for sales promotions, premiums, fund raising, or educational use. For details, write, email, or phone New Concepts Publishing, 4729 Humphreys Rd., Lake Park, GA 31636, ncp@newconceptspublishing.com, Ph. 229-257-0367, Fax 229-219-1097.

First NCP Paperback Printing: April 2002
10 9 8 7 6 5 4 3 2 1

Printed in the United States of America

MIDNIGHT'S DOOR

Jane Toombs

Dara Castaneda stared through the windshield down the twisting curves of the Grapevine where the Golden State Freeway dropped into the San Joaquin Valley. The pavement undulated, not a road at all but a giant snake, she could feel the gray SUV being lifted in its coils, in a moment they'd be crushed inside....

She screamed, clutching at Jo-Jo.

The SUV swerved; he cursed. "Damn near hit a truck. Get her out of the front."

Dara struggled with a red-bearded man, a stranger, who reached from the back and hauled her over the seat. "Take it easy," he drawled. "Nothing's after you."

His voice calmed her a little and she let him put her down next to Cindy. He sat on her other side. "Eric the Red," she said. "Who are you?"

"My name's Nick Owens. Been with you since Castaic."

"Yeah," Cindy put in. "Don't you remember saying we needed thirteen? That's when Jo-Jo spotted this biker at the gas stop. His hog's on the trailer back there."

Dara didn't remember.

"Jo-Jo said redheads were the devil's own and he'd bring us luck," Cindy added.

Dara took a deep breath. She'd forgotten. On purpose. Because of where they were going. Her fault. She never should have mentioned Wolf House to Jo-Jo, who was into Satanism and who knew what else. The ruins were too bloody close to where she'd grown up. Now the twelve of them—no, thirteen with Nick—were crammed into this SUV and there was no way in hell she'd be able to convince Jo-Jo to change his mind about camping out in the ruins of Wolf house and doing his thing. Ritual, he called it. All too soon they'd be passing Vida's grave. Dara shuddered.

Take another upper? She started to reach for her jacket, on the floor in a pile with other clothes. Cindy's black cat, Dido, sleeping atop the pile, opened green eyes and gave her an enigmatic look.

A yes or a no look? Dara caught sight of herself in the long narrow mirror affixed to the side of the vehicle. Dark-circled hazel eyes, long, tangled dark hair, high cheek bones—she looked wasted, reminding herself of Vida and grimaced. Her dead twin was the last thing in the world she wanted to think about, but her thoughts clustered around Vida like blow flies. Her twin, identical except for her twisted body and mind, had died at thirteen. Dara wondered if that's why she'd told Jo-Jo they needed to be thirteen.

Those thirteen years had been long and horrible. Vida had destroyed her family as surely as the 1954 earthquake had leveled Wolf House, something her grandmother remembered and often recounted.

"That's when they all left, the Voleks, those that weren't killed, and good riddance 'twas. We always suspected they were tainted. Specially their twins."

Tainted could mean anything. Like Vida. Dara had left this area when she was eighteen. Because in her dreams her twin mind-called her from the grave. While alive, Vida had never learned to speak, but dead she whispered to Dara at night. After Dara woke up one night and found herself in the cemetery with no idea how she'd gotten there, she packed up and left. For good. So what was she doing back here only two years later?

She could feel her heart still speeding from the last upper, her brain still revved up. She didn't want giant snakes to loom up in front of her again. Maybe lay off taking another pill. Out the side window she could see the Sierra peaks to her right. To the east. When she lived in the Valley, most of the kids she knew went to summer camp in the mountains. Not her. If she was gone for more than a day Vida began her high-pitched screaming that would echo in Dara's head, calling her home.

Those snow-tipped peaks had always looked impossibly serene to Dara, a never-never land she was shut away from as she'd been shut away from the kinds of lives her schoolmates led. Because of Vida. Because no one could quiet her twin except Dara.

Stop remembering. Vida was dead. Buried. Eaten by worms.

"You won't get me!" she cried.

"Come off it," Jo-Jo called from the front. "You're supposed to be looking for the Porterville road so you can tell me where to turn."

"Where's this place we're going to?" Nick asked.

"Ask Dara," Jo-Jo advised.

"Just some old ruins," she managed to say.

"Haunted," Jo-Jo added.

Nick leaned closer, looking directly into Dara's eyes. His were as green as the cat's, she saw. "By a ghost?"

"By something, my grandmother believed." Damn those probing green eyes. She hadn't meant to reveal that. "Why do you care?"

His smiled at her, but not with his eyes. "Hey, I'm number thirteen, remember?"

"The ruins are supposed to be a place they called Wolf House," Cindy put in.

Dara had never seen it standing, but her grandmother had a picture of a big, beautiful old house with a tower.

"Anything left of the place?" Nick asked.

"No," she snapped.

"You told me there were wolf posts where the gate had been," Jo-Jo called back from the front seat.

"Yeah, a couple years ago," she admitted. "Who knows now?"

"They'll still be there," Jo-Jo insisted. "I got this feeling. The wolf is the principle of evil, of the dark forces. Best of all, tonight's a full moon. The proper time to open Midnight's Door."

Jo-Jo called himself a warlock. Whether he was or not, Dara had no notion. She wasn't sure she even believed in warlocks. No question he was into some weird shit though.

"Midnight's Door?" Nick echoed.

"Yeah," Jo-Jo said. "That's why we need thirteen. Otherwise the incantations won't work. Thirteen, like in a coven. And a sacrifice."

"Sacrifice?" Dara asked, feeling goose bumps rise on her arms. She didn't care for even the sound of the word. "Like what?"

"I'll think of something."

Aware Jo-Jo wasn't going to tell her, Dara stared out the side window, spotting familiar landmarks. "Turn right at the next cross road," she said.

Jo-Jo swerved the car off the freeway. Soon they passed oil wells with only a few bobbing slowly. The SUV wound between barren hills, heading east toward the promise of the Sierras, miles away. The groves began, peach and nectarine and citrus. When they reached the older groves, closer to Porterville, wind machines rose tall above trees whose branches bore ripening oranges.

"Sometimes you wake up early on a cold morning," Dara said dreamily, "and you hear a humming like millions of bees, like all the bees in the world are coming, but it's only the wind machines blowing away the frost."

"So you're from around here," Nick said.

She scowled. "Not any more."

Nothing good had ever happened to her here. Apprehension trickled along her spine, warning her it wasn't about to change now. Each time she directed Jo-Jo's turns, she grew more tense.

The gray SUV topped one hill after another, made the last turn, past the cemetery. In the light of the setting sun, Dara saw the small valley below, the green of a pine grove, the remnants of old groves and orchards. Jo-Jo swung onto the overgrown drive, stopped at the gate posts to examine what remained of the marble wolves.

"Perfect," he pronounced. "The vibes feel right and it's near Halloween, when the balance of the world tips toward the dark side. Tonight the door will open, I know it will."

He drove between the posts, the SUV jouncing along the weed-choked drive until encountering a stand of oak saplings it couldn't drive around. "Everybody out," he called. "We trek in from here."

With the sun going down, it was gloomy under the huge old valley oaks whose branches met overhead. Dara moistened dry lips and wished she'd taken another upper. She lagged behind, finally realizing Nick wasn't with the group ahead of her. She stopped and looked back to see him wrestling his Harley from the trailer. He stashed it, along with his rucksack, behind one of the big oaks.

When he saw her watching him, he grinned and loped up to where she stood.

"Waiting for me?"

"Why'd you hide your bike?" she asked.

"Never know when you might need to make a getaway," he said. "Sort of like a gambler's ace in the hole."

She nodded, sort of understanding. After all, he wasn't really one of the group. "Are you a gambler?"

"Depends. What's this Midnight Door Jo-Jo's figuring on opening?"

She shrugged. "He's into dark stuff."

"Does it ever work?"

Dara thought about it. "I think maybe once. But I was pretty phased out at the time."

"Any idea who used to live at Wolf House?"

He sure asked a lot of questions. "A family named Volek."

"Ah."

Why did he sound so satisfied? "You know them?"

"Name's familiar, that's all."

They reached a tangle of bushes and rubble that marked the

site where Wolf House had once stood. Just past there, Jo-Jo had stopped and was ordering everybody around.

"We won't bother with the tents tonight, " he announced. "Better to have nothing between us and the moon. Once we get the fire started, we'll eat." He strode off, heading for the SUV.

Cindy, who had mothering tendencies, took Dara in tow. "You should've brought your jacket," Cindy scolded. "It's going to get cold tonight."

Later, she tried to get Dara to eat, but Dara wasn't hungry. Trying to shake the feeling something really bad was going to happen, she wandered a ways from the others toward an orchard. One of the trees bore a few apples, ripe and red. Because she was thirsty, she picked one and bit into it. The juice was sweet, but when she took the apple away from her lips she saw a worm-hole in the white flesh of the apple.

"Ugh!"

Spitting out what she hadn't swallowed, Dara threw the apple as far from her as she could, imagining the worm alive in her stomach. A hungry worm who'd eat its way through her until it reached her heart...

She crouched and vomited onto the grass.

The sun slid behind the hills to the west and the sky rapidly darkened. Wiping her mouth with the back of her hand, Dara convinced herself that even if she'd swallowed the worm, it was gone now. Not wanting to be alone with night coming on, she turned and made her way back toward the others.

Everyone was gathered around Jo-Jo, forming a circle around the small fire he'd had them build, some sitting on their sleeping bags. Cindy, sitting on her jacket, beckoned to her and Dara slipped in between Cindy and Nick.

"Sit still and listen," Jo-Jo ordered. He remained standing, pacing around the perimeter of the fire. Despite the mild evening and the warmth of the fire, Dara shivered. Jo-Jo didn't frighten her, but being in this place did. Hadn't the worm been a warning?

"Satan is everywhere," Jo-Jo said, his voice solemn and deep. "In the smoke and the wind, in fire and water and darkness. To-night, when I call him, because of this place and this time, be-cause we are thirteen, Midnight's Door will open and who knows what creature of darkness will manifest itself?"

Dara clutched the wooden amulet she wore on a thong around her neck, always under her clothes to keep it from sight. Little use for protection when it hadn't ever protected her before, but holding its familiar shape through the cloth of her T-shirt gave her some comfort. It belonged to her, handed down from her grandmother, not to her mother nor to Vida, but to her alone.

"It's supposed to go to the one who needs its protection," Grandma had said. "In my dream that was you, child. The rune was handed down from my mother to me."

Rune. That was the mark burnt into the polished wood of the amulet. Dara had researched runes and found they came from ancient times. Druids had used them and each symbol had a meaning. She didn't know what hers meant.

"My mother told me her mother said that the man named Quincy fashioned the amulet to protect my grandmother and made her wear it as long as he was with her—three days and nights. Long enough to leave her with child. He never came back. Arrived naked and left naked, for he didn't take along the clothes she'd given him. Like as not he never knew she bore him twins. My mother was the girl and grandmother named the boy Quincy, after his father. He didn't live past babyhood."

Quincy. The name echoed in Dara's mind. Her great-grand-father had left naked, as he'd arrived. How odd.

Dara's attention jerked back to Jo-Jo, now crouched over a sack directly in front of her. He chanted meaningless words, ones she somehow didn't want to hear. She retreated into herself, start-ing to close her eyes. But the moon, rising full and yellow above the pine grove at the edge of the grass and weed-choked clear-ing, distracted her.

"Aglom, Tetragram, Vaycheon, Stimulamathon," Jo-Jo intoned. "I call, you, I call you, I call you."

He reached into a pocket and flung a powdery substance into the fire. Pungent smoke arose, spicy, aromatic. Then he opened the sack and pulled something out. A dark cloth? No, it had a tail. Paws. Green eyes glazed in death. Dido! Dara grimaced, horrified. Jo-Jo had killed the poor innocent cat for the sacrifice.

From beside her Cindy moaned in protest, but Jo-Jo paid no attention.

"Blood and death," he chanted. "I give you the sacrifice."

From beyond the fire, faint and far away, something howled. Dara bit back a gasp. A coyote, that's all, she tried to tell herself. But it hadn't sounded like one.

Jo-Jo tossed the cat's body into the fire. A horrible stench arose, making her gag. An insidious worm of thought circled in her mind. Not Dido, but Dara was meant to be the real sacrifice. There was no place to run to, no place to hide. She was doomed...

She heard her twin laughing from somewhere underground, a laugh that turned into a full-blown howl. No, not Vida. Something else howled. Something evil. Coming closer. The monster from hell Jo-Jo had called up.

One of the girls screamed. A man cursed. Suddenly everyone was in motion, scrambling to their feet. Dara saw Jo-Jo bolt from the fire, heading toward the SUV. She started to get up. Someone's boot hit her head, half-stunning her, knocking her sideways.

She struggled to her feet, hand fumbling for the amulet, freeing it from under her shirt. Protection, she needed protection. All the others were ahead of her, racing for the SUV. She hurried after them. Something howled, so close that she whirled to look, staring, hair rising on her nape.

Leaping toward her from the direction of the pine grove was a huge dark beast, an abomination unlike any animal she'd ever seen. She knew it was coming to kill her.

Though all but frozen with fear, Dara forced herself into frantic motion only to trip on a hidden root and fall headlong, knocking the breath from her. By the time she turned herself over, trying to sit up, the beast loomed over her. It stared down at her with feral yellow eyes. Not at her face. At what? The amulet! She closed her eyes, bracing herself as best she could for the attack.

Moments later, when nothing happened, her eyes popped open and she saw the beast loping back toward the pines. Nick stood over her. Was that a gun in his hand? As he hauled her to her feet, she lost every shred of sanity she possessed, sobbing and shaking, Vida's voice echoing in her mind, calling to her, luring her.

She was only vaguely aware of someone putting a jacket over her shoulders, then holding her wrist, tugging her along, finally halting.

"Dara," a man's voice said so sharply she blinked, looking to see who he was. Red hair. Red beard. Eric. No, no, his name was Nick. His green eyes probed hers.

"Listen up. Everyone's gone. Took off in the SUV. I've got my bike, but you'll have to ride in back hanging onto me. Let go and you fall off and die. Understand?"

There'd been a beast. "Is it gone?" she quavered, terror threatening to swamp her.

"We've got to get out of here. You heard what I said about the bike?"

She managed to nod. "Hang on to you."

"No matter what. Don't forget."

He made her don the jacket he'd put over her shoulders, helped her onto the Harley, then seated himself. Hold on, she warned herself, and gripped him around the waist as he fired up the bike. They jounced over the uneven ground until at last the ride smoothed. As they traveled onward in the dark, she laid her cheek against the back of Nick's leather jacket, clinging to him, inexplicably feeling safer than she had in a long time. Who cared where they were going as long as it was away from the ruins, away from Vida's grave.

Dara had only a dim recollection of the bike finally stopping, of being hauled off and stuffed into a sleeping bag. Was there a tiny fire? She lapsed into sleep without being sure.

She woke to sunlight sifting through evergreen branches. She froze, imagining she was in the pine grove by the ruins, helpless, immobilized in a sleeping bag. Driven by fright, she clawed her way free of the bag and leaped to her feet. Her head swam, shiny black dots shimmered at the edge of her vision.

"Hey," a man said. "What's the problem?"

Nick. He crouched beside a small fire.

"The ruins," she quavered.

He jerked his head. "Down below us. We're in the Sierras."

Dara's knees gave way and she sprawled onto brown pine needles. Sitting up, she gave a long sigh of relief, only realizing then that she felt really lousy. Coming off a high, that's why. She fumbled in the jacket pocket for her uppers, finding nothing but a used tissue. Only then did she realize the jacket wasn't hers.

"This is Cindy's jacket," she blurted.

Nick shrugged. "Whatever. I grabbed the first jacket I saw on the ground by the fire. Took someone's sleeping bag for you too when I realized we were going to be left-behind partners."

"But my jacket had uppers in the pocket," she wailed.

He shrugged again. "Guess you'll do without."

Dara burst into tears. He didn't move, made no effort to comfort her. Eventually, her tears used up, she was forced to use the soiled tissue to mop her face. He didn't care how she felt. Didn't understand. Or even try to.

"Want some stew?" he asked.

She'd opened her mouth to refuse, when her stomach gurgled, warning her it was running on empty.

He dumped some stew onto a plastic plate, got up, and crossed to her. "Here," he said, handing her a plastic spoon.

Dara ate it all, realized she was thirsty and found she had to share a water bottle with him. By then her aching head had cleared a bit. Why was she with Nick? The last she knew they'd been at the ruins and something bad had happened. Everyone ran away and left her for the sacrifice. But Nick had come back. Nick had saved her by bringing her with him.

1 4

"Um, thanks," she muttered. "For the stew and for rescuing me."

He gave her a lopsided grin. "No good deed goes unpunished."

"That's an odd thing to say."

"Maybe."

When she stood up, the dizziness returned. She managed to relieve herself among the trees, then stumbled back to the sleeping bag and crawled into it again, dropping into a dark fog of nothingness.

Nick watched her, figuring it'd take at least a couple of days to get the drugs out of her system. Pure luck she didn't have any on her. He had enough to worry about without trying to deal with a crazy druggie. By this afternoon she'd probably be alert enough not to fall off the bike while they traveled down the mountain for gas and supplies.

But then luck had been running his way ever since Jo-Jo had picked him up in Castaic. He'd been coming to the Valley anyway following a lead he'd spotted in an article in the L.A. Times. Something about a dove hunter being spooked by a strange-looking beast that he swore wasn't a bear.

The ruins of the old Volek place—what a break that was. And Dara. As soon as he'd spotted that rune amulet and saw the beast turn away from her, he knew what he had. Too bad the sight had stunned him enough to make him miss his chance for a decent shot. As special as the bullets were, he couldn't waste any. Still, unknowingly, Dara would draw the beast back to her. Beasts, because he was almost positive he'd heard two howling, not one. Two, what a prize.

As for Dara herself... His smile faded. Her vulnerability had struck him from the first. He didn't think she knew, or even suspected, what the amulet meant. Or what the beast was.

After stocking up, he'd bring her back to this isolated spot and they'd camp in the mountains until one or both of the beasts located her. He doubted she'd object to staying with him since her friends seemed to have more or less dumped her. Not that he intended to touch her. No, she was safe from him that way, even if he couldn't yet be sure she was entirely safe from him in other ways. He was what he was, after all.

A week later, Dara felt better than she had in over a year. She told Nick it was due to the clean air of the mountains, but in her heart she knew the cause was the absence of drugs. Nick, as it turned out, didn't even smoke grass.

She was taking it one day at a time, not planning ahead, but simply enjoying feeling herself again. It could well have been the uppers that made her think she'd heard Vida whispering to her, that made her hallucinate a beast that couldn't possibly exist.

As for Nick standing over her, gun pointed at that imaginary beast, well, he did pack an old Colt. The gun had been his grandfather's, he said, brought along in case of rattlesnakes. He admitted to grabbing it off his bike when he ran back, just in case he had to shoot a coyote or something. According to him, he hadn't seen anything.

She and Nick got along great. He not only made her laugh, but didn't crowd her, didn't try to jump her bones. They took long walks in the pines and firs around their isolated camp and he told her all about what kinds of trees they were. He knew the names of the birds and animals they saw, too.

"How come you know all this stuff?" she asked him.

"Took some college courses in my time."

"Your time? How old are you anyway?"

"Closer to thirty than I like to admit."

"Once I thought I'd like to go to college," she told him. "Didn't work out that way."

"You can't be more than twenty. Lots of time, yet."

She sighed. "I don't think I have that kind of future."

One day they took the bike up to King's Canyon, to the sequoias, which Nick had never seen. "I thought they'd be more like the coast redwoods," he admitted, looking a hundred feet or more up the gigantic trunks to where the sparse green foliage of the branches began. He drew in a deep breath, "Only their scent is similar."

Dara had been here before so she enjoyed getting her chance to show off a little by pointing out the different ways the big trees grew. "See those two sequoias growing close together? They're a loving couple. Now look at those three together—three graces."

"Reminds me of two's company, three's a crowd. " He shook his head. "These trees make us seem insignificant."

Dara had felt pretty insignificant all her life. "Aren't we?"

"No." He flung both arms wide. "I'm king of the hill."

She laughed, half convinced he really was. Nick was anything but insignificant.

This was a new life to Dara, one she might just have a chance of holding onto. With Nick? She couldn't be sure. Experience had taught her not to try to plan ahead, but it was hard not to.

What she looked forward to most was when they sat around a tiny fire at night, sometimes talking, sometimes in companionable silence. It made up for all the camping trips in the Sierras that she'd missed as a child.

That night, Nick said, "How come you always wear that amulet of yours under your shirt?"

"I don't want people to see it," she told him. "They'd think I was crazy for always wearing a piece of wood on a leather thong."

"Where did you get the amulet?"

"From my grandmother."

"Do you know where she bought it?"

"Oh, she didn't buy it. My great-grandfather made it for my great-grandmother. 'To keep her safe,' he's supposed to have said. Big deal, since he left her pregnant after three days to run off naked and never come back. She had to take care of the twins she had later all by herself."

"He ran off naked?"

Dara laughed. "The same way he arrived, apparently. I've got really weird ancestors. Anyway, my grandmother got the amulet from her mother and handed it down to me. 'For protection', she told me. 'Always wear it.' So I do—for what that's worth. Hasn't been much protection."

"How do you know? Maybe it wards off an evil you know nothing about."

She stared at him in the fire's dying flames, their flickering casting shadows that came and went, making him seem like a stranger. "Evil?"

"Don't you believe in evil?"

Dara hugged herself. "Like what Jo-Jo was trying to do? Open Midnight's Door? Yeah, I guess I believe evil exists." After a moment, she added, "Why are you looking at me like that?"

"I don't meet many innocents in this world."

"Innocent? Are you kidding? You have no idea of the things I've done. I'm just lucky I don't have some fatal disease."

He waved his hand as though brushing away her words. "Innocence of spirit is different."

"I'm not sure what you mean."

"Then you'll just have to think about it. "

From somewhere nearby, an owl hooted four times. She shivered. "You know the Miwok around here think the owl catches your spirit when you die."

"We're both very much alive and we're not Miwok. Tomorrow we're off for supplies again. We need to wash clothes, too."

"But we're coming back here?"

"Probably not. I'd like to get closer to one of the rivers."

She sighed inaudibly, relieved. He wasn't going to shake her off. Maybe it was a mistake to get attached to Nick, but she couldn't help it.

"You've done a lot for me," she told him. "Fed me, even bought me clothes." She didn't add that his companionship, his acceptance of her, had also given her a glimpse of a new life. "Some time I hope I can repay you."

"Your company is payment enough."

Touched, she leaned over and kissed his cheek. His hand came up—to ward her off? To hold her? A quiver of anticipation ran through her. When all he did was briefly cover her hand with his, disappointment followed.

Don't expect too much, she warned herself. It's probably best this way.

After that, they moved to a new camp site every week, gradually coming down the mountain until, the fourth week, Nick found what he claimed he'd been searching for. A spot on a rise overlooking a river.

"It's getting colder. Thought we'd be better off at this lower elevation," he said. Which was true enough, but did nothing to lessen his guilt.

The truth was the moon would be full this week. He'd sensed the alien presence of what he was waiting for, though only one and not close, so he'd needed to put Dara within range of what he knew was looking for her.

Damn, he was getting too attached to her, so attached it was hard to keep his hands off her. One touch and he'd be making love to her, which must not happen. He didn't dare lose his head, it was already difficult enough to use her for bait. With the beast so close, he couldn't turn away from his born duty. He'd missed his first chance there in the ruins. He wouldn't miss another.

She hadn't asked him for anything. Not food, nor clothes, nor protection. She hadn't made any effort to seduce him and, unlike most of the women he knew, she made no mention of a future together—or any future at all, for that matter. He'd given her food and clothes anyway to keep her with him. As for protection... Nick sighed. He'd do his best, but as a Stalker, luring the beast close and killing it came before any other consideration.

"This is a beautiful spot," Dara told him as they set up camp.

"Listening to the river will lull me to sleep at night. I don't know when I've felt so good. You know—healthy."

She didn't mention being off drugs and neither did he, though he was sure she knew that was the reason for her improved outlook. He watched her stretch, raising her arms and her face to the sun slanting through the small stand of pines covering the rise. Dara was beautiful. And damn desirable. He couldn't sense any wrongness within her, but with a great-grandfather who arrived and left naked and was never seen again, her heritage was suspect, to say the least. In addition, there was the amulet.

Never mind how much he wanted to bed her, he couldn't. Unknown to her. he was already risking her life. Worse, if what he suspected was true, he might have to kill her. He tried to thrust that thought away from him, but it remained within range, an unpleasant possibility.

That night, as the fire died down, she told him she was a twin. "I don't usually talk about it," she added, "but I know you'll understand."

Her trust choked him.

"Vida's been dead for seven years now. She wasn't born normal and there wasn't anything the docs could do to help." Dara sighed. "No matter how I tried to feel sorry for her, I came to hate her because she never left me alone. Even after she died, I used to think I heard her in my mind, calling to me. That's why I left the Valley. I think it's why I started the uppers, too."

"She was your only sibling?"

Dara nodded. "I thought I felt her in my mind when we camped at the ruins, but that might have been the drugs. Like thinking I saw a horrible beast with yellow eyes. Just like Vida's were. Feral yellow."

Though he'd told her before he hadn't seen anything, Nick hedged now. She'd have to know sometime. "Something howled down there. It scared off the others."

Hugging herself, she said, "I guess I didn't imagine the howling, then. Could it have been a coyote?"

He equivocated. "I don't know."

As if her words had evoked them, a chorus of wails and howls arose from some distance away. Dara shivered and he put an arm around her shoulders, saying, "Those are coyotes. An entire family, by the sound of it."

"I know. I heard them enough when I lived in the Valley. Somehow, though, hearing them now spooks me." She snuggled closer to him.

Nick pointed to the rising moon. "Almost full. They're singing to it."

"The Miwok say Coyote laughs at the moon. He's their Trickster, up to no good most of the time."

"You mentioned them before. A local tribe?"

"In the Valley and the foothills. My grandmother was friends with a Miwok woman named Sawa who wove gorgeous baskets. Sawa used to tell me native stories if I was there when she came to visit my grandmother.

"One was about Kuksuyu, a feathered spirit who might help you, or might not, depending on whether you deserved to be helped. He might even kill you if he was annoyed. You could tell he was coming by the whistling. The Miwok had Kuksu Dancers, who tried to summon him when they needed help. Sometimes he came, sometimes not."

"So they never knew whether they were summoning aid or death. Kuksuyu sounds undependable."

"I guess you need to be careful who you ask for help."

He found it harder and harder to keep his mind on the conversation with Dara pressed so close against his side. He couldn't control the thought that she'd feel even better pressed somewhere else. Before he could clamp down on his need, he caught her to him, his mouth seeking hers. Her lips were soft and warm and welcoming. She tasted of the honey he'd bought to put in their tea and he could smell the fragrance of the soap she used, mixed with her own intoxicating woman's scent.

He wanted, he needed...

No! With great effort he released her, stood and walked to the edge of the rise, where a cliff angled sharply down to the river. As he regained his control, he noted moonlight glinting on the water.

The moon would be full tomorrow night. And he sensed the creature was much closer than before. With luck there'd be an end to it then. Yet even if he killed the beast, what about the other he'd heard by the ruins? The second one. He couldn't leave this area without doing his damnedest to rid the world of both abominations. Which made Dara a continuing problem. In more ways than one.

Left alone by the fire, Dara tried not to feel rejected. He'd kissed her, not the other way around, so it'd been his idea. Hadn't he liked her response? What had he wanted? Something other than he'd gotten from her, obviously.

Maybe, like a lot of guys, he shied away from the slightest suggestion of commitment. But how could one kiss imply commitment? She certainly didn't expect any, even though she'd begun fantasizing about beginning a new life, maybe with Nick. That's all it was, though, a fantasy. He hadn't given her any reason to expect he wanted her in his life once this interlude in the mountains was over.

She closed her eyes, reliving the kiss. A potent one, filled with promise and passion. Residual warmth still pooled deep within her. She'd wanted more, hoped for more. Which wouldn't happen.

That night her sleep was uneasy, despite the soothing murmur of the river. She could tell Nick was restless, too.

The next day, Nick took her on a hike down to the river by a roundabout way that avoided the steep drop from their campsite. Walking along the river, they startled a rattlesnake trying to catch frogs. Nick took a wide detour around it.

"I thought you brought your Colt in case of rattlesnakes," she commented.

"Brought it, but not on the hike. This is his lucky day."

"Or hers."

He slanted her a look.

"Well, it could be either sex," she insisted. "Unless you're an expert who can tell at a glance."

"Anyone who can tell a female from a male rattler would have to get a lot closer than I ever intend to."

When they finally turned back, Dara had worked her courage up. "You kissed me last night," she said.

"Yeah. Won't happen again."

She persisted. "What was wrong with the kiss?"

He paused and looked at her. "This isn't the right time. Or place."

She wanted to ask if there ever would be, but knew better, so all she did was gaze into his eyes, green as new leaves in the spring. He brought the back of his hand up and stroked her cheek lightly and much too briefly.

"You deserve better," he said and resumed walking.

Whatever that meant. Never mind what she deserved, what she wanted was Nick, but she certainly wasn't going to say so.

By the time they made their way back up the rise, Dara needed a rest. So did Nick apparently because he leaned back against a boulder near the edge, staring down at the water. When she saw him close his eyes, she curled up in a patch of sunlight and fell asleep.

That evening, after they finished cleaning up from their meal, instead of sitting by the fire as it died, Nick paced around the camp perimeter.

"What are you looking for?" she finally asked.

"I feel—" He broke off. "Restless," he added after a pause.

The rising moon inched up the sky, lighting the areas not hidden by the shadows under the trees. When Nick strode through a moonlit patch she noted with astonishment he'd strapped on the Colt. When had he done that? And why?

She started to ask him, then held her tongue, suddenly afraid to hear what he might answer.

"You have your amulet on?" he asked as he passed her.

What a strange question. "I always wear it, you know that."

"Take it out from under your shirt. Don't ask me why, just do it."

The urgency in his tone made her obey without question. He paced on, his gaze searching the shadows under the trees. Apprehensive, Dara rose to her feet, looking around. Who was he expecting? Or—what?

"You're scaring me," she whispered.

He slapped the holstered Colt. "This and the amulet will keep you safe."

"From what?" Despite herself her voice rose. "What's out there?"

A long, ululating howl from the pines answered her.

No coyote ever made a sound like that. Dara clapped her hand over her mouth to stop the scream rising in her throat. She was horrified to see Nick disappear into the darkness under the pines, leaving her alone. She could run—but where to? Nowhere was safe.

She inched closer to the fire, her gaze glued to the pines. Suddenly, a dark shape burst from the shadows into the moonlight. The beast! Frozen, she watched, terrified, as it loped toward her. A loud crack startled her. Gunshot? The beast faltered, took a few more stumbling steps and fell forward, almost at her feet, and lay unmoving

As she stared down at it, the body began to change. Dara rubbed her eyes, unable to believe what she was seeing. Must be a drug flash-back. She'd thought a monstrous beast had come at her, but what now lay at her feet was unmistakably a man. A stranger. Naked and dead. Finally she grew aware Nick had reappeared and was standing over the body, Colt in hand.

"You—you shot him," she quavered.

"I killed a Shifter," he told her. "That's my purpose in life. Man isn't meant to shift to a beast and back into human form."

"That's impossible," she cried.

"You saw him, saw the beast I shot. You saw him change back to a man after he was dead."

"I don't know what I saw," she mumbled.

"Yes, you do. You saw a shapeshifter, the same one, in all probability, that scared your friends from the ruins. He couldn't be allowed to live."

Nick holstered the Colt, grabbed the naked man's feet and hauled him over to the cliff face. She stared, appalled, as he tipped the body over. Moments later a splash told her the dead man was in the river.

Dara swallowed. Nick had killed a man and dumped his body in the river. A man he claimed could change to a beast. Unable to process such information, her only impulse was to get away. She turned and began walking toward the road, hurrying faster and faster until she was running.

When she reached the road, she slowed, but continued on downhill, her head in turmoil, no plan in mind.

Eventually she heard the roar of the Harley and realized Nick had come after her. Since there was no place to go, she stopped and waited. He pulled up beside her and she saw he'd packed all the gear.

"We'll camp down below," he told her. "Get on."

What was her other choice? Unable to think of one, numbly, she obeyed, clutching him around the waist because she had to, and closing her eyes as though that could wipe out the memory of what had happened.

She had no idea how long it was before he pulled off the road. When she opened her eyes she saw they were in an old orange grove. Nick got off, so she slid off, too. He tossed her a sleeping bag.

With a sinking feeling, she asked, "Where are we?"

"In an orange grove."

"Yes, but where? I don't want to camp anywhere near the ruins."

"We're not that close."

Maybe not. But how close was too close? She feared the cemetery where Vida was buried couldn't be all that far from where they were. Dara shivered. She didn't like being here, but at least Nick was with her. Though she hadn't yet come to terms with what he'd done earlier, the thought of being alone frightened her a lot more than he did.

Deciding she had to try to sleep, she unrolled the sleeping bag and put it a ways from where Nick had placed his.

Watching her, Nick decided now wasn't the time to tell her he believed there was another shifter like the one he'd killed still roaming around somewhere. He had another silver bullet for that one in the Colt and Dara had her amulet. If he stayed alert, they should be safe enough.

He tried to stay awake, but found himself dozing off. In the night he woke with a start, realizing he'd fallen into a deep sleep for a time. He checked his watch. After midnight. Glancing over to where Dara should be sleeping, he blinked. Where the hell was she?

Rolling out of his sleeping bag, he strode over to hers, drawing his breath in when he saw she'd left the amulet behind. Cursing, he picked it up, studied the rune for a few seconds, then slipped it into his pocket.

Why had she taken the amulet off? Where could she have gone and what for? Not to the ruins. Where else? Think, man, what else did she tell you?

Something about a twin. Yes, Vida, her dead twin. Buried in a cemetery around here somewhere.

Was it possible—? But why would Dara visit a cemetery in the middle of the night? The hair on his nape rose as he remembered her saying after Vida was dead, her twin had talked to her in her mind. Called her in her sleep. Once she'd awakened and found herself in the cemetery.

With no other clue to where she might be, he had to follow up on this one.

Dara woke to find herself in the cemetery, walking toward her twin's grave. At first she thought she must still be dreaming, especially when she heard Vida's voice in her mind. *I'm here, come to me, let us lie heart to heart as we did before we were born.*

She stopped beside the headstone she knew was Vida's, and her hand automatically reached to clasp her amulet through the cloth of her shirt. But the amulet wasn't there. Frantically, Dara reached under her shirt, searching. It was gone.

Heart to heart, Vida's mind whisper continued. *Take off your clothes and lie on my grave so we can be together. So I can reach you.*

Was she awake? Dara wondered dazedly. Had she wandered from the orange grove to the cemetery in her sleep? Where and when had she taken off the amulet? She never left it behind.

Come to me, we must lie heart to heart.. Vida's insidious whisper paralyzed her will. Without willing it, Dara began to disrobe until she was naked, then stretched out prone on the grassy grave mound.

Now we can be one, the way we were meant to be. We can change and run together in the night.. Vida's frightening mind whisper was the last thing Dara heard.

When Nick finally found the cemetery, it was close to two in the morning.

In the moonlight he searched through the headstones for the right grave, swearing under his breath every time he stumbled on the uneven ground.

Was he on a wild goose chase? If he didn't find her here, he had no notion where to look next.

He'd reached the far end of the cemetery when he saw what looked like a body lying on the ground. He conquered a momentary frisson of superstitious fear. The dead didn't crawl out of their coffins. Ever. Dara? Impelled by dread, he hurried toward the body. Naked. Clothes scattered around. Reaching down to turn the body over to make sure it was Dara, her skin felt so cold he shuddered. She couldn't be dead.

When he finally located a faint pulse, he sighed with relief.

He pulled out the amulet and dropped it over her head, yanked on her jacket and gathered up the rest of her clothes. He needed to get her back to camp as fast as he could and warm her up. He told himself the faint cry that came as he strode away from the grave carrying Dara must have been a night bird. Vida, dead and buried, had no voice.

At the orange grove, he zipped the two sleeping bags together and stuffed Dara, naked except for the amulet, inside, then stripped and got in with her, zipping them up. He wrapped his arms around her, holding her close, lending his body heat to warm her. When her skin stopped feeling as chill as death, he relaxed a little and, though he didn't intend to, exhausted, he slept.

He dreamed of a woman's hands caressing him, of feather-light kisses teasing his lips, of the soft erotic feel of breasts against his chest. By her scent, he knew the woman was Dara. Aroused, he gathered her closer and woke to find himself holding her in his arms. The sky was gray with pre-dawn. Before he could form another thought, her lips found his and he forgot everything else as he lost himself in the kiss.

She still tasted of honey and of herself, infinitely tantalizing. He needed more, needed everything. By the way she pressed against him, from her little moaning gasps, he knew she was offering him what he wanted. Any vestigial remnants of caution burned to ashes in the heat of his desire.

Her breasts were made for a man's caresses, the curve of her hip for driving him mad. By the time he rose above her he was beyond all reason.

She welcomed him inside, her inarticulate sounds of pleasure an assurance he was driving her up along with him. The sensuous spasm of her release sent him flying over the edge.

Holding her afterward, as she eased back into sleep, he tried not to think about what he was and what she might be. Or what he would have to do if his worst suspicions were true. She was Dara. His for the moment.

He must have dozed, because the next he knew the sun was up.

Dara, lying next to him, smiled, saying, "Hi."

Much as he wanted to, Nick forced himself not to haul her back into his arms. To resist the temptation, he had to crawl out of the sleeping bag. "Do you remember how you got here?" he asked as he donned his clothes.

Her smile faded. "I—I had a nightmare about the cemetery."

"No nightmare. That's where I found you, face down and naked on your twin's grave. It got cold last night; you could have died of exposure." He had to tell her for her own protection, but the lost look on her face stabbed him to the heart.

"Not a dream, then," she whispered. "Vida said she needed to be a part of me."

"I won't let it happen again," he assured her. "With our sleeping bags zipped together, you can't leave without me being aware."

"What if it doesn't have to happen again?" Her voice was so low he could hardly hear the words. "What if—if Vida—?"

"That's not possible." Even as he spoke he realized he wasn't sure. Shifters existed. Stalkers existed. Why not twins who could become one? A moment later he shook his head. "Vida died seven years ago. She's in her grave. Buried."

Dara sat up, the sleeping bag wrapped around her. "But she calls to me."

"Now?"

"No. Last night. And before. When Jo-Jo brought us to the ruins. She told me I was a—a sacrifice."

"You were on drugs then."

She grimaced. "You're thinking I had a drug flash-back last night. When I left the Valley two years ago I wasn't on drugs and I left here because Vida kept calling to me. " Unzipping her side, Dara emerged from the sleeping bag and grabbed her clothes, turning her back to Nick. As she started to dress, she paused and lifted the amulet from around her neck, dropping it onto the bag.

"Why did you do that?" he asked.

"Turn my back? I didn't want you watching me dress."

"I meant take off your amulet."

She half-swiveled to glance at him, then down at the discarded amulet.

"It was bothering me."

"How?"

"Why're you making such a big deal out of this?"

"You told me you always wore the amulet for protection."

Her laugh was brittle. "Some protection. First the beast, then Vida."

"The beast didn't harm you the first time."

Fully dressed now, she turned and glared at him. "So you lied to me."

Nick shrugged. "You were coming off a drug high. I figured if you knew you actually did see a beast, it might tip you over the edge."

Dara opened her mouth to deny it, then paused to think. Much as she hated to admit he could be right, she hadn't been in the best of shape for a few days there.

He reached down, picked up the amulet and offered it to her. When she shook her head, he asked again, "Why?"

"It irritates my skin," she said finally.

"Wear it outside your clothes."

She sighed. Obviously he was going to persist, so she might as well put it around her neck again. "Okay." Accepting it from him, she slipped the thong over her head, the amulet coming to rest between her breasts on the outside of her T-shirt. She moved her shoulders uneasily, for some reason not liking the feel of it.

"Do you know what the rune burnt into the wood stands for?" he asked.

"No," she admitted.

"Without going into its runic meaning, it's meant to keep you protected against the evils of shapeshifting. That's why the beast in the ruins didn't harm you."

"Against the evils of shapeshifting," she repeated.

"So keep the amulet on and in plain sight," he advised.

"But you killed the—the thing, whatever it was."

"You saw it change from a live beast to a dead man. Why can't you accept that Shifters exist?"

Dara shivered, feeling as though something dark had settled into her mind. She did not want to go on with this discussion. "Are we staying here again tonight?"

He shrugged.

"Why not move to the ruins? Since you killed whatever it was that prowled there, we have nothing to fear." Even as she said the words it seemed to Dara that they belonged to someone else. Yet she'd felt compelled to say them.

Nick stared at her. "I thought you didn't want to even be near the ruins.

"Why the sudden change?"

"I don't know." Which was true. "Maybe to prove something to myself?" That rang false. Dara turned away so he wouldn't see her confusion.

Whatever her reason, she'd unknowingly keyed in to his agenda, Nick thought. If there was another shifter in the area, likely enough he'd be near the ruins. And the moon was just off full, enough left yet to trigger a change. Dara would be in no more danger than she'd been on the rise above the river. If a beast prowled tonight, the amulet would keep her safe while he killed it.

He couldn't leave the area until he made sure no other alien beast ran under the moon. One of the advantages of being a Stalker was that he'd be able to sense a shifter long before the beast got close to them. While, on the other hand, Shifters couldn't sense Stalkers.

"Okay, we'll camp at the ruins tonight," he told her. "Pack up."

They showered and changed clothes at a truck stop, then found a laundromat to wash what was dirty. It was late afternoon before Nick drove the Harley between what was left of the wolf posts and stashed it behind one of the old oaks again.

"I much prefer being here without Jo-Jo," he said as they set up the night camp.

"I'll never forgive him for killing Cindy's cat," Dara said. "I always wanted a kitten, but Vida screamed without stop if anyone brought a cat into the house. How she knew was a mystery. But she always did. I think she wore my folks out so that they just gave up."

"Where are they now?"

"They both died when I was eighteen. No reason to stay around here after that."

"Especially since your dead twin had begun whispering to you."

She nodded. "Do you know you're the first person who ever believed me about that?"

He grimaced. "I got a first hand view of the result last night. I meant it when I told you it won't happen again."

"I believe you, but—" Her words trailed off and she twisted the thong of the amulet in her fingers. "I wish I could take this off," she muttered.

"Promise me you won't."

She sighed. "Oh, all right."

That night, after eating, they sat around the dying fire.

"You're wearing that gun again," she said.

"Makes me feel more comfortable."

"You're the most close-mouthed person I've ever met," she complained. "You never talk about yourself. You pretty much know all there is to know about me, but what do I know about you?"

"My life isn't all that interesting."

"Well, do you have parents? Siblings?"

"My mother is alive, though I'm not sure where she is at the moment, we're not that close. She and my stepfather travel a lot. No siblings."

"Where do you live?"

He gave her a lopsided grin. "No fixed abode."

"A wanderer like me. No job?"

"My grandfather left me enough money to live on." Along with the Colt and the molds for the silver bullets to fit the gun. Nothing but silver could kill a Shifter.

"Why do I feel like I'm having to pry all this out of you?" she asked.

"I don't like to talk about myself."

"Big surprise." She was twisting the thong of the amulet in her fingers again.

He started to say something when he caught a flicker of movement from the corner of his eye. He leaped to his feet, whirling to look, hand on his holstered Colt. A dark figure stood not five feet away from them. It wasn't the beast.

"Who the hell are you?" Nick demanded.

"Just an old Indian," the man said softly. "They call me Running Bear."

The moonlight showed Nick he wore his hair in braids and that he was definitely old. "What do you want with us?" Nick asked, hand still on the Colt.

"Peace," Running Bear said. "I come unarmed. My people live not far from here. Close enough so I heard the roar of your hog when you turned into this accursed place. A bad spot to camp. Unsafe. I came to warn you."

Nick scowled. "Are you telling me we can't?"

"You can choose to ignore me. At your peril." With that, Running Bear turned and made for the pine grove.

Did the old man know about the Shifter? Nick wondered. He thought of hurrying after him to ask but decided not to.

"I'll bet he's a Miwok medicine man," Dara said. "Not 'just an old Indian.'
What did he mean by accursed?"

"What do you think?"

"That beast," she said. "But it didn't stay here, it came after us. After me."

Which was true. "The beast is dead," he reminded her.

She shivered and hugged herself. "Somehow I don't think that means the curse is lifted."

"You wanted to camp here."

"We're both going to sleep in the zipped-together bags, aren't we?"

"Wouldn't have it any other way."

"Then it's okay." She stood, came close to him and gazed up provocatively. "Will it be 'at my peril?'"

He reached for her. "What do you think?"

Soon they were snuggled together in the sleeping bags, his Colt within easy reach. Not naked this time, but that didn't deter Nick. Tonight he'd make the advances.

With Nick holding her close, Dara forgot the apprehension brought on by the medicine man's visit. When he kissed her, she opened to him, thrilling to the sensation of being tasted, breathing in his own special scent. It had never been this way with any other man. He made her feel she was dissolving with need, just from a kiss.

She'd stripped down to a night T-shirt that came to mid-calf, and when his hands slid under it to caress her breasts, she moaned with pleasure. As he explored her secret places with fingers and tongue, the world ceased to exist except for her and Nick. Nothing else had any reality.

"Please," she whispered, hardly aware she was speaking, on fire at her core, her need rising with his every touch.

When they came together she cried out, already beginning the glorious upward spin of release. She rose up, up, higher than she'd ever been. Rockets went off in a grand explosion and then she drifted down along with Nick, until she lay in his arms.

"Did we touch the moon?" she murmured.

"And more."

She wanted to keep talking, to try to tell him how she felt, but sleep tugged at her so insistently, she gave in. And dreamed of Vida.

Now, Vida whispered. *The moon calls to you. Feel the moon and obey.*

Dara wanted to obey, longed to feel the moon, but something

held her back, something pressing down over her heart. She struggled to rid herself of the weight, finally freeing herself and tossing it aside. Carefully, stealthily, she inched down the zipper and eased from the sleeping bag. Clad only in her night T-shirt, she headed for the pine grove. Before she reached the trees, something howled.

"Yes," she cried, "yes." Flinging off the shirt, she raced into the trees toward the sound, ignoring the wrenching within her.

Nick woke abruptly, the howl echoing in his head. He tore himself from the sleeping bag, grabbed the Colt and leaped to his feet just as a white-clad figure neared the trees at the edge of the pine grove. He swung around to stare at the sleeping bag. Only Dara's amulet lay there. He grabbed it and slung the thong around his neck.

"No!" he shouted at the figure now disappearing into the shadows under the pines. "Come back!"

Wearing nothing but his jeans, he raced toward the grove. Just short of the trees he found Dara's discarded sleep shirt. There was no trace of her, no matter how hard he searched. Worse, after a time the howling began again, in the distance, coming from two different beasts.

Sick at heart, Nick made his way back to the camp and pulled on the rest of his clothes. Had he been wrong about Dara? Either she was a Shifter, or else they'd tumbled into a nest of the abominable beasts and she was out there without her amulet. Unprotected.

Dara woke in the morning naked and cold. Rocky walls surrounded her. It looked like a cave. Yes, she could see daylight at the cave mouth. Where was she? Next to her a naked man snored. Not Nick. She bit back a scream. Spotting a nearby filthy blanket, she wrapped it around her nakedness. She couldn't get away because the sleeping man lay across the cave opening. He looked somehow familiar. Terror gripped her when the river. The man who'd been a beast before he died.

How had she gotten here? The last she recalled was being at camp and Vida whispering to her. Dara groped for her amulet and realized it was gone. She was no longer safe from evil. Somehow she must have gone through Jo-Jo's Midnight Door.

The man's eyes opened. Feral yellow eyes. She scooted farther away from him, fetching up against the cave wall.

We ran in the night, Vida whispered. *With you I can change. We can change.* Vida's mind whisper frightened Dara almost as much as the naked man in the cave with her. Ran in the night? Change? Dara hugged the dirty blanket to her.

"I don't harm you," the man told her, his gutteral voice seeming to struggle with each word. "Won't."

She swallowed, not daring to believe him.

"My brother," the man added. "Did you see my brother?"

Dara shook her head, ignoring her mental vision of Nick shoving a dead man over the cliff, a man who looked like this one. A man who was also a beast?

We ran under the moon, Vida whispered. *We changed and ran.*

By now Dara noticed dried blood on her hands and she could no longer tamp down her horrible suspicion. No, impossible! Yet here she was naked in this awful cave with—with a man who might be something else. How did she get here?

"Tonight we run to find my brother," the man said.

As if not looking at him could change what he was saying, Dara turned her face away. Her gaze fell on a raw, partially eaten haunch that looked like it came from a deer. Bile rising in her throat, she scrambled around the man, barely making it out of the cave before she vomited, again and again. When her stomach was finally empty, she realized the day was slipping into twilight. How could it be?

The last she'd known she'd been at the camp with Nick. At night. Had she somehow slept through the following day in the cave with that man? Now a new night was coming and she couldn't remember what had happened in- between. She shuddered as she noticed him peering from the mouth of the cave.

"Moon comes up soon," he told her. "We change and hunt again."

Again? The implication brought on a new wave of nausea.

We'll mate with him after we change, Vida whispered. *I want to know how it feels. Different than with your man.*

Dara, sickened further, realized that somehow Vida had become a part of her and could feel what she felt. Worse, her twin must be controlling her mind and body.

"No!" she cried. "I won't!" Yet what could she do to prevent it from happening once Vida took control? Her skin crawled at the very notion. Without conscious volition, her hand reached for the amulet. No longer there. No protection.

"Night comes," the man said.

What would happen to her when the moon rose?

She caught sight of something moving toward them in the gathering darkness. Even before she could hope it was Nick, miraculously rescuing her, the man called out, "Grandfather."

"Quail Man." She recognized the voice of Running Bear.

The old man approached the cave. "You can't keep the woman," he said. "You have a wife in the village."

"Not for me," Quail Man said, "She runs under the moon like my brother. She's for him."

"Your brother is dead," Running Bear said.

She stared at the old man. How did he know?

"The woman comes with me." Running Bear leaned closer to peer into her face. He laid his hands to each side of her head, then let her go and stepped back. "Darkness crouches within you, tainting your heart," he said. "You must not stay here."

"I don't want to," she cried. "Please take me back to where I was camping in the ruins. Back to Nick. I don't know what happened, don't know how I got here."

Running Bear made no reply. He reached into a leather pouch hanging at his side and sprinkled a dark, aromatic powder over her head. Ignoring her sneeze, he grasped her hand and led her away from the cave.

"No, Grandfather," Quail Man called after them. "My brother—"

"I tell you your brother is dead." Running Bear tossed the words over his shoulder as he increased his pace, tugging her with him. When they reached the edge of the trees, he broke into a lope. "Hurry," he told her. "The moon must not catch you here or you're beyond help."

She stumbled along as best she could in her bare feet, clutching the blanket to her with her free hand. Vida began to whisper to her, but for some reason the words were too fuzzy to quite understand. Was it because of the painful wrenching inside her?

Oh God, she was changing, changing into—what?

Running Bear was talking to someone, then he shouted at her, "Drink this. Now. Fast."

Dara opened her mouth, gagged on the bitter liquid running down her throat, but forced herself to swallow it. She, in turn, was swallowed up by utter blackness.

———◈———

Nick didn't dare move from the ruins in case Dara might return and find him gone. He'd looked for her all day, fell asleep while he was eating supper, woke up to darkness and continued the search, Colt in its holster. As the moon rose, he heard a beast howl. Only one this time. What had happened to Dara? Or was it her? He understood now that he didn't know if he could bear to discover she was dead. But if what he suspected was true, she wouldn't be dead, but she'd be a Shifter. What then? Wouldn't he be compelled to hunt her? Kill her? The thought sickened him.

Hearing the howling come ever closer, he climbed into the crotch of a big valley oak and waited, gun in hand. After a time, the beast loped from the darkness under the pines in the grove, heading into range. Nick took careful aim—never waste a silver bullet—only to find he couldn't pull the trigger because he couldn't identify the sex of the Shifter. What if it was Dara?

Only when the beast was well past was he able to tell it was a male. Too late for a decent shot. He'd failed his sworn duty, violated the Stalker code. He waited, but the beast didn't return.

Nick spent much of the night searching—in vain. Just after dawn, he was sitting on his sleeping bag, his head in his hands, when someone said, "I warned you."

He jumped up and confronted Running Bear. "What the hell is that supposed to mean?"

"Your woman is safe. I'll take you to her. She needs clothes."

Nick gathered some of Dara's things. Once he had them in hand, Running Bear headed for the pine grove.

Nick caught up to him. "What happened to her?"

The glance Running Bear threw at him was caustic. "You know, hunter of moon runners."

"What did you call me?"

"What you are."

If the old man knew about Stalkers, then he knew about Shifters.

"You've killed one," Running Bear said. "You must not kill the other. He's the last. Now that his brother is dead, we can cage him when the moon is full. The dead twin was the stronger, my granddaughter's husband the weaker. He's no threat."

"Shifters are an abomination," Nick protested. "If he lives, more will be born."

"Not from Quail Man. Is your woman an identical twin?"

"Her twin died seven years ago."

The old man shook his head. "Her twin's spirit is undead."

"That doesn't make sense." As his words echoed in his mind, Nick remembered Dara telling him how her dead twin whispered to her. Had Vida's spirit actually lured Dara to the cemetery a few nights back? He couldn't forget how he'd found her lying naked on Vida's grave.

"Neither do moon runners make sense. Nor you, hunter of moon runners. I met your kind many years ago, searching the area for stray Voleks. They killed one."

"I learned about the Voleks as a child," Nick admitted. "A Shifter family."

"They no longer live in the valley."

"At least by that name," Nick said.

"Your woman harbors darkness within. It must be removed or she will be lost. Quail Man is ours, one of the People, we take care of him. She is not. If we don't rid her of the darkness, will you allow her to live, Hunter?"

Being called Hunter bothered Nick, even though that's what he was. And he couldn't deal right now with what might have to be done about Dara.

"My name is Nick," he told the old man. "Hers is Dara."

Running Bear stopped walking. "It's good to know names. Soon we come to my village. I need your promise you won't harm Quail Man. If you don't agree, you doom Dara. We'll hold a Kuksuyu ceremony for her, but Quail Man's the only one who'll be able to sense when the dark spirit leaves her."

Nick had no way of knowing if all this wasn't pure hogwash, though he recognized the word Kuksuyu.

"Can Kuksuyu ever be trusted?" he found himself asking.

Running Bear looked at him oddly. "Can any spirit ever be trusted?"

An equivocal answer. Nick didn't know what to believe, but a Miwok medicine man ought to have a few tricks up his sleeve. Or at least Nick could hope so. There didn't seem to be any other hope.

"You have my word about Quail Man," he said.

"As the moon shrinks, Quail Man will come back to the village. He'll be himself, so won't need the cage. Which is good, because Dara's in it." Running Bear resumed walking.

"You have her in a cage?" Anger tinged Nick's words.

"For her safety as well as ours. The other within her is dangerous."

"She isn't hurt? The beast didn't harm her?"

"He did not. Her feet are bruised from walking barefoot, nothing more. I don't know what damage her spirit has suffered."

Nick reached under his shirt and drew out the amulet he'd worn since Dara disappeared, leaving it behind. "She took off this amulet before she—" He found he couldn't bring himself to say the word that would label her as his deadly enemy.

Running Bear slowed to look at the amulet. "She lost her protection."

Nick nodded. "If I put it around her neck again—"

"No. Not until the ceremony. The twisted spirit within her could force her to destroy the amulet. You wear it until then." Running Bear offered him a crooked grin. "Might change you some, Hunter. Do you good."

"What is this Kuksuyu ceremony?"

"Taught to my people by the Old Ones. Bad spirits plagued my ancestors, too. Uneasy spirits who couldn't rest. The ceremony needs the afflicted one's heart mate. Dara is lucky I found you."

Heart mate? The old man called him that?

"I'm not—" he started to say, then hesitated. Just how did he feel about her? Heart mate sure wasn't the word he'd use, but he did care what happened to Dara. Cared a lot more than he'd ever intended to. "You mean you expect me to be a part of the ceremony?" he asked.

"Who else?" Running Bear said.

As they emerged from the pines an owl hooted four times. Moments later a huge white bird flew soundlessly past them, so close that Nick could almost feel the brush of its wings.

"Ah," Running Bear said. "The white owl tells us what we need to know. We need not further disturb his hunt for belly food tonight. We will see him again. Ask no more questions."

Nick had a lot of them, but he kept quiet the rest of the hike to the village. Though the old man had warned him, the sight of Dara lying on a pallet in a steel cage at the far edge of the settlement struck Nick to the heart.

"How can you say she's dangerous?" he demanded of Running Bear. "The moon's not up."

"The dark spirit forced a change the night before I found her," Running Bear said. "Medicine we gave her will prevent her from changing her shape again during this moon time, but it can't dislodge the darkness within her."

His words confirmed what Nick knew in his heart. Dara was a Shifter. Hadn't he heard her howling in the night? His natural enemy. She seemed to be sleeping at the moment. How small and helpless she looked. Running Bear left him sitting on the ground beside the cage, watching her.

As soon as the old man was out of earshot, Dara opened her eyes. "I knew you'd come," she told Nick. "Get me out of this cage and we can leave this accursed place."

Nick eyed her uneasily. She sounded different and she didn't look him in the eye as she spoke. "I brought your clothes," he said, rising and thrusting them through the cage bars. "Why did you run off?"

"Vida whispered to me again and I must have tried to find her and got lost in the woods. Running Bear found me, dosed me with some foul tasting stuff and locked me in here. I want out!"

He knew she was lying. "You left your sleep shirt behind," he said. "And your amulet."

"Vida seems to want me naked." She unwrapped the blanket around her enough so he got a glimpse of her breasts. Smiling slyly, she added, "Like you do."

Something about the way she acted raised the hair on his nape. This was and yet wasn't Dara.

"You shifted," he said bluntly.

Her smile broadened, became challenging. "Do I look like a beast?" She stood up, dropped the blanket and stood naked before him.

"Get dressed," he said and turned away, sick at heart.

"Please let me out," she begged. "I'll do anything you want, Nick. Just open the cage." The tremor in her voice got to him. If he didn't look at her when she spoke, he could imagine he was hearing the Dara he'd known before she'd changed.

He couldn't let her out, not as she was. Steeling himself, he glanced over his shoulder. When he saw she was almost fully clothed now, he faced her again.

"Look at me, Dara," he said.

Her eyes met his briefly, then glanced away. He hoped his shock wasn't obvious. Her eyes, instead of the changeable hazel he remembered, were amber-colored. Feral eyes. Hadn't she once told him Vida had yellow eyes? But Vida was dead. How could she become a part of her living twin?

Uneasy spirit, Running Bear had said. The talk of spirits made Nick uncomfortable. Spirits were intangible. Who knew whether or not they existed, Kuksuyu included?

"Will you let me out now?" she begged. "You can see I don't belong in this horrid cage."

"We have to wait until Quail Man comes home," he told her finally.

"What's he have to do with it?"

So she'd heard the name before.

Nick decided he might as well tell her the truth. "He's a part of a ceremony you need to go through before I can set you free."

"Ceremony?" her voice rose. "What kind of ceremony? You told me once we weren't Miwok. We're still not. Why should I have to wait for Quail Man, just to go through some stupid Indian ceremony? I might starve to death before then."

"I'll see you get something to eat." With an excuse to leave, Nick strode away from the cage. No human should ever be caged, he thought, still disturbed by seeing her imprisoned. On the other hand, Shifters couldn't be entirely human. Which led him to wonder, for the first time, if Stalkers were.

He found Running Bear sitting on a mat under a valley oak. "Dara's been fed," the old man told him. "I'll ask the women to bring her more to eat. Sit, now, and ask me your questions."

"You claim no more Shifters will be born," Nick said. "What's to prevent Quail Man from fathering a whole crew?"

"We took care of that long ago. Many moons ago, one of our women was raped by a man who'd been seen running as a beast.

We killed him. When the woman proved pregnant, we meant to kill his seed, but she begged for the life of her child, twins as it turned out, saying they were a part of our people. She spoke truth. What we did, when the boys were old enough, was take them for the operation that makes a man sterile. No babies ever will come from Quail Man. Or his twin, the one you killed, Hunter."

"I was born to kill Shifters," Nick said.

"You were taught this, yes. I'm not so sure about born. For us here in the village, Quail Man is no threat. He has a good heart and will submit to swallowing the medicine and being caged during the moon time. Once he is gone, we will have no more who change shape."

Thinking this over, Nick conceded that the Miwok had taken care of the situation as best they could without killing the twins.

"I'm going back to the camp site, gather up my gear and ride back here on my bike," he said.

"You will sleep in the village?"

Nick nodded. "I'll give Dara her sleeping bag and put mine next to the cage."

———※———

The night began quietly enough. Clouds obscured the waning moon. No howling disturbed sleep. Nick had just drifted off when the whispering began.

"I'm cold, Nick. Let me out so we can zip our sleeping bags into one and be together. You know you want me. Please, Nick."

The worst of it was he did want her, even if she wasn't quite Dara. But he was unpleasantly reminded of how Dara had told him Vida whispered in her mind.

He stood it as long as he could, at last taking his sleeping bag and moving far enough away so a whisper wouldn't reach him, but, if she needed him, she could call and he'd hear. After a long time he dropped into a deep sleep. Nightmares plagued him, ones where twisted, deformed creatures whispered in his ears, changing back and forth from monsters to diseased humans that silver bullets wouldn't kill.

44

Morning had never looked so good. He was rolling up his sleeping bag when one of the Miwok came to tell him Running Bear wanted him. It took Nick a minute to realize the man, dressed in jeans and flannel shirt, looked exactly like the man/beast he'd killed.

"Quail Man?" he blurted.

The man nodded, then loped away.

Nick had left his Colt locked in the compartment of his bike so he wouldn't be tempted to break his word to the old man. It made him uneasy to realize he was so close to a Shifter he'd promised not to harm. Because of Dara. He understood now there was little he wouldn't promise to see her overcome her sickness, whether of the spirit or whatever and be herself again.

Was it possible? He had to take the chance. Without his own Dara back again, life looked pretty damn bleak and pointless.

When he reached Running Bear, the old man said, "We begin the ceremony at dusk. You're not ready. Because you aren't of the people, you didn't hold a vigil in your youth, all alone, waiting for a spirit to come to you. You being *oyeai*, white, might think of it as an epiphany. Whatever. So you go now, with no food or drink, into a lonesome place and wait. For your heart mate's sake, we'll hope you find success before you return at dusk. Do you know where your lonesome place is?"

If he had to do it, he had to. "The pine grove near the ruins," Nick said after a little thought.

Running Bear nodded. "Because the Voleks planted those trees and your kind killed so many Voleks, it may work for you if you open your spirit." He reached to place one hand over the other on Nick's head for a moment. "Go."

Nick left his bike at the village and walked. When he entered the pine grove, he became acutely conscious of the crackle of brown pine needles under his boots and the snap of the occasional stepped-on twig. Too loud. He stopped, lifting his head to see rays of sunlight creeping between the thickness of the boughs. Aromatic scent filled his nostrils. Looking around, he chose a tree that appealed to him and sat at its foot, back to the bole. As he did, a red squirrel scampered up a neighboring tree, pausing part way up to chatter at him, the intruder.

When he didn't move, the squirrel finally fell silent and vanished into the branches. He thought over what he knew about Indians—Native Americans. Some tribes in the Midwest, as he recalled, believed that an animal came and spoke to them when they underwent their vigil as a youth. Was the squirrel an omen? It was red, like his hair.

Too simple. Nothing resembling an epiphany.

Silence surrounded him. He tried to blank his mind and succeeded so well he dozed off.

He sat in a field. A dark-haired man with golden eyes stood over him. Though the man didn't speak, Nick sensed what was unspoken. That he was trespassing on this man's property. Sergei Volek's property. Pine trees would be planted in this field someday.

Sergei beckoned and Nick rose, following him. Suddenly they stood in a room lit only by firelight where two dark-haired babies lay in separate cradles. Twins. A man who resembled Sergei hunched over one of the cradles, knife in hand. With a pang of horror, Nick realized he meant to kill the child. The baby opened its golden eyes and smiled at the man. The knife fell to the fur rug under the cradle and the man began to weep.

Somehow Nick knew that baby was Sergei and that Sergei's father knew what a Volek twin could become, but was unable to kill his children.

The scene shifted to a filthy pen in a cold, barren land where a young boy, malnourished and nearly naked, crouched like an animal. Nick watched while a bearded Sergei freed the boy and thwarted those who tried to follow and kill them. He understood that boy was Sergei's grandson.

Then Nick found himself in the hall of a large house. Wolf House, where the Voleks lived. He was alone except for a young woman who crept ahead of him. She opened a bedroom door and stepped inside. He knew instantly that she was a Stalker and what she meant to do.

*He watched as she killed as many Voleks as she could before she was
herself killed by one.*

*Sickened by the slaughter, he turned away and was once again in
the pine grove. Night lay thick about him and somewhere in the
darkness a Shifter prowled. It was his duty to kill the beast. He had
only a knife, but it was silver and would poison the Shifter. Suddenly
the beast leaped toward him. He buried the knife up to the hilt in its
chest, knowing he'd reached the heart. The beast fell at his feet. A
stray moonbeam shot through the boughs overhead and illuminated
Dara's dead face...*

"No!" Nick screamed, waking himself up. Sunlight still slanted
through the boughs, but at a different angle than earlier. Late
afternoon. He struggled to rid himself of the shards of nightmare, but they clung so persistently that he feared if he closed
his eyes he'd see her dead face again. Not Dara. Never Dara.

His cry had disturbed the squirrel. It appeared on a branch,
stared down at him, chattering, chewing him out properly for
being where he shouldn't be.

"I don't hunt squirrels," he said softly, which did nothing to
pacify the little animal.

No, he hunted Shifters, killed them without mercy. Like the
woman Stalker in Wolf House. He thought of the father, poised
to kill his own twins for fear of what they might become and
grimaced.

"Taught to be a Stalker," Running Bear had corrected when
Nick had said he was born one.

Though Nick had thought his unhappy childhood memories
were firmly buried in the basement of his mind, they rose up
before him, unhappy ghosts. His mother, weeping, telling him
of the divorce and that he must stay with his father

"For you are what he is. I only hope someday you can realize
you are also part of me."

He hadn't understood at the time and deeply resented her leaving him and his father. As a young boy, he'd tried hard to please
his father, even though he hadn't wanted to learn how to kill

people. Hadn't wanted to learn how to kill, period. His father had taken his belt to him, more than once.

Taught, yes.

He still had to numb his mind, to psych himself into killing.

He hated to kill.

Nick blinked, shocked by his own thought. Long moments passed before he realized what he'd had was an epiphany of sorts.

After a time he rose and made his way through the grove toward the village.

By the time he reached the settlement, afternoon shadows were long, pointing toward dusk. He wanted to talk to Running Bear, but the old man took one look at him and shook his head. "I can see you are different. I don't need to know how. The sweat bath is ready, you must take one with us."

Hunched in the low-ceilinged dwelling with seven men, steam rising around them, Nick finally was able to forgive his mother for leaving him alone with his father when he was a child. She, who could hardly bear to swat a fly, would have found it impossible to live with a killer. Obviously his father hadn't revealed what he was until he began training his son to kill. Their son. Nick knew now his mother was a part of him, too.

As he dressed after emerging from the sweat lodge, Nick felt as though he was inhabiting a strange dream. The feeling intensified when the drumming began and he saw a man dressed in a cape of bright feathers dancing around one of the four small fires to the right of where Dara, no longer in the cage, lay naked and motionless on a pallet. Another man, his feather cape all black, danced around the fire to her left. Two more, one in white feathers, the other wearing an owl headdress danced at her feet and head.

Kuksu Dancers? No doubt, since Kuksuyu was a feathered spirit.

The old medicine man, draped in a bearskin, crouched beside Dara. He motioned Nick to him, telling him to kneel on her left side. "Take the amulet from your neck and put it around hers. "

Raising her head so he could put the thong over it, Nick realized from the dead weight that she must be drugged. "Can't she have a blanket?" he asked in a low tone, hating to see her naked. "She'll get cold."

"Any covering will interfere. No more questions. Place your left hand, the heart hand, over her heart and do not move it no matter what happens."

Nick obeyed. He expected her skin to be chilled, but instead, it seemed hot. Was she running a fever?

Quail Man, dressed as Nick had seen him earlier, in jeans and flannel shirt, approached and crouched beside Running Bear. The medicine man rose and, chanting in a language Nick assumed was Miwok, began stroking the air above Dara's body with a long white feather. Quail Man watched each stroke intently.

A weird high-pitched whistling began, raising the hair on Nick's nape, even after he realized it came from the dancers. Unless it heralded the approach of Kuksuyu himself. Nick was no longer certain what he believed. Each of the dancers must have thrown some kind of herbs into their fires because a pungent smell arose, strong, but not unpleasant.

The scent, the chanting, the regular beat of Dara's heart under his fingers and the mesmerizing strokes of the feather in the air combined to send Nick further into a dream world. Dusk settled in, blurring outlines while still light enough to see.

Running Bear replaced the feather with a bone knife, ancient by the look of it, his chant becoming louder as he made passes over Dara's head with the knife. Nick felt his left hand, pressed over Dara's heart, grow colder and colder, until numbness set in. Suddenly Quail Man pointed his finger at a twisted wisp of mist gathering above Dara's body. At that moment a huge white owl swept over her. When it disappeared into the gathering darkness, the mist was gone.

"The evil has fled from her," Quail Man said softly.

"The death owl bears the unquiet spirit to the land of the dead, where it belongs," Running Bear affirmed.

Dara's eyes opened. It was hard to be sure with the uncertain light, but they looked hazel again to Nick as she stared up at him and called his name.

He reached for her, gathering her into his arms, and stood, holding her. A woman standing nearby motioned to him, so he followed her, carrying Dara into a house.

"I'll help her dress," the woman said.

As Nick waited outside, Quail Man approached. "I'm happy for you," he said. "My own heart mate is my life. I know you killed my brother, but I forgive the death. You were driven. I understand driven."

Nick was speechless. Staring after Quail Man as he walked away, he realized he'd was never again going to kill a Shifter. He didn't know why the Stalkers had taken up such a vendetta, but, for him, it was ended. Never before had Nick even considered that Shifters might not wish to shift, but couldn't help themselves. Driven, as Quail Man had said. Just as the Stalkers were driven.

Later, with Dara nestled against him, Nick listened to Running Bear's story of the Volek clan who lived in the house now in ruins and the strange taint that darkened their lives. Because the Miwok had always lived somewhere near Wolf House, their lives had been darkened, too.

"The old stories tell us that Quail Man and his brother were not the first of Volek blood to contaminate our people," the medicine man said.

"So you believe those with Volek blood still live around here?" Nick asked.

"Volek men were no different than any other men when it came to women. Why shouldn't they have left children they didn't know of behind?"

"Quincy," Dara said. "My great-grandfather. Could he have been a Volek?"

Running Bear nodded. "Had she lived, your twin would have been one who changed. You carry the blood, but you are not one. Her spirit entered you for a time and drove you into the change. Kuksuyu sent the owl to bring her to rest. She won't trouble you again."

"Kuksuyu helped me?" Dara said wonderingly.

"He found you worthy."

"I can feel I'm free of Vida," Dara said, clutching her amulet. "She—she took over, so that I couldn't get past her."

"Don't let your life be tainted by this," Running Bear advised. "Whatever her twisted spirit whispered to you was not the truth, but lies. What the heart knows is the only true worth."

He glanced at Nick. "You found something of worth in your vigil. Never lose it."

Nick knew he had to fully explain what he was—no, what he had been—to Dara, to admit he'd had his own reasons for joining Jo-Jo's group. He'd used them, used her. Looking at her, her eyelids already drooping over unmistakably hazel eyes, he was aware tonight was not the time. Not after what she'd been through. Tomorrow, when they left the Miwok village, he'd confess. Would she forgive him, as Quail Man had? He couldn't be sure.

"I owe you Dara's life," he told Running Bear. "In a different way, mine as well."

"We all were put on this earth to help one another," Running Bear said. "See that you don't forget the lesson you learned."

<hr />

The next morning, Nick pulled away from the Miwok village on his bike. Behind him, Dara leaned her cheek against his leather jacket , feeling safe for the moment. They'd camp, he'd said, by the ocean. Far away from the Valley, from Vida's grave and the ruins of Wolf House. Yet she had to carry her own concerns along with her as unwelcome baggage.

Though she vaguely remembered being caged, she didn't recall the ceremony that had freed her of Vida, nor, thank heaven, the night she'd spent running under the moon. What troubled her was that, both times she and Nick had made love, her twin's dark spirit had been with her. Was it actually Vida and not Dara who'd mated with him?

Maybe not. She'd been wearing the amulet both times, so she was in control, not Vida. It had protected her, after all. Which was why Vida had made her take it off. But how could she ever be sure Vida hadn't instigated the lovemaking?

When they finally reached the spot Nick had told her about, it was as wild and isolated as their Sierra camps.

"You have a talent for finding these places," she told him. "I would have sworn there wasn't anything like this between Frisco and LA. Not accessible, anyway."

"They're disappearing fast."

Though the day was mild, the wind off the water was cool. She helped him set up camp on the side of the sand dunes away from the ocean. After they ate, they sat near the dying fire as they'd done so many times before.

"What is it about a fire that makes you feel protected?" she said.

"Racial memory from the old caveman days," he suggested.

"I suppose." She wanted to ask what was ahead for them—but was there going to be a them?

"I have to tell you something," Nick began.

When he didn't go on, she asked, "What?"

"You know about Shifters." Again he paused.

"More than I want to, yes."

"I'm a Stalker. We kill Shifters."

"I know that—I saw you kill one. But what do you mean you're a Stalker? Is it some kind of organization?."

"Not exactly. I've been thinking about it and my belief is that Shifters and Stalkers are two sides of the same coin—one exists because the other does. Neither is the norm, as humans are."

"Good grief, Nick, you're as human as—as anyone." She'd been going to say "as I am," but caught it back. Carrying Shifter blood, was she entirely human?

"I don't think I am," he said. "My mother was, though, so I'm half-human, anyway."

She smiled at him. "Good enough for me."

"You don't understand. Stalkers are trained from birth to kill

Shifters. It's our destiny."

Dara grimaced. "Sounds depressing."

"I joined Jo-Jo's group because he told me he was going to some old ruins where Wolf House once stood. I was following up on a lead about a strange beast seen in the San Joaquin Valley and it sounded as though Jo-Jo might have a shortcut to finding it. Which turned out to be true, though I missed my chance to kill the beast there. Then I realized the beast appeared not because of all the nonsense about Midnight's Door, but because you were there with that amulet. So I used you as bait to lure the Shifter to me again and did kill it."

"You used me as bait?"

Nick didn't look at her. "Rotten deal, I know. I did figure the amulet would keep you safe, but that's no excuse."

Hurt and angry, Dara tried to order her thoughts. It *was* rotten of him. And all the time she'd thought he was so wonderful, had been so grateful he'd given her a chance to straighten out her life. She started to say so, then remembered what happened after he'd killed the Shifter. Hadn't Nick rescued her from Vida's grave? Without him she might have died there of exposure. Hadn't he helped Running Bear rid her of her twin's unquiet spirit?

Another thought occurred to her. "How come you didn't kill Quail Man?"

"I've given up being a Stalker. I know I carry the blood, but that doesn't mean I have to be one, any more than you have to be a Shifter. You're the reason I examined my life. When I feared you might be a Shifter, I knew I could never hunt you down and kill you."

Tears filled her eyes, banishing the hurt and anger. He did care about her. "I can't blame you for what you did. You saved my life."

He reached for her. More than anything she wanted to be in his arms, but she drew back.

"What's wrong?" he asked.

She blurted out the truth. "I carry Shifter blood; I can't take any chances on bearing a Shifter child. Thank God I didn't get pregnant when we made love before."

Nick laughed.

"I don't see anything amusing about it," she snapped.

"Quail Man can't pass on his Shifter blood because Running Bear saw to it he and his twin had vasectomies when they were young teens. I can't pass on my Stalker blood because I did the same thing when I was twenty because I'd made up my mind never to teach a child of mine to kill. I'm sterile; you're in no danger of getting pregnant."

"Truth?"

"Truth. I'm through lying to you. Running Bear called me your heart mate and that was also the truth."

Heart mate. She liked the sound of it, the implication that there'd be a future for them. Together.

"What with all these truths," he said, "I figure maybe we can find a place we like to settle in and get you that kitten you've always wanted. What do you think?"

More than an implication—a declaration!

She held out her arms and he caught her to him. When his lips found hers, the kiss, deep and long and passionate, told her how much he wanted her. And she found another truth there. If Vida had been a part of their lovemaking before, she wasn't now. And never mind Shifter and Stalker. This was Dara and Nick and no one else. Nothing else.

Heart mates. Forever.

DEMONKILLER

Myra Nour

BRETUCK'S GIFT

Azra worked quickly on the clay, her strong, deft hands shaping the form without hesitation, making her creation appear effortless. It was not that she was a great artist. No. She had some small talent, true. But it was the fairy blood running through her veins, much diluted from her great-grandmother, yet still potent that made the frail shape seem to take on a life of its own.

Such was the magic that could be imbued into a figurine molded from the special properties of the akla clay when shaped by one trained in the fairy arts. She smiled gently. Her son, Bretuck would be very pleased with it. She could picture his happiness as his large, yet delicately made hands clasped the statue to his chest. In those hands, she already saw the markings of a healer. Not that any of the villagers, except a few close friends, would ever let him touch them with the gift of health.

To them, he was born under a curse, conceived as he had been by a demon; a soldier, dreaded enemy, one of the violent Hessitor race. Men who captured the villagers for working the crystal mines of their homeland and slew indiscriminately those who opposed them.

Unfortunately, her people, the Coihlar were immune to the

deadly fumes of the crystal caves, making them invaluable as mining slaves. Her child, born from the pain and anguish of his beginnings, would inherit power from her, the human Coihlar blood, as well as the cursed blood of his father. From the villagers Bretuck had received only superstition, hatred, and by some tolerance, but to her, he was the truest joy in her life.

DEMON'S CURSE

Her mind skimmed over pleasanter, recent memories, back to her darker days. Back to the time of "un-Bretuck". That day, the most profound one of her young life, had started out wondrous on one hand and the worse ever, on the other. She had marveled at the sparkling crispness of the air as she left the cottage that morning, going to fetch water for her mother's sponge bath.

There was an earthy smell and that of growing things, a very pleasing mixture to her fairy blood. The forests around the village sang and moved with wildlife, as if the creatures had come out on this first fine spring day to celebrate the ending of the long harsh winter.

As Azra retraced her steps to the cottage where her mother lay ill, three days now, she hoped spring's arrival would revive momma as well. Being the only healer within a weeks journey, momma had to do her own healing, which she did when her illness began. But there were times when Azra watched with anxious eyes as her mother burned with fever and mumbled frightful curses to the four winds.

Azra knew some healing practices. She knew to cool momma's body with dampened cloths and how to brew a strong broth for her to sip. But momma's fever burned as bright as the hearth on a winter's morn, and she was as weak as a newborn kitten. The smell of sickness underlay the herbs she crushed and scattered to counterbalance the ill humors.

Wishing she were a little older, more knowledgeable, Azra sponged momma's fever sweat from her. There was no recognition in her mother's lovely golden eyes this morning—they shone like twin suns in the grip of her hot flesh and the darkened cottage. If she were a young woman instead of the young thing she was, with breasts that barely thrust against her dress, she would know so much already.

The student learned, but rudimentary things — some common healing practices, a few magic tricks — until they reached the true beginnings of their power. A girl had to reach the fullness of womanhood before her powers flowed through her veins, ready for the arts of healing and magic to be passed on to her. Boys had similar time frames.

Azra had looked down at her thin frame in disgust. She had barely begun her monthly blood flow. She was many, many moons away from her time of true learning. She had sighed and brushed momma's curly hair gently away from her cheek. She stared at her mother a moment, remembering that momma had made her memorize the most important magic a healer could give to her chosen village. There were tricks of fairy power to confound an enemy and keep them from discovering the village. Of course, Azra would be unable to use any of them for a long time, but momma insisted she learn them anyway.

She bit her lip as she remembered it had been the first morning of momma's sickness. Had her mother had a premonition? Azra paled at the thought. Did momma think she would no longer be around to protect the villagers? The alarm horn sounded, blasting through the cottage's side window, cleaving the quiet as sharply as the thunder of a winter storm. Her head snapped up in reaction, as quick as a deer who hears the careless hunter struggling through the underbrush.

Azra's heart rose into her throat and the bosom of her dress fluttered slightly as she peeked fearfully from the window. All clear. Maybe it was but a nervous guardsman? Maybe he had heard a deer or wolf passing through the bushes and panicked?

Taking a deep breath of the fresh air wafting through the opening, Azra was glad the villagers had set a guard anyway.

Momma was in no condition to foresee the Hessitors coming, and she was too young. So the villagers did it the old way, the way before the fairy folk had come into their lives, making their harsh existence better and safer. It was the time when the people needed a healer/magician the most, to sense the enemies approach and prepare a spell for their arrival. One of the spells momma had made her memorize but days ago.

Just when Azra's erratic heartbeat slowed, she heard the clash of sword against staff. Beastly yells erupted from men's throats and screams of women and children rose shrilly, fouling the cleanness of the sparkling spring air. She glanced at momma. Her features seemed more shrunken than but a moment before, as if she wished to withdraw from the cruel sounds that pierced the quiet safety of the cottage. Azra knew she couldn't move momma in her condition and certainly she did not have the strength either. Her momma would be limp, dead weight made heavier by its inertia.

Maybe they would be safe? The cottage was at the farthest reaches of the village, surrounded by the forests from which fairies drew much of their power. The next instant the thought was shattered as a fierce Hessitor warrior burst through the door, his huge body filling the frame. The sour smell of beer, the tangy odor of fresh blood, and that of an unwashed body invaded the small cottage, driving all other odors before it.

For a second the warrior's face was hidden in the shadow from the great oak outside, and Azra saw the gleam of fire where his eyes were located. He took one step and became immersed in the sunlight from the window, and there was the barest impression of knee length boots, suede pants, a chain mail shirt, and long hair.

His eyes flicked in her momma's direction, but seemed to dismiss her as undesirable prey. His face was a blur to Azra as the large Hessitor approached. She trembled and knew not what to do. But it seemed the warrior did — he launched himself at her. Azra's bones were jarred out of place as he forced her onto the floor in one great predatory leap, uncaring his weight almost crushed her.

She tried to fight, but the warrior brushed aside her efforts as easily as she batted away annoying flies from her face on a hot summer's day. Azra waited for the death blow, then looked up in confusion as she felt the warrior fumbling with his clothing. Hessitor's usually plunged a sword immediately through any-one who showed the markings of fairy blood. They were fearful of the magic as well as angered by the fairy's ability to hide a village from them. Azra couldn't help the faint moan that es-caped her lips as she felt his true intent. Her momma groaned like a beast in agony, as if she shared her daughter's pain.

Looking into the Hessitor's demon bright eyes for a heartbeat, Azra saw he *was* frightened of her, but kept stabbing at her with his man's weapon, as if he could purge his fright through com-pletely overcoming her with his own kind of power. He would kill her with his iron sword afterwards. She did not need her power to read this in his eyes.

A shadow fell between their bodies. Azra barely glimpsed her father's dear face and his raised staff with the carved spear point before a stream of hot blood spewed over her. He disdainfully pushed the dead soldier off her, noticeably looking aside as he helped her to her feet. Azra ran the few steps to her mother's bedside, her knees trembling as she knelt with a sudden plunge. Her momma's lovely eyes stared upward unseeingly. She was dead.

She would never know if it were simply momma's time, or if the battle had edged her closer to the precipice. Maybe Azra thought glumly, momma had still been able to feel the close connection between them, and the pain had been too great to bear.

With head drooping like a wilted flower, Azra wept silently. Her father knelt slowly beside her, placing a hand on her shoul-der, silent comfort in their shared grief. He shook her gently after a brief moment, telling her they must be off, must hide in the forests until the enemy left. Azra arose in numbed acceptance, too used to obeying her father to disagree now. She barely noticed the drying sticky blood on her dress, or the mixture of blood and warrior's leavings that had run down her thigh.

The village had been lucky this time. A few were slain, a few taken as slaves, but most came out unscathed. The guards' vigilance had paid off—most of the people had heard the alarm in time to run off and hide in the woods. She was not so lucky. Azra knew when next her cycle time came and went, even though the warrior had not killed her, he cursed her even from his grave. She carried a bastard Hessitor offspring, spawn of a demon race.

WITCH'S PURGE

At first she tried fairy curses, hoping to purge the creature from her body, but she had no true power yet. The child remained, locked in her womb, mocking her with its astounding growth rate.

One more time she tried to rid herself of the Hessitor curse. She traveled deep into a part of the forest she'd never seen, had only heard whispers of. The villagers thought she knew not of this place, the witch's hut wherein the servant of the dark handed over magic for those with the right coin. They went for poison to kill an unwanted child, for love potions and other things which a healer would never consent to do.

The trees surrounding the glen where the witch was reported to live were bent over and twisted into odd shapes, as if they suffered arthritic pains. It was dusky dark under those snake-like contortions of limb and leaves and smelled of mold and dampness under the deep purplish shade. Azra felt sure sunlight had never touched the earth beneath the overhanging giants, yet the sun had seared her shoulders before stepping into the trees gloom but a moment before.

At first glance, she thought there was an overgrown hill nestled between the giants, but in reality, it was a profusion of vines and greenish-black creepers crawling into and over a tiny hut. A small door was barely distinguishable between the virulent growth, but someone kept the doorway cleared. Before her hand descended on the cracked wood, an ancient sounding voice called for her to enter. Her nostrils flared, offended by the strange smells emanating from within, the sickening mingling of ancient magic making it worse. Dark power. Dark magic. She shivered in reaction.

She found a haggard old woman with lank hair dragging the ground, sitting on a small stool and stirring a smelly concoction in a hearth blackened pot. The interior was darker than the tree shadows, relieved only by the hearth fire, which threw out shoots of sparks and faint light. It lit the witch's face and Azra realized she'd held her breath for a horrified moment, for the old crone looked an ogre in its lair.

The woman grinned widely, showing two bone white teeth, everything else in her mouth blackened or greenish with decay. Azra shivered as she realized how the witch's appearance replicated the hut's exterior, and the old sorceress knew well the image she created.

"Fairy child, come to the old witch for help, eh?" She cackled and waved to another stool across the hearth.

Azra hesitated, unconsciously touching her stomach.

"Oh, want to be rid of the demon's curse."

She jumped, wondering if the witch had the power to read thoughts. "Yes, I need to be rid of the...Hessitor's spawn!"

The old woman raised her eyes at Azra's vehemence, then leaned forward. "I've never had a fairy ask for my potions." She laughed merrily. "Puts me in a right good mood, it do." She jumped up sprightly for one so old and went to where the deepest shadows lay.

Azra felt light-headed. The tiny room was filled with the odor of strange herbs and weeds, which she saw were hung to dry from the rafters. Now that her eyes had adjusted to the dimness, she spied a bat hanging upside down amongst the herbs, its wings were spread as if ready to take flight, but it hung captured by death and several strings attaching it to a beam.

The scent of wet fur and animal droppings filled her nose. She wondered if rats and other vermin nested in the shadows, or if it was the old witch that smelled so rank. Azra crushed something underfoot. Looking down she saw frogs lining the stones of the hearth. Her foot had ground one of the dried husks.

The old woman crowed happily and Azra glanced up as a log flared on the hearth and the firelight pierced the darkness surrounding the witch. She took a small vial from the back recesses of a filthy, web bedecked cabinet, clasping it within her gnarled, clawed hands as if it were elfin gold. Suddenly she exclaimed, "Yea 'ave stomped one of me curse frogs."

She scuttled like a giant beetle to where Azra sat. Her skin crawled and she wished to be gone, wished she'd never come at all.

The witch shrugged and swooped down over the shattered frog, seeming not to notice as Azra scooted back frantically. Each tiny fragment of stiffened frog skin was carefully gathered into the witch's knotty hands, then every piece held up for a quick glance as if it were a gem before placing it gently back into her palm.

Returning to the hearth, the old hag took a fingertip pinch of the frog and dropped it into the pot. "No harm's done fairy. You might as well pull your heart out of your stomach." She grinned, a death skull come to life. "I needed to crush the frog anyway."

Azra shifted on the stool, scuffing her foot against the dirt, hoping none of the frog's potential curse rubbed off on her.

"Done," the witch put down the thick handled spoon she'd used for stirring the brew. "Some unlucky fellow will find his man's desire shriveled for a spell." She shook her head solemnly, but the guffaw that escaped her wrinkled lips spoiled the illusion of her concern.

"Don't yea wish we could give the Hessitors a goodly dose of this?" she waved to the pot and eyed her.

Azra couldn't squish the gleam of satisfaction that arose in her, then blanched in horror when she saw the witch had read it in her eyes.

"Yes, we be not that different, only work for different masters."

Azra stumbled off the stool. If the old witch wanted to play games she would leave, potion or no. Sensing her determination, the witch's eyes twinkled with hidden knowledge as she handed the vial over. She cackled merrily as Azra got ready to leave, poking happily through the large basket of food and herbs she'd brought as payment, the witch uncaring that her filthy hands left smudged trails of grime in their wake.

Home! She breathed deeply of the fresh herb scent within her cottage. It seemed a safe haven after the stifling, evil atmosphere of the witch's abode. Azra had spent a long time sitting, staring at the vial, holding it up to the light to try and see through its murky contents. It was liquid, but such a pitch-black color, not even the bright sunlight falling through the window could penetrate its bottomless depths.

Shivering, she took a small sip of the witch's brew. Its taste was bitter, horrible. She spit it out instantly. Azra's frightened breath came in short bursts as she warily placed a hand on her stomach. She had heard a scream in her mind and she knew from whence it came, and it was the presence of that flickering life which made her spit the witch's brew out.

Azra looked where she had spewed the black poison, shivering again as she saw the wisps of evil magic curling upward from the damp spot. She could smell the dark magic. Taking a thick cloth and healing herbs, she scrubbed the spot thoroughly; rubbed until the boards glowed a pale yellow color next to the dark brown wood surrounding it. Then she buried the vial in a deep hole beyond the confines of the village, for distance was an important factor of safety when magic and potions of the dark arts were involved.

Her back ached and she kneaded it thoughtfully then placed her hand once more on her small hump of a stomach. Was this child more fairy than beast? Azra didn't know, wouldn't know until its birth, but she had decided, she would wait.

BRETUCK'S ARRIVAL

Her pregnancy had been easy, her bulk on such a small frame the only hindrance to her work. Azra had kept her face expressionless as the birth pains started when her time approached. She told her father and friends she planned to go but a short distance into the forests to pick herbs. The villagers shook their heads in worried agreement, knowing it might disturb the healing magic for a mere human to tag along on her search.

Her father wore a worried, resigned expression. She thought he guessed her intent, perhaps he too thought it best for her to have the child in secrecy, away from the prying villagers' eyes. Azra went deeper into the woods than she had told the others she intended, not wanting a villager to stumble on her birthing by accident. She must be the first to see the baby and make her own judgment. It even surprised her the baby was born in but a few brief hours. Azra had already laid out all the necessary cloths, cleansing herbs and a small sharp knife. She had borne a son, a healthy one from the look of him. Azra didn't allow herself the luxury of looking further at the baby until after she took care of cutting and tying the cord, then thoroughly cleansing them both.

She lay down on a blanket made from soft curly lamb's wool, the babe lay cradled in her arms in a smaller version of hers. She touched the fine thatch of red hair on his head, then her own curly locks. At least he had inherited the fiery tresses of the fairy clan. She stroked a finger gently across his downy cheek, then counted every toe and finger, holding each one in wonder. How tiny, how perfectly formed each one was.

"Bretuck," she said softly, trying it out loud for the first time. It sounded right to her, even though her son made no response. He was a beautiful baby. Azra noticed a flash of color fly overhead. Looking up, she saw a blue bird perched on a branch just above their heads. Her body jerked in surprise when a tiny object fell and landed on Bretuck's stomach. The bird had dropped something.

She picked up the red holly berry and glanced up questioningly at the bird. "A gift for the young fairy," the blue bird chirped, fluffing his feathers gaily. Azra shook her head in wonderment. You'd think the little fellow had made the berry himself. Birds could be such boisterous "peacocks". She absently tucked the gift into her pocket.

Azra spent the rest of the short evening feeding the baby and herself, and getting acquainted with him. Bretuck hadn't opened his eyes yet, not an unusual thing for a newborn, but she waited anxiously for it. Her son's whole future, perhaps his very life, hinged on the color of his eyes. She settled down for the night, tucking them both into the warmth of the wool blanket. The night creatures whom she'd spoken with earlier agreed to alert her to any intruders.

She pulled as much power as she could from the forest surrounding her, but it would take much to regain the loss of energy during childbirth. The first shadow of dusk fell over the land, when it happened — Bretuck opened his tiny unfocused eyes.

A chill shot through to her very bones, but it was not the night air. Bretuck's eyes were the demon red of his father's. Tears dripped unheeded, wetness soaked her bosom. It was not fair! He was a perfect child, a beautiful healthy son. The aura of power shining from him was very strong, even the blue bird had seen it right away.

She sat in numbed silence for a long time, then her mind filled with plans. These thoughts had been with her ever since she had bonded with Bretuck, she had simply not called them to life until they were needed. Unlike humans, fairies bonded with the life within them months before the birth, when the life force of the fairy blood within the child made itself known. Once she'd felt that connection with the unborn Bretuck, Azra had already made her mind up that no villager was going to murder her child or force her to do it.

It was rare that there were births from rape. Most women were dragged off to be slaves, and even if raped first, were still taken by the Hessitors. It was the occasional women who escaped the warriors such as she had, who bore the bastard child. Even these were generally accepted as long as they inherited human eye coloring, and she had never heard of a fairy bearing a Hessitor child.

With a shiver she recalled her momma's dire warnings against a joining of fairy and Hessitor blood. She also remembered her grandmomma mumbling of dark curses if such a thing were to happen. Why had they not told her more? Perhaps they felt she were too young at the time. Azra hugged her own body in misery. How she wished momma were here to give her comfort and guidance.

Looking down into the bright red eyes of her child, Azra went over the legends in her mind. Of the few births of such children as her innocent son, only a handful had been born with the fire colored eyes of their fathers. All of these infants were killed. Even her dear momma had taken part in such a ritual, traveling to a distant village, one without a healer and giving a demon-eyed baby the potion of eternal sleep.

A young Azra had been shocked. Her momma had gently explained it was a preferable method than strangling or drowning as was the popular custom in villages far away. Then her momma and grandmomma, who had still been alive at that time, had sat her down and warned her of the demon curse. The villagers half believed the legend of the Sartwor demon to be just that — a legend. The Sartwor was used as the "boogie man" to scare little children into obedience.

But the two powerful fairy healers let her know in firm convincing tones the legends were truth. That if a baby with the red Hessitor eyes were allowed to live, it could turn into the fearful Sartwor demon. Her Grandmomma personally knew of one such case and had heard of another in her youth. The two children, who had been allowed to live because the villagers were too kind-hearted or the mothers' too well-loved, had changed into Sartwor demons.

MYTH?

Azra had left her momma's cottage, tears of sadness threatening to fall. She loved little children, it seemed unfair to her even then, their fate was so ordained. But she had not needed to listen further to her elders. She knew the legends as well as any villager, only she now knew they were truth.

The reality of the Sartwor was wrapped in myth and mists of times past. No one knew by what magic the two demon-eyed children had transformed into the Sartwor. This creature was said to be huge and horribly ugly to look upon, that it was evil, murderous in its rage, and it would kill anyone in its path. One child of eons past had slaughtered all of its fellow villagers. The other child who had turned into the Sartwor demon had been stopped by large numbers of men fighting together against it.

Azra's shoulders straightened unconsciously as she again looked into the smoldering red eyes of her infant son. She stroked his soft cheek. No one, regardless of legends or truth, was going to injure Bretuck. She smiled gently when the baby's fingers curled around her finger as she played with his tiny hands. Surely they would see the power that shone from him, he was good. She felt it with every fiber of her being.

A family of blue birds flew by, calling a greeting as they passed. Remembering the gift, Azra fished the berry from her pocket. She looked from the berry to Bretuck's eyes, astounded at how they matched as if preplanned by some unknown force. She glanced to where the birds had disappeared in the forest's heavy foilage. It almost seemed the blue bird had known of Bretuck's eye coloring. Azra laughed to herself, she was being silly. Birds didn't have any power. Nevertheless, unwittingly, he had given her the first offering for Bretuck's acceptance. A gift from woodland friends was considered special, more so if it was the first offering.

Reaching in her pack, she withdrew her son's *raqu* prepared by her before his birth. It was a small amulet bag, sewn from the silky fur of a rabbit her father had found frozen in the snow. A healer would not eat of an animal's flesh nor wear the wrappings made from her woodland friends. But it was considered lucky to make the raqu from the fur of an animal found dead, as if the amulet might retain some connection with the spirit of the previous owner. Azra had felt the rabbit was right for Bretuck's raqu, maybe the creature's gentle spirit would help waylay the fears of some of her fellow villagers.

That was her thought before she'd seen her son's damning eyes. Now, not even the raqu's spirit could help her baby. But an infant's first acceptance must be from his mother, thereby the bestowing of a gift had a special meaning. The significance of the gift was even more important if the baby were born with fairy power.

Azra carefully placed the red berry inside the bag and pulled the strings shut tight. She draped the raqu around her son's neck, where it hung to his tiny chest. His chubby arms shook in a reflexive movement, but to Azra it appeared he approved of his raqu.

Now, she had to win the acceptance of the villagers and be offered a gift by someone in the village to signify acceptance. It would be Bretuck's second offering to his amulet bag. Others would be added as special events occurred in his life. Azra touched her own raqu, which hung between her breasts, then gripping it tightly, she sent a silent prayer to the being of light.

THE TRUE DEMON

———— ❖ ————

Azra suckled the babe all through the day, increasing his strength and continuously pulling power from the forest around her to build up her own. She was worried, knew her vigor was not returning quickly enough for the trek back to her village.

As twilight seeped into the landscape, a large silver wolf stepped from the bushes and peered at her with its intelligent gaze. Azra noted the female's elongated nipples, probably she'd recently weaned a litter of pups. She stretched a hand toward one of the most magnificent creatures of the forest, calling the canine to her side.

The wolf stood patiently as Azra explored her soft fur with her hand and did not turn away when she stared into its golden eyes. She communed silently with the female, who as quietly, agreed to allow the fairy to draw from its vast reserves of energy.

The imposing predator stretched out beside her. Azra, wrapped in her blanket, Bretuck cuddled in her arms, lay side-by-side with her new woodland companion, her fingers curled into the thick fur. She felt the great beast's heart beneath her caressing fingers, guided her power to tap into its center, and drew gently from its sustenance.

All night they lay thus, fairy and wolf, bound by magic and motherly instinct. In the morning, the she-wolf rose slightly unsteadily, then shook her body vigorously, as if shaking off the effects of the fairy magic.

"I hope you are not too weak." She spoke softly, thanked the creature with eye-to-eye contact.

Like a flitting of a swift bird through her mind, she picked up the wolf's thoughts, "Weak, rabbit renew strength."

Azra dipped her eyes in acknowledgement of her gift and to hide her distress that a precious bunny would lose its life soon. So it was ordained in the life cycle of the forest and its denizens.

After the silver form slipped silently into the foliage, she arose, surprised by the immense pulse of power that surged through her small frame. The she-wolf had been strong indeed, perhaps the dominant female in her pack. Azra was more grateful than ever her call had been heard by such a majestic beast.

She gathered her things, then bundled Bretuck securely to her breast as she started the long journey home. She was only a little weary once arriving at the villages' outskirts. No one saw her at first, not until she stood near the plaza's edge, then a flow of humanity ringed her suddenly.

The village elders broke through the crowd. Weta, the leader, spoke with his official voice. "Show us the child."

Azra was frightened for Bretuck, but also an unexpected determination and iron-will flushed through her being. Ever since her pregnancy had weighed heavily on her body, her fairy power had been gaining strength at a remarkable rate. In secret, she'd practiced her magic, those taught to her by her mother, and other acts gleamed from her mother's ancient texts.

Now, as she unwrapped Bretuck and held him high above her head for all to see, she gathered her powers about her like a shield. It glimmered and crackled. Her hair stretched outward in reaction to the currents flowing through her body.

People gasped in the crowd, and whether it was her appearance or Bretuck's, she didn't care.

"Death to the Demon." Weta pronounced.

"Death to anyone who tries to harm my baby," Azra stated solemnly, letting the power permeate the air and crack sharply.

More gasps. Suddenly the villagers parted and her father stepped forward. He met her gaze, his eyes were sad but steady in their loyalty. She handed Bretuck over when he reached for her son. Her father examined the infant carefully, then turning to his neighbors, proclaimed, "He is a fine baby boy."

"But his eyes!" Someone shouted nervously.

Her father shook his head. "True, they are red, but also he is part fairy. Much power emanates from him."

"You cannot judge, you are bigoted in his behalf," Weta said.

"I am. But, who better to judge his potential than he who was married sixteen years to a fairy and whose child is one so gifted?"

"It is the law." The leader insisted.

"I don't think she agrees it is fairy law." Her father nodded in her direction.

The villagers turned as one, stared at her stubborn, power-tinged stance, many turned their eyes away in discomfort.

"The Demon must die!" A large, brutish man pushed forward and several other people joined him, including some women.

Now Azra understood the true face of the Demon. It was not her son with his ruby eyes, but the ugly hate-filled glares and prejudice that saturated the very air, an invasion of superstition from her people that infused the plaza with evil.

THE ACCEPTANCE

The small group edged forward, their hatred shimmering about them like a shield, but it would not help them.

"Step back," she commanded, thrusting on arm toward them.

When they didn't stop, she let a stream of electric-charged power shoot from her fingertips. It struck the dirt in front of the big man's feet, causing a cloud of dirt to spiral up and coat the belligerent villagers. The group coughed furiously, then faded into the crowd.

"There is another law." Her father suddenly shouted, gaining everyone's attention.

Weta stepped from the crowd and faced them, a smug expression flooding his features. "That's right, the law of acceptance."

Azra knew he thought no one would step forward to give her child a gift of acceptance, thus securing his place amongst the villagers, whether most of them agreed or not. She worried her lower lip with her teeth. Her father couldn't give acceptance, being a relative negated participation. She picked out several childhood friends among the wash of faces, but the young women turned their eyes downward in shame. They were not brave enough to go against Weta and the whole village.

Silence reigned. The only movement was villagers shifting their gazes from one neighbor to another, challenging expressions on many, they did not wish anyone sympathetic to her plight, to step forward.

A small figure pushed through the people. It was Hanla, her father's best friend, close enough to her family she'd called him uncle all her life. Hanla was a wizened old man, barely topping her own height. His grandmother had been fairy, only his size reflected this heritage. His hair was a nondescript brown, his eyes a dark green.

"I give acceptance," he said loudly, his tone firm.

Shocked looks overcame many villagers' faces. The elders were clearly displeased. Nonetheless, Weta would not neglect his duty. He said, "How do you show acceptance?"

The old man fumbled in his side pack, brought forth an object too tiny to see properly, then plopped it unceremoniously into Weta's outstretched palm.

"It is a twin of Bretuck's raqu." Hanla had an air of pride in his tone.

Weta examined the tiny gift, frowned, then with an angry clench of his jaw, handed it to her.

Azra was overcome with joy. The gift was a miniature rabbit, carved with care and great artistry, which Hanla was famous for producing. Its nose was caught in mid-twitch, and it held a carrot between its paws. It even had thin whiskers and individual hairs were carved in such a manner, its fur looked real.

"It's beautiful," she whispered, giving her uncle a smile of pure joy. Balancing it on her palm so it sat on its haunches as Hanla intended, she held it out for all to see.

"Acceptance." Sheris, another dear friend of the family spoke up loudly, striding through the people, taking up position next to Hanla.

"Acceptance." Another shout cut through the clean, somnolent air. This time, Vaya stepped forward, making a third in the triangle of acceptance that was village law and tradition.

"The child is accepted." Weta proclaimed, his countenance denying his words by every agitated twitch of his face and body.

The crowd dispersed slowly, many hateful stares thrown at Bretuck's tiny red locks before they left.

Tears shimmered in Azra's eyes as she examined the diminutive gift, it was anything but a small present. So perfect. How could he have known? She glanced to Hanla, warmth flooding her senses at the kind face that met her gaze.

Perhaps he'd already carved the rabbit long ago, maybe as a gift for someone's birthday. But, somehow she didn't think so. It felt special, made just for her son, but it would be impolite to ask Hanla the truth.

She opened Bretuck's raqu, kissed the wondrous gift, then dropped it carefully inside. An image came to her mind, of Hanla sitting by the hearth at night, perfecting the beauty he created with his talent. She knew in her heart, whether by fairy power or strength of friendship, Hanla had started carving the acceptance gift when her time neared.

Her son's life was saved, his place in their society cemented by her friends' love and loyalty, and the lovely wood carving which replicated the spirit of Bretuck's raqu.

She went up to her friends, tears running down her cheeks as she thanked each in turn. They patted her hands, kissed her cheek, and gave words of love and encouragement.

It was all she needed, after the acceptance, this gift of true friendship and love. The air suddenly seemed clearer, sparkled with good spirits — the whiff of evil dispersed, at least temporarily.

As Azra walked beside her father to her cottage, the one he and others had built shortly before Bretuck's birth, she mulled over many thoughts and worries. She knew gaining her son's real acceptance would be a long, hard struggle, but perhaps with friends, such as had shown their loyalty today, the battle could be won eventually.

METAMORPHOSIS

Bretuck was an astoundingly beautiful baby, who laughed frequently and cried only when he was hungry. Several of Azra's lifelong friends finally gathered up the courage to stop and chat with her and smile at his winsome face. Alas, it was only when Bretuck slept they could show such bravery. Once his eyes opened, visitors shuddered and made some excuse to leave.

Her son might have won some villagers over eventually, even with his eerie eyes, if it'd not been for the other "strangeness" that quickly showed up– separating him irrevocably from other infants.

He was six months old, and although the situation was tough, Azra had hopes one day things would even out. She'd put Bretuck down for a nap while she picked herbs in her garden. The small window above his crib allowed her to hear his every sigh, and would alert her to his awakening.

She enjoyed this time alone. After Azra picked the herbs she needed for little Setra's cold and medicinal blossoms for Hanla's arthritis, she went ahead and chose other plants to restock her stores. Many illnesses had struck the village lately, none serious, but aggravating to the recipients.

Azra had been disturbed some of the nastier elements in the village had started rumors that her son threw a malevolent cloud over the place. Her presence and ability to quickly cure the ills seemed to dispel the issue, but she worried about future times. What would happen if her normally healthy people contracted a serious sickness? What evil portents would they then heap on her innocent son's head?

She paused, knees digging into the sun-warmed earth and listened. Bretuck's steady breathing wafted to her clearly through the window. No restless shifting came from him yet. Azra surmised her son needed a long nap. Glad for this brief reprieve — Bretuck was a very active child – she decided to prune and weed her garden while he got the required sleep his body demanded.

Azra glanced toward the cottage much later when a loud gurgling sound floated to her. Bretuck was awakening. She checked the sun's descent, surprised he'd slept over two hours, a rare occurrence for her little dynamo.

Jumping to her feet, she popped her knees and stretched the kinks from her back, then grabbed a brightly colored flower, Bretuck loved them so. The darkness inside made her blink and stumble against a chair leg on the way to the crib.

The blossom dropped unheeded to the floor as Azra stood in shock staring at what lay in her son's bed. A large, blob-looking substance reposed on Bretuck's goose down mattress. Had someone kidnapped him and placed this strange looking object in his crib as a cruel joke?

"Bretuck," she said loudly.

He could not answer vocally of course, but there was a slight nudge against her mind as she felt his presence. Closing her eyes and concentrating, Azra sensed her son's being very close. She quickly searched the cottage, but he was nowhere in sight.

Confused, she again focused her powers and felt Bretuck nearby. Stretching her hand forward, Azra consolidated her energy into a direction finder. Her hand pulled her forward until her knees banged painfully against the rough-hewn crib.

Azra opened her eyes, stared down at the ugly object, which rested upon her son's sheet. It was greenish-brown and appeared to be composed of a hard material. Examining it carefully, she realized two things – it looked like a giant cocoon and it was only slightly longer than Bretuck's body length.

Her hand trembling, Azra touched the immense cocoon and jumped back in fear. She'd felt Bretuck's essence coming from within the mass. Stilling her shaking limbs, and fear, she placed her palm against the hard, oddly warm substance, and concentrated.

Bretuck's quintessence came through loud and clear. He was sleeping and in no pain. Azra withdrew, sat down in a chair she'd pulled up, and stared at the cocoon. She didn't understand, but knew whatever process her son was going through, it was normal for him.

Her father came by that evening and found her in the same position, gazing transfixed at the cocooned Bretuck. He was as shocked as she, but being a practical man, took her personal state under supervision, as well as helping keep an eye on his grandson. He made her take short breaks to stretch her legs and get something to eat, otherwise, she'd have sat, waiting patiently for her son to awaken from this strange new process.

Her father agreed the wisest course, was to let people think Azra had come down with a head cold, little Bretuck too, that they were isolating themselves in order to not contaminate the villagers.

Three days this went on. Each morning she awoke from an exhausted, restless sleep to discover the mass had shifted and changed shape. It had elongated and grown in width, so that on the third day, it filled Bretuck's entire crib with its odd appearance.

Finally, on the evening of the third day, gurgling noises began emitting from the cocoon. Bretuck appeared to be waking up. Azra placed her hands just above the hardened substance, wondering if she should tear it open. While she hesitated, a rending sound like that of fabric tearing erupted into the quiet cottage. A long rip appeared along the length of the cocoon's surface and she watched in surprise as one of Bretuck's feet punched through the tear, then the other foot kicked through the membrane. Azra grabbed both sides of the opening and pulled mightily. It held for a few seconds, then fell to the sheets with a graceful ease.

She thrust the clinging material from her son's face and body, then grasping him by the middle, tugged him from the sticky interior of the cocoon. Azra held Bretuck aloft, unconsciously mimicking his acceptance day. He would need acceptance all over again, if not in a ceremony, at least informally from the villagers.

It was her lovely son she held at arm's length, but he had changed. Even beneath the clinging material still coating his body, she could see this change. He was approximately the size of a two year old, instead of the six month infant who had cocooned himself in some unfathomable method.

Bretuck had undergone metamorphosis.

CHANGLING

Her son laughed, reached his chubby arms toward her. Azra held the tears inside and clutched him to her breast fiercely. He was still her sweet innocent baby, in spite of his astounding appearance.

She'd bathed and fed Bretuck when her father arrived. He was shocked, but swung the enthusiastic child up in the air when his grandson waved his arms for a "pick me up".

She filled her father in on the details of Bretuck's "de-cocooning" as they watched her son play about their feet in growing wonder. He stumbled at first, but soon was taking tentative steps around the small cottage, grasping furniture for support. He grabbed a corn-husk doll on the floor, took several stronger steps than previously and dropped it clumsily onto her lap.

"Doll."

Azra sat in stunned shock, felt the pull of her father's gaze and saw he was just as dumbfounded as she.

"He talks."

She shook her head slowly. "And walks."

"He's the size of a two year old." Her father said, as if they both needed to hear it voiced aloud.

"He went into the cocoon with the abilities of a six month old and came out a toddler." She chewed her bottom lip. "It must be the dem...Hessitor blood." Azra was glad she caught her near slip-up. She never wanted to call her son that horrible word the villagers used against him.

"Yes, but how are we going to explain this to the others?"

Her father's expression was as worried as she knew her own was. "We'll just do the best we can," she waved at the precocious Bretuck, who was examining a box, trying to pry the lid off. "I'm afraid his physical appearance will throw them into a panic, no matter what we say."

"Maybe...we should consider moving to another village?" Her father's gaze bathed Bretuck in loving support.

"No. I'm not going to let them run me off from my home." She patted his hand. "Besides, I have a feeling other villages may be even worse. They wouldn't know me."

He sighed, resignation lighting his features.

So it was, Bretuck's metamorphosis did throw the villagers into a panic at first, but no one dared harm him. Of course there was always adults supervising him. The three faithful friends guarded Bretuck, along with her father, so at least two adults were always present when she was taking care of the sick or gathering medicinal herbs.

Although she never completely shook off her worry, at least after a time, Azra felt confident Bretuck wouldn't be murdered outright. When he passed by, villagers made signs for blocking evil and turned their gaze quickly away. No one tried to harm her son, but neither did they try to get acquainted with Bretuck or truly accept him.

The fact her son had no children to play with saddened her, but the five adults filled in as playmates. She'd notice Bretuck watching other youngsters tussling and chasing one another, but so far he didn't seem to miss the interaction.

Time passed quickly, more swiftly than she would have thought.

A year and a half flew by. Bretuck was two years old in chronological years, but had reached those capabilities long ago. He continued to grow, but at a normal rate.

Azra was not shocked when she found Bretuck cocooned again, but perturbed. How big would he come out this time? Would she still have her baby to love and cuddle?

A dark cloud passed over the sun and a somber thought wedged its way into her mind. What if he changed into the Sarwor demon this time?

Again, her father took up watch duty with her, patting her shoulder comfortingly. She felt more on edge than the first time. The cocoon grew each day, just as it'd done earlier. Five days they waited for Bretuck to emerge.

When the rending sound came this time, Azra tore the substance back with anxious hands. She sighed in relief when a human face appeared once the sticky stuff was wiped away.

It was her son, much bigger, but still the same sweet smile and bright, intelligent ruby eyes. Her father helped her bath Bretuck, who chattered up a storm the whole time.

They exchanged glances over his head. His language skills were much more advanced, in-keeping with the six-year old body he'd metamorphosed into.

The villagers didn't like this transformation anymore than they did the first, but at least they seemed used to it. Life went on as before. Azra looked after the peoples' sicknesses, and Bretuck lived a solitary existence, filled with older friends. Azra managed to keep the village safe from invasion by utilizing the spells her mother had insisted on teaching her on her death bed. By doing that, she was very valuable to her village. So, even if not accepted, Bretuck was tolerated for her sake.

Trying to throw a semblance of normalcy into her son's life, Azra had planned a birthday party for him. One couldn't host a party without gifts. She knew her father and their family friends had already made presents. Thus, Azra had traveled deep into the woods to make this special gift to mark Bretuck's second year

MAGICAL BEINGS

A squirrel and a blue jay quarreled noisily over her head, snapping Azra out of her reverie. Laughing, she brushed a leaf off the top of her head and glanced up. The squirrel stopped his antics when he saw her amused face. The jay ruffled his feathers as if to say "see there" and flew off. The squirrel got in one departing chitter at the bird then scampered toward the tree hole at the branch's junction.

Probably going to tell his mate all about his encounter with the fairy folk. Azra smiled to herself. She loved squirrels. Loved their funny little faces, the cute way in which they ate nuts, their quarreling over every branch as if they owned the whole forest. But they could be such nosy little people sometimes.

She smiled at her own wandering thoughts. It was the Villagers' fault, telling amusing stories of elfin magic until she had infused her favorite animal with some of their long lost characteristics. Elves. The first true magic folk, here even before the fairies, now vanished so far back in time, no one could recount the last sighting of one. Their magic lived on now only in stories and superstitious beliefs.

Fireflies seen dancing in the moonlight were believed to be elf spirits. If the bole of a tree grew strange knots, the people would see a face amongst the bark and were convinced an elf lived in the tree's spirit. Often times Azra came across strange offerings at the base of old oaks: copper bowls with fragrant oat-cakes or other delicacies inside, perhaps a brightly colored bead necklace, or a small bottle of priceless perfume.

The villagers believed the elfin folk came out at night and danced under the moonlight, accepting their gifts as their due. If Azra passed by the same bowls much later, sometimes the cakes had dissolved in the rain leaving a mushy mixture, the beads faded to a dull grayish color, or perhaps a drift of flower scented perfume was all that remained. Azra had heard the people whisper of these offerings, of how the giver must have offended some woodland sprite, their offering refused.

There were other times when Azra found the gifts gone the next day and she wondered if a mischievous child, too young to truly believe yet, had made off with the offerings. More than likely, one of her playful forest creatures or a fairy bent on a little harmless fun. One thing Azra did believe might be possible, the myth that elfin blood ran through some humans. She had come across a few who had a soft aura of magic around them.

Whether it was true or not, the Hessitor race had one more notch against them, a reason for fairy and human alike to hate them. The Hessitors' violent ancestors had wiped the elves off the face of the land, leaving only their legends behind. Elves had been too sure of themselves, too ready to have fun and not take matters seriously. And they liked and trusted humans too much.

The Hessitors had some magic of their own. Their wizards, famous at that time for dabbling in the lost black arts, had helped track down the elf clans. Elves were valued for only one reason, their gold. Everyone knew they had stashes of it, mountains of it, if legends could be believed. The elves tunneled through the mountains using elfin magic and stockpiling gold as if it were wheat. Gold was their source of power.

The squirrel came back, chattering to her, asking what she was about. Yes, Azra thought, why am I musing away the afternoon? This is what I really came for, Azra explained to her inquisitive friend, unfolding her hands so he could see. She looked at the delicate creature cradled there, still astounded by the magic of such a creation. The squirrel was quite unimpressed and wandered off, fussing at a crow this time.

After some few intense moments of further concentration, Azra looked down with satisfaction. The tiny deer stood alert, as if searching the forest ahead for hunters, its ears cocked. She had finished it while her memories flowed through her. It was the best way to make an elfin-life creature, letting the mind roam free while one's hands and the power guided you in the making. Elfin-life! Azra smiled. Another gift from the humans — naming fairy magic after the elves.

Without the aid of magic the small statue would still have been beautiful, but it was more than a lovely art object. The deer's muscles stood out rigidly, yet with a fluidity of movement as if it were ready to run any second, and its eyes twinkled with a hidden life and knowledge. It was not truly alive, something Azra had not the skill nor inclination to attempt, yet it came as near to a live animal as a statue could without breathing.

Azra gently wrapped the deer in a soft cushion of lamb's wool brought expressly for this purpose. It would not do to break the dainty statue before setting it in Bretuck's grasp, gift from her heart, molded by love and fairy power. It was to celebrate his sixth, yet un-sixth birthday. Her son who was the equivalent maturity and size of a large six year old, but who had only lived to see two winters so far.

She carefully tucked the thickly padded wool covering into her healer's bag, its leather sides grown bald with use, its sides bulging from the herbs she had gathered today. Azra patted it fondly. The bag was part of her inheritance from her mother, passed down from her mother before her; the healer's badge of office and priceless to her.

No, the lovely deer would be safe, protected as it was. Breaking, killing the villagers would say, of a thing with a elfin-life would bring a witch's curse of bad luck. She did not know if she believed this superstition, but knew she could not think of injuring the tiny thing.

Azra took a deep breath, closing her eyes for a few seconds, letting the peace and beauty of the deep forest flow through her, energizing her. The smell of honeysuckle and gardenia blended into a soothing aroma, and the bird song was hauntingly beautiful, their trills taking on a chorus of synchrony. They were always glad for an audience of the fairy folk. She could feel the presence of a rabbit beneath the cover of a nearby bush, too shy to come out and say hello, yet watching her intently.

Azra grabbed a handful of sun-warmed earth, letting its sustenance flow through her. Cracking her eyes, intending to coax the timid rabbit from cover with a succulent clover leaf, she started in surprise as she noted the sun's advance. Azra hadn't realized her activities had taken so long, nor that she'd let so much time slip by. The land lay bathed in a rich golden glow, color strewn in dappled drops over much of the trees.

PORTENTS

She couldn't stop the worried frown that flashed suddenly across her face as she turned quickly and started for home. The birds stopped singing abruptly, cocking their heads questioningly as they saw her expression, and the rabbit hopped off nervously.

It was not good to be gone from the village's borders for long tracks of time. She must ever be wary and alert. Azra chided herself as she kept up a ground eating pace. In her heart she knew it was the clay and promise of a special gift for her son, plus the rare herbs, which grew only under the immense old oaks in these parts of the woods, that drew her here today.

Yet, she couldn't help feeling little pangs of guilt. It had been a long time since she had escaped the rigorous duty of watching over her son and the safety of the villagers. She had lingered longer than was necessary, first dancing under the thick shade of the trees and communing with the woodland creatures, ever before her hands touched the akla clay.

She was miles from home but making good time. Azra was blessed with a healthy, strong body even though she appeared too frail with her tiny stature and delicate bone structure—mark of her fairy blood, this double twining of size and strength.

Azra was perhaps two miles from the village when a quivering alarm flushed through her entire body. She took a deep steadying breath, hoping it was not what she felt it to be, yet knowing it was. She stopped and closed her eyes, concentrating on the danger she felt with every nerve ending in her small frame.

Her sudden intake of air and opening of her huge golden eyes were all the indicators of her quickening fright. It was them — the Hessitors — they were very near the village, if not already upon it. Azra took off in a fast sprint, causing a family of cardinals to wheel in alarm, their red flight circling through the trees like a ribbon of blood. She noted the birds passing with fatalistic acceptance. The woods were giving her a clue even as she felt the pains of death shoot through her. Her people were being slaughtered even now.

Only one power could see through the veil of invisibility she'd cast around the village, and pierce a door through it. The Hessitors had a powerful sorcerer with them.

Drawing on her vast reserves of power, Azra infused her body with extra energy so she could keep up the mile-eating pace. She became frustrated at the length of time it seemed to be taking, yet she knew in reality she was moving faster than she'd ever attempted before. Her body ran while her mind wheeled free like the birds, circling in its distress, round and round with memories.

FIGHT FOR BRETUCK'S LIFE

As she continued to run through the forests, Azra's mind flitted over her memories quickly. She knew them so well there was no need to linger. It seemed as though she had been thinking of her past a long while, but knew it was the swiftness of which she wished to arrive at the village that caused her to feel this way.

It helped to keep her mind occupied, to ward off rendering it less powerful when she came to the village. She must be ready to help her people. Her memories did not drag her down. But thinking about what may be going on right now with her people, with

Bretuck, would make her sick with worry and perhaps lessen her magic's effectiveness.

The love for her unique son ran through her breast, beating stronger as her memories awakened old feelings of protection. Thus, when Azra stopped near the village's border, she was ready for battle.

Several blood-splattered bodies lay strewn indiscriminately in the central plaza, screams and sounds of fighting cut through even the thicket behind which she hid. Seeing neither villagers nor the enemy, Azra stepped cautiously into the exposed air, then took off at a sprint when she was not attacked.

Passing cottages, she noticed signs of fierce fighting everywhere – broken spears, furniture scattered about as if thrown, and trails of blood. In the distance, a villager engaged a huge Hessitor, but she could do nothing to aid his fledgling efforts. She must find Bretuck; that was her first and only thought at that point.

Racing into her father's abode, Azra skidded to a halt so abruptly, her dress flapped outward in front of her. Panting shallow breaths, she gazed with shock at the destruction, much worse than outside. Overturned and shattered furniture was flung about, broken dishes littered the floor, food and drink splattered the walls. But worst were the large splotches of thick blood bathing the walls. It also flowed over the food as if it were some colorful topping and coated the floorboards in slick gelatinous globs.

Holding her nausea at bay, Azra approached an upended, rough-hewn table. Spying a man's limb sticking out behind it, she drew near slowly, then instantaneously threw up when she found a detached leg, the ragged flesh clearly torn from the body. Shaking and not feeling up to the task of exploring further, but knowing she must, she rounded the table edge.

The scene meeting her shocked eyes was beyond her comprehension. Bodies lay scattered in discarded heaps of flesh, most so dismembered, she had a hard time recognizing their identity. Physical pain lanced through her heart on finding her father sprawled against the wall, his face the only untouched tissue on him.

Azra knelt in the blood and gore, gently touched his face briefly, then finished her survey of the room quickly. She had no time for grief now. Bretuck may still be alive. Moving swiftly to the door, she took a few deep breaths. The room reeked of blood and death, but at least this near the entrance it was less so. Her eyes ran skittishly over the room one last time. Four humans were dead — Sheris, Vaya, and Hanla — three dear people who had befriended she and Bretuck when they needed it the most. Her father made up the fourth. Thank the being of light, her son's body was not among the slaughtered victims.

Steeling her trembling limbs as best she could, Azra centered her powers and reached for contact with Bretuck. She found none and tried to push back the terrified response that brought, instead she concentrated on his essence, which still lingered in the cottage. His passage had left traces.

She saw her father and friends through Bretuck's eyes. They played games with him and fed him delicious treats to keep his thoughts from his absent mom. She could feel her son's happiness, but also his eagerness for her return, so his birthday party could truly get under way.

The images hazed, flitted away, then came hammering back with frightening clarity. Bretuck was confused and curious, but the adults terrified at the sudden appearance of Hessitor warriors at the door. The pictures merged, became disjointed and then swirled, making Azra feel queasy. Through it all she saw snitches of the enemy shouting with savage joy as they beat the three men and fondled Sheris. Then she felt Bretuck's surprise when the enemy laid eyes on him.

He was picked up, tossed in the air, passed back and forth between them, then set on the table. One of the men was dressed in a long robe, surely the sorcerer. He pulled a small pack from his waist thong, gazed at her son merrily, then took a piece of a dark, sickly-green root and plunked it in one of the cups. Stirring it with his finger, the man kept up a cheerful conversation with Bretuck, then handed him the drink. The curious child downed the drink after some encouragement.

Her son's vision became blurred and reddish-tinged. A pain hit her precious son's spine, one so intense as to put birthing pains to shame. Azra cried out verbally, gripping her middle in empathy as shards of agony shot outward into Bretuck's vulnerable body.

She almost lost contact through her son's fall backwards onto the floor and his subsequent rolling about on the boards in tortuous spine-twisting spasms. Azra wanted to reach out and hold Bretuck, wanted to kill the Hessitors with every curse of magic she could muster, but could do neither. What was had already passed.

She thought she'd lost contact, then realized Bretuck had blacked out, for she could still feel the faintest essence of his being. Then, abruptly the contact was shattered, yet she received new images, seemingly from a different person, a large being it seemed. She tried to break contact, but was held as surely as if she'd stepped onto a floor full of strong glue.

Azra watched through the giant's perspective and saw its killing rampage as it tore the cottage and the inhabitants apart, except the enemy, who'd strangely but wisely, run from the cottage. She felt its deep rage, an overpowering confusion, and a pulsating drive to kill. The rending murderer ran through the door after finishing his slaughtering spree and Azra was able to break the connection.

Plunging to her knees, she threw up, over and over, empting her insides, wishing she could cleanse her memory as effectively. Shaking all over as if she had the ague, Azra stumbled out of the carnage house, too shocked for tears, but they burned in her chest and screams lurked just behind her numbed senses.

Staggering a few steps, she cleansed her lungs with fresh air, then pointed her trembling legs towards the faint sound of battle. Nearing the villages outer cottages, she was jolted to discover more dead villagers. Some had clearly been run through with swords, but many were torn apart. It made no sense. Hessitors wanted slaves, unless they had decided to make an example of her people, thus demonstrating violently to other villages resistance was futile. This they had been known to do, but rarely.

Azra picked up a discarded club, its heavy weight giving her small comfort. She struck a Hessitor on the head as she came up behind him and one of her people engaged in fierce hand-to-hand combat. The man nodded grimly, then speared the downed enemy through the gut, twisting and pulling, making it more painful. Paling, she walked away towards the harsh, terrified screams nearby.

THE SARTWOR

Rounding a tree, she came face to face with a scene from hell and what must be an escaped beast from its bowels. A huge, hulking creature stood over the mangled and torn remains of several villagers. Its skin was a dark green, knotted with strange configurations of flesh on its skin, as if its muscle fought for dominance and pushed upward into the flesh from beneath. A weepy wetness made the skin shiny and oily. It reeked of slaughtering pens where the leavings had rotted for a day in the hot air.

The putrid ripe odor caused Azra to grab her nose and also gained the beast's attention. As its eyes pinned her location, she was frozen, couldn't move if her life depended on it — and it did. The gaping mouth filled with two-inch horrific jagged teeth opened as if pleased with her presence. Blood, bits of flesh and dripping strings of saliva drooled from its jaws as it started toward her.

"Tarsha!" She commanded loudly, thrusting both arms outward at the same time. It was a powerful word, one used to immobilize. The nightmarish creature shook its head slightly, as if she had muddled its thoughts temporarily, then thudded the few steps it took to be within striking distance.

One solitary tear trickled down her cheek as she whispered, "Bretuck, I'm sorry."

The beast stumbled, then straightened, a stunned look crossed its grotesque face.

"Bretuck," she said louder, wondering if her son's name worked as a talisman against the hell-beast.

The thing's mouth gaped, then worked up and down furiously, slimy ooze from its maw flung outward in disgusting long strings. A gurgling "augh" poured from its rasping throat.

Azra felt stronger, less terrified, as if she'd stumbled on its Achilles heel. She thrust out her hands again and screamed Bretuck as loud as she could.

The thing screeched in agony, plunged to its knees with a crash and lifted its tortured eyes to hers with a pitiful expression, if it were possible with such a beast. A quiver of responding pity flashed through her, and horrified at her reaction, Azra took a step backward. The monster thrust his arms foward and cried out.

"No!" She shouted silently, then screamed "no" aloud. "It can't be," she screamed at the thing. How could it cry out "mommy" in an inhuman voice, yet still have a twinge of her son's tone, and cause such a surge of motherly instinct within her breast.

Sure she'd truly slipped into hell itself, Azra took back the step forfeited, then another. The large misshapen head was level with hers as it kneeled and she had a clear, earth-shaking view of its eyes. Red demon eyes! Rage, fear, sadness and anguish all mingled together in their depths.

"Bretuck?" She whispered.

The beast within whose frame her son's essence was trapped, cried a hoarse version of "mommy" again. Tears soaked her bosom as she stretched one hand toward him. It looked at her hand, then at her face, fear flashed, a message she interrupted correctly – he was afraid to touch her – fearful he'd tear her apart.

"Bretuck," she said in a firm, loving voice, flipping her hand toward him for emphasis.

The creature closed its eyes, shook its misshapen head vigorously, as if it were trying to shake off the effects of demon possession. The Bretuck Demon threw its head back and let loose a nightmarish scream. Its body twitched and jerked as it went into spasms.

Abruptly, a slit appeared in its stomach, accompanied by a rending sound, reminding Azra of the cocoon ripping open. An object wriggled through the slash, covered in greenish ooze. It took her a moment to realize it was a hand.

"Bretuck," she said, stepped forward fearlessly, kneeled and grasped that frail human hand firmly. She balled all her love and power into one thrust of energy aimed at the beast and pulled with all the strength she could muster. She was afraid to push the Sartwor's flesh apart, since she didn't know how connected it might be to her son. She knew though, Bretuck was trapped inside the hellish beast's body just as surely as he'd been caught inside the cocoon.

The jagged, putrid green cut lengthened, then suddenly widened from stomach to chest. It gaped like a huge, open infected sore. A second hand and arm flailed from within the creature and Azra grabbed Bretuck's other wrist. Red curls tipped with green slime popped through the tear as her son struggled to push his way out.

Like a baby emerging from the womb, Bretuck's upper body plunged in one swift movement completely out of the beastly container. Azra tugged again and Bretuck flopped into her arms, slippery, but securely held nonetheless.

His arms clutched her neck in a death grip. She patted and soothed him with loving words as she eyed the thing that sprawled lifelessly on the ground. It was flattened and had fallen backward in a tumbled spill of clawed limbs, looking like a monstrous puppet cast to the side after the puppeteer finished with his performance.

Spying a small group of villagers who'd banded together in the distance, Azra struggled to her feet. It was then she realized Bretuck had undergone metamorphism again. She could not lift him in her arms, he was as tall as she now.

She gently pushed her son's desperate grip from her and turned his much slimmer face up to her. "We must leave. Can you walk?"

He shook his head in acknowledgement, his ruby eyes filled with fear and horrid images that floated unseen behind his sweet gaze, but which she felt with every fairy sense in her being.

Tucking him near her body, with one arm about his, they began to walk away from the scene of carnage. Unfortunately, there was no direction she could choose where Bretuck did not see evidence of his rampage. Unthinking, she turned him toward her cottage. The strewn and dismembered bodies were less evident at this end of the village.

Azra sat Bretuck in a chair while she snatched clothes, a few precious magic books and keepsakes. He watched her the whole time, his eyes gleaming eerily like an animal in the darkened cottage.

She paused, checked the forest's perimeter. No villager was in sight. Centering her powers, Azra zoomed her psychic eye back to the Sartwor's body. Many battered and injured people were gathered around the monster, discussing it. She heard her name and withdrew back to the cottage.

It was possible she could say she'd killed the beast with her fairy powers, not much of a deviance from the truth. The Demon would get attention off her son, even with his new metamorphous, but she couldn't take the chance that some stray villager had seen Bretuck change into the creature of destruction.

Securing the pack on her back, she gently pulled her son from his frozen position in the chair. He still did not speak, but his eyes spoke for him, and neither could he seem to detach them from her frame, as if fearful a glance away and she'd disappear.

Azra chose a path near the back of the cottage, a winding overgrown trail that plunged deeply into the dense forest. One she knew well, but was infrequently traveled by the villagers. It was too heavily roamed by wolves and bears for their comfort, but would aid her cause in keeping Bretuck safe.

She turned for one last glance at her home, she knew she'd never see it again. Squaring her shoulders, Azra shrugged off any sadness. Their future lay ahead, whatever that entailed. Hopefully, they could find some isolated place where Bretuck could grow up safely. He'd never have the carefree existence of many children, but at least she could make sure no one harmed him.

She threw little overt glances at her "new" son as they walked along. By his physical build and facial features, she guessed him to be near twelve years old. He was no longer cute and chubby, but was edging toward handsome. He would be a lady killer when grown.

Azra smiled for a moment, then realizing the depth of that thought, a shiver rippled through her body. Would he be a killer when he grew up? Would the Sartwor Demon reappear at some future date?

She unconsciously squeezed his hand, Bretuck returned the gesture with one of his own and a loving smile lit his face, shining through the slime that still covered portions of it. Azra pulled her resolve about her like a shield. Somehow she would find a way to help her precious son.

THE JOURNEY BEGINS

Bretuck was a quiet companion, which was a good thing since stealth may be as important as swiftness in their flight. Only occasionally did he break the rhythm of their walk with a comment about a bird, perhaps a question about an animal hugging the path as they passed.

They walked for hours, taking breaks when Bretuck tired. He was stoic, never complaining, but his step would falter, alerting her to his need for refueling his flagging strength. He was normally an extremely strong child, but after each metamorphous, he needed time to regain his energy.

Azra picked a handful of wild strawberries and they shared the tasty treat, along with homemade bread during one of their breaks. Bretuck's laughter drew her attention like a shot. A blue bird hopped about his feet as her son scattered the crumbs from his bread.

"Blue birds are special to me."

He didn't answer, simply turned those extraordinary eyes toward her, curiosity temporarily pushing the pain from them.

In a low voice, she told him about the blue bird who'd given him the first gift for his raqu. Bretuck fingered his amulet and watched intensely as the bird sought every tiny morsel.

"Do you think it's the same one?"

This question made her realize there was still much child in her son. It pleased her. "Who can say," she answered mysteriously. "Maybe he's a guardian."

"Do you really think so?"

The look in his eyes was so intense, so hopeful, she didn't want to shatter whatever fledgling comfort it seemed to give him.

She ruffled his hair, stopped when she noticed her fingers sticking in his stiffened locks. "The woods are full of mysteries, most humans will never know the secret to unlocking them."

"And we do, being part fairy?"

She nodded, put one finger to her lips. The blue bird had hopped onto Bretuck's knee, cocked its head back and forth several times, then with a chirp, flew away.

"What was it saying, mommy?"

"Goodbye, and thank you for the delicious snack."

Bretuck giggled and she laughed with him. It was good, this sharing of feelings other than dark-laden thoughts and deeds.

"Now, help me pack up the food." He did and in a few moments they were on their way again. But not many minutes went by before Bretuck's steps started dragging again. She stopped.

"I'm sorry, I feel so weak." He sounded so pitiful, as if it were all his fault, not just the inability to walk as far as they needed to, but everything that went before. She read this in the demeanor of his body and great sadness in his ruby gaze.

Azra decided to distract him. "Come on," she stuck out one hand and gripped his nearer one. "Not much farther." She lowered her voice as if about to impart one of the forest's great secrets, in a way she was. "There's a hidden place up ahead, off the trail."

After a few minutes, she said, "See, here's the marker." She parted a bush with both hands, showed him the faint path that broke through the underbrush.

"What is it mommy?"

She had captured his interest. "Come on, you'll see."

She got on her knees, plunged through the thick growth, then stood up after a few feet. A much smaller path wound from the thicket through which they'd pushed into a darker part of the woods. She plunged ahead, turning often to make sure he followed right behind. Bretuck's eyes were huge and shone like beacons in the thickening dusk.

They had to often walk sideways, but at least didn't have to resort to crawling on their knees anymore. It was further than she remembered and poor Bretuck was lagging behind more and more. Finally, they broke through into a small clearing.

Azra held his hand as he gazed around. On the other side of the clearing, a tiny creek meandered through the area, pooling against the base of a huge rock cliff, forming a small pond. The cliff was jagged, cut with steps formed by nature. Her eyes went up the face of the rock, just as his did and she smiled at his indrawn breath.

A ledge topped the cliff, and peering at them over the rim was a family of wolves — large silver and black beasts, those of legend — creatures who created fear in humans, nothing but a welcoming peace in her. A litter of similar-colored pups played about the adults' legs.

She was glad she still clutched Bretuck's hand, for he started forward and she pulled him back. He turned to look questioningly at her.

"We must ask permission to share their water."

He nodded wisely.

Azra closed her eyes and communed silently with the pack, who readily gave them permission to share in their bounty. Still holding Bretuck's hand, she led him to the pond, then dropped it and unpacked some items. The wolves stretched out atop the ledge, head on paws and watched them with interest.

She waded into the water and waved her son to follow, he was reluctant, the night was approaching and the water had cooled to a chilling degree. She quickly unclothed him and soaped his body with the flower-scented bar she'd unpacked. Bretuck shivered, but stood quietly as she scrubbed the disgusting gook from his body, then his hair. She was glad the soap was made by her hands, thus would disintegrate in a few minutes, instead of mess up the wolves drinking pond with scum. The natural spring would also cleanse the dirt in a few minutes with its swift flow.

Azra rubbed his body vigorously with the extra change of clothes she'd brought for herself, helped him redress quickly, then wrapped him in his sleeping blanket. Next, she started a small fire to warm him up.

As they sat next to the cheery blaze, sharing their supper, Bretuck asked, "What am I?"

For a moment she was stunned. He'd never asked about his origins before, but then neither had he ever turned into a monster.

"You are part fairy, human, and...Hessitor."

"And the Sartwor?"

She waved a hand of dismissal. "That was a fluke."

"Are you sure mommy...positive it will never return?"

She couldn't answer.

His face turned darker, his thoughts deeper. "Am I bad?" The fire picked up the glimmer of tears in his eyes, but they never spilled, just sat there like shimmering reflections of pain.

"Oh Bretuck," she pulled him into her arms, gave him the only comfort she could. "You're not bad," she whispered into his soft curls.

"Then what am I?" He spoke against her dress.

She pushed him gently back, so she could gaze into his face, and placed both hands on his cheeks. "You are a boy who has ancestry different than other people we know."

He nodded and whispered, "No one else makes a cocoon."

She dropped one hand and picked up one of his, turned the palm upright. "And no one else has the power I see in you."

"Was it the power that made...me change into the Demon? Will it happen again?" His voice became shrill with nervous excitement.

"I can't lie to you, I'm not sure, but I don't think so."

"A lot of...things are fuzzy, but mommy, I remember hurting people...I think I might have killed grandpa."

"No! I don't believe it was you." At his confused gaze, she said, "Remember, the warrior gave you a nasty drink, that caused the Sartwor to appear." She brushed his hair back from one temple.

He nodded, his eyes haunted.

"Bretuck, you are not the Sartwor Demon." He watched her face, his gaze hopeful. "Remember how you were nestled inside the cocoon, yet you were not part of the cocoon?" At his nod, she continued. "I think...that is the way it worked about the Sartwor too. You," she pressed a finger lightly at his chest, "Were trapped inside the beast."

He sighed, closed his eyes a few seconds. "I'm tired," he said.

She settled them for the night. Not long after Bretuck fell into a fitful sleep, his constant flailing of limbs and frightened mumblings caused her to resettle his head in her lap. Azra stroked his hair, sang low-keyed songs, and finally used a light fission of power to send sleep messages to him.

THE SEARCH

Bretuck's eyes had a less haunted look in the morning. His ruby gaze brightened slightly when she set out their meal. Breakfast was sparing, but good. They refreshed themselves at the pond, then waved goodbye to their benefactors, the wolves.

Azra choose a new path, one that would bring them in a winding fashion upon a different trail than the one they followed yesterday. She didn't want to take a chance that some vengeance-filled villagers were on their track. She really hoped her people thought she and Bretuck were torn apart by the Sartwor. It'd create much less problems for them in their new life. Rumors had a manner of wedging their way into the most unlikely of places.

That day, they reached the outskirts of a small village, but she didn't like the appearance of the populace. They looked like ruffians. Perhaps they were really a band of robbers who used a village as cover. Azra had heard of such places, they were to be avoided.

She didn't have any choice though, they were out of food, she'd have to barter with the natives to obtain the goods they needed. Securing Bretuck a safe distance away, she entered the miniscule plaza and began announcing cures and treatment for the sick.

People seemed surprised a stranger had slipped unnoticed into their midst, but none asked her to leave. Fairy descendents were not common in every village and their powers for healing were always welcome. A crowd soon gathered round, and Azra handed out herbal remedies in exchange for food. She visited a few cottages with anxious relatives, bandaging wounds with healing poultices and diagnosing ailments. From these individuals she received payment in a soft woven blanket, which would come in handy, a bright colored spinning toy Bretuck would love, and a multi-colored scarf for her.

She had started for the village's fringe, when a great bear of a man stepped into her path. He introduced himself as the village leader, and Azra could well believe he led a band of criminals.

"Why not stay a bit, you've been so helpful to my people."

"I can't." She walked around him, but he stuck out a brawny arm and stopped her again.

"I would advice you to step aside," she commanded.

"What are you going to do about it, if I don't?"

Smiling slightly, Azra let loose a tiny ball of energy. It struck the man's toes on one foot, sizzling with electric-charged joy as it leapt from toe to toe before fizzling out. He stood while the fairy power ran over his foot, then his dumbfounded look was overcome with a loud shout, and subsequent hopping about.

She made a quick retreat, no use getting some of the men interested in hunting her for sport. She ran swiftly, stopping at a distance away, clutching her stomach and giving the belly-laugh she'd been holding in free reign. Bretuck's curious face appeared around the trunk of a great elm. She didn't realize she'd run that far.

"Are you alright?"

"Yes," she waved him over, sat down on a log and patted the seat beside her. "I've got a funny story to tell you." Indeed, her son's eyes were merry after the telling, he even laughed a bit, but most dear to her heart was the smile that stayed on his face afterwards.

"Now, I've got some wonderful goodies." Azra opened her pack and spread the blanket on the ground, then put out more than enough food for lunch. They shared flaky biscuits covered with jam, a tasty fruit drink from a gourd, and two chicken legs, which a good housewife had fried up fresh. It could have made two meals, but she felt they needed some rejoicing, things had been too glum for too long.

"Dessert," she announced, spreading her palm and showing Bretuck the colorfully wrapped candies.

"Oh," his eyes got larger.

"Only one each, after each meal."

As she and Bretuck savored the wondrous flavor, she thought about the couple who'd given her the candies in exchange for treating a nasty looking leg wound on the husband. Looked like a sword cut to her, but she had cleansed it, wrapped it in healing poultices, and instructed the wife how to make more. The man had nodded toward a lovely wood-carved box, and his wife had opened it reverently, giving her a handful. These delicacies seemed too rich for the family living in that tiny cottage. Farmers indeed!

After they finished and repacked everything, she withdrew the toy from a side pocket and placed it in his hands. Bretuck's face lit with joy, but he frowned when he couldn't get it to spin atop the dirt.

"Soon we'll have a home where you can play with your toy."

He smiled and spying a spray of color spilling from the pocket, pointed to it.

She laughed and removed it. "Someone decided I needed to dress more like a gypsy."

"Put it on mommy."

She complied, tying the ends behind her neck. Bretuck clapped his hands. She stood and curtsied. The rest of the evening was just as pleasant. Most of the trail they followed was wide, as if domesticated animals wore the path down. This allowed them to stroll along hand-in-hand, singing, laughing, simply enjoying nature's bounty and each other's company.

The next few days Azra was to recall her words "soon we'll have a home". They ran across other villages in which she questioned the peoples' livelihood, just as she did at the "robber village". Several places were pleasant enough, but it didn't take long to hear rumors about the Sartwor. In other villages, the people were sloven, their cottages unkempt and fields weed-grown messes— not an atmosphere she cared to raise Bretuck in.

Each place, she only stayed long enough to gather the supplies they needed. In a few communities, she ran across other fairy descendants. They'd visit briefly and share treatment secrets, but then she'd be on her way.

Thus, for weeks they wandered from village to village, finding not one containing all the elements Azra required. She was getting tired, as was Bretuck. Physically, they were fit, but they just yearned for a place to call home.

One particularly beautiful morn, they ran across a tiny cottage in the woods, but no village was in sight. Entering cautiously first, Azra was pleased to find it empty, and it appeared to have been for some time. She waved Bretuck inside. He immediately went to the small fireplace and started clearing it of junk.

It was only one room, but had a sturdy bed made of logs in the corner, the mattress had fallen between the wood slats and looked like it was a nest for rats or some wild animal. What once had been a crude table for one and the accompanying chair, were broken into pieces in the other corner. Azra watched with a smile as Bretuck sorted through the dining set, selected several branches and took them to the fireplace. In no time they'd have a welcome blaze. It was a chill morning and made her worry anew about finding a home before winter truly set in on them.

Finding a small whisk of a broom, she quickly brushed off the rock ledge in front of the fireplace, placing their pack upon it. "What do you think?" Bretuck cocked his head upward from his kneeling position. "I like it. Can we stay here...for a while?"

A NEW HOME

"We'll see," she ruffled his locks. "Let's warm up and have a snack, then I'll check the area."

He nodded, concentrating on starting the fire. He well knew the routine.

It was nearly noon by the time she decided she'd better be off. It had been so pleasant, sharing the warmth of the fire and good spirits the place evoked. Bretuck didn't protest when she led him to a secure spot some distance away. The cottage's welcoming presence might invite a stray hunter to enter.

Following a well-worn and wide path, Azra came across a village about a mile from the cottage. She stood at the edge for some time, watching the people and examining everything. The villagers seemed very pleasant, there were many smiles and laughter as they greeted one another. The cottages were neat, the fields properly tilled. It reminded her of her birth village.

This made Azra even more leery than normal. She couldn't allow any fond feelings for her birthplace to influence her inspection of this place. When she approached the plaza with a sparkling fountain in the center, she was almost immediately surrounded by excited people, and quickly discovered the villagers were a healthy lot. Several frowns crossed different peoples' faces as they tried to think who may need the fairy's attention.

"Old Tahra needs medicine for her arthritis." An elderly woman spoke up.

A gaggle of happy folks followed her to the cheerful cottage the woman led her to. The villagers politely waited outside while they entered. It took her no time to stir up a pot of herbal tea for the sweet old woman, but she stayed for a while, enjoying the two elderly women's pleasant company and sharing some delicious cookies. Luckily, the woman she'd treated pressed her to take several treats with her. She happily tucked two in her pack for Bretuck.

When she exited the house, the villagers had thought of two more slight cases that required her attention: a young mother who neared her birthing time and could use some words of comfort, and a young boy who had a small infection on one leg. Both were taken care of in no time.

In spite of the fact Azra felt her services weren't needed in any urgent manner, the people were enthusiastically sincere for her help, and she received little wrapped packages of food in gratitude.

She spent sometime visiting different homes and going with several farmers to gaze at their bountiful fields. The people were proud of their pristine village, and rightly so. Azra did none of this to entertain herself. She soaked up every little tidbit of gossip and chatter. She spent a few hours in the village, but at no time was the Sartwor Demon mentioned. This was a good sign.

The elders approached her, asked if she'd be interested in taking up residence in one of the cottages. A villager had died recently, leaving a cottage available. They insisted on showing her the charming little house and it would have been tempting under normal circumstances, but she couldn't bring Bretuck into the village, nor let any of them know about his presence.

She explained that she was looking for a new home, but hadn't had time to make her mind up yet. "Being fairy, I feel more comfortable surrounded by the forest." People around her nodded in understanding. "If I were to decide to stay, there's a small cottage I ran across outside town, on my way here. Who does it belong to?"

"It's yours, if you wish," the elder smiled happily. "It belonged to a widow who passed on years ago. No one else has been interested in living so far from the village."

"May I stay there a few days until I decide?"

"Please do." The old man said, several others chimed in with the same answer.

Bretuck was thrilled when she got back and shared everything she'd learned. They still were unsure as to whether they could stay permanently, but couldn't seem to stop themselves from preparing the cottage as if they were already the owners. They dusted and took out trash, used an old shirt, wetted down, to scrub the walls and floors.

Every day for three days, Azra visited the village and took care of the few ailments and injuries that occurred with the people, all the time listening carefully. Still, not one person mentioned the Sartwor. That evening, she told her son she'd decided to stay, at least for a while and see how things worked out with the locals.

She had informed the elders of her decision before returning to the cottage that day, and was surprised the next morning when a knock pounded on the door. She peeked outside the tiny front window and was shocked to see a group of villagers gathered out front. She hurriedly helped Bretuck slip out the back window, checking first to make sure no one would spot him.

After letting the group in, she was inundated with gifts: cleaning tools, a set of dishes and glasses, a fresh smelling mattress stuffed full of goose down, and a small, finely woven rug for the hearth.

She was overjoyed and chatted with the people, when several men nudged into the small room carrying a sturdy table and two matching chairs.

"This is too much," she exclaimed, but her remarks were waved away merrily. Two heavy-set, matronly women quickly wiped the oak tabletop to a honey gleam, then set the table as if she were expecting company.

Tears glimmered in her eyes. "Oh, thank you, it's perfect."

After some small talk, the people excused themselves, leaving a fragrant loaf of fresh-baked bread in the center of the table as their parting gift.

She watched them depart and when sure all had vacated the area, excitedly waved Bretuck inside. He was as thrilled with their new accessories as she. Of course her son immediately sliced the soft bread and with a smile, Azra took down the last of the jam to spread on the delicacy.

They had a peaceful evening in their new, little home. It was even chill enough for a cheerful fire. They warmed their hands and toes, then roasted chestnuts she'd found earlier. It was the end to a perfect day, and she hoped, a beginning for a pleasant future.

HEALING HANDS

———⋇⟨◈⟩⋇———

Things went along so smoothly in their new home, sometimes Azra wondered when something disastrous would happen. She couldn't help this attitude. Every time life had come into a rhythm back in her home village, a new development with Bretuck threw things out of kilter. It wasn't his fault of course, and this time not one villager knew about him. Still she worried, and watched her son carefully.

She taught him how to tread softly in the woods, so no human ear could detect his presence, and showed him areas it would be safe to play. His favorite was a tiny creek that meandered in crooked spurts some distance behind the cottage. It showed no evidence of human trespassing, probably it was too small to gain the villagers interest. There was a nice sized stream which flowed near the village, one in which they drew water, washed clothes, and fished.

Bretuck's creek was too small to support fish, but many crawfish, frogs, and salamanders called it home, making it a perfect playground for a little boy. He'd come in every evening, clods of mud clinging to his clothes, knees scuffed and dirty. She'd simply shake her head and dust him off before letting him into the house. Azra thanked the being of light for having a spring-fed well outside, which made washing clothes frequently so much easier.

Her routine included visiting the village every other day to check on current patients, aid new ones, and to distribute medicinal herbs. She also cast a spell to protect the village against a Hessitor invasion, although they were rare in these parts. Her larder stayed well-stocked from the villagers thankful, gracious payments. Slowly, her little house became filled with various items that made life more pleasant: a butter churn, a delicate lace table cloth she brought out only on special occasions, and a brass jewelry box, which must have come from a city and she had no need for, since she owned no jewelry.

But, the box made a nice decoration on the shelf running above the fireplace, and other little knick-knacks the ladies had given her dressed the place up. The homey cottage was becoming their real home. She felt truly happy for the first time in a long while and thought by Bretuck's countenance, he did too. Her son smiled frequently now, as he'd done in his earlier years. It confirmed her opinion that she'd chosen the right place for them to settle.

They awakened one morn to a white landscape—winter had arrived. This didn't stop Bretuck's outside play. She was glad he was such a healthy child and enjoyed the outdoors. Forts and funny figures sculpted from snow now joined his regiment of play. Azra got pulled into several snowball fights, and later admitted to herself, she enjoyed them as much as her son.

The heavier material the village ladies had given her, came in handy to make Bretuck warmer play clothes. She even made him a nice jacket from an old quilt. He still trampled through the snow daily to his favorite place, the creek. She cautioned him against falling through the thin ice, although he couldn't drown in ankle deep water, it might give him a chill that could bring on sickness.

One particularly chilly day, Bretuck returned from the creek and convinced her to go back with him. The minute stream had frozen all the way through, and her son showed her how to take a shambling run and skate down its narrow path. Taking a deep breath, she managed to stay on her feet a few seconds before landing on her rear, but it had been great fun. They spent at least an hour sliding down the creek's icy bed. It was an afternoon she'd not soon forget, and one Bretuck brought up with chuckles quite frequently when they bathed in the hearth's warmth on long, freezing winter nights.

The promise of healing powers she'd seen written in Bretuck's hands at birth, began to show up. He brought home a rabbit with a broken limb. Although she tried to temper his enthusiasm with caution, they bandaged the leg, bundled the frightened creature in rags and placed him in a box near the hearth.

The next few days, Azra would come up quietly behind her son and see him stroking its fur in a mesmerizing manner. The bunny did recover and in such astounding time, she wondered if Bretuck had used his powers to hasten its healing. Much to her son's delight, once they released the rabbit upon its full recovery, it did not run off, but took up residence in a hollow log in front of their home.

She couldn't approach the timid thing without it skittering into its log, but anytime Bretuck came near, the rabbit would hop about his feet like a dog. It heartened her to see her son make a friend, even if it was a member of the animal kingdom.

After the bunny, Bretuck regularly brought injured animals

into their home for care. A bird, half frozen in the snow recovered in no time, but as with the rabbit, it made a new home in the oak outside.

The next patient was disheartening to her kind-hearted son. Bretuck had rescued a lovely red fox from a hunter's snare, one back leg was mangled and infected. It hung on two agonizing days, even her son's healing powers couldn't save it. He didn't bring any more creatures in that winter.

Springtime brought a welcome relief from the cold and a renewal of Bretuck's interest in treating injured animals. Many reptilian creatures found their way into the tiny cottage; a turtle whose shell had been dented, perhaps by a child wielding a large stick, and a snake who had a large lump in its body. Bretuck thought it hilarious when she explained the snake had simply swallowed a meal. She insisted he take it back outside immediately. Lizards, frogs, and numerous small mammals followed.

The most memorable and irritating patient of their makeshift hospital was a large, ugly toad. Bretuck saw it by the creek and noticed it had not eaten for several days. How could he be certain, she wasn't sure, but she believed him. The brown-green, wart covered thing was as big as her whole hand and sat like a large blob, its stomach spreading in a mushy puddle about it. It simply stared at her from the hearth stones where her son had placed it.

"I think he's just old," she commented.

"But, I can't let it starve."

She sighed. "I guess not." She smiled at him, "Do your magic then."

And he did, waving his hands around the frog, then sealing its squat body between his palms and concentrating. Azra was surprised to see a slight aura surrounding Bretuck's hands. His powers were indeed increasing.

Afterward, he opened the front door, letting a few flies in and one bee. The toad totally ignored all the insects buzzing about the room. She finally shooed the bee out and swatted the flies.

The next day, Bretuck used his powers to cloak the toad again within the aura. This time when he let in several flies, the toad eyed the insects with interest, then with a zap of its long tongue, flicked all three in quick succession.

"Yeah," he clapped with glee.

"Yes, yeah, now we have an easy way to rid the cottage of bugs."

"Mommy," Bretuck laughed.

They still started the fire on chilly spring nights. The toad would sit with eyes gleaming eerily and soak up the warmth. The combination of toad with a fireplace brought up unpleasant memories of the old witch she visited. Azra frowned at the toad and caught herself as she shuffled back from the hearth. She wasn't going to move. If anything, he was going to leave.

The next day, she left the front door open all day, but the toad didn't move, simply gobbled up the insects that flew inside. That's how an ugly toad came to be a house pet.

BRETUCK MAKES A FRIEND

Bretuck had been gone all morning, playing in the creek. It was past lunchtime and he'd forgotten again. Azra decided to slip up on him quietly and surprise him at play. Perhaps she'd be lucky and see him practicing his healing arts on some small animal.

Treading softly, she peered around a bush and saw her son placing a stick on a makeshift dam he apparently was constructing. How delightful, she thought.

"I need more mud," Bretuck said aloud.

"I've got it."

Azra was shocked to see another boy of similar age approaching her son, carrying a dented bucket in one hand, oozing mud sloshed over its rim.

She watched the two for a while, building a dam together in

companionable unity, then slipped away as quietly as she'd entered Bretuck's realm.

She called loudly, and after a few minutes, her son appeared at the forest's edge, dirty from head to toe, a happy grin splitting the mud across his face.

Knowing he'd wish to return to his dam building, she gave Bretuck a wash pan to rinse his hands and face, then brought his lunch outside.

"Can I have a sandwich to take with me?"

She nodded and went inside to fetch the extra sandwich, which she knew was for his friend and handed it to her son wrapped in a cloth. She watched him run swiftly back to the trail that cut through the woods to the creek. She'd thought all the extra requests for food, had been his increased appetite, now she knew what it was truly for — his friend.

Friend. What impact that one little word held, more so for her son. He who had been ostracized from play with other children, led a lonely life except for her and previously a handful of older companions. Azra hugged herself, feeling such joy radiate through her, she could barely contain it.

But, then other thoughts invaded, those of a worrisome nature. What if the boy told others of his friend with bright red eyes? She sighed. She would have to speak with Bretuck about this friend.

The opportunity presented itself that evening when her son held the ugly toad in his hands and spoke softly to it.

"I'm glad you've got a friend there." She nodded toward the toad.

Bretuck laughed and set the creature back on the hearth. "He's not the only one. There's rabbit."

"And?"

"And...bird."

"No others," she asked gently.

He turned toward her. "What do you mean, Mommy?"

Stroking his hair softly, she said, "I planned on surprising you today at the creek, I saw the other boy."

"Oh," his eyes dipped down for a second, then returned to her face. "Are you mad?" His ruby eyes gleamed in the firelight.

"No," she glanced in the creek's direction, as if she could still see it through walls and the dark. "I'm just worried."

Bretuck stroked the toad with one finger. "Mommy, he's a good friend, he'd never tell."

She examined his features. He was sure of his conviction, she just hoped the boy felt loyalty as strong. "How...long have you been playmates?"

"When winter set in, he came to skate on the creek."

"How did he even know of it? It's pretty well hidden."

Bretuck smiled and waved one hand. "This was his grandmother's cottage."

"Bring him here tomorrow, so I can meet him."

"You're not going to bug him about stuff, are you?"

"Bretuck, I must be sure he understands how important your secret is."

"OK," he grumbled good-naturedly.

When Azra met the boy, named Celib, the next day, she was very pleased with his deportment. He was polite, cheerful and seemed genuinely fond of her son. When she brought up the subject of Bretuck's eyes, Celib's got hugely round in excitement.

"I think his eyes are neat."

She smiled. "That is true, but you must understand that no one else but you can know about Bretuck's eyes."

"I understand," his face was solemn, more grown-up in its expression than she would have thought possible. "He told me some people might try to kill him, just because his eyes are different."

She couldn't help herself. She grabbed Celib up in a swift hug. Bretuck groaned and the boy wriggled to be free, his face flaming when she undid her arms.

Azra watched them run off, two young boys on the verge of adulthood in a few years, drawn together by play, their friend-

BEST/WORST OF TIMES

Now that she knew about the boys' secret friendship, their relationship became easier. Celib ate lunch with them everyday and seldom were the boys late any longer. Although Celib was human and had no healing powers, he had a gentle soul that made him a perfect companion for Bretuck's healer duties.

Celib helped by holding down nervous patients and speaking softly to them while Bretuck worked his magic. He brought any injured creature he found to her house, where they would be worked and worried over by the two boys. Azra aided by giving them poultices for cuts, while Celib became quite proficient at setting limbs.

It was a wonderful time for all three of them. Bretuck's healing activities brought them even closer, having something in common to share. Celib slipped into the relationship with ease, almost became another son to her and brother to Bretuck.

They'd been living in the cozy cottage a year, fall was upon them and the leaves were turning to golden red splendor, when everything fell apart. One morning a wide-eyed Bretuck came running into the house.

"What's wrong?"

"It...it's Celib's younger brother, he followed Celib this morning."

"Did he see you?"

Bretuck nodded.

"Where's Celib?'

"He took his brother home, he's coming back here afterwards."

She gave her son a biscuit as they waited nervously. A tap on the door and peek outside assured her. She let the anxious looking Celib inside.

He didn't wait for them to ask him a question, but in a loud voice that squeaked out, said, "You've got to leave."

"What happened?" She asked gently.

"That stupid little brother." Celib's eyes brimmed with unshed tears. "I talked to him all the way home about keeping...things secret." He glanced at Bretuck with a sad expression. "He blabbed it to dad as soon as we got in the house."

"What did your father say?"

"Nothing, he left and I followed him." Now those tears slipped slowly down his dirty cheeks. "He went to some of his friends, they're organizing men with weapons."

Azra jumped up, her look spun around the charming room. So many things she loved—most would have to be left behind. Her gaze landed on her sad-faced son. Truly, he was the only loved object she need worry about securing.

"Bretuck get the blanket off the bed and pack only items you need or care about."

She grabbed her old, worn pack and started stuffing hastily wrapped food into it.

"What can I do?" Celib asked.

She stopped long enough to gently caress his cheek. "Keep an eye out for company."

The boy nodded solemnly, then stationed himself at the front window. Azra efficiently packed up all the food within the cottage, then started on her herbs. She noticed Bretuck standing over a pitifully small stack of items piled in the center of the blanket. "Gather your clothes sweety."

Next, she grabbed her own clothes, thankful she'd washed the day before, and stuffed them into another pack made from the thick blanket given to her recently. Azra tied the pack on her back and the blanket at her waist, then helped Bretuck secure the other blanket at his waist.

She gazed around the lovely little room, deeply saddened they had to leave once again. "Are we forgetting anything," she spoke softly.

"Toady!" Bretuck ran over to the ever-present, squat resident of the hearth.

"I'll take care of him," Celib said, his eyes never wavering from his duty.

"Thank you," her son handed the toad gently to his friend. "Will you check on my bunny and bird too?"

"Yes." Celib turned for a brief moment and stared into Bretuck's face. "I'm sorry."

"It wasn't your fault."

"I hear them, you must go." He exclaimed, pushing Bretuck toward the back of the cottage.

Azra climbed out the window and waited for Bretuck. She heard their farewells, spoken with grown-up words, barely held in tears caught in the tone of their voices.

Her son perched on the window. "I'll never forget you."

"Me neither." Celib called as hard fists pounded on their front door.

Hearing heavy footsteps crunching the leaves at the side of the house, she pulled Bretuck into a thick cover of underbrush. There wasn't time to properly hide, nor could they hope to put distance between themselves and the men without being seen.

Azra cast a quick spell, one that would make them invisible for a brief time. She listened to the men inside throwing objects around, as if Bretuck could hide behind that tiny table or under the soft mattress. Dishes crashed and objects were flung against the walls. Clearly they were expressing their frustration by tearing her cottage apart.

The angry mob outside trampled the bushes, shouted, and generally milled about like mad bulls. One man discovered the tiny trail leading to the creek and called to the men inside, who exited quickly. The group disappeared down the path in a huddle, looking like some great angry beast stomping its way down the trail.

Tears sprang to her eyes, but she brushed at them angrily. They had no right! It reminded her too painfully of her flight from her birth village. Making sure the men were far down the pathway first, Azra gripped Bretuck's hand tightly and went cautiously around the cottage. How she wanted to look inside but refused, knowing it would break the last of her heart.

She quickly chose a trail leading away from the cottage and the village.

A HARSH WINTER

They walked for hours, taking short breaks to recuperate, but by nightfall they'd traveled some distance from the village. This time, Bretuck was not newly recovered from metamorphous. Instead he was strong and didn't lag behind at all. Azra decided not to light a fire, even though the night was chill, she was afraid some of the men might be tracking them and a campfire would be a dead give-a-way. She did feel secure though, since an owl living in the tree above them promised to alert them to intruders, and his senses were far sharper than her own.

The next day their journey followed the same schedule, and the next, until nearly a week had passed. She didn't realize how hard she'd been pushing herself and Bretuck until he suddenly said, "Don't you think we've thrown off anyone following us?"

She stopped and looked at him, really examined his tired features, the dark circles under his eyes, and the discouragement in his shoulders.

"I'm sorry, we can take the whole day off. How would that be?"

"Fine." He unearthed a rock with his shoe and kicked it across the trail, his whole demeanor clearly indicating everything was not fine. His world had been turned upside down once again, just when he truly was enjoying his childhood for the first time in his life.

She heard a stream in the distance and guided their steps in that direction. Finding a miniature waterfall at the trail's end was delightful. Bretuck didn't crack a smile, simply nodded in acknowledgement as she pointed to the gurgling spring. They used it to wash up and although it was freezing cold, it felt wonderful.

Her son didn't seem inclined to entertain himself as he did back at his creek by seeking amphibious residents. He propped his back against a tree and stared at the water. Azra pulled out a thin volume containing old folktales and started reading out loud. Bretuck tried to act like he was bored or didn't care, but soon she noticed he was listening carefully, and after a while asked a question here and there during a story.

They did have an enjoyable day, and she made sure they had a large, cheery fire that night. Unfortunately, the next day, Bretuck's glum face was back again. She tried to make jokes, and referred to the folktales several times, but he only grunted in response. Finally, Azra too settled in silence, trudging along, placing one foot before the other, trying not to think.

Their lives fell into a routine, traveling all day, stopping for a few days when they ran across isolated villages. She'd trade her skills for the goods they needed, but didn't feel they had traveled enough distance to risk settling down, even though a few villages were promising.

Winter hit swiftly one night. They awoke shivering to snowflakes coating their bodies. For the first time, Azra was unsure what to do. Saying a prayer to the being of light, she concentrated her powers and asked for guidance. Gathering their supplies quickly, she led the way down a small, winding trail, unsure why she'd picked it, but following her gut instinct anyway.

Her toes were feeling numb when unexpectedly they practically ran into a wood structure. Struggling through the snow banks that had accumulated, Azra saw a very tiny hut, perhaps a hunter's resting place. Waving Bretuck behind a tree, she tapped, then entered the small dwelling. It didn't take but a glance around to realize this place had not seen human occupation in a very long time. Cobwebs draped the corners, giving them a hazy appearance. She stuck her head out the door, but a shivering Bretuck was already coming toward her.

She shut the creaky door, but had to prop it closed with a large log to get a snug fit. She was so thankful there was firewood piled in a corner, even though there was not a fireplace, there was a pit in the center of the room. Azra started lugging wood to the pit and Bretuck jumped in and helped start the fire. Soon they were warming their half-frozen fingers and toes gratefully.

She coughed. The room was getting a little smoky, but it was breathable. Looking up, she saw a hole in the ceiling where the smoke curled lazily upward. There was enough firewood to keep the blaze going all night. They had just enough room to spread their blankets on the dirt floor to sleep. Surprisingly the earth floor made a decent bed, albeit a hard one.

The next morning, Azra trudged through the snow, choosing a well-worn, wide path, hoping it led to civilization. After several hard miles of walking, a small, dismal village appeared at the end of trail. The people weren't the friendliest they'd met, but appreciated a fairy's presence—there were many sick residents.

She was exhausted when she stumbled through the door to the hut that evening, but at least she'd gathered enough food in exchange for services, to last them a week. Her toes and fingers were numb. When a blazing fire met her entrance, Azra felt as if every nerve ending in her body leapt with joy.

Bretuck ran to her, gave her a quick hug around the middle, then took her pack and placed it next to the fire. "You look tired."

"I am," she smiled weakly. "Did you get bored?"

He shrugged and waved at the hut's interior. "I kept busy."

Gazing around in surprise, she saw he had been a busy little boy. All the cobwebs were gone, the dirt floor had been picked clean of debris, and he'd even dragged in two thick logs, which were set one on each side of the fire.

"Thanks for cleaning up." She patted the log she eased down on to. "Make pretty good chairs."

"I guess," he stared into the flames. "You deserve real chairs...like the ones we had." His red gaze came up, wetness and pain glittered in their ruby depths.

She got up and knelt in front of him. "Bretuck, I don't need things, only you."

"Why? I've only brought you heartache."

Azra gently gripped his jaw. "No, you have not, we cannot account for others' behavior. But you brought joy and love into my life."

His look was puzzled.

"You know how much I loved my father?" At his nod, she said, "You remind me of him — the way you walk, your love of animals, your kind heart, even the fact you hate tomatoes."

At those words, he smiled. "I am a lot like him."

"Yes, and have you ever known a better man than he?"

"No," he whispered, his eyes lighting with joy for the first time since fleeing their home.

She opened her arms and he plunged into them, they embraced for long seconds, then Azra pushed back. "Let's eat this delicious food I brought."

He laughed with delight as they laid out their supper.

They fell into a routine that winter, with her making the arduous journey to the village once a week when snow didn't make it impossible, while Bretuck kept the wood chopped and stacked to keep them warm. They both had given thanks that first week when they discovered a worn but serviceable hatchet behind the hut. Her son began caring for injured animals again and sometimes Azra stood and shook her head in wonder. The room was at times alive with running, jumping and slow moving creatures of every description.

He also occupied his time by studying the fairy arts contained within her mother's precious volumes. The first time she discovered Bretuck reading, without her showing him even the rudiments of it, shocked her to the core. The abilities he'd "inherited" from his father were much more powerful than she'd guessed. Regardless of his strange capabilities, she was happy to find him most evenings squinting over books in the false light shed by the fire.

It was a harsh existence for them. Sometimes they went to bed hungry when the snowdrifts prevented her weekly trip to the village. One particularly frigid, snowy week breathed frosty newness to the ice storm that followed on its heels.

Azra was truly worried for the first time. They had gone to bed hungry the night before, and she didn't know when she could travel again. She barely managed to tug the old door open, it was stuck so solidly. She stared dismally at the achingly lovely landscape—white wonderland shimmering like diamonds had been flung in giant handfuls over everything. Its fatal beauty spelled more hunger ahead.

REPRIEVE

Snow was fluttering down in a peaceful silence. She turned and the corner of her eye caught a patch of bright red – out-of-keeping with the pristine white surrounding it. She pulled. A tightly bundled blanket released so suddenly from the snow's clutch, she pitched backward onto her bottom. Azra plunked it down gently by the fire, not sure what to think. Who had left it? How had it gotten here?

"What is it, mommy?"

"I don't know. Let's see." She unwrapped the ends after they thawed a bit, pulling the edges back carefully. Little jars filled with multicolored goods tumbled out. Her jaw dropped.

Bretuck pointed and counted aloud. "There's thirty! Can we open one?" His hungry gaze pulled her from her reverie.

"Pick one." She watched him wrestle with a jar of preserved squash, great satisfaction flushing his face when it opened under his prying fingers.

"Mmmm, smell." He held the glass container under her nose.

It smelled as scrumptious as anything she'd ever sniffed in her life. She tickled his side. "Let's eat it instead." They both took turns dipping eager fingers into the yellow gift and savored each bite as an individual delight. It wasn't enough to fill their bellies, but it did assuage their hunger.

"Can we open another?" Bretuck asked.

"We better not," she stared at the closed door. "I don't know how many days it will be before I can return to the village. Why don't you get us a few tubers."

He sighed, but got up and fetched the wild vegetables from the corner where they were stashed.

"I know you're...we're sick of them." She ruffled his hair as he placed them carefully near the coals at the edge of the fire. "But, they're the only thing that's kept us from starving some days."

"I know," he threw a small stick into the blaze. He turned and eyed the pile of jars. "Where did they come from?"

She smiled. "I've figured that out." She picked up a bottle stuffed full of pretty green peas. "I remember seeing shelves full of these yummy vegetables when I helped a farmer, Hira, and his family."

"What did you do?"

"Delivered his first born son." She stared into the fire. "It was a difficult birth, the mother and perhaps the infant would have died without assistance."

"The father must have thought you saved them."

"Yes," she nodded. "His gratitude is bountiful and given with much effort." She placed the precious jar back carefully with the others.

"He must have used snow shoes," Bretuck said wisely.

"I suppose you're right." She stood and stretched. "Help me stack the jars in the corner, then if you'd like, I'll read you a story." In no time they had the bottles safely secured in the corner.

Azra didn't know how Hira had guessed their plight, but she was very grateful herself. He was a lifesaver, literally. Each day the ice remained and snow often drifted in fluffy accumulations over the top of the treacherous mix. And every day they opened one jar of a delicious vegetable, accompanying it with the abundant tubers, staving off starvation, if not stomach grumbling hunger.

They were down to the last jar when Azra opened the door and stood in pleased surprise and stared at the dripping, melting mess that was flooding the area in front of the hut. The sun washed her body with welcome warmth.

"Bretuck, come look."

He made a great leap and splashed freezing water over her feet, but she didn't care. Her son was suddenly a little boy again, enjoying water puddles, and getting drenched before they ran inside to warm up by the low-banked fire.

The next day she made the journey to the village, folks were as happy to see her as she was to see them. Many coughs and colds had run rampant through the hamlet, arthritic pains flared, and more than a handful of cuts and scrapes received poultice treatments.

Azra whistled a happy tune as she neared the hut and an excited Bretuck ran to meet her. Her pack was full of nutritious food, they ate that evening until they were full, probably several meals worth in one sitting.

Life got back into a pleasant routine, and spring had broken through the cold with a blast of warm air that caused flowers to open hesitant blooms earlier than normal, and flocks of birds to fill the oaks outside.

She was inside, sewing a new shirt for Bretuck when she heard him scream "Mommy". She threw the material aside and skidded to a stop just outside the door. Her son was frozen in fear. Facing him was the farmer who'd left them the food.

The man was turned in her direction, so she saw his frightened, angry expression. He had a bow in one hand. It was pointed at Bretuck, but no arrow was notched in it as yet. Two rabbits were tied with twine to his waist, clearly he'd been out hunting. Dropping a small bundle he held in the other hand, the man quickly stuck an arrow on the bow.

"Stop." She screamed.

The bow dropped a few inches and a puzzled look overcame him. "Why?"

Azra eased a few slow steps, until she stood protectively behind Bretuck. "Because, he is my son."

The farmer gazed at her, then back down to her son. "But he is a Demon."

"He is harmless, and I know I cannot convince you otherwise, but I love him, just as you love your own son."

Something in the man's face shifted, perhaps it was the reference to his child, which she'd mentioned on purpose, hoping to nudge his fatherly instinct. The bow dropped completely to his side.

"You know you must leave." He stated in a flat voice.

She nodded. "You will tell the others."

His eyes shifted to her son, for a second a flash of sadness rested there. "No, I would not dishonor you that way. But, now spring has arrived, some villagers will make the journey here when they need cures."

"You are right." She sighed and placed a hand on Bretuck's shoulder. "Time to move again."

"It's OK, this place was too small anyway."

She smiled and pinched his cheek gently. "You know, *you are right*." She nodded her head toward the hut. "Let's go get our things and look for a better place." She was going to say goodbye to the farmer, but he'd already slipped back into the woods.

It was an easy packing job this time. Bretuck had two bunnies and a bird, which were resting up from injuries, but they were ready to be released. They stood, hand in hand and watched the creatures hop and fly off.

"Look, there's something over there."

Azra and Bretuck approached the brown object cautiously, then she said, "It's the bundle Hira was carrying." She squatted and flung back the tied ends, expecting to see more dead animals, but finding a nice selection of his scrumptious preserved vegetables.

She glanced up at Bretuck. "I guess he was bringing these to me." She smiled. "There are a few good-hearted men in this world. And now we have some goodies for break time."

Her son's eyes were happy. He loved the vegetables. His gaze went to the trail where Hira had disappeared earlier. "He was a good man, wasn't he? He didn't shoot me."

She could only nod, tears clogging her throat. Her son was made more happy by the fact a grown man didn't murder him in cold blood.

NEVER ENDING JOURNEY

They traveled for weeks at a time before stopping briefly at various pleasant villages, those that offered an isolated cottage and allowed them privacy. But, people would hear of her skills and eventually come knocking on her door. It was too danger-ous, Azra would gather their things and they'd be gone soon after villagers frequented her home with requests.

It was a wonderful time to be on the road. Spring was in full swing, flowers bloomed everywhere, and the air was crisp. Their treks through woodland trails was pleasant indeed, with the ser-enades of birds and soothing sounds of nature — the whoosh of soft winds through the majestic trees, busy rustlings of small creatures going about their daily business, and the sun beating on their shoulders with warm massages, not heated blasts of its rays.

Bretuck was more cheerful than the last time they traveled, and this made her happy. Still, she'd come upon him some eve-nings, after she'd searched the surrounding woods for wild herbs, sitting and staring into space. Something in his face and hunch of his shoulders told her he was lonely. He was probably missing Celib, or perhaps his patients. It was difficult to doctor animals when they walked a great distance every day.

After she packed away her herbs and placed their supper out, Azra got an idea. She searched slowly through Bretuck's carefully wrapped items in his pack. He look puzzled at her actions but watched her inquisitively.

She held up a tiny object. "Did you forget this little fellow?"

"Oh," he took the small clay deer from her hand gently. "I did," his face flushed with guilt. "I don't know how I could?"

"You've had a lot on your mind...lately."

Bretuck stroked one finger down the statue's back as if it were real. "Thank you for reminding me." He smiled at her sweetly. "He was my only friend for a long time."

She turned away quickly to hide the tears that sprang to her eyes. She knew he did not forget the faithful, older friends he'd had back at her village. The deer was the only "friend" at that time that was young like him and of a small size. In a way, it substituted for the children he could not hope to attain as friends.

For the next several days, she'd find Bretuck alternately studying her books intently, or stroking the statue thoughtfully. She wondered where his thoughts lay, but he seemed content, so she didn't pry.

One morning they ran across the fringes of a village and quickly withdrew a safe distance, then Azra visited it to refurnish their supplies. It was a hamlet laden with sicknesses—she was late returning their camp that evening.

Bretuck was propped against an oak, laughing and talking in a low-tone to something that flitted swiftly back and forth between his feet. It was about the size of a rat and Azra thought her son had acquired a new patient, although the creature seemed too fit to be sickly.

"You've made a new friend?" She said with a smile.

"No," he grinned. "An old one." Bretuck looked down between his upraised knees. "Come on, don't be shy, you know Mommy."

She sat down on a large tree root across from him, curiosity getting the better of her. A tiny shadow merged from the darkness under her son's body, took a few tentative steps, then suddenly pranced forward into the faltering sunlight. It was the deer. It was alive!

"Bretuck, you did it. How?" Her eyes raised in wonder to her son's radiant face.

He shrugged. "I've had lots of practice centering my power when I heal. I just concentrated all my energy and commanded 'life' as I held the statue."

She shook her head in amazement. "Truly, your powers increase every day."

"Yes, they do." His eyes looked wise and suddenly much older than his years. "I can heal, I can make a clay figure come to life, but I cannot change the hearts of men."

Azra busied herself with preparing supper. She had no easy answer for her troubled child.

Just as quickly, Bretuck's mood changed back to joy as he played with the little miraculous deer. Soon, the miniature creature was springing about her feet as well, making her laugh.

Her thoughts that night were alternately sad and happy, but at times swirled about her head like a whirlwind. In the morning, she told Bretuck the direction of her thoughts.

"The fairies!"

"Yes, I think...hope they can come up with a way to help you. If we cannot change the thinking of those around us, perhaps the fairy folk can change something about you, that will make you acceptable to them."

"You mean my eyes?"

She nodded. "If they could change the color with magic." Her words trailed off, it sounded so fantastic, but fairy magic was more potent than anything else in this world.

"I think it's a great idea." He smiled and clucked his tongue, Bretuck's signal for the deer to jump onto his palm. "Even if they can't help, I'd love to see true fairies."

Their journey after that took on a purpose. They headed in the direction her grandmother had told her of many years ago, where the fairy clan was located. A secret place, unknown to human hearts and eyes.

Azra was unsure herself of the exact location, but she knew it was far, and once she got close, she would feel a "pull" that would guide her to them. Their pleasant springtime travels turned into an uncomfortable hot summer trek, thus, they kept to heavily overgrown woodland trails to ward off the heat.

She returned from a hunt for herbs one morning to find Bretuck once again cocooned. Azra sighed and sat down beside the hard casing enclosing her son in its embrace. She was glad they'd chosen a well-hidden place for their camp the night before, enclosed in thickets of briars and underbrush. There was no way she could lift or drag the cocooned Bretuck to a safer spot. The mass surrounding her son was heavy in itself, add Bretuck's weight to it, and it became impossible to budge at his present size.

She didn't leave his side the entire time, which stretched into a nail-biting two weeks. Every morning, just as previous times, the cocoon had grown larger. By the end of the second week, the mass was long enough to contain a full-grown man.

Would her precious Bretuck emerge a man? If so, would he resemble his father in temperament? Or, would he ever remain her sweet son? Azra rubbed the rigid material thoughtfully. Whatever size he emerged, she didn't think he'd still be a child.

This led her thoughts down the path of his brief childhood. They'd had so little time together as mother and son, yet that time had been rich with experience and love. She had spent the majority of those hours playing, talking, and caring for Bretuck. Only her brief excursions later to gather supplies kept her from his side.

She took a deep breath and listened to the strange gurgling sounds that emitted from the cocoon, as they had been doing the last two days. Somehow, she felt his time to emerge was near. Whatever metamorphosis gripped Bretuck's form this time, she would love him just the same.

Azra nibbled on wild strawberries, thankful they were plentiful in the bushes surrounding them. The berries, plus the overflowing pack of food she'd had on hand, kept her from having to leave Bretuck alone.

A ripping sound broke the silence. She turned anxious eyes to the cocoon and waited.

ADULTHOOD

Azra leaned over but pitched backward in a fast scrabble when a fist shot up through the cocoon, punching a large tear in the fabric. Her heart thudded in her chest. It was large, a man's fist.

The appendage withdrew, then each side of the substance was gripped by two hands and pulled apart in one mighty rip. A "swooshing" sound erupted when the seam lengthened and widened instantaneously. The figure inside sat straight up. Covered in the slimy green muck, he was unrecognizable.

Still she hesitated, holding the blanket she had ready in frozen limbs. He swiped at his eyes, then turned to her and blinked. Ruby eyes stared back at her, then he grinned. Suddenly recognition lanced through her at that familiar smile and distinctive eyes.

"Mother, it's good to see you."

"Bretuck," she breathed in relief.

She stood and held the blanket outward, averting her eyes from his slimy, naked body. Big or little, Bretuck would be embarrassed to be seen in such a state. He wrapped the material around his waist securely, grabbed his pack up, then headed directly toward the stream nearby.

Azra laid out the last of her food, then quickly gathered a large portion of strawberries and added them to the serving. He was gone quite a while and she remembered how hard it was to scrub the scum off, even with a sponge and soap. Bretuck had these items in his pack.

A snapping twig alerted her and she watched her son, her now grown son, step into the clearing. He was tall, well over six feet, and devilishly handsome. His red curls had softened into auburn waves and it had lengthened, touching the tops of his broad shoulders. His slightly chubby cheeks had hardened into a square-jawed face with finely molded lips.

Of course his red eyes looked disconcerting. One expected green, blue or brown orbs to be shining from such a beautiful male visage. Yet, even with his ruby gaze, he was breathtaking. If not for the legend of the Demon, Bretuck would have a hard time fending off interested women.

Now she'd finished inventorying her son's new look, Azra burst out in laughter. The shirt was set to bust at the seams, it pulled so tight across his muscular chest, and it rode well above his bellybutton, while his pants were split at the bottom and hit his legs just below the knees. The drawstring was the only reason they fit his slim waist at all, even then, he barely had enough string to tie the ends.

"You like," he placed one hand on his hip. "It's all the rage this season."

Azra laughed so hard tears ran down her cheeks and she had to hold her stomach. Bretuck joined in, and after they got their sudden flare of silliness under control, she patted the log next to hers. "Aren't you hungry?'

"Starving."

The eager look in his eyes pleased her. She handed him a new selection each time he gobbled down the previous one. "If you can stand those clothes for now, tomorrow I'll see if I can trade for some material."

"That would be wonderful mother. Thanks." He leaned over and gave her a quick peck on the cheek.

Part of her was sad she would no longer be called "mommy", but another part was proud he'd turned out so magnificently, and besides, it'd sound silly for a grown man to call her "mommy".

They caught up on things that evening, even though there wasn't much to tell. She'd treated a few animals that'd wandered near, and she and the deer had become good friends.

"Where is Kira?"

Azra glanced around quickly. "She was here asleep, just before you emerged. She must have been frightened off."

"She'll return, won't she?" His gaze was troubled, and although it was a far cry from the teary-eyed look they would have held earlier, he was clearly still Bretuck. He loved the deer and his heart would be broken if she'd run off.

They both heard a slight rustling at the other side of the clearing and turned expectantly. Kira stepped nervously from the bushes and Bretuck called softly to her. Her ears flicked forward and she cocked her head questioningly in his direction. Again, he spoke softly. This time she snorted, made a quick leap into the air, it seemed a leap of joy, then ran swiftly to his feet. Bretuck picked her up gently and they spent some time getting reacquainted.

The next day, the villagers seemed surprised Azra requested material instead of food, but they complied anyway. After she acquired the goods she wanted, she visited the last of the sick people and accepted the proffered food gratefully.

Bretuck was studying one of the magic books when she returned but laid it aside for a bit to watch her sew him a shirt. Of course it had to be fitted too, but he didn't seem to mind her making him stand like a scarecrow with arms stuck outward as she measured his frame.

She handed him the completed shirt to try on before starting on the pants. He looked wonderful. His biceps bulged below the sleeveless arms, and he left the strings untied on the shirtfront. It was still very hot weather.

It took longer to finish the pants, and Bretuck had thoughtfully readied supper while she squinted in the failing light. She pitched the pants to him later, and with a grin he popped behind a bush to change. She shook her head in satisfaction when he emerged, the pants fit well.

"Bretuck, I've been thinking."

"About the fairies?" He interrupted with an eager look.

She knew he yearned to reach the fairy clan. She shook her

head. "No, about our journey there."

His gaze was just as inquisitive.

"You're grown now." She waved a hand at his form. "All the gossip running through the villages is about a Demon child. They will not be expecting an adult."

"What are you saying mother?"

"That, I think we can walk the more traveled roads. We'll make better time, and it's not as hot as it was last month."

"But, my eyes."

She nodded. "If you gaze down every time we pass others, as if you're in deep thought, they'll not see your eyes."

"That's true," his countenance cleared. "I'm game if you are."

Indeed, their trek down the wide road made for two-lane traffic, usually wagons or donkeys laden with goods, made walking much easier and faster. Bretuck's act of being in deep thought worked well. The majority of people they passed were intent on their own business and at the most waved a friendly hello.

A few people stopped them to ask for assistance with ailments, but they concentrated on speaking to the fairy. Bretuck strolling off to the side as if studying the landscape ahead went unnoticed.

For weeks they traveled in this pleasant manner. In the evening, instead of camping out with other travelers, they plunged into the woods for a distance and set up a solitary campsite. A few chatty folks had tried to walk along beside them and strike up conversations, but planning ahead saved them. Bretuck would start coughing furiously and Azra would explain he had a contagious lung disease she hadn't found a cure for yet. The fellow travelers would quickly excuse themselves.

Only one incident upset the pleasure of their journey. They ran across a man with a wagon who was standing at the back of the small vehicle, leaning over something inside. His face was torn with worry.

Azra stopped to speak with him while Bretuck strolled off to the side. She approached her son a few minutes later. His gaze met hers—he knew something was very wrong.

She sighed. "The man has a little girl in the back of the wagon. He was taking her to the nearest city to see a doctor."

"What's wrong with her?"

"Fell from a tree yesterday and has been in constant pain ever since." She placed one hand on her son's nearer arm. "Her injuries are beyond my capabilities."

He glanced at her briefly. "Try to keep him distracted."

They approached the wagon together and Azra explained to the man that her traveling companion was a healer. The disturbed father gladly stepped aside and let Bretuck examine the girl.

"Her injuries are deep...but perhaps I can help."

Azra kept the man's attention away from her son's downcast head as he moved his hands over the girl's abdomen, his healing aura spreading outward from his hands.

Unexpectedly, lightning clashed loudly overhead, heralding a storm, and causing all three adults to glance skyward. Bretuck swiftly looked downward, but apparently not fast enough. The man screamed "Demon" and pointed at him.

Azra glanced hurriedly around and was glad to see no other travelers shared the road with them at this moment. "He can help your little girl."

The man's response was clear. He fumbled in the back of the wagon, bringing forth a long, hefty spear.

Bretuck grasped her arm and pulled her into the trees near the road, backing away slowly, keeping his eyes on the man the whole time.

THE FAIRIES

Neither one of them ever mentioned the incident, but each knew it had disheartened the other. They walked down little traveled trails again. Azra was too fearful the man was spreading the word about a man/Demon trekking up and down the common roads.

Their journey continued for weeks. Finally, one morning she felt something tugging at her, as if an invisible string was tied to her waist and someone stood at the other end, constantly yanking on the thin thread of attachment. Azra knew they were near the fairy clan and gave herself over to the unseen hand that drew her steps forward. For several days, they continued thusly, with her walking ahead by gut-feeling alone, and Bretuck following faithfully behind.

Then, one day, Azra, who was in the lead, walked into a tree line that "hummed". The vibrations flushed through her whole body and tingled all the way to her toes. She turned to Bretuck. "There's a cloaking spell here."

He nodded. "I can feel it."

They pressed forward, and broke through heavy foliage into a pristine valley carpeted in thick, lush green grass. An endless variety of flowers in every conceivable color range were strewn in an awesome display of beauty.

The sun was bright overhead, warm, not hot, and the air was crisp. Azra wondered why this particular valley seemed a few degrees cooler than the surrounding areas they traveled through, then noticed the mountains ringing the area. Perhaps winds off the high peaks blew in chiller air, thus filling the valley with a pleasant temperature and fresh air.

"Mother, look." Bretuck pointed to the middle of the vast meadow.

"Oh." She held her breath for a second, the sight was so wondrous. Hundreds of large butterflies flitted up and down, back and forth. Their large wings were gossamer sheaths of silver and sparkled under the brilliant sun like shards of mirrors cast into the sky.

"Come on," she whispered. "Let's get closer."

She stopped in mid-step when they rounded a large tree many yards away, one that blocked their view until they passed its wide breadth. Bretuck screeched to a halt beside her. Azra was mistaken. They weren't butterflies, but fairies. Hundreds of fragile, tiny figures flew about in a melee of transparent wings and acrobatic skills that were astounding.

"We've been awaiting your arrival."

She shut her mouth instantly, gazing down in wonder at the small figure, which had appeared right in front of them. It was a man, no more than half her four foot, eight inch size. He wore a robe that touched the ground, but his silvery wings were folded neatly in a straight line behind his shoulders. His face was wrinkled with age, but his eyes spoke of wisdom beyond that of human elders.

"We've traveled a great distance to find you."

He nodded. His sage eyes examined them both. "We have heard tales of the daughter of fairy and human union, and of her son. You are welcome to stay as long as the need exists."

Azra was curious as to the exact meaning of his words, but then fairies were known to talk in riddles. Whose need? Hers? Bretuck's? The fairies?

"I knew your grandmother, before she left us to marry into the human realm." Another tiny figure appeared beside the man, a woman this time, and even smaller than he.

She smiled uncertainly at her, not sure how fairies felt about marrying outside their clan. But the petite woman stepped forward and touched her hand briefly, then said, "I will enjoy getting acquainted with the granddaughter of my old friend."

"Come, you must be hungry and tired." The old male fairy waved them to follow. He headed straight toward the center of the mad melee of flying fairies.

Azra's senses were overcome with wonder. The miniature figures flitting about them like the most brilliant of dragonflies were fairy children. All had the silvery wings, long red curling locks and amber eyes that shone as brightly as gold, but their sizes were as varied as the individual features on each mischievous face.

Some were the size of the two elderly fairies who escorted them others ranged the size in-between. Azra was fascinated by all of them. But the tiny mites who were no bigger than her whole hand, gained most of her attention. They seemed to represent the fairies from which legends sprang, in reality, they appeared to be the youngest of the fairy children. Laughter, giggles, and whispers were a constant barrage of noise around them as they proceeded.

Many times as they traversed carefully through the tiny bodies, fairy children would hover in front of their faces like hummingbirds, their cherub faces merry and curious. More than once, she felt the soft brush of a silken wing against her cheek, almost as if the children were using their wings to give them a kiss of hello.

Azra thought it strange, but very interesting, that Bretuck had more than his share of female fairies hovering about his face in a constant, ever-shifting flow of excited, tiny figures.

When they reached the other end of the valley, a line of impressive, majestic oaks were at the end of the short trek.

The elder fairy turned to the flock of children who'd followed them. "Go play children, you can visit with them later."

Reluctantly it seemed, the tiny figures left in groups, dozens of dazzling bodies flitting off together. A shaft of discomfort shot through Azra, there was a group of elder fairies facing them. Would these solemn-faced beings welcome them as readily as the children and their escorts?

It didn't take long to find out. One by one, the older fairies came forward and bid them welcome. They were shown a luncheon set out on a grassy knoll just for them. The food was natural items gathered from the woods around them: a variety of berries, tubers, an interesting salad mixture, a tasty bun, and of course fresh, sparkling clear water. The fairies disappeared briefly as they ate their fill, then reappeared once again when they finished.

"You need rest." The elder who'd first greeted them spoke.

Azra didn't know how he knew, unless her tiredness showed in her face, but she was glad for their consideration. She felt as though she'd fall down in fatigue any moment. The excitement of meeting the fairies and being a part of the brilliant array of flying children had drained the last of her strength.

THE GREAT HEALER

———◆❖◆———

The elders took them to the base of a great oak, one of the huge trees lining one end of the valley. It was at least fifteen feet across, a giant. One of the fairies stood facing the trunk and spoke a few low-toned words she couldn't hear. A hole shaped like an arch opened. Another cloaking spell, she realized.

They followed the original two escorts into the dark interior. It was a large hollowed out space, empty of anything except a narrow staircase carved of wood spiraling upward on one side.

"Watch your step." The old man said, cocking one eye meaningfully at Bretuck's large frame.

Azra was enraptured with the living space contained within the tree. Each spiral of the staircase led to a different level, where flooring had been attached to stretch across the width of the trunk. These areas were furnished with thickly padded pillows she guessed were used for sitting upon, and richly woven rugs covered the wood flooring. A few levels seemed devoted to cooking areas, with pots, pans, dishes, and cups scattered about.

No fairy was in sight, and Azra guessed rightly that fairies preferred being outdoors unless the weather forbade it or when night fell. The elder confirmed this during his conversation as they ascended ever upward.

Finally, they stopped before another opening. This one admitted sunshine into the interior. They stepped out onto one of the immense branches. Peering down, she estimated they must be about midway up the tree, for there were many branches below and above them.

Walking a few more steps, Azra realized so much more than their location on the tree. The branches on their level and above them were alive with fairies and structures. Ladders carved of wood stretched from this branch to others above them, their coloring and shape blended with the tree around them, making them almost invisible.

The elder guided them into the nearest structure, which stretched from the branch they stood on to the next great limb on the same level. It was more flooring with living space. Hammocks made of tree vines were visible, only because the padded material resting upon the vines stood out. Azra's mother had told her fairies liked their creature comforts, and now she saw it was true.

"You may rest here, the premises are unoccupied at present."

She thanked the elder and they sank gratefully onto the pleasantly comfortable hammocks. Upon awakening, Azra was surprised to note the sun's advance, and that they'd slept away several hours. A snack was placed upon the table set between them, and they downed the delicious offering in no time. Just as surprising, their escort reappeared soon after they stirred.

He asked if they wished to continue their visit, and they readily accepted. They climbed up to the next branch level and their escort let them explore as they willed. At each structure, the curious residents jumped up to meet them—they were friendly and old.

Only a few fairies they ran across were younger, and they were laid up due to sickness. The older fairies would be by the side of each young patient, giving assistance. They stopped to speak with each ill person, and Azra would ask what herb or treatment was being done. The healer took it as she intended, that she wanted to learn, and as a compliment to their ability as a healer. One tiny fairy girl, who was no longer than her arm from wrist to elbow, was deathly sick. Azra might not be able to distinguish fairy folks' ages yet, but she could see this child was still very young. Her cheeks were rounded in the same manner as a human child of less than six years old.

The healer was very worried by her expression. She answered Azra's questions, but then turned to Bretuck and laid a hand on his arm. "Can you help my granddaughter?"

Her son knelt by the low-slung hammock, gently felt the child's limbs, then ran his hands up and down her body. His ruby gaze came up to meet the old fairy's worried stare. "She has...a growth of some kind, here." He placed one hand over the girl's chest. "It makes it hard for her to breath, correct?"

"Yes." The old fairy patted his hand. "Use your power."

Bretuck bowed his head, concentrated his unique energy. A pale blue aura shimmered around his hand. His brow creased and droplets of sweat gathered on his forehead.

Azra watched with hope and pride. She got a feeling of some-one behind her and whirled to see a group of older fairies watch-ing with their curious golden eyes wide with anticipation. Glanc-ing back to her son, she was amazed at the healing aura—it had changed to a deep blue.

It seemed an eternity Bretuck knelt by the little girl, but it could have been no more than an hour. Patience was pervasive. The fairy audience didn't move a muscle or utter a word. They knew her son's concentration must be all consuming and unin-terrupted for what he was attempting.

A soft sigh rose in the air and all turned as one to stare at the tiny fairy child. Her eyes blinked, then opened wide, her amber gaze flitting upward to latch with wonder onto Bretuck's face. She placed both her exquisite little hands on top of his one large hand.

"You have healed me."

"Is it so?" The grandmother edged close to Bretuck and peered down at the child.

"I...don't sense anymore growth." He moved his hand slowly across her chest, his eyes glazed in an inner focus.

"May we confirm this?" The elder who'd first met them, stood behind her son, as well as several more of the older fairies.

Bretuck got slowly to his feet and moved to the side. Five elder fairies gathered round the child, moved their hands over her body, their power of concentration shimmered about the group like a silver-blue shield.

After a few minutes, the fairies turned to those waiting, their attention on Bretuck. "She is healed."

A sigh erupted from many throats. The next instant, the air was filled with whispers and chatter, it sounded as if the whole tree was filled with birds calling to one another in human speech. Glancing about, Azra saw fairies on branches above them leaning over to peer at the activities below, their arms waving in excited gestures.

It took some time after that to explore the rest of the giant tree. Every resident wanted to touch Bretuck and congratulate him. By the time they retraced their path to the trunk's entry point, her son's eyes glowed with happiness.

They were met outside by a great mass of constantly moving bodies, fairy children as well as adults flitted here and there as the news spread. With so many fairies gathered in one place, Azra noticed her earlier presumption about the tiniest fairies being the younger children, was off. The adult fairies ranged from half her size all the way to the length of her lower arm.

The congregation of elders who'd first greeted them appeared. Their male escort, the one they were most familiar with, spoke, "We are most grateful for your powers of healing and the gift you have bestowed on our community."

Bretuck flushed, slightly embarrassed she knew, by all the attention. He opened his mouth, then quickly shut it.

Probably, he was going to say "it was nothing", but thought better of such a profound statement.

The fairy continued, "We know you came here seeking help from us, what it is, we cannot say." He smiled genuinely at her son's surprised look. "We have many magic powers, but mind-reading is not among them."

Giggles like the tinkling of delicate bells emitted from the crowd and Bretuck chuckled.

"But, know you this, Bretuck, healer of the greatest power, son of the fairy Azra and a Demon warrior." He paused to let the words sink in, then said, "Whatever your need is, the fairy clan will try to aid you in fulfilling."

She was shocked by the old man's blunt words in reference to Bretuck's heritage, as was he by his expression. But, then she realized the wisdom behind those words, speaking them made their reality less powerful. Bretuck's brow smoothed, and she thought he'd puzzled out the insight as well.

"Thank you."

The elder nodded at her son. "But, first, we celebrate the return of one of our daughters," he gazed gently at her. "And the healing of Izlali."

SALVATION

The fairies knew how to party better than anyone she'd ever been around in her life. Food set upon blankets spilled over in mounds at the base of each giant tree, and revelers went from tree to tree, picking and choosing various treats to enjoy. Pastries laden with sweet bits of chocolate and sprinkles of an unknown colorful tasty topping abounded. Azra was convinced the tastier goodies had to be made with fairy magic because they were so mouth-watering delicious.

Bretuck brought Kari forth so she could enjoy some of the tasty vegetables proffered. If she'd thought the place was noisy before, she was mistaken. Once the tiny deer was spotted, the volume became almost unbearable. Gossamer wings brushed against their bodies, trying to squeeze in to see and pet Kari. They left behind a wake of perfumed essence. The poor deer soon was cowering behind Bretuck's legs and he put her back in her cozy bed he'd made long ago in his pack. Sassy fairies argued with him, outraged to be deprived of such a wondrous being. Finally, he promised to bring the deer for another visit tomorrow.

A tart alcoholic drink was abundant. Tipsy fairy giggles frequently filled the air, and many wobbling figures whooshed by, barely missing running into her.

At night, the darkness was lit by brilliant firework displays, while the daylight was filled with dazzling shows of acrobatics from fairy children darting about. The young fairies picked up on the good spirits of their elders, their play became even more invigorated than normal. Even the air appeared to have a sparkling haziness to it and she wondered if fairy dust was being thrown about indiscriminately.

By the end of the third day, Azra was more than ready to call it quits on having so much fun. Bretuck too, wished to move on to more serious matters—mainly what had brought them here in the first place. But, he enjoyed being the star amongst such a stellar group of special individuals. His ruby eyes glowed with happiness.

On the morning after the revelries ended, several of the elders approached them. Moya, the elder leader who'd been their escort, said, "We have come to ask what favor we can grant your son." Azra looked to her son, who immediately explained what they wished. The fairies seem unaffected by his strange request, as if they'd been expecting it. They spoke in low whispers, then Moya said, "We may be able to help you learn to change your eye color, but we need to make a short journey to gather a nugget of elfin gold, the only object powerful enough in this world to attempt such magic."

"Elfin gold," she said. "I thought…" Her voice trailed off at the patient look on their faces. Apparently fairies knew where the treasure of a long-dead race was stashed.

"Of course, not even elfin gold could help, if it were not for the power your son has."

She nodded. "I saw it even at his birth."

The old fairy smiled hugely, a hint of mischief glimmered in the fold of his lips and twinkle of his sun-colored eyes. "His power is so great, it shines from him in a constant dazzle; one so blinding it hurts our eyes to look at him directly too long."

"It does?" she whispered. Glancing at Bretuck, she sensed his magic as always, but did not see a blinding brilliance.

Moya patted her shoulder. "Don't worry yourself, my daughter, your eyes have been dulled by living with humans, and watered down with human blood."

Azra's cheeks heated, then she got herself under control. The old fairy meant no disrespect to her human roots. He was simply speaking a fact.

He turned his attention to her son. "If you are ready, we have packed supplies for the journey."

Bretuck nodded, then said a quick goodbye to her. Azra watched the tall, handsome man and three tiny fairies leave. They made an odd group, but a powerful one. She prayed to the being of light that at long last her son would find help.

She fretted for two days while they were gone. Would the fairies be able to help her poor Bretuck, or would he once again be disappointed by life's hardships?

A trill of fairy voices alerted her to their return, and she exited the tree trunk where she'd been caring for a sick elder. The group was surrounded by so many silvery wings, they were almost invisible for a while. It took some minutes before she could gain Bretuck's side.

She held her breath, then let it out in a rush. Her son's head towered over the fairies, his amber eyes shining like the purest gold. She couldn't speak, her throat clogged with emotion, so she simply grasped his hands.

"Mother, it worked." His deep voice was filled with joy so deep, only she knew from what depths it'd sprang. When his arms came around her in a tight hug, the tears flowed unchecked.

More celebration erupted that night, she and Bretuck joined in more heartily than they had on the previous one. Two more days they stayed with the fairies. Azra restocked their supplies while Bretuck sequestered with the elders and practiced maintaining his new eye color.

Their goodbyes were long and drawn-out. There were so many fairy folk to see, and many who they'd grown close to in the short time they visited. Finally, they pulled reluctantly away the tiny fingers of children who hovered about them, and paused at the forests' edge. They waved a last goodbye to the gathering of dazzling, beautiful beings who thronged in a tight mass of bodies, whether they stood on the lush grass, or flew in the air above the heads of those below.

Azra pushed through the humming shield and waited for Bretuck to follow. They turned as one and glanced back. A lovely meadow and pristine valley met their eyes, but no fairies were visible. Sighing, she started down a narrow trail, hoping at the end of this journey, they could at long last find a home.

JOURNEY'S END

They traveled for months. Fall was fluttering around them with its constant shedding of gold, red, and orange foliage. Their wanderings had been aimless at first, but then something about the mountain ranges that surrounded the fairy clans' homeland drew her, and they headed toward the high peaks.

During their travels, they had decided that mother and son were inappropriate terms any longer. Bretuck looked to be of the same age as she. They re-termed themselves sister and brother, words they had to practice diligently at each village they ran across. By the time they ended their trek, calling each other siblings had become easier. In private, they still were mother and son, but in public they had to ever be aware of their adopted roles.

Bretuck used his time wisely, practicing his powers of concentration in relation to his eye color. Curious, Azra had asked to see his power source, the elfin gold, soon after they left the fairy's territory. Her son had obliged happily, carefully picking up the nugget nestled in his raqu. It was barely larger than Bretuck's thumbnail, a misshapen glob of sparkling golden metal. Yet, she could feel the power emanating from it. Azra started to touch it, but thought better of it, and withdrew her hand. She didn't want to take the slightest chance of dampening the magic.

The journey became difficult, more so than ever before, but at its end their reward was worth the effort. They discovered a lovely village located in a verdant valley between craggy mountain passes, reminding them of the fairies' stronghold. It also reminded her of her birth village: the people were friendly, the cottages charming, and the lands fruitful. Most important, the legend of the Sartwor Demon was seldom mentioned, and Azra found no evidence the people knew of a fairy and her Demon son.

They stayed several days with a host family before deciding they did wish to make this place their new home.

Azra had no more fears concerning her son's eyes. He could control the color throughout the day with ease. Only at night, while he slept, did his ruby orbs glare like beacons. Since they shared a room and it would be unthinkable of the family to barge in unannounced, discovery of Bretuck's secret was virtually impossible.

Azra stood unobtrusively by the plaza's fountain and watched her son. He lounged against the bole of a tree, enjoying a juicy orange. People paused frequently to chat with him, or make appointments for him to visit a sick relative. In just the few days they'd been in the village, his reputation as a healer had spread like wildfire.

Young women gathered round him like bees seeking to suck from the orange's sweetness, but it was not the fruit they wanted. Bretuck fended off their flirtations with charm, but not even once while she watched, did he break into a pleased smile.

She knew his thoughts. They'd spoken quietly of this very subject several times over a campfire on their journey here. Bretuck wanted to marry one day, wished for all the comforts of a home and children, just as many of his peers had already attained. But, he feared his lack of total control at night forbade such thoughts, at least for now. What if he were to find the love of his life, he'd posed the question to her one day, and she awoke one night to see his Demon eyes shining into hers.

While they visited and pondered their decision, Bretuck treated a very important patient, one whose true value was not known until later. It was an old woman, the wife of the village leader. They'd been married over fifty years and were very devoted to one another. The leader was consumed with worry, and frantically asked her son to help.

Azra felt as though they'd shot back to the past briefly when Bretuck pronounced the woman had a growth in her lung. Just as before, he concentrated for a long period, and when he finished, the old woman was cured.

The leader was ecstatic. His wife was everything to him. He insisted on giving them a cottage to live in as payment for such a gift. Used to such thankfulness, they accepted graciously. But, when the old man led them to a cottage with one large living area and two bedrooms, she tried to kindly refuse the gift. It was too much she thought. After much going "back and forth" in the discussion, Azra gave up and accepted the gift. The leader was wealthy and had inherited the cottage from a relative recently. He really had no need for it, and would rather give it to them than stockpile more wealth.

They soon discovered the village was more interesting than they had first surmised. It was surrounded on all sides by smaller hamlets, and a large city was located just the other side of the nearest mountain. The neighboring towns were interested in this particular village because the people grew the largest and tastiest of fruits and vegetables. Once a month a large bazaar was set up in the plaza. Merchants from surrounding villages, and even some from the city, brought their wares to be sold.

Now that this had become their home and their reputation as healers spread quickly, sick people were brought to town frequently by concerned relatives. Their home soon became filled with all the comforts that made it cozy, their larder was bulging, and since they regularly cured rich folks as well as the poor, they began to be paid in coin too.

Everyone in town noticed the small squadron of mounted knights that escorted a very wealthy gentleman into town during bazaar weekend. He spent the night at the Hobb's Inn, the only one in town, known for its cleanliness and hearty food. She wasn't to discover he'd come to see her, in order to get herbal treatments for his gout, until the morrow.

Having money for the first time in her life was wonderful. Bretuck didn't seem to care one way or the other. She could wander the bazaar to her heart's content and purchase any item that struck her fancy. But, she ran into something that peaked her interest in a way she'd never considered before.

She was sorting through an exquisite selection of fabric a merchant had brought from the East; silk wonders embroidered with tiny stitches that must have caused the creator much eye strain.

"Can I purchase one of those for you, pretty lady?"

Azra turned at the deep voice, slightly miffed for some reason, but also flattered. It was one of the knights. His chain-mailed chest was broad, his legging-covered thighs muscled. He was also only about a foot taller than she, something rare for a knight. They usually were more in the proportional range of her son.

Her eyes came up to his face and she was sucked into the most beautiful pair of blue eyes she'd ever seen. Coupled with his shock of unruly blonde locks, he was breathtaking.

She didn't remember much after that, except they ended up rambling the bazaar together, and she didn't let him purchase the material, but took home a good piece of it with her own earnings. He tried to get her to meet him later for supper at the Inn, but she refused, and she wasn't sure why.

It shocked her all the way to her toes when she again came face to face with the handsome scoundrel the next day. It was he who personally escorted his rich master to her house for treatment. They were to leave afterwards, and something in her chest felt tighter when he told her. But, before he mounted his majestic horse, he slipped something into her hand. Unfurling her palm, she saw a lovely red and black hair ribbon. As she waved goodbye and watched his departing figure, she realized it was his colors.

Somehow, she was not surprised when he showed up at the bazaar the next month. His excuse was he needed more herbs for his master, but she knew it was she he'd come to see. That evening, she accepted his invitation to dine and wore a simple red gown, with the black and red ribbon tying her curls into a pony tail at her nape.

Azra danced a little jig when she arrived home and hugged herself. She was so happy. She tiptoed into Bretuck's bedroom, a habit she'd never been able to give up, checking on him. He was sound asleep. She'd heard from gossip at the bazaar that the great healer had a very busy day.

She kissed his cheek gently so as not to awaken him. He mumbled in his sleep and his eyes opened sightlessly, as they often did from his childhood. Red, like tiny lanterns. Azra sighed. If only Bretuck's life could be more normal, as hers was starting to be.

THE DEMON DIES

It was but a month later, her wish came true. Her son's sleep was extremely restless. He'd treated a baby whose birth defects internally spelled its early demise. All Bretuck could do was give it a peaceful night's sleep. She treaded softly into his room, knelt and placing her hand on his forehead, breathed a sleep spell onto his sweet face. Before he succumbed, his eyes opened. Azra was shocked to find the lovely amber shade of his daytime guise.

Three more nights she snuck back into his room, carrying a small candle shielded by her hand, so as not to awaken him. Each time, Bretuck's unknowing, golden gaze shone under the taper's light. The next morn, she informed him of her discovery. At first, he thought it was a fluke, but she finally convinced him it was true. Bretuck's power seemed to be holding sway over his eyes even at night.

It took several days to really sink in, but finally her son began to act different. His sleep was less restless and he seemed more content when around others during the day.

She was perched on the edge of the village fountain, idly swishing her fingers through the cool water, watching her son covertly. He was leaning against the stone wall that surrounded the town. Several lovely girls were giggling, vying for his attention. For the first time, Bretuck smiled broadly, without caution, his manner flirtatious.

Finally, after all their travails and heartache, there was hope for her special son, maybe a love with a special girl. As there will perhaps be love for me too, she thought with a secret smile, as her bold knight made his way across the town square toward her.

Bretuck's laughter drew her eyes once again. How handsome he was, how powerful a fairy/wizard. Once he was almost lost to her. But it was not her fairy powers that had pulled him back from the brink of being damned forever with the Demon curse. Azra realized the truest truth. It was not magic or spells, nor swords and brawn which killed the Demon that awful day, but a mother's love for her son.

THE END

THE TOWER

Jennifer Dunne

CHAPTER ONE

General Bayard urged his horse up the final hill leading to the baronial seat of Kittern. His new home. At last, after years spent conquering, defending, and marching through others' lands, he finally had a barony of his own. If he could keep it. And if the previous Baron's soldiers did not resist the change of ownership.

He halted at the crest of the hill as he viewed the modest castle for the first time. His lieutenant, Cheval, rode up beside him. The two of them sat gazing in silence at the broad stone walls of Kittern castle, nestled in the valley below, while the two dozen troops escorting him fanned out around them.

"Not much to look at," Cheval finally said.

Bayard shook his head. "What were they thinking, to build the castle in the valley? No wonder King Ulrich's forces have conquered so much of Suddalyk if all of King Jaeger's people are so inept at defensive strategy. The castle should have been built on this rise, with clear lines of sight in all directions."

"That forest is a problem, too." Cheval gestured to the dense greenwood that filled the valley to the west of the castle. "They've let it grow up too close to the wall."

"I'm no stranger to clearing brush."

Bayard hefted his shield, decorated with his personal device of a sword hewing ivy against a field of blue, commemorating his rescue of young Prince Ulrich that had earned him his knighthood so many years ago.

The jest fell flat on the humorless Cheval. Not for the first time, Bayard looked forward to being reunited with his friend and steward, Eduard, whose ready sense of humor had lightened a number of dark campaigns.

Cheval frowned. "The men can clear the brush, my lord. You have more important duties."

"Well do I know it."

King Ulrich's commands echoed in Bayard's memory. First, he was to take possession of the castle, either peacefully or with the help of the soldiers escorting him. His primary charge, and the one he'd communicated to his troops, would be to make the castle defensible before the spring brought a renewal of fighting. His secondary charge was to subdue and pacify through any means necessary the lands of his barony and the new land grants from what had been the four surrounding baronies. If he succeeded, the King would grant him leave to remain upon his new estates. Bayard intended to succeed.

He eyed the castle's defenses and judged them woefully inadequate. The low curtain wall might stop sheep from accidentally wandering into the gardens between the bailey and the main keep, but it would do nothing to stop a determined assault. The iron gate sat flush in the wall, with no sentry posts to provide defensive cover.

"The curtain wall will have to be raised and widened, a second gate added behind the first, and sentry towers created to watch over the double gate. There may not be enough hands to build everything that needs to be built before Spring."

"Indeed, the castle seems deserted," Cheval observed.

No sentries stood watch beside the flimsy gate or patrolled the shoulder high wall. No soldiers trained in the empty bailey. Yet a wisp of smoke rose lazily from the L-shaped keep's southernmost chimney, proving that someone still inhabited it. From their position here on the ridge, there was no way to determine if the inhabitants were hiding in fright, or concealing warriors for a surprise attack once he and his men were within the castle walls.

"Eduard rode out ahead of us, so the castle inhabitants expect our arrival. They might be laying in wait, hoping to spring a trap. But it's more likely that the former Baron emptied his castle to support the ill-fated campaign against King Ulrich, and the commoners fled. Eduard may well be the only living soul inside an empty castle."

"They might have magical defenses," Cheval suggested. "The empty keep could be an illusion meant to lull us into false confidence."

Bayard shrugged. Kittern was a small barony, unlikely to squander its treasury on magical defenses when conventional defenses were so much more reliable and less expensive.

"There's only one way to find out. Unfurl the flags."

The standard bearer threaded dowels through the top and bottom of the King's banner, then hung the shield showing a crowned bear on a red field from the tip of his lance. Bayard's personal device hung below the King's.

He signaled his troops and rode forward, the column following, with the standards clearly visible to anyone guarding the castle. Bayard's pulse thrummed with pre-battle excitement. Now they would discover if the Barony of Kittern planned to acknowledge him as their new lord, and Ulrich as their rightful king.

They were within arrow range of the castle gate when the keep's door opened. Bayard tensed, but no armsmen ran to their castle's defense. Seven men in servant's garb, of all ages and builds, hurried at a fast walk through the gardens and bailey to meet Bayard's troops at the gate. Eduard was not among them.

Bayard flexed his fingers and rested his hand on the hilt of his sword. Behind him, he heard the soft shift of leather and steel that indicated his soldiers were also readying themselves for a possible attack. The servants carried no obvious weapons and were on foot while he and his soldiers were on horseback. If they meant to defend the castle rather than welcome him to it, his troops would make short work of them.

The servants reached the castle gate just before Bayard and his troops. Six of them arranged themselves into a line, while the seventh threw open the gates. It was to be a welcome, then. Bayard let himself relax slightly but remained cautious. Eduard was not among the greeters.

The man who had opened the gate stepped forward and bowed, then called out a greeting. "General, welcome to Kittern castle."

On cue, the rest of the men bowed.

Bayard rode up to the group, his troops fanning out into a defensive pattern that would give them room to maneuver.

"I am the new Baron Kittern," Bayard announced. "Who are you? And where is my man, Eduard?"

"Severin, my lord, steward of Kittern." The man rose from his bow, revealing a pleasant, intelligent face that looked little older than Bayard's. "Your servant, Eduard, is in his quarters, having taken ill after his hard journey to reach us in time for us to prepare for your arrival."

"How ill?"

"He is nearly recovered, my lord."

Bayard grunted. He'd believe the steward's tale when Eduard confirmed it, and not a moment sooner.

"Who are these others?"

"Huntsman, chief groom, captain of the guard—"

Bayard raised his hand, cutting off the introductions when he saw the man Severin had named captain of the guard. The old man looked like he could have fought in the army of King Jaeger's grandfather.

"You train with your men?" he asked.

The old man squinted at him. "I have no men, my lord. They went to fight with the last Baron, as did my son, their Captain. The guard now consists of half a dozen young boys still learning to use swords."

If this oldster had lost his son in the war, he might well want to strike back against those who caused his loss. And if the son had retreated with King Jaeger, Bayard did not want the father passing details of Kittern's defenses to him. In either case, the man could not remain as captain of the guard.

"I will review your trainees' progress tomorrow, and you can transfer command to my lieutenant. He will be the new captain of the guard. Your boys will train with my men."

The old man bowed acceptance of Bayard's command. The steward began to introduce the rest of his staff, but Bayard stopped him again. The old man might be a potential traitor, but for now, he was Bayard's man, and Bayard would not simply turn him out into the cold when a new captain claimed his quarters.

"Do you have other children you can live with?"

"Yes, my lord. Two daughters in the village."

Bayard nodded and signaled Severin to proceed. When the introductions were complete, one key position had not been mentioned.

"You have no cook?" Bayard asked.

"She refuses to leave the kitchen," Severin admitted. "We arranged for a banquet to welcome you to the castle, and she insists her underlings will ruin the meal unless she personally oversees every aspect of its creation."

The excuse sounded plausible, since cooks were notorious for running their domains like tiny independent fiefdoms, but Bayard didn't like it. He would watch the cook closely for signs of treachery.

Bayard turned and issued orders to his troops. "Gage, take five of the men and secure the walls, then set up a guard rotation with the remaining troops. Jerard and Rodell, go with the groom and see to the stabling of our horses. Cheval will accompany me on a tour of the keep. Dace and Leandre, secure the baronial chambers and take the first watch. Everyone else, carry the gear into the guard quarters."

He dismounted, handing his horse to Rodell, and strode to where the steward waited. "You will take me to see my man Eduard, then on a tour of the remainder of the castle. The rest of you may return to your duties."

His men struck their breast plates in salute, while the servants bowed. The confusion of men and horses quickly resolved itself into small bands of soldiers and servants heading to their assigned duties, while the remaining soldiers efficiently removed saddlebags and piled them neatly on the ground before handing the horses to Jerard and Rodell.

Severin nodded to Cheval and bowed to Bayard. "If you will follow me, my lord?"

Bayard and his lieutenant followed Severin toward the keep, the steward giving a running commentary as they walked. Bayard tuned out the discussion of the various herbs and vegetables planted in the gardens and focused his attention upon the keep.

An impressive four stories in a rough L shape, the upper three stories boasted large multi-paned windows, the topmost in dormers extending out from the steeply pitched roof. The keep's builders had made a token gesture toward defensive considerations by using arrow slits instead of windows on the ground floor, and by banding the door with iron. It wasn't an impossible design to defend, but much would depend on the style of embrasures inside the windows. He'd reserve judgment until he saw them for himself.

Severin stepped through the door into a dim entry room. Bayard followed him, instinctively stepping aside and placing his back to the wall while his eyes adjusted to the relative dark, even though he sensed no one else in the room. It would be the perfect moment for an attack. The castle's builders had known a thing or two about defense after all.

As if anticipating Bayard's reaction and not wishing to provoke him into any displays of aggression, Severin stood in the center of the room where he was clearly visible. Perhaps that was why, even though he seemed to be the servants' leader, he'd said nothing when Bayard dismissed the old captain of the guard. Bayard wondered what Eduard had said about him that so intimidated the servants.

"This doorway to your left leads to the storage rooms," the steward announced. "The stairs at the far end of the room lead to the grand hall. And the doorway in the corner opens onto the central spiral connecting all four floors and the two wings of the keep."

"I will see my man Eduard first," Bayard said.

Severin led them up the central stairs to the fourth floor, then exited into the shorter wing. A single room stretched from wall to wall. Eduard lay on a pallet in the center of the floor. The side walls slanted inward, meeting over his pallet, and three dormer windows bathed him with gentle afternoon sunlight.

Bayard went into the room to kneel at his man's side. "Eduard?"

"My lord?" Eduard opened his eyes and sat up with no sign of strain or weakness. "I delivered the message, my lord."

Bayard smiled. "Yes, you did. The castle was ready for my arrival. But I was told you had taken ill."

"On my way here, I was caught in a storm and took a chill. It turned to fever, and I feared that I would fail to deliver your message."

"But you did."

"Yes. My quest was successful." Eduard smiled faintly then turned serious. "The castle staff nursed me to health with the skill and attention due the knight I should have been, not the servant I am. I could have asked for no better care. But I am still weak, and they insist I sleep."

Bayard summoned his lieutenant to his side and said softly, "Take Severin and inspect the battlements that encircle this floor. I wish to speak to Eduard with no chance of being overheard."

"Yes, my lord." Cheval returned to where the steward waited in the doorway and repeated Bayard's orders. The two disappeared into the spiral stairwell. A moment later, Bayard heard the door to the battlements open and close, then the heavy tread of boots upon the stonework outside.

He turned to Eduard. "You may speak freely now. Is that the truth of what happened?"

"Yes, my lord. The Kittern servants have been extremely kind and helpful."

"You are healing as fast as you should? You do not suspect them of adding sleeping herbs to your food, or other tricks to keep you from watching them as closely as you normally would?"

"No, my lord. Although..."

"Go on."

"When I first told them that you were to be their new baron, they did not seem as concerned as I had expected."

So Severin's attitude was not all Eduard's doing. Interesting. "How so?"

"Even if they are the finest of servants, and have no fear of you finding their service lacking, they should have wondered if you would be bringing your own retainers who might displace them. I had expected them to worry about changes you might require to the running of the castle. I had planned reassurances for all these fears and more before I arrived. Yet they expressed no concerns, reasonable or otherwise. It was almost as if they did not care who held the position of Baron."

Bayard frowned as he considered Eduard's words. "You think they do not expect me to hold the title for long?"

"Perhaps. But I have seen nothing to indicate that they plan a revolt."

"The King warned me that there were rebels in the area still loyal to King Jaeger. If the castle staff knows of a planned attack, that would explain their behavior. Whichever side wins, they win, too. If the rebels succeed, the staff claims they were assuaging my suspicions. If the rebels fail, the staff claims their loyalty is proved by their fine service."

"Poor service would make you suspicious after the fact, even if the servants were not involved," Eduard agreed. "But wouldn't they be concerned with whether you were an unfair or suspicious man?"

"Perhaps. Perhaps not. Who knows what goes through a Suddalyk mind? When you are well, you can mingle more freely with the servants and try to learn their secrets. In the meantime, I will keep my guard up and not let them take me unaware."

"Yes, my lord."

Bayard smiled and patted Eduard on the shoulder. "Now, rest. I will see that a plate from tonight's feast is brought up to you."

The door from Eduard's room led onto the landing of the spiral staircase. Ignoring the opposite door that accessed the larger wing of the keep, Bayard turned and stepped through the small, iron-banded door leading to the battlements. He breathed deeply of the crisp air. Kittern castle was clean and well-maintained, but like most keeps, it smelled of old smoke and too many people. He assumed he'd get used to the smell eventually. The Heavenly Pair knew, he'd accustomed himself to worse stenches on campaigns.

To his right, one of his soldiers had already established a guard post at the corner of the battlement, looking over the road they'd traversed this morning as well as surveying part of the forest behind the castle. Bayard walked toward him, pausing to inspect the steeply slanted roof. The wooden shingles fit tightly on top of each other, with no splitting or curling, and no signs of moss or rot. Yet Bayard wished the roof had been made of inflammable slate.

He bent to look inside one of the windows, pleased to see that the interior wall narrowed to barely a hand span before flaring on the opposite side. It allowed plenty of light, but an enemy's arrow would have trouble getting through to the room inside.

Cheval and Severin rounded the corner, returning from their tour of the battlements. He waited for them to approach, noting Cheval's discreet nod of approval.

"Severin, explain this roof to me." Bayard waved a hand at the expanse of shingles, broken by the brick chimney and two dormer windows flanking it.

The steward's forehead creased. "What aspect of the construction concerns you, General?"

Bayard wondered if the use of his military title signaled the steward's displeasure at the implied criticism of his keep, or if the steward, momentarily confused by Bayard's question, had forgotten to adopt his usually servile attitude.

"The slanted roof makes the rooms inside more cramped than they need to be. I had to duck my head along the sides of the room where Eduard is. Why?"

Severin smiled. "My lord, you are unfamiliar with the weather of this region. It rains very heavily, sheets of water that are nearly impossible to see through. The rains are brief, but would flood a flatter roof. Instead, the water flows off the roof, and through the drainage holes in the battlements."

Bayard knelt and examined the floor. Now that the steward pointed it out, he could see that the battlement slanted ever so slightly away from the keep. Wide holes bored in the stonework, previously hidden by the shadow of the battlement walls, also angled away from the keep.

Bayard closed his eyes, remembering how the battlements looked from the bailey. They had appeared to be supported by decorative stonework, with no sign of openings. These holes obviously did double duty as machicolations through which defenders could surprise an enemy by pouring hot oil upon them in times of attack, and as drainage spouts in times of peace.

Bayard straightened. This castle looked insecure, but it actually had decent defenses. Rather than reassuring him, that fact troubled him. If the castle could have been defended against King Ulrich's claim upon it, why hadn't it?

He was still musing about that question when he followed Severin around two corners of the battlements to the west side of the keep. In a tone similar to that used by soldiers displaying treasured swords or fine destriers, the steward announced, "The forest."

Bayard stared in awe. Trees in every shade of green imaginable stretched in all directions, fading to meet the shadowed horizon in the distance. This was no tame wood or carefully manicured hunting preserve. The mass of greenery exerted a subtle power, as if it laughed at the humans' puny attempts to make themselves secure at its fringe. Unless the castle staff were extremely vigilant, the forest would reach out and grow right over the keep.

Shaking his head, Bayard dismissed the fanciful thought. It was only trees. The golden haze that seemed to hang over it, thwarting his efforts to clearly see its full extent, was no doubt merely a trick of the late afternoon sun reflecting off the leaves. But just to be on the safe side, he'd post a guard on this side of the battlements as well.

When Severin suggested that they resume the tour, Bayard gladly went back inside the keep. His esteem for the steward rose with each room they visited.

The baronial chambers were hung with costly tapestries, and intricately embroidered silk screens separated the working space from the private space. More tapestries graced the great hall, where servants were setting the high table with gleaming silver services. Most surprising of all, the store rooms under the keep were fully stocked for the coming winter, filled to bursting with salted meat, wine, and grain. Even if none of the more expensive furnishings had been stolen, Bayard would expect some of the food to disappear, gone to feed hungry relatives in the village.

They returned to Bayard's chambers, to find one of his guards arguing with a maid holding a basket of kindling.

"But the fire needs to be lit in his lordship's chambers," she insisted.

"I told you, no one goes into the General's chambers without his permission."

"Let her pass," Bayard said.

The guard saluted and stepped away from the door. "Yes, my lord."

"Severin, make a list of who enters these chambers, when and why. I will review it, then make certain my guards can recognize the servants who need access."

"Yes, my lord."

The girl finished lighting the fire, and put her tinderbox back into her basket. She curtseyed to Bayard, then hurried from the room.

Bayard sat in the largest chair, gesturing for Severin to take one of the others. "The keep is in far better condition than I expected."

The steward bowed his head. "Thank you, my lord."

"It has been my experience that when a castle changes ownership, most of the castle's stores and furnishings find new owners among the previous inhabitants. Yet it appears that little if anything has been stolen here. I surmise that you are responsible for that."

"The former Baron instructed me to keep all in readiness for his return. I was just doing my duty."

"Yes, and with regard to that duty, you do realize that Eduard is my steward?"

"He indicated as much when he arrived, my lord."

Bayard studied Severin's face, but the steward could have been talking about the likelihood of rain for all the expression he showed. He certainly didn't look like a man afraid that he was about to be relieved of his position. Something was definitely strange here.

Bayard considered offering the castle steward's job to Severin. He needed men he could trust. But he also needed men capable of fulfilling the duties he assigned them. Eduard would be too busy organizing the barony to supervise the castle staff as well, and none of the soldiers under Bayard's command had experience as a steward. Perhaps Severin knew that, and that's why he was unconcerned.

"King Ulrich has expanded the land of this barony," Bayard continued. "He has granted me six fiefdoms that used to belong to other barons, as well as Kittern itself. Eduard will have the baronial stewardship, overseeing the other fiefs. I will need someone to oversee the running of Kittern castle. You have proven able at the task. I would like you to continue for now, until I make a final decision regarding the stewardship."

Severin bowed his head again, showing no surprise at Bayard's request. "Thank you, my lord. I will endeavor to maintain the castle to your satisfaction."

"That's settled, then. You can give me your oath of service at the feast tonight."

The steward's head snapped up, his eyes wide. "No, my lord. I regret I cannot."

Bayard shoved back his chair and stood, his hand gripping the hilt of his sword, ready for treachery. "Who claims your service, then?"

"Kittern."

Severin's calm response cooled Bayard's rising battle frenzy before it could start. He blinked, trying to make sense of the steward's answer.

"You serve Kittern?"

"Yes, my lord."

"But I am Baron Kittern now. The previous Baron is dead."

"I know, my lord."

"Then you serve me."

"No, my lord. I serve Kittern. The barony, not the baron."

Bayard released his sword and began pacing his chambers. "How can you serve land? It makes no sense. Land cannot give orders. Land cannot collect tribute or taxes. You must serve a man."

"With all respect, my lord, I do not serve a man. My oath has been given to Kittern, and it is Kittern that I serve."

Bayard cursed. "What of the other servants? Are they all sworn to Kittern as well?"

"Yes, my lord. With the exception of the guards and soldiers. Those were sworn directly to the baron."

Bayard did not understand how such a procedure could possibly work. "Is that the custom in Suddalyk?"

"No, my lord. Only in Kittern."

"Your King did not object?"

Severin hesitated. "I do not believe the King knew how things were done in Kittern. The Baron understood."

"And I have inherited his customs as well as his title. Well, there will be time to change things later." He shook his head. "For now, an oath ceremony is expected. I will accept oaths of service from the captain of the guards and his charges prior to the feast. An old man I am dismissing tomorrow, and six boys too young to do anything but run errands. Still, they are better than nothing. See that they know what to say, and seat them at the head of one of the tables."

Severin bowed. "As you wish, my lord. Is there anything else you will need prior to the feast?"

"No. You may leave me."

The steward bowed again and departed, leaving Bayard with his gloomy thoughts. He sat down in his chair again and stared into the fire, his sword resting across his legs.

"How am I going to hold the barony, when I cannot even control the keep?"

CHAPTER TWO

———✦❦✦———

The next morning, Bayard began investigating the contents of the keep's records room. Specifically, he was reviewing the sheaf of detailed maps Severin had provided that showed land owner-ship, crop plantings and yields, grazing rights, and other infor-mation vital to the running of a barony.

He almost flipped past a map of the forest game trails, but something on it caught his attention. Stepping closer to one of the multi-paned windows, he held the paper up to the light and squinted at the tiny print in the center of the single large clearing deep within the forest.

"Old Keep. No hunting here," he read. What old keep? King Ulrich's grant had mentioned only Kittern castle. Perhaps it was no longer in use, which is why the new King did not know of it. If it was still sound, it would be a perfect base for any rebels.

Bayard strode into the antechamber, where Severin labored over the accounts, and brandished the map in front of him.

"Severin, this map mentions an older keep."

The steward carefully blotted his page. "Yes, my lord, from when Kittern was a frontier outpost. When it became a barony, the current castle was erected."

"If it is part of Kittern's defenses, I must inspect it."

"It is little more than a crumbled ruin, my lord. You would find it no use for defense."

Bayard narrowed his eyes at the steward. Severin had said he would find it useless for defense, implying someone else might find a use for it. For defense? Or were they using it for other things? Perhaps some of Kittern's wealth had been removed from the castle before his arrival, after all.

"Nevertheless, I wish to see it."

Severin sighed. "Very well. I will arrange with the game keeper to escort you. Would two days hence be suitable?"

"No. It will not." He would give Severin no time to warn the rebels, or anyone else that might be using the old keep. "We leave immediately."

"But my lord! It is nearly half a day's walk to the old keep, and the sun is already half way to its height."

"It is barely a candle mark past dawn," Bayard corrected him. "But I agree that we should not waste a full day trekking to the keep and back."

Severin smiled and relaxed. "Very wise of you, my lord."

"The map clearly shows game trails leading to the keep. We will ride, and combine the trip with a hunt."

Severin paled. "No, my lord. There is no need."

Bayard brushed his fingers across the hilt of his sword, seeking the reassurance of cold steel. The steward clearly knew someone was using the tower. Bayard would give him no time to warn them, no chance to betray him. This was his land now, and he would allow no one to challenge his rule.

"We leave now."

Severin bent his head in acknowledgment and rose, but Bayard's desire for a quick departure seemed destined to be thwarted. He found his lieutenant in the bailey, putting the soldiers through their paces, and berating them for their clumsiness when they slipped on the rain-softened ground.

"You should not risk yourself," Cheval insisted, speaking softly so that their argument would not carry to the soldiers. "This is a scouting party, facing an unknown number of rebels. Wait until you know what you face before you ride with the troops."

Bayard glanced toward the forest, shielded from his sight by the reassuring bulk of the keep. The forest disturbed him, and he would be happier if he never had to enter it. But such weakness was not permissible in a general, whose soldiers depended on his clear thinking for their lives. If danger was going to come from the forest, he would enter the forest and seek it out.

Bayard shrugged. "I can't be certain there are rebels at the old keep. It may be nothing more than the crumbling heap the steward claims. But something about it disturbs him. I need to inspect it myself, to understand any possible threat."

"Very well. I can see I won't convince you to follow the course of good sense. At least let me ensure you are well protected." He waved a hand at the training soldiers. "A dozen men should be sufficient if you come upon the rebels unawares."

The thought of entering the forest surrounded by that much steel warmed the cold spot in Bayard's chest. "It is likely nothing. Tell the men to bring light bows, and when we have finished at the keep, we will do a bit of hunting. See that they are ready to leave as soon as possible."

Cheval saluted and began barking orders to the troops. While he oversaw the soldiers' preparations for departure, Bayard and Severin located the game keeper in the kennels, feeding his hounds.

"His lordship wishes to ride into the forest," Severin announced. "To hunt."

The man continued dispensing bones to the dogs. "Hunting is done for the year."

"I'm not seeking a boar or hart," Bayard offered. "Small game, birds or hares, would serve as well. We won't need the dogs."

The game keeper shook his head. "Storm last week, brought down trees and branches. Can't take horses into the forest until the trails are cleared."

"Then we can clear the trails as we go," Bayard snapped. "Finish feeding your hounds and make ready to depart."

The game keeper hesitated, then finally said, "Aye, my lord."

Bayard turned to leave the kennels but stopped in the doorway when he realized Severin was not following him. Instead, the steward was having a whispered conversation with the game keeper. Stepping carefully, so that his boots would not give him away by rustling or breaking the straw, Bayard edged close enough to hear them.

"Not right," the game keeper grumbled. "We should tell him."

"No. We don't know how he'd react."

"But if we warn him—"

"We say nothing." Severin turned, startled to find Bayard beside him. "My lord! I thought you were going to the stables."

"Obviously, I did not. What should you warn me of?"

"It is nothing, my lord."

Bayard glared at them both. "It didn't sound that way."

"The trails may be unsafe for the horses. The recent rains will have made the ground soft and unstable."

The steward faced him with a clear gaze and open face, but long years of experience told Bayard the man was lying. Or rather, while what he said might be true, it was not what they had been arguing about.

There was no need to press the steward, however. Bayard already knew there was something he should be concerned about in the forest, and that Severin knew what it was.

Soon the party was riding toward the edge of the forest, bows in hand. Almost immediately, one of the soldiers had to dismount to drag a thick branch out of the path. The game keeper had spoken the truth about the condition of the trail.

And he was still speaking. In fact, the game keeper had muttered ceaselessly since they'd dragged him away from his hounds.

"Not the proper season for a hunt. Not the proper time. All the hunting's done for the year. Not right to hunt now."

Finally, as they rounded the first curve, blocking out sight of the castle, Bayard turned to him and snarled, "Keep quiet. Or my first trophy will be your wagging tongue!"

The game keeper glared at him but kept silent. The entire forest seemed to hold its breath. No buzzing insects or calling birds disturbed the silence that reigned beneath the gold and green trees. Even the jangle of harness and the crunch of their horses' hooves upon fallen leaves seemed somehow muted and distant.

The soldiers dismounted to clear two more heavy branches and a sapling that had become wedged across the path at knee height. But then the obstacles ceased, as if the worst of the storm had struck the edge of the forest, or the movements of animals had already cleared the trails deeper within.

Bayard called to Severin and the game keeper, who knew this land best. "We seem to be past the storm damage. Is it safe to move the horses to a faster pace?"

The steward traded a look with the silent game keeper before answering, "Perhaps a fast walk."

Bayard frowned. "What other dangers must we be wary of, that we should not trot?"

"The ground is soft, and the leaves a slippery footing."

"In the forest itself, perhaps. But the packed dirt of this trail is as hard as baked clay, and the leaves are dry and brittle." Even now, the steward tried to delay them with lies and half-truths. "We will move forward at a trot."

"There is a greater chance of injuring a horse on an unexpected branch if we ride too quickly."

"There is a greater chance of getting caught in the forest after dark and needing to spend the night in the old keep, if the horses move no more quickly than a man walks," Bayard countered.

Realizing that Bayard's temper hovered dangerously near the breaking point, the steward subsisted into silence, although he looked no happier than the game keeper. Bayard gave the order to his men to step sharply, trotting when they could see the trail ahead and slowing to a walk when the twists of the trail blocked their sight. The party continued riding in the eerily silent forest until well past noon. Then Cheval called out, "I think I see something. There, through the trees."

"Weapons at the ready," Bayard ordered. "Forward."

They entered a large clearing and beheld the old keep. It was a round tower, two stories in height, built of stone. The parapets had crumbled, strewing blocks of stone in a ragged circle around the keep, many of them overgrown with grass. The first floor stood open to the elements and forest denizens, as the door had long since rotted away or been stolen. No rebel in his right mind would think of using it as a base.

"As I said, my lord, a crumbling ruin, of no use to you," Severin said.

Bayard dismounted and approached the keep. "I grant you it has crumbled. But I have yet to determine its usefulness."

"You're not going in, my lord, are you? The tower is unsafe."

Ignoring the steward's latest protest, Bayard summoned one of his soldiers as an escort and the two of them entered the keep. The single room of the first floor was filled with piles of leaves and small bones, indicating some animal had been using it as a den. The soldier poked at some of the piles with his sword, but found only more leaves.

They climbed the stone stairs to the second floor, moving carefully and testing each step. The large blocks were built into the wall of the tower, rather than curving about a central support, but seemed surprisingly sound.

The second floor was divided into two rooms, with the door between them still intact. Bayard glanced at the rusted fixtures on the walls and mentally restored them to paint a picture of this space as a well-equipped guard room with swords, shields and crossbows hung on the walls. That meant the space beyond the door would be the lord's chambers.

The door swung open easily, and they entered the room. The door concealed no wealthy treasure trove. In fact, it looked more like a secret trysting place. The room held a bed, of ancient construction but with fresh bedding, and an equally ancient table flanked by two chairs. The dried remains of a bouquet of flowers littered the table top. He supposed it was equally likely that the room had been used by a hermit or a rogue soldier, but some indefinable atmosphere hinted at warmth and stability rather than solitude or furtiveness.

He peered out the arrow slits, and saw only the clearing below and the trees surrounding the clearing. As it stood, the tower was of no use to him. He smiled grimly. But now he knew where he would get the stone to begin reinforcing the curtain wall around his castle.

"I have seen enough." Bayard led the soldier out of the tower to find Severin waiting nervously by the open door.

"As I told you, my lord, of no use."

"No, it will be very useful for Kittern's defense. I will tear it down, and use the stones to reinforce the castle walls."

The game keeper choked off a protest, but Severin shouted, "No! My lord, you cannot!"

A shocked murmur ran through the soldiers, and they lifted their swords, in case the steward tried to run from Bayard's justice.

"You dare to tell me what I can and cannot do?" Bayard asked.

Severin seemed to realize he had gone too far and bowed deeply in apology. "Forgive me, my lord, for speaking so. But this tower is well known by the people of Kittern. Legend states that any couple who make love in it will conceive a child. In all my years, I have never heard of the magic failing. Who knows what binds the magic? It could be the very stones themselves. And that is the least the magics attributed to it."

Bayard shivered, assailed by a vision of Kittern castle, overrun by screaming, shrieking brats born from every tumbled servant. "Very well. I will summon a mage to inspect the tower, but will not touch it until the stones are deemed safe."

"You are wise, my lord."

Understanding clicked into place. This was the secret the steward and game keeper had debated confessing. If they had tried to tell him this story back at the castle, he would have dismissed their tale and suspected their motives. But having seen the tower for himself, he knew it hid nothing of value. And yet, such a simple secret did not explain their fear.

"This forest will yield something of value to me this day. If not stones for my wall, at least game for my larder."

"But my lord, the stores are full. Even with you and your men at the castle, the food will last the winter," the game keeper protested.

"Will you now try to dictate to me, with stories of a magic larder or enchanted deer?"

The game keeper paled. "N-no, my lord."

"Very wise." Turning to his soldiers, he ordered, "Mount up. We hunt."

The game keeper led them further into the forest. He tried a few times to dissuade Bayard from continuing, claiming that it was too cold, too bright, or too damp for animals to be active.

"If you are such an inept game keeper that you can not find a single animal in this entire forest, I shall tie branches to your head for horns, and chase you through the trees."

"Yes, my lord. I mean, no, my lord. I mean, yes, I will find you an animal to hunt, my lord."

"Good."

To Bayard's surprise, the game keeper did discover a young buck. It bounded across the trail. Bayard loosed an arrow, striking the deer but not killing it. He could hear it crashing through the trees in a mad dash as he dismounted.

"We'll have to run it down. You six, mind the horses. The rest of you, come with me."

The trail of blood and broken branches was easy to follow and soon led to the fallen deer. It kicked weakly as Bayard approached, trying to rise and continue running.

"Well fought," Bayard said softly, pulling out his sword and stepping behind the buck for the killing blow. "Die with honor."

The deer's blood sprayed out in a glistening arc, and the game keeper fell to the ground with a low moan. Bayard stared as the man rocked back and forth, muttering to himself, as if the death of the deer had deprived him of his wits.

The soldiers backed away from the game keeper, looking to Bayard for guidance. Meanwhile, Severin knelt and tried to reason with the man, reassuring him that Bayard had killed a buck and not a doe, as if that made any difference.

"Take this deer back to the castle," Bayard ordered his soldiers. "And Severin, you take that fool of a game keeper back. Cheval, you and I will rejoin the others."

Bayard considered the logistics for a moment, then selected another soldier. "Rodell, come with us."

As they walked back to the horses, Bayard gave Cheval more complete instructions. "I want you leading the party back to the castle. Keep an eye on the steward. He knows more than he says. Particularly watch for any places he tries to avoid."

"Yes, my lord. What about the game keeper?"

"Watch him as well. If he causes trouble, you may kill him at your discretion."

Cheval saluted. "As you command."

His lieutenant seemed to have nothing else to offer, so Bayard quickened his stride, outpacing Cheval and Rodell in his eagerness to leave the strange scene behind him. They must have thought he was out of earshot, because Cheval muttered to Rodell.

"I thought following the General into retirement would be easy. If things keep on as they've gone so far, come Springtime, I'll be begging the King to let me rejoin the army and fight a nice, sensible attack."

"It's not as bad as that! So he has a tower of enchanted coupling and a game keeper who faints at the sight of blood. It could be worse."

"How?"

"He could have an enchanted game keeper who faints at the sight of coupling!"

They were both laughing as they rejoined Bayard and the soldiers waiting with the horses. He pretended he hadn't heard their comments, and secretly wished his friend Eduard was well enough to accompany him, so that he had someone to jest with.

Bayard led his half of the soldiers further down the trail. He hoped to surprise another deer, but did not care if they found nothing. His thoughts kept him occupied, puzzling the mysteries of

Kittern and its people.

He rounded a curve in the trail and saw a deer standing in the middle of trail, upwind and facing away from him, some twenty yards distant. Drawing his bow, he took careful aim. A circling hawk voiced a hunting cry, startling the deer into motion, and Bayard's shot went wide.

"Foul timing," he muttered and retrieved his arrow.

Soon enough, they encountered another deer, and again, the hawk's cry startled it into motion before Bayard's arrow could strike. The forest seemed empty of deer after that, and Bayard decided that they may as well turn for home.

"It grows late. Let us return."

They turned and followed the path back toward the tower. He did not expect to find any more deer, but the presence of a hawk indicated there should be small game nearby. He scanned the trees carefully as they rode past, looking for signs of roosting birds. Soon, his vigilance was rewarded with a flock of pigeons.

The birds took wing, and he tracked their flight, aiming for the more difficult shot into the air. Still, with an entire flock whirling overhead, his chances were good of hitting something.

Then the hawk swooped out of the sky, diving through the center of the flock. The birds scattered in all directions.

"That is the last time!" Staring into the sky, Bayard kept his eye on the wheeling hawk, and loosed his shaft at it. It screamed in pain, and dove toward the ground, far away from him. Its cry seemed to echo on the still air, until it was abruptly cut off.

A cloud chose that moment to pass across the sun, chilling the trail in shadow. He heard muttering behind him, as some of the soldiers whispered prayers of protection. Bayard kicked his horse into a trot and thundered up the path, anxious to get out of this accursed wood before twilight fell.

They reached the place where their party had split up, the trail now marked with spatters of blood. Soon after, the tower hove into sight.

"Hold, General!" the soldier riding point cried.

Bayard curbed his horse and scanned the clearing. There, a bit of light blue fabric caught his eye. Issuing quick orders for a defensive formation, he drew his sword and rode into the clearing.

A beautiful noblewoman lay sprawled on the ground, blood pooling beneath her and soaking the fine silk of her bodice and sleeve. Bayard knelt beside her and placed his fingers against her throat.

"She lives," he said. "Two of you, check the tower and make sure it is still empty. The rest of you, search for signs of whoever attacked this lady or any companions she might have had with her."

The two soldiers he had dispatched to inspect the tower quickly returned. "It is safe, my lord."

Bayard lifted the woman into his arms. She weighed less than a suit of armor. Carrying her into the tower and up the stairs, he entered the bedroom and lay her on the bed. His knife made quick work of the woman's gown, cutting away the blood soaked fabric to reveal her wound, a deep puncture clear through her shoulder.

"The gown is already ruined. It won't matter if I cut it further."

She did not respond to his muttered explanation, and offered no resistance when he slashed long strips of fabric from the hem of her skirt. The first he soaked in water from his water skin. Gently, he used the damp cloth to wipe the dried blood away from her wound. It was clean, with no bits of fabric or soil that he could see which might cause it to putrefy.

Folding two other strips into pads and pressing them on either side of the wound, he wound a final strip around them and around her shoulder, pinning her arm to her side and holding the cloth pads in place. It was important to immobilize her arm, as he knew from Eduard's bitter experience. Eduard had continued to use the arm he had injured in a training accident when they were both squires, and it had never healed properly, leaving him unable to carry a shield, and thus to become a knight. This woman would never need to carry a shield, but a crippled arm might prevent her from finding a husband, if she did not have one already.

When he had done what he could for the woman, he pulled one of the chairs over to the bedside and began his vigil. She had much to explain when she awoke. Who was she? Why was she alone? Who had she been meeting? Surely a noblewoman would not be seeking to become pregnant by a man other than her husband, and if her husband hoped a visit to the tower would cure her barrenness, why did they not travel together?

No, more likely she hoped the legend of the tower would explain her presence, should any discover her. But her real reason for being here was likely to be something else entirely.

Bayard frowned, wondering who had attacked her and left her to bleed to death. He did not think robbers frequented the forest, although they might be recent arrivals. Far more reasonable, however, to assume she had been set upon by whomever she came here to meet. And only she could tell him if that person might prove a danger to him as well.

His thoughts chased each other around his head to no end as the room gradually darkened. One of the soldiers brought a lantern for him and set it upon the table.

"Will we be staying the night, my lord?"

"No," the woman said, opening eyes as blue as her gown. "You shall not stay."

CHAPTER THREE

The woman started to sit up, then fell back with a moan.

"Do not move," Bayard cautioned her. "Your shoulder has been wounded. I bandaged it while you slept, but any movement might make it bleed again, and it will certainly pain you."

"So I noticed."

He expected tears or irrational demands, as he would from any of the Nord D'Rae noblewomen he'd had the misfortune to encounter during his brief appearances at court. Her dry humor took him by surprise. It was a reaction more fitting to one of the women soldiers he had fought against in the high hill country, and he found himself wanting to like her. But he couldn't take that risk until he knew more about her.

Noticing her nervous glances at the waiting soldier, Bayard ordered him out of the room. Perhaps she would speak more freely if it was just the two of them.

"Can you tell me anything about who attacked you?"

"I did not see his face. I barely saw him at all, other than a glimpse out of the corner of my eye. For all I know, you could have been the man who did this to me."

Bayard stiffened. "I am not in the habit of assaulting ladies."

"Well, I'm not in the habit of being assaulted. Today seems to be a day for breaking old habits."

"My men and I were hunting in the forest and discovered you lying in the clearing. There was no sign of the man who attacked you." Bayard shook his head, wondering why he was bothering to defend himself, when he should be questioning her. "Who are you, and what were you doing in my forest?"

"Your forest, is it?" She laughed, a lyric trill like bird song that ended on a gasp of pain as she stretched her pierced shoulder. "You and your men are likely the only ones who believe that."

"What do you mean?"

"These lands have belonged to my family since long before the first Baron of Kittern tried to claim them. His line has ended, but I am still here."

Bayard glared at her, but his intimidating scowl appeared to have no effect on her.

"Are you threatening me?" he asked.

"Are you threatened by the truth?"

"You are not speaking truth, you are speaking riddles."

She sighed and closed her eyes briefly. "My name is Feronia. I was merely going about my business, taking care of the forest that is my birthright when I was attacked. The shock unnerved me, and I do not recall anything else until I woke on this bed."

"Your birthright? Then, you have no brothers? No parents?"

"No one to whom I may be ransomed." A wry smile twisted her lips. "I may choose to spend my time in the forest, but I know how the world outside it works."

"You are not a captured enemy, to be ransomed." Even as he said the words, Bayard wondered if that was true. If Feronia truly had a claim to the forest land, she might be working with the rebels to bring about his downfall.

"I am pleased to hear that. So what do you intend to do with me, since we can not simply stay here chatting until my shoulder heals?"

"Where do you live? Can I contact your household or servants to take you home and look after you?"

"No. I live alone, as I am yet unpaired, and keep no servants."

"But you are of noble blood?"

"I find nobility has more to do with one's actions than with the number of servants one keeps, don't you?"

His cheeks heated, but he held to his line of questioning. "Who is your guardian?"

"I am my own guardian." She glanced at her shoulder and sighed again. "Although I am usually much better at guarding myself. I was taken by surprise."

Bayard blinked, startled at this difference between Nord D'Rae and Suddalyk customs. In his country, a noble maid would have a guardian until she married, or until she was strong enough to take and hold the reins of power for herself. Feronia did not have great physical strength. He had seen that much when tending to her wound. Yet there were other kinds of strength, and he would do well to beware.

"You say your family claims this forest. Has no one ever disputed your claim?"

"Of course. The Barons have ever been greedy, wanting to place their name on our land. We let them. What difference does a name make? It is still our land, and the people know that."

"The other nobles recognize you?"

She trilled another laugh, although careful this time to remain still. "The common people of Kittern respect the true ruler of this land."

Bayard's eyes widened, as Severin's explanations suddenly made sense. "They swear their loyalty to you, not the Baron."

"Yes."

"King Ulrich has conquered this land from King Jaeger. Do you pledge your loyalty to the Nord D'Rae King?"

"I swear fealty to no man."

Bayard rose and paced the room, trying to order his chaotic thoughts. If she refused to swear fealty to King Ulrich, she was a rebel traitor and must be dealt with, subdued if possible, and killed if she could not be controlled. Yet she was not loyal to King Jaeger, and the Suddalyk rebels would follow her lead. If he could ally himself to her and win her support, he could neutralize the rebels without a single battle.

Returning to the bed, Bayard sat beside her and clasped her uninjured hand. "Lady Feronia, despite the common people's beliefs, the nobility control the countryside, and they do not recognize you. Marry me, and you shall be a baroness, a ruler in their eyes. You will have a fine castle, with plenty of servants to guard and look after you. Not only is the barony a rich one, but I have considerable wealth of my own, which you would share as my wife."

She shook her head, wincing as the motion pulled at her injured shoulder. "I have no need for your wealth or your castle. And I care nothing for the opinion of nobles."

"What can I offer you, then?"

"Refrain from hunting in my forest. Make it a place of peace, and I will marry you."

Bayard's temper snapped. Bolting to his feet, he snarled, "I am the ruler of this barony. I will not allow my servants to order me about, and I will not take orders from you. This is my tower, in my forest, and my word is law. You will marry me. Your only choice is how long you will stay imprisoned here before you accede."

He stomped out of the room and slammed the door shut. The soldier who was waiting for him saluted smartly, no doubt hoping to turn Bayard's wrath from himself as a target.

"Guard the door," he ordered. "This tower has just become a gaol."

The soldier saluted again and moved to station himself in front of the door. Bayard nodded. Then he went downstairs to receive the other soldiers' reports.

"What did you find?" he asked.

"Nothing, my lord. Only the one pool of blood, no spent weapons, and no signs of where the attacker or attackers went to."

"According to the lady, she was surprised and attacked by a single man. It appears they were not working together, but I will take no chances." He pointed to one of the soldiers, Dace. "You and Roald will stay here tonight and guard the tower. He is already on watch. Make certain that no one enters, and the lady does not leave."

The soldier saluted. "Yes, my lord. Will our horses stay with us or go back to the castle?"

Bayard considered, studying the clearing. "There is enough grass for them to graze on that they won't go hungry for one night. You can stable them inside the tower."

Dace saluted again and went to collect his and Roald's horses. Bayard turned to the rest of the troops.

"Tell no one what you have seen this afternoon. If anyone asks, we had no luck hunting after killing the deer, gave up, and rode back to the castle. We left two soldiers to guard the tower as a precaution until it can be made secure."

"Yes, my lord," the soldiers chorused.

Satisfied, Bayard led them back to the castle. As soon as they dismounted, Severin rushed out of the keep to meet him.

"My lord, was your hunt successful?"

"No. Has the game keeper recovered?"

"Yes, my lord. He is a fine game keeper."

Bayard raised his hand, cutting off the rest of the steward's defense. "We will discuss this later."

They feasted on fresh venison, but Bayard got little pleasure from the cook's efforts. His thoughts were busy with the puzzle of the lady in his tower.

The next morning, after he broke his fast, he packed water and wine skins, a loaf of bread, and venison sausages. Taking two soldiers as escort, he rode back to the tower.

"Any difficulties?" he asked Dace.

"No, my lord. The lady attempted to leave the tower last night, but we explained that she was to remain as your guest. She was singing earlier, but you did not forbid that."

"Singing? Might she have been communicating with someone in the forest?"

"I do not think so, my lord. Her song had no words. It was just a pretty tune."

"Very well. Your replacements are here. You two will return to the castle with me, when I finish speaking to the lady."

Taking his gifts of food and drink, he entered the tower room. Feronia was standing by the arrow slit, gazing out. Her right hand rested against the wall, while her left arm hung at an awkward angle beside her.

"Lady Feronia. How is your shoulder this morning?"

"Healing." She did not turn. "May I leave now?"

"Will you agree to marry me?"

"So that you may imprison me in your keep instead of this tower? I think not."

He set the food on the small table. "I brought you food and drink to break your fast. I do not wish you to suffer."

"I suffer every hour I am away from my forest." She turned and glanced at the food. Her blue eyes filled with tears. "But I will marry you if you promise to stay your hand, and forbear hunting."

Bayard threw the wine and water skins to the table. "You are my prisoner. You will not dictate terms. Perhaps you will change your answer in another day."

He returned to the keep, out of sorts and irritated. The woman had no understanding of her position, that she tried to dictate terms of surrender to him. He was being gracious, asking for her agreement, because he wanted an alliance. A local noblewoman would serve him well as a wife, and if the common folk believed she had some authority, they would be more likely to accept his rule. His purpose would be better served by having the people see them as a unified force. But he did not need her agreement. A forced marriage was better than no alliance at all. Surely she could see that and would realize she had no bargaining power? Perhaps a full day of reflection would change her mind.

He entered the keep and headed for his chambers, and found Eduard making his way slowly down the center stairs. He ran up the stairs to his friend's side.

"Eduard! You are recovered."

"And not a moment too soon. I was growing heartily weary of that room." He grinned. "Although, should you ever want a detailed analysis of how the roof of the keep is constructed, I have memorized every beam and joint."

Bayard hesitated, then asked, "How long did it take you to grow weary of the room? So much so that you would do anything, even something distasteful, to leave it?"

"After my fever broke, you mean? Three days, perhaps four." He tilted his head, eyeing Bayard with a penetrating look. "Why do you ask?"

Bayard glanced up and down the open stairwell. "Let us go to the records room. We must set our strategy for ruling the barony."

As they entered the records room, Severin hailed them from the antechamber. "My lord, I understand that you are posting a watch at the old keep."

"Yes. While I agree with you that it is useless for defense, it could be used as a staging area for someone wishing to attack the castle."

Severin shook his head. "You need have no worries. The forest is protected. No attack will come that way."

Eduard's eyes widened. "Protected? There is magic upon it?"

The steward glanced from Bayard to Eduard, as if uncertain whether he was supposed to speak to the baron's man if the baron was right there.

"As steward of the barony, Eduard will need to know as much as I do," Bayard said. "You may answer him."

"Very well. There is a magic in the forest, yes. The forest guardian sees all that happens within her borders. She will allow nothing that would harm Kittern to remain within her domain."

"That is my domain, now," Bayard corrected.

"Of course, my lord. You are the baron, and own the land." Severin hesitated. "But it is hers as well. She is the land."

"And to which of us have you sworn loyalty?"

Severin paled. "I would never betray Kittern, my lord."

"What if this guardian should be killed? To whom would you owe your loyalties then?"

"My lord, do not speak of such things! To destroy the guardian would be to destroy Kittern itself."

"I loathe magic." The sooner he penned his request to the King, the sooner a mage could arrive to banish the unwanted taint of magic from his new home.

Bayard pointed toward the stairwell. "Go to the kitchens and fetch wine and food for us. We will be in the records room."

Severin bowed and scampered off. Eduard followed Bayard into the records room, his eyes alight with curiosity.

"What was that about, Bay?"

Bayard lowered his voice, so that he could not be heard by any guard chancing to walk past the windows on patrol. "I know the guardian of whom he speaks. She is imprisoned in the old keep. That is why I have set a guard on it."

Eduard stared at him. "You captured a magical being?"

"She is no magical being, just a noblewoman. If she has any magical gifts, she has not shown them to me." Bayard closed his eyes briefly and sighed. "My hunting party came across her in the forest, wounded and bleeding. If destroying her truly would destroy Kittern, it seems my enemies are even now moving against me."

"But if you didn't know she was the guardian, why did you imprison her?"

"I wished to marry her."

Eduard laughed. "Oh, yes, I can see how that would win the lady's heart."

"It was not my intent. She was wounded, as I said. The tower contains a chamber that is yet sound, and was the nearest place to care for her. And as I did not know who she was or why she was on my land, it seemed safer than taking her into the castle."

"But that does not explain why she is now your prisoner."

Bayard smiled. "She has fire. She attempted to dictate terms to me."

"Ah. Now I understand." Eduard sat at the map table, causing Bayard a brief sting of guilt for keeping his friend standing when he was so recently out of his sick bed. "But now that you know who and what she is, what will you do with her?"

"It is more important than ever that I make a formal alliance with her. I will be better able to protect her as my baroness, and I do not intend to see my barony destroyed." He drew out the chair beside Eduard and sat down. "You have always been gifted where women are concerned. What would you counsel?"

Eduard considered. "You said she had been injured. Was her gown damaged?"

"Yes. The shoulder was soaked with blood, and I tore the skirt to make a bandage."

"Give her a new gown, then. It will show that you are considerate of her comfort."

"But where am I to find a gown?"

"Did the former lords and ladies of this castle not keep clothing? Surely they must have chests of old clothing stored somewhere."

"A good idea. I shall ask Severin when he returns."

The steward chose that moment to enter the room, leading a kitchen scullion bearing wine, bread, cheese, and cold strips of venison.

The food was laid out on the map table, and the scullion dismissed. "Is there anything else, my lord?" Severin asked.

"Yes. We have been discussing the contents of the keep. What of the former barons' personal possessions? Where are those?"

"There are some tapestries in the store rooms. The last baron had no baroness, so the lady's chamber was converted to an infirmary. The furniture for her, her maid, and the child are also down in the store rooms. And there are a few chests filled with old clothes, training weapons, and the like."

"I will look those over this afternoon."

"As you will, my lord."

The next morning, Bayard rode eagerly to the tower, his saddle-bags filled with gifts for the Lady Feronia.

As he approached, he heard a haunting melody echoing through the trees. It spoke to him of sadness, futility, and despair. Yet at the same time, it was almost unendurably beautiful.

His horse tossed his head, snorting, and pawed the ground. He gave a nervous sidestep, as if something in the trees spooked him, and broke into a canter. Bayard leaned back in his saddle, pulling steadily on the reins to slow the beast to a walk. Behind him, he heard the two soldiers escorting him struggling to control their own mounts.

They entered the clearing. Bayard stopped, staring up at the keep. The song was coming from the top of the tower. Feronia was singing.

The melody faded to silence. Bayard lingered for a long moment, hoping she would begin singing again. Chuckling at his own foolishness, he dismounted. He was not here to listen to her sing, no matter how beautiful her songs. He was here to make her his wife. If Severin's beliefs had even the slightest truth to them, he could not afford to kill her, which meant he had to find a way to control her. Marriage seemed the best solution.

Carrying the saddlebags over his shoulder, he entered the tower and climbed the stairs to her room. The soldiers saluted him, reported no difficulties, then departed to join their replacements, leaving him alone with Feronia. He took a deep breath, resolving to master his temper no matter what she might say, and entered her chamber.

As before, she stood looking out the arrow slit, her left arm useless at her side.

"Have you come to set me free?" she asked without turning.

"I have come to tell you that you are to be my wife. As baroness, you will have the freedom of my castle and keep, and the barony under my protection. And the people will be united under one rule. My rule."

"But that is no freedom at all."

"My lady, I have spoken to my steward. He believes that your life is tied to the health of my barony. Were my enemies to kill you, they would destroy the barony. Is this true?"

She sighed and turned to face him. "If I were to die, Kittern would die as well, yes."

"Then you must see that it is my duty to protect you."

"I told you, I am capable of protecting myself."

Bayard pointed to her shoulder. "Your condition implies otherwise."

"The man who shot me was not of Kittern."

"You remember who attacked you, then?" Bayard tamped down the spike of fear that rose at her words. What was someone not of Kittern doing on his lands? Had one of the other barons objected to losing their lands to him?

"I told you, I did not see his face. But had he been a man of Kittern sworn to me, I would have known him without needing to see him."

The mention of her magical power discomfited him, and he changed the subject by laying his saddlebags over the back of a chair. He took out the food and drink first.

"I have brought more wine and bread for you. And cheese."

She smiled, and her face seemed to glow with the gentle emotion. Bayard found himself wanting to do or say anything that would continue to please her. He also wanted to yell at her and shake her, and force her to stop using whatever arcane power was influencing his mind. But he suspected that in this case, her only magic was her beauty.

He opened the second saddlebag and shook out the gown. "I also brought you a new gown, to replace that one, which is ruined."

Feronia brushed the fingertips of her right hand over the blood-stained bandage wrapped over the torn shoulder of her gown, her eyes on the gown in his hands. "I should not accept that from you. It is a gift beyond the hospitality of your prison."

"It is a gift freely given. I have fresh bandages, as well. My intent is to see you restored to health."

She smiled sadly. "That your barony might be restored?"

"We did not start well. But I truly wish you no ill. I will do what I can to ensure your health, comfort, and safety."

Feronia approached, taking small, tentative steps, like a deer entering a clearing. Bayard held his breath, and remained perfectly still, lest any movement startle her into flight. Her right hand reached out, caressing the delicate seed pearls embroidered over the dark green velvet bodice, stroking the fine green wool of the skirt. She lifted her left arm to reach for it, then hissed in pain.

"I fear I can not take it, for I can not get into it. Unless you are willing to play the part of a lady's maid?"

Her wistful expression overcame all consideration of the inappropriateness of the suggestion.

"Of course, my lady. Only tell me what I must do."

She favored him with another glowing smile. "Thank you. First, this gown must come off. The laces are in the back."

Bayard circled behind her and gently lifted her hair out of the way and over her right shoulder. It smelled of honeysuckle.

Fighting the urge to bury his face in her hair, he untied her gown's bow and loosened the lacing. The gown slid off her right shoulder, but the bandage held it onto her left.

"These bandages are knotted tightly, and I can not undo them one-handed," she said. "You must do it."

"I will need to untie them from the front."

"Very well."

Keeping his eyes fixed on the knotted cloth, Bayard worked at the stiffened fabric until it came apart in his hands. The bandage fell to the floor. So did her gown.

Bayard caught his breath. She wore no chemise beneath the gown. Her body was beautiful, as perfectly formed as any statue he had ever seen. Yet unlike a statue, her muscles were fluid beneath skin softer than the softest rabbit fur.

He snatched his hands away, realizing that he had allowed his fingertips to stroke her.

"My apologies. You are yet a maid, and I had no right."

Feronia lifted her right hand and cupped his cheek. Her touch was the gentle brush of a bird's wing.

Shocked, he looked into her eyes. Their clear blue depths held no censure or condemnation, only a sad longing.

Hesitantly, watching her for the first sign of unwillingness, he raised his hands and gently stroked the skin above her breasts. When she did not object, he covered them, brushing the rosy nipples with his palms. Slowly, he rotated his palms, feeling her nipples pebble beneath his caress.

"It is said," he whispered, "that this tower is enchanted. Any coupling within its walls results in a child. If I were to claim your maidenhood and get you with child, you would have no choice but to marry me."

She caressed the side of his face, trailing her fingers around his ear and furrowing his hair. Bayard shuddered beneath her touch, more delicate than any he had ever experienced, all the more prized for its rarity.

"All I ask is that you approach in peace."

Bayard slid his hands down to her waist, encircling her hips. His thumbs dipped low to brush the softness of her hair, and he lowered his head to kiss her breasts. Her head tipped back and she sighed.

"Never would I hurt you, my lady."

She slipped from his grasp, backing toward the bed. He thought at first his answer had displeased her. Then she lay down   on   the bed and beckoned to him.

"Approach in peace."

He quickly shed his clothing and joined her on the bed, kneeling between her legs. He approached in peace, and with her, found a peace and joy greater than any he had ever known.

Afterward, lying beside her so as not to risk disturbing her injured shoulder, he rested his hand on her womb, where even now a child might be quickening.

"I wish that I could spend the rest of the day here with you. But duty calls me back to the castle." He idly traced a spiral on her soft skin. "You could return with me, if you would consent to wed."

"I must dress."

Hoping her answer indicated a willingness to return to the castle with him, Bayard sprung from the bed. He pulled on his own clothing, then helped her into the new gown, guiding it over her wounded arm. He held the other sleeve so that she could slip her good arm into it, then laced it up the back.

"Well? Now that you are no longer a maiden, are you willing to be my wife?"

"Now that you know the joy of peace, are you willing to forswear violence within my forest?"

Bayard snarled. "It is not your forest. It is mine, as part of the barony of Kittern. And I will not have you order my actions like a common vassal. I will hunt when and where I like, and I will defend my borders wherever necessary."

"Then I will refuse to wed you."

"Then you will stay here until you agree. If being locked in a tower does not sway you, you will change your mind when you are great with child."

He stormed out of her chamber and slammed the door. Sooner or later she would consent to be his wife. She had no choice.

CHAPTER FOUR

———◆◇◆———

The next morning, Bayard brought Feronia a gift of one of the tapestries he'd found in the store rooms, as well as her daily delivery of food and drink. When he arrived at the tower, he found one of the guards lying bound on the floor outside her door, with the other guard watching both the door and his unconscious comrade.

"What happened?"

"It was the lady's song," the remaining guard said. "When Gage heard it, he went crazed, trying to reach her."

Bayard frowned. "This is the first time he has stood guard here?"

"Yes, my lord."

"Did her song affect you?"

"I felt sadness, but no more than I would sitting around a campfire singing to fallen comrades."

That matched Bayard's impressions of when he heard Feronia singing. Then he recalled that the song had affected more than just him. His horse had also been restive.

"How do your horses react?"

"We had to picket them in the clearing. I was afraid they might make themselves lame, kicking the tower walls."

Bayard knelt and untied the guard on the floor, noting the rope burns on his wrists and bruises on his face. Jerard sported matching bruises.

The attention woke the guard, and as soon as his hands were free, he stood and saluted. His head was bowed, and he refused to meet Bayard's eyes.

"My lord, I failed you."

"It is not your fault if you succumb to magic. But you have made me aware of a flaw in my plans. Do you still feel a need to go to the lady?"

"No, my lord. It was only while she sang. I felt that she was suffering, and I had to stop her pain."

"How?"

"I ... don't know, my lord. I just thought that if I could get to her, I could do something."

This was no doubt how she controlled the commoners. Bayard nodded and dismissed both guards, sending to wait with their replacements in the clearing. Gage hurried out, but Jerard lingered.

"My lord, she is a powerful mage to possess a man's mind as she did Gage's. You should not be alone with her."

"I heard her song as I rode up, and suffered no ill effects from it. I have nothing to fear from her magics."

Jerard hesitated but could think of no other argument. He saluted and disappeared down the stairs.

Entering Feronia's chamber, Bayard confronted her immediately.

"Who are you trying to summon with your song?"

She turned from the window. "No one. I greet the dawn with song. That is all."

"What manner of song is it, that it clouds men's minds so? One of my men turned upon his comrade, injuring them both in his efforts to reach you. No doubt you heard the commotion."

She gave a one-shouldered shrug, although she winced as the movement tugged on her wounded shoulder. "It is just a song."

"Will you sing for me?" He dreaded the thought of exposing himself to her magic, but trusted that his will was strong enough to resist her ensnarements.

"So that you can determine if my song poses a threat?" Her smile was sad, but he thought perhaps a glint of teasing shone in her eyes.

"Will you sing?"

Opening her mouth, Feronia began to sing. The song had no words, yet he understood her as well as if she had spoken. She missed the freedom of roaming the forest, and longed to return. She was hurt, and afraid, and alone. But perhaps, for a while, not lonely.

Bayard felt himself drawn to her, but not because of any magical power she possessed. He reacted as he would to any beautiful woman who was suffering and in need of comfort which he could give.

Dropping his gifts on the table, he crossed the room to stand beside her at the arrow slit. As she finished her song, he lifted a hand to gently brush her hair from her face.

"My lady, you have no cause for fear."

"Have I not?"

"I would never hurt you. And I would give you anything you desired to comfort you." He smoothed his palm over the velvet bodice of her gown, and she arched into his touch. "Fine gowns, glittering jewels, rich tapestries. I brought one today that I thought you might enjoy."

She leaned forward, pressing against him, and rose onto her toes to look over his shoulder. "Is that it, on the table?"

"Yes." For the first time, she had shown an interest in one of his gifts. Although he longed to remain pressed closely against her, he could not afford to lose this opportunity. Reluctantly, he turned and guided her toward the table.

She reached out and touched the rolled tapestry. "May I unroll it?"

"It is heavy. Let me." Bayard shook out the tapestry, revealing a woven scene of a woman in white, blessing the lake. Stylized representations of fish, ducks, and other waterfowl also received her blessings.

Feronia's eyes widened. Extending one finger, she stroked the woman's face with reverence. "It is my mother."

He had chosen more wisely than he could have dreamed.

She turned to face him, and he saw tears glittering in her eyes. "I have been so lonely since she died."

"How long ago was that?"

"Five, maybe six years. I'm not quite sure. It all blurs together."

"She was the forest guardian before you?"

"As her mother was before her, and my daughter will be after me."

Bayard glanced at Feronia's slender waist. "Your daughter?"

"Eventually. When I have one." She stepped closer. "I would like a daughter."

"My lady," Bayard answered, spanning her waist with his hands and drawing her closer still, until only their clothing separated them. "I will do everything in my power to grant your desire."

He carried her to the bed, ever mindful of her wounded shoulder, and once again planted his seed within her. Afterward, as he had the day before, he lay beside her, stroking her soft skin and admiring her beauty. Her eyes were closed, her face glowing with a faint smile, and he dared to hope she was happy, and at peace.

She opened her eyes and turned her head slightly to look at him. Bayard noted that the motion did not seem to cause her pain as it had just a few days ago.

"Your shoulder is healing quickly."

"Yes. I expect I will be able to move the arm in a few more days. But it will be weeks yet before it can bear my weight."

He stroked spirals on the skin above her womb. "And when will you know if you are with child?"

"Also a few weeks." She placed her hand on top of his, lacing their fingers. "We should not be idle during that time."

Bayard chuckled and leaned forward to kiss her temple, dropping more kisses down her cheek and along the line of her jaw. "I told you, I would do my utmost to grant your desire."

Feronia sighed and turned her face away from him. "Any desire but one."

"My lady, I will give you anything you wish. But do not seek to control my actions. I have given my allegiance to my King. He and he alone may command me."

"Then it appears we are at an impasse."

"And duty recalls me to my keep. But before I leave, is there anything you would like me to bring you tomorrow?"

When she turned to him, her eyes were filled with longing. "Are there any other tapestries of my mother?"

Bayard hesitated, torn between wanting to see her glowing smile again, and knowing he dared not promise her something he could not fulfill. "There are other tapestries of the forest, but I did not pay detailed attention to the depictions. I will look, and if there are any more with the woman in white, I will bring them."

She smiled then, as radiantly as he could wish. "Thank you."

When Bayard left the tower, he found Gage once again bound, although this time he was awake and sitting on the ground, tied to a tree. The two replacement guards stood over him, looking nervous.

"The lady sang again," Jerard explained.

"You may untie him. She will be silent until we leave." Bayard frowned. The two guards he'd brought with him today seemed unaffected by Feronia's song. But if he chanced to assign two guards who were both susceptible to her magic, they would release her. Or worse, they might find themselves moved by her songs the same way he was. If one of them pledged to renounce the path of violence, would she marry him, and allow him to father the daughter she desired?

Bayard could not take that chance. She would be guarded by wood and steel, not men.

"A new door will be needed, to seal the tower." He stood in the doorway, measuring it against himself. The lintel brushed the top of his head when he stood at his full height, and with his shoulder against one jamb, he could rest his palm against the other with his arm outstretched.

Turning to the new guards, he said, "I will send a carpenter. If he arrives today, watch him carefully, and see that he does not learn of the lady's presence within the tower."

"What if she calls out to him, or sings?"

"Then you will have to kill him to keep the secret. Advise her of this, and she will remain still."

The guards saluted. "Yes, my lord."

Bayard mounted and rode away from the tower without a backward glance. But his spine prickled, and he knew Feronia watched him from her prison. If she heard his words, no doubt she would be shedding tears over the violence to come in her beloved forest. Yet Bayard's first thought had to be for his barony's defense. If his enemies were trying to injure Feronia, he could allow no one to know where she was.

The gentle voice of truth suggested that he might feel the same way even if Feronia's life was not tied to his barony's continued health, but he dismissed the notion. Her health was tied to Kittern's. He need consider nothing else.

———⁕———

When Bayard reached his keep, he found Eduard and Severin in the records room, discussing the barony's taxes. They both stood when he entered.

"My lord," they chorused.

"Eduard. Severin. How are the plans to improve Kittern's defenses coming?"

"The stone has been ordered," Severin answered. "The first wagons will be arriving within the fortnight."

"Will weather impede delivery?"

"No, my lord. We have mild winters in Kittern. The roads will remain passable."

"What of the workers?"

"We will hire them from the nearby village and put the word out that we are looking for laborers." Eduard handed him the list of potential workers, as well as a detailed analysis of how much each type of worker should be paid. "I had hoped we could go to the village this afternoon, if you are agreeable."

"You are well enough to ride?"

Eduard grinned. "You'd have to tie me down to keep me from riding."

His comment reminded Bayard of the soldier who'd tried to respond to Feronia's song. "In addition, we will need to commission a carpenter to build a new door for the old keep, and the smith to fit it with a lock. I should also meet the village leaders. It would be best to send a messenger now, to give them notice and allow them some time to prepare."

Eduard nodded and walked out of the room, calling down the stairway for a servant.

"You are locking the old keep, my lord?" Severin asked.

"I trust that will not interfere with its magics. And it will free my soldiers from having to do guard duty. When the barony is secure, I will reconsider opening the keep to the people who wish to take advantage of its power."

"As you will it, my lord."

Bayard nodded, pleased that the steward knew when arguing would be futile. He began looking over the notes Severin and Eduard had written. "Will we find a master mason in the village?"

"Yes, my lord. Kittern is a prosperous village."

———⋙◆⋘———

"We're coming up on the village outskirts now," Severin said over his shoulder to Bayard and Eduard, and Bayard signaled the soldiers following him to close ranks. Their horses rounded the last bend, revealing neat cottages with well-tended gardens. Low fences protected the gardens from hungry sheep.

The cottages changed gradually to houses, then larger houses that were almost small keeps. People lined the road, eager for their first glimpse of the new baron. And Bayard was equally curious about the people he now ruled.

The procession stopped in the village square, where the village's leaders waited to welcome Bayard. A young boy ran forward to hold their horses, bowing to each of them, even the soldiers.

Bayard approached the leaders, Eduard at his side, while Severin performed the introductions. Not surprisingly, three of the village's most important people were the heads of the weaving and dying guilds, and the chief vintner, but there were also the owner of the largest herd of sheep and the head of the trading guild.

"Welcome to Kittern village," the woman who led the weavers said, presenting him with a small pillow woven in a pattern of sheep, grape cluster, and tree. It was done in white, blue, and green, the colors of Bayard's personal device, and he took the similarity as a favorable sign.

"Thank you. I am here to find laborers to work at the castle. I am increasing the walls."

The leaders glanced at each other. Finally, the sheep owner said, "My lord, why? Kittern is protected. You do not need higher walls."

Eduard bristled and started to step forward, but Bayard halted him with a light touch on his arm. "It should not matter to you why I want this done, simply that I do. I am willing to pay well all who work for me. My stewards will arrange the details."

The village leaders grumbled to themselves but clustered around Eduard and Severin to discuss who they planned to hire. Meanwhile, Bayard moved a short distance away, surrounded by his soldiers, and allowed the rest of the village's important people to introduce themselves to him.

"Ferron, the master mason, my lord," a middle-aged man with scarred hands introduced himself.

"Ferron. I have work for you at the castle."

"I heard, my lord. You want the walls raised." His expression said clearly that he thought it was a foolish desire, and a task beneath his skill.

"Yes, but I also want a proper gate constructed, with watchtowers at either side. For that, I need a master."

Interest kindled the mason's eyes and he leaned forward. "Round or square?"

"Round."

"Embellishments?"

"Crenelations at the top, and spy holes on the arch over the gate." Bayard held out the pillow he'd been gifted with. "This pattern, carved on the arch, would show all visitors the wealth of Kittern."

Ferron bowed deeply. "I would be honored to build it, my lord."

"See my stewards to arrange what you will need."

More people introduced themselves to Bayard, a master chandler, scribe, jeweler, miller, and glasswright. He was impressed. Although it called itself a village, the wealth and skills in Kittern were greater than in many small cities.

"Parvell, my lord. Master carpenter." The man had the look of a tree, with brown and weathered skin, and thickly muscled arms and legs. His brown and green clothing added to the effect.

"I have a job for you, too."

The carpenter frowned, struggling with the idea of how wood could be used in castle walls. Finally, he said, "You want stone for your walls, my lord."

Bayard just nodded, having dealt with enough similar intellects in the army to know correcting the man's mistaken assumption would be a waste of time. "In addition to the castle walls, I am repairing the old keep. It needs a new door."

The man smiled. "Fine job, that. Wise of you to repair it, my lord."

"The door is as tall as the top of my head, and as broad as my shoulder to my hand." Bayard demonstrated the dimensions, and the carpenter nodded, mumbling under his breath. "See my stewards to discuss what you will need."

Parvell bowed and made his way to the cluster of people surrounding Eduard and Severin. The next man was young, barely into his twenties, although his broad, muscled shoulders and arms and leather apron marked him as the smith.

"Trey, my lord. Journeyman smith."

"Journeyman? Not master?"

"No, my lord. The master has gone to Sylveron, and left me in charge of the smithy. He didn't know you would be visiting the village."

Interesting. The barony of Sylveron had lost a large fief to Bayard. He would expect Sylveron to wish the new barony of Kittern to fail. They may well have been behind the attack on Feronia. Were rebels from Sylveron working with the master smith?

"Does he have family in Sylveron?"

"Two daughters and a sister, my lord."

"Is he originally from Sylveron, then?"

"Yes, my lord. He's told me often how he learned his trade in

Sylveron, but that he had to move to Kittern to become a master. Our old smith died in the summer fevers five years ago."

Bayard wondered if the summer fever had been what killed Feronia's mother, or a symptom of her passing. He resolutely pushed all thoughts of Feronia from his mind and concentrated on the smith before him. If the master smith's loyalty was questionable, he would rather the journeyman did the work he needed.

"I am restoring the old keep. The master carpenter is building a door. I need it fitted with hinges and a lock."

"Hinges are simple, my lord. What kind of lock?"

"Something to seal the tower when it is not in use."

"It will go on the outside of the door?"

"Yes."

The young smith scratched his chin, considering. "I could make a bar for the door, and padlock the bar so it could not be lifted without opening the lock. Would that be all right?"

"That will work well. See my stewards for anything you require."

Bayard dismissed the smith, pleased to see that no one else wished to speak to him. He stretched and turned to rejoin his stewards. It had been a very productive trip. Feronia's tower would be sealed, and he had a suspect who might be leading the rebels.

The next day, Bayard arrived at the tower early enough to hear Feronia singing. She sang of sorrow so deep, it was a wonder her heart had not shattered. He spurred his horse forward, charging across the clearing, vaulting off the horse before it had stopped. He ran up the stairs, and almost impaled himself on the guard's sword before the man recognized him and lowered the blade.

"Your pardon, my lord!"

Feronia's song ended, freeing Bayard of the compulsion to rush to her. He paused to gather his thoughts, and his escort caught up to him, carrying the gifts he had left on his horse.

"My lord, you left these behind in your haste."

"Thank you." He took the saddle bags and tapestry, then waved dismissal and entered Feronia's room.

She turned from the arrow slit, and he could see the shiny tracks of tears upon her alabaster cheeks. "Is it not enough that you must lock me in this cage? Now you seek to render it barren of life, trapping me in cold, unfeeling stone?"

"What do you mean?"

"I heard you speaking to your soldiers yesterday. You plan to replace the guards with metal locks. I will be the only one left alive in this tower."

"Do you speak to the guards?" Bayard struggled to make sense of her complaint. The guards should not have spoken to her, but he had not explicitly ordered them not to.

"No. At least, nothing beyond asking them to empty the chamber pot. But I know they and their horses are nearby."

"But a sturdy lock will provide more protection for you than the guards."

"A lock is not alive!" She spun away from him and returned to the arrow slit, her forehead resting on the stone above it as she pressed her face to the opening. "I can see the forest, but it is too far away. I cannot feel it."

Feronia's shoulders quivered, and her right hand, pressed against the stone wall, clenched as if she would claw her way through the stone to the forest beyond.

Bayard came up behind her and slipped his arms around her waist, pulling her against him. "You are not alone now. And if it distresses you so, you shall never be alone. What do you need? Plants? Animals? I will bring them to you."

Feronia turned within his arms and tilted her head back to look at him. Fresh tears glittered on her cheeks, but her blue eyes shone with hope.

"I thought you meant to break me," she said.

He brushed the tears from her face. "I mean to make you my wife. I have no wish to break you."

Hesitantly, she lifted her good arm and threaded her fingers through his hair. Cupping his head, she pulled his mouth down to hers and kissed him.

As he had every other day, Bayard lifted her and carried her to the bed. But this time, instead of merely letting him make love to her, she made love to him in return. Bayard had thought the joy he had found previously with Feronia could not be equaled, but the ecstasy of her willing partnership far surpassed anything he had experienced before.

"Feronia, ma—"

She lay a finger across his lips, silencing him. "I cannot agree to marry you until you agree to make my forest a place of peace. No hunting, no fighting, and no threatening to kill innocent craftsmen to warrant my good behavior."

Bayard's face heated. Phrased that way, his instructions to his soldiers yesterday did sound extreme. But their lives were worth nothing compared to hers, and he would do whatever was required to see her safe, to keep his barony safe.

Her finger still pressed against his lips, preventing him from voicing his protest. She smiled sadly, as if she knew what he would have said.

"I understand that violence is your nature. You are a general, conditioned to see all situations as battles. But I will not allow my forest to become just another battleground. So do not ask me again. I will be forced to refuse you, and that will cause both of us pain."

She lifted her finger. Bayard considered pressing her, then realized she was right. Until the situation changed, asking her to wed him could only result in anger and hurt feelings. But when she knew for certain that she carried his heir, the temple would marry them regardless of her wishes.

Confident of his strategy's eventual success, he smiled and acquiesced. Rising from the bed, he went to the table and unrolled the new tapestry he had brought her.

"Come, see the gift I have for you today."

CHAPTER FIVE

"We have to assume they will be reluctant to pay their taxes, my lord," Eduard said.

Bayard ran a hand over his face, tired beyond thought at the convoluted construction plans they had been analyzing all afternoon. How was he to build up Kittern's defenses if he had no revenue? "All of them?"

"The baronies that formerly owned these four lords' fiefs were captured by King Ulrich, and granted to loyal Nord D'Rae noblemen. They recognize your right to the land. The lords will pay their taxes to you. Not the lords on this side." Eduard tapped the map twice, illustrating his point. "The barons that formerly owned these two fiefs each arranged with an envoy of the King to give away one of their fiefs in order to maintain their rule of their baronies. But the barons do not believe you can keep the lands, and the lords of these fiefs know it. The lords will not pay taxes to you if they fear they will have to pay them again to a second baron when they are reconquered."

Bayard studied the map. The two baronies in question were Devarot and Sylveron. "Sylveron again. It seems I find them at the center of all my problems."

"Again? What other problems have they caused?"

Bayard explained about the attack on Feronia and the missing smith.

"But you have said the guardian did not recognize her attacker. And visiting relatives is not treason."

"Perhaps." Bayard sighed. "I may just be suspicious with no cause. But my suspicions have kept me alive through plenty of risky campaigns in the past."

A soldier thumped on the doorway and saluted. "My lord, a

messenger from the King has arrived."

"Show him in."

A dusty messenger, clad in the burgundy and blue colors of the Nord D'Rae royal house, knelt before Bayard and extended a rolled parchment. "General Bayard, Baron Kittern, King Ulrich sends greetings and this message."

"I am honored by the King's regard, and trust all is well with the King and Dalthar."

"The King is well, but he is not in the capital city."

"He is not?" Bayard had merely given the customary response to the messenger's greeting. He hadn't expected an answer.

The messenger nodded. "He has come to put down rebel activity in Sylveron, and replace the traitorous Baron with a more loyal one. No doubt his message will explain the details."

"No doubt." Bayard took the parchment and unrolled it on top of the maps he'd been studying. "Go to the kitchens and refresh yourself. I will summon you when I have readied a response."

The soldier escorted the messenger out of the room while Eduard hovered nervously beside Bayard, waiting to hear the news.

"He has approved my request for a mage to investigate the tower's claimed magic."

"That is good news. Why do you look so grim?"

"Because he will bring the mage as part of his entourage when he comes to visit in one month's time. He believes that will be sufficient time to restore order to Sylveron."

Eduard blinked. "A royal visit? To Kittern? In one month?"

"Yes. He does not say as much, but I am certain his intent is to evaluate Kittern's defenses, and determine if we are likely to fall prey to Suddalyk rebels as well. If we fail his evaluation, I will once more be riding at the head of a division of troops come Spring." Bayard glared at the parchment. "Kittern is my home now, and I shall not lose it."

"Does he say anything else?"

Bayard scanned the missive again, sifting for clues to the King's thoughts. "He asks about alliances, and whether the people here are loyal to their new rulers. If I tell him that I have made alliances without informing him, he will think I am conspiring against him. Yet if I say I have not, he will think I fear and distrust the nobles surrounding Kittern."

"You do distrust them."

"But I should show some progress." He rubbed his face again. "When will the first stoneworks be going up for the new towers?"

"A month from now."

"Very well. We will host a celebration a month from now, in conjunction with the King's visit, and invite all the knights and nobility from the entire barony. That will give them the opportunity to see that I am enhancing Kittern's strength, while I take their oaths of fealty. And I can feel them out for possible alliances under the watchful eye of the king."

Eduard nodded. "Shall I write the invitations?"

"Not yet. We will wait until the King approves the plan. I'll compose the missive now."

<hr />

Dawn found Bayard leading his escort through the forest, laden with empty baskets in addition to bags of food. Whenever he saw a likely looking growth of ivy, ferns, or other ground cover, he would stop, dismount, and cut out a section with his knife, complete with the soil it was rooted in. When he had filled all of the baskets, he led his escort to the tower.

Feronia's eyes widened when he carried the first armload of baskets inside her chamber. As the two soldiers followed him inside with their own loads of greenery, she broke into a radiant smile and clasped her hands over her heart.

Bayard dismissed the soldiers, closing the door behind their hasty retreat, and turned to her. "You can move your arm!"

"My shoulder is healing well. And you have brought half of the forest to me!"

He returned her smile, pleased that he was able to make her happy, and anticipating a suitable reward. "Where would you like your plants, my lady?"

"By this arrow slit." She pointed to the southern one. "The sun shines strongest through here."

He arranged the baskets as she directed, smiling indulgently when she reached forward to brush some of the leaves with her fingertips, or to lift a trailing ivy vine to the opening in the wall.

As he expected, when she finished caressing the plants, she turned and bestowed the same attention on him, and he was well rewarded for the morning's efforts.

Lying beside her on the bed, Bayard stroked her soft skin that it seemed he could never get his fill of touching. "I will not be able to see you tomorrow. I must meet with a delegation from the temple. Among other things, we need to confirm the schedule of the visiting priest and priestess who travel quarterly to the castle. The meeting will take all day."

"You have a life outside of this tower."

"As could you, if you would—"

Feronia pressed her finger against his lips, silencing him. "We agreed not to speak of that. Tell me instead of your plans for the castle. What happens when the priest and priestess visit?"

He described the decorations Severin had shown him that would be hung in the great hall, to transform it into a temple. Many people from the village and surrounding countryside and everyone in the castle would attend the service, including the cook and kitchen servants, so there would be no midday meal. Bayard would have some light refreshments, probably bread and cheese, then receive petitions from the villagers. Those villagers not wishing to speak to him would go out to the bailey and have their own repasts.

"Some will bring wares to trade, and lay them out on blankets, turning the day into a small fair. Nothing so grand as we'll see next month, when the nobles come."

"Which nobles? And why?"

Despite his normal reticence, Bayard found himself telling Feronia all about his plans for the coming celebration and the arrival of the King. Ulrich would have no patience for Feronia's situation. If Bayard could not demonstrate that he controlled her, the King would order her killed.

Bayard distracted himself from that grim thought by describing the plans being made to host so many people in Kittern's small castle. To his surprise, he heard himself telling her what those visiting nobles would never know, his reasons, hopes, and fears. She would never betray his confidences, isolated in her tower and soon to be his wife.

"Ulrich is a strong king, and the kingdom prospers beneath his rule. But that strength is purchased at the price of constant vigilance. Any possible threat is destroyed before it can grow too strong. I have served him well these past years, and led his armies to many victories, for which he rewarded me with Kittern. I must be able to hold it, in order to remain. Yet if I hold it too successfully, he will fear that I plan to lead my own forces against him, and find some pretense to strip me of lands and title."

Feronia hesitated, then answered, "You will make a good baron, for all that you were not born to Kittern. You prepare to fight, but to protect, not to destroy. Is there any way, aside from marriage, that I may help your efforts?"

Bayard's heart leapt. She had made the first step toward an alliance. Although he wanted her as his lady, he would take any alliance, and build on that basis until he convinced her to marry him. He needed to accept her offer with a suggestion for aid that was neither beyond her reach nor insultingly menial. Unfortunately, she had heretofore been evasive regarding her skills and abilities as forest guardian.

"I do not know enough of your powers to judge."

"The birds and beasts of the forest obey me. I can see through their eyes, and hear through their ears. I can command the plants of the forest to speed or slow their growth. I know whenever someone enters the forest, and if they are sworn to me, I know why."

Bayard gazed at her in awe. Feronia had recited her abilities in a matter-of-fact tone that left no room for doubt. Those skills would be the pride of all but the most powerful of mages, yet he sensed that there were other abilities she possessed, that she had chosen not to share with him.

"Your forest borders the fief of Stone Valley, which used to belong to the barony of Sylveron, and is now part of Kittern. Do you know their minds when they enter your forest?"

"No. They may belong to your barony of Kittern, but they are not of Kittern."

Bayard frowned. "How can they belong to Kittern but not belong to Kittern?"

"They belong to your Kittern. Not mine."

"Because they do not live in the castle or Kittern village?"

"Because they do not honor my forest. To the wide world, you and your men are Kittern now. But to me, you will not be men of Kittern until you believe as the people of Kittern do."

"Yet you are still willing to help me?"

Feronia rose from the bed and threaded her way between baskets of plants to look out the arrow slit. "I guard the forest and by extension the people of Kittern. I told you that I was aware of the events of the world outside my forest. Your King Ulrich has taken many baronies from King Jaeger. Come spring, King Jaeger will try to take them back. Kittern falls at the southern end of the disputed region, and will be one of the first fought over. If you are strong, the fighting will pass Kittern by. If you are weak, the peace of Kittern will be destroyed as first one side then the other lays claim to the castle. I help you to help my people."

"A well-reasoned argument. And one I might have believed, had you delivered it to me, rather than the wall."

Bayard joined her by the arrow slit and gently turned her to face him. When she continued to look at the floor, he lifted her chin until she finally met his gaze.

"What other reason do you have for helping me?"

She gazed at him in silence for so long that he feared she would never answer, but eventually, she said, "I do not want your King to take you away."

"No more than I desire to leave, my lady. Together, we shall defend all of Kittern's lands and people." Leaning close, Bayard kissed her lightly to seal his pledge. "My current concern is that agents of Sylveron seek to harm Kittern. Can you watch the forest for people not of Kittern, or those of Kittern whose loyalties are not true?"

She lifted her injured arm. "My powers will not be at their fullest until I am wholly restored, but I will watch for intruders. That much I may do from within this tower."

Over the course of the next two weeks, the tower's guards were replaced by the sturdy lock and door Bayard had commissioned, allowing him to spend as much time with Feronia as he desired without causing comments among his troops. Instead, he and Eduard rode out from the castle every day to inspect the far-flung properties of the barony. At some point, their paths would diverge, with Bayard riding to Feronia's tower while Eduard continued alone. They would meet up again when Eduard returned, and ride back to the castle together, allowing Eduard time to report anything of significance he saw. Bayard should have inspected all of his holdings himself, but he trusted Eduard's judgment, and made a point of ensuring he visited any major landowners before he and Eduard parted company.

One thing that became clear, which the maps had obscured, was that the tower was truly in the center of Kittern. The distances varied with terrain, but the time required to travel by horseback from any point on the border to the tower remained constant.

Another thing that became clear, at least to Bayard, was that Feronia had fallen in love with him. She eagerly ran to meet him when he entered her tower, and seemed to want nothing more than to spend hours attending him, sharing pleasure or listening to him talk about his efforts to improve the barony, and the arrangements for the coming celebration.

Yet the last few days, he had sensed an underlying sadness that she refused to discuss. Her shoulder had healed, and she had regained full use of her arm, a fact which she had demonstrated most exuberantly. But that very demonstration had served to distract

Bayard from further commenting on her restored health, something he realized only after he had thought back on the day's events later that evening.

He wondered at the possible cause of her sadness now, as he entered her tower, and was immediately distracted by the tower's transformed nature. The first floor had been swept clean. All that remained of the detritus that had filled it was a neat pile of ash and a newly fashioned stick broom.

Bayard hurried up the stairs to find the second floor equally transformed. The table and chairs had been moved to the outer room, and stood bathed in a wide swath of sunlight from an arrow slit. The two tapestries depicting Feronia's mother hung on the interior wall, flanking the door to her chamber.

Almost fearful of what he might find within, Bayard stepped into her chamber. A riot of vines covered the walls and twined around the corner posts of the bed while ground cover carpeted the floor, blooming with a profusion of flowers unlike any he had ever seen. Scarlet trumpets hung beside white star flowers, while tiny blue hearts' remembrance peeped from beneath the concealment of their rounded leaves.

Feronia stood in the center of the room, watching him enter. "Do you like it?"

"It's magnificent. But how...?"

She shrugged, dismissing the impossibility of spring, summer and autumn flowers blooming at the same time, on vines that had not existed the day before. "My powers have returned."

Turning away from him, she trod as lightly as a sunbeam across the hearts' remembrance carpeting the floor, and climbed upon the bed. Bayard stared with amazement at the undisturbed flowers. She had spoken of her powers, but he had never truly understood what she meant. She did not own or command the forest, as a man might own or command land through the strength of steel and stone. She lived and breathed it, and was a part of it, as inseparable as the soil and sun.

Feronia opened her arms, beckoning to him. "Make love to me, here, in the heart of my forest."

The hearts' remembrance pulled away, green leaves sliding over tiny blue flowers, to clear a path to the bed. She called to him, as the flowers' nectar called to bees in the summertime, and he was equally helpless to refuse. Briefly, he questioned the wisdom of allying himself with a power so outside his scope of understanding. But as he joined her on the bed, he dismissed the thought as unimportant. He did not need to understand or control her power, since she would no more turn her power against him than he would ever turn his might against her.

Their joining was all that Bayard could dream of, yet in the stillness afterward when he caressed the soft skin of her face, he felt tears upon her cheeks.

"Feronia! What has distressed you?"

"Willingly would I share my forest and myself with you, but only if I may have your solemn vow. Will you promise to stay your hand and forswear all violence within the forest's borders?"

He blinked in confusion, wondering why this question should reduce her to tears now. "You were the one who demanded we not speak of this."

"Then I am the one who may rescind that demand. Will you give me your pledge of peace?"

"You know I cannot. I must remain free to defend Kittern's borders, including the land of your forest."

Feronia gestured with a broad sweep of her arm, indicating the flower-bedecked room. "You see the extent of my powers. How can you doubt that I am capable of defending the forest without recourse to your steel?"

"You were not able to do so this past month."

"The attack surprised me. That will not happen again."

"How can you know that? What if your enemies find another way to take you unaware?"

She rose from the bed and walked to the arrow slit, looking out over the forest the way she always did when she was troubled. Bayard followed her, carefully nudging the delicate hearts' remembrance aside with his feet. He was half way to her when she spoke.

"I was not attacked by enemies. I was injured while giving aid and did not consider that I might thus be putting myself in harm's way. I will not make that mistake again, therefore, I will not inadvertently be injured."

An icy rage suffused Bayard's being. Unlike battle rage, which spurred him to great physical displays, this rage froze him where he stood. He had to struggle even to force words past his numb lips.

"How long have you remembered the circumstances of your injury?"

"I have always known the circumstances. It is the identity of the man who shot me that I did not know."

"But if you had told me the identity of this other you were aiding, we could have questioned him or her. Perhaps that person saw something you did not."

Feronia smiled wryly. "I think not. Besides, it does not matter who shot me. He did not mean to injure me, and I have forgiven him."

"Intentional or not, you could have been killed. I will not have such lawlessness in my barony. He must be found and made to pay for his crime."

"Then I shall never tell you more of what transpired that day, for I do not want him to suffer."

"I will find out who shot you. And when I do, he will suffer as he should."

Bayard glared at her, but Feronia simply shook her head, immune to his posturing.

"My defense extends even to those others might consider unworthy."

Bayard's eyes widened, as he recognized the extent of his blindness where she was concerned. "All along, you have asked me to pledge myself to you, to allow your defense of Kittern to reign supreme over my own. I never asked for a similar pledge from you. If you swear to me that you keep no further secrets from me, and that you will direct your defenses as I command, I will forswear all violence within the forest's borders so long as you are able to marshal your defense."

Her hand dropped to rest against her stomach. "I regret, I cannot make that vow."

Although he had spent his life among soldiers, Bayard was not unfamiliar with women. He recognized the instinctive protective gesture of a mother-to-be.

"This is the secret you would keep from me? That you carry my child?" he shouted.

Eyes wide, Feronia backed up against the wall. The plants around Bayard's feet writhed with her distress, yet the hand that remained raised to shield her unborn child from his wrath answered more eloquently than anything she could say.

Connections fell into place like a row of tin soldiers.

"That is why you were so eager for my pledge, so that you could cease resisting our marriage, and our child would not be born a bastard."

She still did not answer, merely watching him as if she expected him to attack her. He considered grabbing her and dragging her back to the castle, but realized he would never make it through the forest with her as his prisoner. She needed to be bound to him as his wife before she left the tower.

"You have lost your gamble, my lady. The priest and priestess will be here tomorrow for the quarterly service. They will gladly administer the wedding vows to a pregnant woman and the father of her child, regardless of your approval. We shall be married, and I will hunt and fight in the forest as I see fit."

"I will not have my daughter shot by accident in one of your hunts!"

"Never fear. My daughter or son will ride to the hunt with me, not run wild through the trees like you."

Feronia stiffened. "I will see my forest destroyed, every tree shattered and every plant burnt to ash, before I will see my daughter slaughtering animals for pleasure."

The scarlet trumpets that wound around the bed post untwined themselves and whipped toward Bayard's legs. He dodged backward, trampling delicate flowers in an effort to avoid the lashing vines. Now was not the time to argue with Feronia. He'd give her a chance to cool down and see reason before returning with the priest and priestess.

As he rode away from the tower, her scream of fury echoed through the clearing. It sounded eerily like the hunting cry of a hawk.

The next day seemed to drag on forever as Bayard joined the people of Kittern for the lengthy religious service, then sat through a mind-numbing array of petty disagreements requiring his judgment. At last, all disputes were settled, the villagers went home, and the castle inhabitants gathered for a well-earned feast.

The priest and priestess were given the places of honor beside Bayard. Discussion of the latest news from the other villages and castles they visited on their rounds lasted throughout the meal, finally ending just as the pudding was served.

Eduard had discovered earlier in the day that he and the priestess were from the same region. The two of them now returned to telling tales of their youth and finding common acquaintances.

With the priestess occupied, Bayard waited until the servers had departed, then asked the priest, "Tell me, what is required for a wedding service?"

The man beamed. "Are you inquiring for yourself, my lord?"

"Marriages are a time-honored way to cement alliances."

"Indeed, indeed. The covenant between man and woman echoes the covenant between the Heavenly Pair to create life. A marriage ceremony's simplest form takes only a few minutes, as the man and woman simply recite their vows before a priest and priestess. A full state wedding may take all day, and involve six clergy, up to a dozen acolytes, and the reading of lengthy legal documents. No doubt you would want a modest state wedding, with one pair of clergy and acolytes."

"Could a brief ceremony occur first, with a formal ceremony following?"

The priest winked. "Eager to get on with the benefits of marriage, are you? You're not the first. Double ceremonies are often done among the nobility."

"What if the couple have already indulged in, as you put it, the benefits of marriage?"

"It doesn't matter, unless there is already a child. Then the couple is considered married in the eyes of the Heavenly Pair, and we merely observe the formalities for legal purposes." The priest shrugged, and spooned a helping of pudding into his mouth. "The man and woman don't even need to recite their vows, simply be present while the vows are read by the priest and priestess."

Perfect. Bayard hid his smile by eating a spoonful of his own pudding. The cook's normally excellent dessert tasted like sawdust and glue, keeping him from the moment when he and Feronia would be married in law as well as deed. The morning could not come soon enough. If it weren't for a lifetime in the army that had trained him to sleep whenever and wherever he could, he doubted he'd be able to sleep at all tonight.

He set down his spoon. "There is more I wish to discuss with you, but I must leave the table so that my curiosity does not trap my household in the hall all night. There is someone else I would like to include in our discussions as well. Would you and your priestess accompany me on a short ride tomorrow morning before you depart?"

"I have no other requests on my time, but I cannot speak for her."

Bayard turned and caught Eduard's eye. He ended his tale, and asked, "Are you ready to leave the table, my lord?"

"First, I would like to invite the priestess to accompany the priest and me for a ride tomorrow."

She gave him a searching look, no doubt wondering at the odd request, but demonstrated her practical nature by asking no questions. "I am honored, my lord."

Bayard rose, dismissing the hall and granting them leave to stay or go as they chose. As he headed up the private stairs to his chambers, Eduard ran to his side.

"What are you doing, Bay?" he whispered. "Is it not enough you go haring off to visit your lady every morning? Now you must drag the clergy along to witness your folly?"

"She is with child," Bayard returned in a voice too soft for the priest and priestess to overhear. "I ride tomorrow to make her my wife and will bring her back to the castle to remain at my side from now on."

Eduard stopped, startled, then broke into a wide grin. "The tower's magic has lived up to its reputation."

Bayard returned the smile, recalling the many magical hours he had spent there with Feronia. Now that he no longer needed to use it as a prison, he might let villagers benefit from its potency. Or he might keep it to use as a pleasant retreat from the castle if he and Feronia wanted to escape from the duties and pressures of baronial life.

His eagerness led him to summon the priest and priestess to break their fasts in the predawn quiet, and the three of them rode out of the castle at first light. The previously chatty priest was reduced to monosyllables by the early hour, although the priestess remained quietly alert.

Bayard quickly abandon his pretense of speaking to the priest and priestess once they had entered the forest, pressing his horse to make the familiar journey in record time. He slowed as he entered the clearing, staring at the silent and somehow forbidding tower. Arriving this early, he had expected to be greeted by Feronia's song.

Dismounting and tossing his horse's reins to the grass, he left it to graze while he unlocked the door. The priest and priestess rode up behind him and also dismounted.

"Are we to be favored with an explanation yet, my lord?" the priestess inquired.

"Soon." He pushed open the door and went inside. All was as he had left it earlier, and yet, the first room felt unwelcoming in the cold light of morning.

He hurried up the stairs to the guard room, passing the table and chairs huddled by their dim arrow slit, and burst into Feronia's room.

"Fero—"

Bayard stared in shock at the room, littered with withered vines and desiccated flowers that appeared to have died years ago. The breeze of his entry crumbled half of them to dust.

He scanned the room for any sign of life. Feronia was not sleeping in the bed, or anywhere else in the room. She was gone. Somehow, she had found the means to escape the locked fortress. She had escaped him.

He struggled to breathe, unable to comprehend his loss. How could she have disappeared? The stone tower and sturdy lock had held her securely even after her magical powers had returned to her. Unless she had been capable of escaping earlier, and chose instead to stay.

But then why had she left now? Yes, they had quarreled. But she loved him. He knew she did. Their quarrel, repeating the positions in which each of them had become entrenched, did not seem sufficient cause for her leaving. It was as if yearly border raids had suddenly escalated into all out war, and he had no idea what provoked it. She was the one who had forced their conflict into the open, knowing his position, and knowing nothing had changed.

He shook his head. Something had changed. She had discovered that she was carrying his child. Was it possible that she would sacrifice her freedom for the sake of her child, and it was his demands to raise the child as a Nord D'Rae noble that had convinced Feronia instead to flee for the sake of her child?

Crossing to the arrow slit where she had so often stood, he looked out over the forest. As he stared out into the overcast gray morning, one hand braced upon the wall where she had rested hers, a flash of white on the sill caught his eye.

Bayard picked up a white feather, banded with brown and speckled at the tip. A hawk's wing feather.

Clutching the feather in numb fingers, his knees buckled, and he fell to the dust covered floor.

A hawk. That was how she could escape him. She could turn herself into a hawk. A hawk like the one that had followed him, spoiling his hunt, on his first day in the forest.

Bayard buried his face in his hands. He had asked her to trust him, assuring her that he would never hurt her, when his was the arrow that had struck her from the sky. A shot fired in spite and anger at the hawk that had chased away his intended targets.

"Ah, Feronia. Forgive me. I didn't know."

Her words made sense now. Now, when it was too late to tell her that he had resisted her demands out of pride and fear of her growing possession of his heart and mind. He would have done anything for her, but pride and the same spiteful anger that had nearly been her downfall had refused to let him say so. He had to have her on his terms. Instead, he had lost her completely.

A new terror gripped his heart. Had he lost the child as well? Hawks did not give birth to live young. Did Feronia's transformation kill the unborn child she carried?

"My lord," the priestess called from the doorway. "Are you in need of assistance?"

A dry laugh escaped his tight throat. The aid he needed, she could never provide.

Painfully, he climbed to his feet. He cast one last look around the room, burning it into his memory, then walked out the door.

"I regret calling you out on a useless errand," he apologized to the clergy as he locked the tower door. "There was no need for your services after all."

CHAPTER SIX

———⟡———

Bayard threw himself into the running of his barony and the preparation for the King's visit with a single-minded dedication that allowed no time for stray thoughts of Feronia to intrude upon him. He began before the first light of dawn and worked long into the night, often falling into an exhausted sleep sprawled across a table full of papers. He fought to keep from dwelling on his loss, but the presence of the nearby forest preyed upon him, constantly hovering at the edge of his awareness.

Only Eduard knew the truth of what drove him, and his good friend and steward knew no way of easing his pain other than letting time run its course. Eduard consoled himself with ensuring Bayard always had a plate of Cook's good food to warm him, no matter the hour of his rising, and mastering the art of rousing Bayard just enough to stagger to his bed without fully waking him. Bayard was grateful, but could not express his thanks without mentioning the cause of his distress, which he refused to speak of.

Now, listening to the blare of trumpets that heralded the King's imminent arrival, Bayard wondered if his preparations would be sufficient. He found that he didn't care. It did not matter if the King recalled him to duty in the army. Without Feronia, Kittern was no longer an idyllic haven from the world. It was a torture chamber that forced him to confront his failings on a daily basis.

He turned to Severin, standing beside him on the battlements. "Is there anything else that needs to be done?"

"No, my lord. Your possessions have been cleared from your chambers. All is in readiness."

Determined to keep his thoughts from straying to Feronia, Bayard focused on the hubbub surrounding the King's arrival. Giant silken tents had been set up for his entourage on the grassy sward outside the castle, a far cry from the simple canvas army tent Bayard recalled the young Prince Ulrich carrying in his father's campaigns. Yet the King's journey to put down Sylveron's rebellion had been as much an appeal to the common people as it had been a display of strength. The people expected pageantry from a king, and Ulrich was too shrewd to deny their vision of a glorious king. It did not matter that his loyal followers would be freezing in the thin tents so unsuited for winter travel. At least the tents Bayard had given his own troops when he turned them out to make for visiting nobles had been heavy, serviceable army tents.

Two heralds crested the hill, banners waving and horns sounding. The main body of the entourage appeared shortly afterward, moving in a remarkably orderly fashion for a nonmilitary caravan. Then a large white horse sprang forward, the rider kicking him into a gallop as he surged past the heralds. They lowered their horns and urged their own mounts forward, but could not catch the white horse.

Bayard grabbed Severin's elbow and pushed him toward the stairs. "Run. The king comes."

They spiraled down the stairs, hands brushing the wall to keep them from falling in their haste. They burst out of the keep's door just in time to take their places at the head of the nobles clustered within the bailey before the king rode through the gate, his heralds trailing behind him.

The lords and knights bowed to varying degrees, as befit their stations. As the baron of Kittern, Bayard could have welcomed the King with a similar bow. Instead, he chose to respect the military aspect of the King's visit, and executed a half-bow with a sharp salute.

Ulrich laughed. "I come to see my new baron, and find my old general in his stead."

"I serve you however you will it, your majesty. As does my barony. Welcome to Kittern. All that I have is yours."

The King kicked his feet out of his stirrups and leapt off his horse. A stable boy, bent nearly double in obeisance, scuttled over and grabbed the reins.

"I see you are enhancing the wall and building guard towers. What else are you doing?"

"The property can best be viewed from the battlements, your majesty."

"And we can also speak in private, hm?"

The King snapped his fingers at the heralds, and they blew another blast on their horns, signaling the gathered nobles to rise. Pitching his voice to carry on a battlefield, the King called, "We recognize your loyalty and look forward to receiving your oaths of allegiance tomorrow."

Bayard wondered if the King was using the royal "We" or if he meant the oaths would be sworn to both himself and Bayard. Either way, it was a break from the tradition that said the nobles of his barony swore their allegiance to him, and he pledged fealty to the King. Did the King feel he had reason to distrust Bayard? Or was he already planning to replace him as Baron in favor of his skills on the battlefield?

"Tomorrow, your majesty?" Bayard asked. He knew better than to voice any of his other concerns. "Is it not customary to preside over the oath taking at your welcoming feast?"

Ulrich snorted, and waved an arm to encompass the massed knights and nobles. "Look at them all. It would take forever, and we have more important matters to attend to. Tomorrow is soon enough."

The King strode into the keep, hesitating briefly in the entry hall.

"The fastest route to the battlements is up the spiral stairs to your right," Bayard said.

They climbed the stairs to the top floor and cleared the guards from the battlements so that they could speak in private.

"Your message hinted that you were considering a marriage alliance," Ulrich said.

Bayard started, surprised that the King had deduced that from his carefully worded missive. "I don't believe I said that."

"But you did not say you weren't considering it," Ulrich countered. "And that amounts to the same thing where politics is concerned. Have you chosen the lady yet?"

Bayard found his gaze drifting disrespectfully away from his King, and out to the forest. He sighed. "My suit was refused."

"Is the lady already engaged to another?"

"No, your majesty." Bayard forced himself to look at the King. "She would only accept a husband willing to live in peace, and the situation with Suddalyk is too unsettled for me to make such a rash promise."

Ulrich nodded. "That was wise of you. A woman with no understanding of warfare is an unsuitable bride for a general."

"Or a former general."

"It is not yet spring, and you have not yet demonstrated that you can hold the barony."

"Sylveron may have had trouble with rebels, but Kittern will not," Bayard assured him. "When King Jaeger attempts to retake his lands, Kittern's defenses will keep his army from setting one foot upon Nord D'Rae soil."

"A noble sentiment. But your castle wall is far from the boundaries of your land."

"The wall protects the castle, but magic protects the land. The original keep is rumored to hold all manner of enchantments within its stones. That is why I asked for a mage to investigate it."

"Do not rely too heavily upon magic," Ulrich warned. "It did not protect the last baron."

"I do not expect it to protect me." After all, Feronia had made her opinion of him clear. "But it will protect the land, and that is what matters."

A hawk's sharp cry pierced the air. Bayard rushed to the edge of the battlement, scanning the sky for a sight of the bird. Was Feronia here?

Ulrich laughed. "Searching the sky for omens now, Bayard? The rustic life has turned you into a country simpleton."

Bayard turned reluctantly from the wall. There was no way he could explain Feronia to the King. If Ulrich believed him, he would no doubt order Bayard to execute her for treason. It was better for him to say nothing, but his silence burned at his soul.

"My wits are as sharp as they ever were, your majesty. Tell me of your campaign in Sylveron and I shall prove it."

Their talk shifted to a discussion of Ulrich's recent battle against the rebels, and the shifting political climate. They continued talking until the sun touched the far hills, and they went inside so that the King could refresh himself before the welcoming feast. Bayard had lost all appetite for it.

When they gathered in the hall for the feast, Bayard sat at the King's right hand, and the King's mage sat on his left. The high table was rounded out by Eduard to Bayard's right, Ulrich's steward to the mage's left, and three of the lords whose fiefs belonged to Kittern on either end of the table. Lesser nobles and knights sat at the central low table, ranging to the merest castle servant seated at the low tables nearest the walls.

When the main course was served, Ulrich asked Bayard, "Stew instead of a roast? You have strange notions of a feast."

"The meat was dried, your majesty. Stew is the only way to serve it." Before the King could comment on that oddity, Bayard said, "There is no fresh game to be found in the forest during the winter."

"Nonsense. I heard a hawk's cry this afternoon, and where there are hawks, there is game." Ulrich grinned. "Now I understand why you were searching so eagerly for a sight of it. After months of stew, you must hunger for fresh meat. We shall have a hunt tomorrow, and satisfy your craving."

Frigid water pooled in Bayard's gut. Feronia was in the forest! "Your majesty, the oath taking ceremony is tomorrow."

"They've waited this long. They can wait another day. Besides, if the hunt goes well, we may be back in time to hold the ceremony in the afternoon."

"We are not likely to find anything. A mouse or sparrow that can appease a hawk's hunger will not serve for a human's dinner."

"You have a huntsman, do you not? Send him out early to find what trails he can. Surely he can discover something in such a large forest."

"But—"

"I have said that we will hunt. Do you gainsay your King?"

"No, your majesty. It will be as you will it."

If the King would not listen to reason, he left Bayard no choice. He would find the game keeper and deliver the King's message. Then he would slip out to the forest and try to find Feronia, to warn her of the King's plan.

<hr />

That night, after the king was settled in Bayard's chambers, his entourage had returned to their tents, and the visiting nobles had returned to their own cramped quarters in the infirmary and the guard room, Bayard slipped out of the castle, and walked into the forest. He wouldn't risk his horse in the darkness. If Feronia was watching him, he did not need to go far into the trees. If she was not, riding all the way to the tower would do no good.

As soon as he was within the dark embrace of the trees' shadows, he began calling to her. Softly at first, his voice gathered volume the further from the castle and King's guards he traveled until he was shouting her name.

"Feronia, if you can hear me, the King intends to hunt tomorrow. I cannot dissuade him. Please, hide yourself, and any of your creatures you wish to protect."

He walked the forest trails for over an hour, shouting his message, until he began to grow hoarse. Reluctantly, he retraced his steps back to the castle.

Safely inside the wall, he tracked down the game keeper, who was as expected with his hounds.

"The King has ordered a hunt for tomorrow," Bayard said.

The man nodded but said nothing, in marked contrast to his previous encounter.

"I tried telling him that it was the wrong season for hunting, but he wouldn't listen." Bayard paced nervously back and forth, agitating the dogs, until he realized what he was doing and stopped.

"You know the local lore."

"Aye, my lord."

"And the forest guardian?"

After a long pause, the game keeper admitted, "Aye, my lord."

"What forms can she take?"

The game keeper studied him intently. "Why would you be wanting to know?"

"Answer the question!"

"She can be anything in the forest — bird, beast, even tree. Most oft, though, she's a hawk or a doe."

Bayard nodded, and touched the hawk feather tied to a leather thong that he wore hidden beneath his tunic. "You must not find any prey for the King to hunt."

The game keeper smiled. "Aye, my lord."

Having done all that he could to protect Feronia, Bayard retired to the chambers he was sharing with Eduard for the duration of the King's visit. Eduard was waiting for him.

"Where have you been? I searched the castle for you."

"Preparing for the King's hunt tomorrow. Has the King been looking for me?"

"No."

"Good."

Bayard turned away and pulled off his overtunic, signaling an end to the conversation.

"I hope you know what you're doing," Eduard muttered, then left him in peace to find what rest he could before rising for the King's hunt.

The next morning, the bailey was filled with chaos as nobles on horseback milled aimlessly or jockeyed for position closer to the King. Bayard waited patiently by the King's side, until Ulrich declared himself ready and the heralds bleated a departure on their horns.

The game keeper and his hounds entered the forest, Ulrich and Bayard behind them, and the rest of their party strung out all the way back to the castle gate.

"What do you think he will find?" Ulrich asked. "I'm hoping for a boar. Not good eating, but an exciting hunt."

"I've heard of no boar in this forest," Bayard said. "And as I said last night, this is not the season to hunt. I do not wish you to waste your time, your majesty."

"Nonsense. This isn't like a Nord D'Rae winter, where the ice and snow drive all the game into hiding. There is no snow on the ground. They should be moving about."

Bayard had no answer. He considered telling the King the truth, but Ulrich was more likely to try to find Feronia and kill her, just to prove she had no power over Kittern, than to respect the magic she commanded. The truth would solve nothing, and only lead to more problems.

Bayard kept silent, but prayed all the animals were well hidden. Feronia most of all. If only he could be certain that she had heard and heeded his warning.

After an hour of riding through the forest, slogging along muddy game trails and seeing nothing of more interest than a small songbird, petulance replaced the King's earlier cheer.

"What sort of forest is this, empty of game? Order your man to find something."

"Your majesty, he is doing his best. I told you last night, there is nothing to hunt here in the winter." Bayard hoped the cold and lack of game might convince the King to return to the keep. "Perhaps we should turn back."

"Perhaps the constant chattering of the flock of sycophants that surrounds me has scared away the game. We should split up into smaller parties."

Bayard swallowed nervously. If they traveled in a single group, the men would all wait for the King to take the first shot at any game. But if they broke into smaller groups and spread throughout the forest, some of them were bound to find animals and shoot them. Bayard could not watch them all.

"I don't think that's necessary, your majesty. Why don't I send the game keeper further ahead, and we can see if that works any better."

Ulrich shrugged. "Try that. But if it doesn't work, we split up."

Bayard sighed, recognizing the mule-headed stubbornness of the King's tone. There was no reasoning with him in this mood.

"Yes, your majesty."

Riding up to the game keeper, Bayard said softly, "Range far ahead. Perhaps a glimpse of a buck will satisfy the King, and he can give chase without injuring it."

The man whistled some commands to his hounds, and they sprinted away. He followed at a fast jog.

Bayard circled back to the King, just in time to see the King draw his bow. He glanced over his shoulder.

A doe had stepped into the trail after the game keeper and his hounds had passed. She did not bound away, merely watched Bayard and the King from large, sad eyes. Bayard froze, overcome with dread. Feronia!

"Out of the way," the King ordered. "You're blocking my shot."

He moved his horse to the right, and Bayard matched the movement with his own mount. At the same time, he rode forward, so that he could make a grab for the King's bow if necessary, blurting out the first thing he could think of.

"You must not shoot that doe, your majesty. This forest is ensorcelled, and part of the enchantment curses anyone who kills an animal outside of the hunting season."

"I don't believe in curses."

The King leaned to the side and fired.

"No!" Bayard lunged, reaching for the bow with his free hand, but the King had already released his arrow. The arrow glanced off of Bayard's arm, diverted by his leather gauntlet, and pierced his sleeve rather than his flesh. The sharp tip scored his forearm with a line of fire that welled blood, but did no lasting damage.

The fury distorting Ulrich's face promised to rectify that mistake.

Bayard heard branches rustle as the doe bounded away into the safety of the trees. The arrow had not struck her. That was all that mattered.

Knowing how little time he had to placate the King's temper, Bayard leapt from his horse and fell to his knees on the trail before Ulrich.

"Your majesty, forgive me, I beg you. But I could not allow you to become cursed by magic if I could prevent it."

The nobles behind the King reshuffled their ranks, as prudent men withdrew lest the King's anger find them as targets, and blood-thirsty young hotheads angled for a better view of the day's only sport.

The King's fury dissipated, replaced by a mild bewilderment. "You honestly believe this prattle. You have become simple-minded."

"Not simple-minded, your majesty. This is one of the magics I requested your mage to investigate. All of the locals know it for the truth. Only turn, and see." He pointed at the rest of the hunting party.

Ulrich turned in his saddle and looked back at the others, quickly noting the same thing Bayard had seen. Not a single man outside of the King's entourage had strung his bow.

"Oh, get out of the mud," the King said, then laughed. "The only one to catch anything in today's hunt will be you — a cold."

Bayard responded with a nervous chuckle but quickly climbed to his feet and remounted his horse, resolutely ignoring the fiery pain in his arm.

"Call back your man and his dogs. There's no point getting cold and muddy if you'll only spoil any other shot I have." The King's eyes glittered with repressed anger, and Bayard realized his good humor was merely a show for the attending nobles. "We can discuss this further someplace warm."

"Yes, your majesty."

"If I did not know you so well, this morning's dramatics would make me question your loyalty. One could say that you raised your hand against me."

"Never, your majesty. I am your man, as I have always been." Bayard lifted his bleeding arm crosswise in front of him, as if riding to battle. "I merely strove to block your arrow, forgetting in the heat of the moment that I did not carry a shield."

"The shield that commemorates another rescue in another forest. You repeat your past glories."

Ulrich's tone made it clear he was teasing, and Bayard relaxed for the first time since he'd seen the King pick up his bow. He began to hope that both he and Feronia would survive the encounter.

As they rode back to the castle, Ulrich said, "Since you are so eager to sacrifice yourself for my safety, you can cement my authority in this region by forming a marriage alliance."

"As I told you last night, my efforts—"

"Which is why I have decided you shall marry a daughter of one of the former Suddalyk lords."

Bayard swallowed. This was his punishment, then, to be denied all hope of ever marrying Feronia. "As your majesty wills."

"Good. I will announce my decision tonight."

⚜

Bayard stood beside the King's chair as the last of the nobles filed up to kneel before the King and swear their allegiance. The six lords whose fiefs belonged to Kittern had repeated the oaths they'd given Bayard to the King. In a break with protocol, the knights and lesser lordlings who owned at most a single manor and a few peasant cottages had also given their oaths directly to the King, rather than swearing to him as their overlord. It seemed the King was taking no chances, and still questioned Bayard's fitness as Baron.

After receiving each oath, the King asked the nobles about their marriageable offspring.

"My middle daughter turns sixteen this spring," Sir Beale said. "She is reckoned both beautiful and talented, and we hope to secure a fine match for her."

Ulrich nodded. "If she is as talented as you say, consider Lord Delmon's second son. He is of an age, and has property near your own."

"Thank you, your majesty."

The knight bowed deeply again, as well he should. A knight's daughter aspired to marry into landed nobility, and would be thrilled with a third or fourth son. Here he had been offered a match with a second son, who might well inherit a sizable portion of his father's estates. Suggesting the match cost the King nothing, but easily cemented the knight's loyalty. And Lord Beale, whose wife had died after giving him six sons, would disregard his prospective daughter-in-law's lower station if she could help run the household.

Bayard admired the King's canny use of his underlings' personal situations, much as he might admire a well-played game of chess. Yet he realized, more strongly than ever, that to Ulrich, all of these people were simply pawns to be played to his greatest advantage. He did not actually care about any of them, past caring how they could be used to further his own ambitions.

The thought threatened to drive Bayard into despair. How would the King best use him? As baron or as general? Married to a Suddalyk bride that he would constantly need to suspect for treason, or as a jailor for the good behavior of a Nord D'Rac bride's father? Each possibility seemed worse than the one before.

A whispered commotion in the back of the hall caught his attention, as well as that of the King. A knot of local nobles clustered around the door bowed as one, revealing the woman who stood in their midst.

"Feronia," he whispered.

The nobles broke apart, making way for Feronia to walk the length of the hall. Suddalyk knights and nobles bowed as she passed, whispering explanations to the confused Nord D'Rae nobles who stood beside them. The whispered words reached Bayard just before she did.

"The lady of the forest."

"The guardian of Kittern."

She stood before the King for just a moment, resplendent in a gown of green velvet and wool embroidered in gold thread with a repeating pattern of Kittern's sheep, grape and tree symbols. Then she sank to the floor in a graceful curtsey.

Ulrich smiled and gestured for her to rise. "I do not recognize you, lady. Have you come to swear your loyalty?"

"I own no lands, and command no warriors, your majesty. What could I possibly pledge to you?"

Bayard heard the King's robes of state shifting but couldn't tear his gaze from Feronia's beloved face. She looked well, and happy. The light was back in her eyes.

His gaze dropped to her trim waist, but it was too soon for any sign of their child to be visible. If his arrogant actions had not killed it.

Feronia folded her hands in front of her waist and smiled softly. The unborn child yet lived. Her transformation to hawk and, he suspected, deer, had not injured it.

"You are mistaken, Lady Feronia," the King said. "I believe you command at least one warrior."

Bayard started guiltily and turned to face the King. Ulrich was studying him intently.

"This is the lady of whom you spoke, Baron?" Ulrich asked.

"Yes, your majesty."

"It would seem, Lady, that your presence here indicates you have changed your mind about the Baron's suit."

Feronia bowed her head. "I have."

Bayard's heart leapt, and he took a half-step toward her, until he recalled the King beside him.

"I was given to understand that you refused his suit because he would not put aside his sword and shield. Will you now give your blessing for his fighting?"

Feronia lifted her head, and tears glimmered in her eyes as she looked at Bayard's wounded arm. "Who am I to deny him sword and shield, when their lack may injure him in his sworn duty?"

Ulrich frowned. Bayard's bandages were not visible beneath his court finery. The king must be wondering if Feronia knew of today's hunt, or if she was speaking figuratively.

"You say you have no lands, no warriors. Who is your family? What benefit is it to me to give a baron in marriage to you, when I might use a marriage to cement an alliance with one of the other noble families?"

"I am now the only remaining member of my line. I bring no siblings or cousins to your banner." She drew herself upright, and an invisible mantle of power settled around her, charging the air. "But my line is the lifeblood of Kittern. With my support, the land will prosper. Without my support, it matters not who you name to rule, or how many warriors he commands. The land itself will rise up against him, and he will fail."

The King lifted an eyebrow and smirked, clearly humoring her. "And how will that happen, when you have no warriors?"

"I have no warriors beneath my command, true. But I command the beasts of the field, the birds in the sky, and even the plants and trees. I can deploy thousands of troops — antlered stags, fierce wolves, mighty bears, and fast hawks, as well as a host of lesser beasts and birds — and weave the branches of my forest into an impenetrable wall. I need no provisions, no pay, no supplies for these troops. I need no masons or laborers to build this wall."

As she spoke, the chair upon which the King sat began sprouting tiny branches and bursting into leaf. The King jumped to his feet and stepped away from the metamorphosing chair.

The field of energy Feronia had gathered around herself dissipated, and she became once again just a beautiful woman. "Can any other noblewoman offer you as much, your majesty?"

Bayard held his breath. Even in his wildest dreams, he had never guessed at a tenth of her power. No wonder she was held in such awe. Surely the King could see the wisdom of an alliance with Feronia. But had she made herself sound too powerful? Would Ulrich now consider her a threat that needed to be destroyed?

"I don't trust magic," the King said, glancing back at the chair which was once more just a chair. Gingerly, he resumed his seat.

"You are wise," Feronia said. "Magic is not something to be trusted. It is a force of nature, like the sun and the rain. It can give life, or it can destroy, and it does not care which. That is why those who guide the magic are needed."

"Then the question is, can I trust you?" Ulrich rubbed his chin, thinking. "You are too powerful to remain independent. I must either kill you or bind you permanently to my service."

A muffled murmur of outrage whispered through the assembled Suddalyk nobles. They had just sworn their loyalty to the new King, but if he ordered Feronia's death, how many would rise to her defense?

Bayard's fingers twitched. He forced himself to remain still, though his every instinct screamed at him to grab the ceremonial sword on the table before the King and rush to his lady's defense. But he could best serve her by giving the King no reason to doubt his loyalty. Silently, he prayed to the Heavenly Pair that the King choose the course of wisdom and accept Feronia's offer.

"Will you swear honor and fealty to me?" the King asked.

"I will swear to loyally support my husband in all his endeavors, including his fealty to you, as part of my marriage vows."

Ulrich stared at Feronia, trying to intimidate her with his presence and the veiled threat of his power. She gazed placidly back. Neither intended to give ground. A bead of cold sweat rolled beneath Bayard's collar and down his spine.

"You are not just a powerful mage, you are a canny trader," the King finally said. "Very well. If you bind yourself to Bayard, his vows will bind you to me."

Bayard struggled to find his voice in a suddenly too tight throat. "Lady Feronia, will you do me the honor of consenting to be my wife?"

"With great joy."

The hall erupted in cheers. The King touched Bayard's sleeve, gaining his attention amid the tumult. Bayard bent down to hear him.

"You realize that this ties you to the barony of Kittern. I dare not leave such a powerful force unattended."

He was a general no longer, then. From now until he died, he would spend all his days within the borders of his barony. With Feronia at his side.

"You will never regret your decision, your majesty."

THE END

HONORBOUND

Robin Bayne

CHAPTER ONE

The birds had stopped singing, hiding instead in the muggy silence which preceded every great disaster. There were no sounds save for the clap of rifles against thighs and boots trudging through tall July grass, and the occasional grunt of men laboring in the heat. Dek watched, mouth open, as hundreds of human men marched directly toward each other, each struggling to stand proud despite the heavy suits already limp from the sun. Half approached from the east, wearing thick coats in various shades of blue, and the others from the west, into the rising sun, their uniforms an assortment of muted browns and greys. All of them looked determined.

Determined to kill each other.

An explosion ripped through the morning and Dek ducked instinctively, then peered through the tree's limbs to see what had happened. Lucky for him he'd landed in the old oak again, vegetation he'd learned about before his first mission. Its bark bit into his skin as vibrations from the ground shook his perch. Shells burst in the air, leaving hovering clouds of dust.

A row of blue coats had fallen at the far side of the field, at the back of their ranks, and cannon fire ripped again through the hot, humid atmosphere. On the grass below, but away from the fighting, a female screamed. Dek watched as she rose, seemingly intent on getting to the soldiers, but an elderly man held her back.

Now guns fired openly, more men fell, twisting in agony as they dropped, and Dek's gut clenched. What little air there was reeked of smoke and the pungent scent of death. Beneath him, the by-standers watched, a few sobbing. Did humans treat battle like the-ater? Though their records showed some residents of Washington had come to watch this first battle, he didn't recall reading that women had been present during skirmishes in their history books.

Time passed, or perhaps stood still, wearing on as the men re-loaded, staggered, fell, etching ribbons of scarlet on the field. Dek saw no man turn and run, no retreats attempted, no giving in. It almost seemed that the soldiers tried harder with every comrade who fell, as though a friend's death were a personal insult instead of a casualty of war. Shifting his position, careful not to lose balance, Dek was uncomfortable, physically and emotionally, finding it hard to draw in any air. Alana had warned that the moisture in the air here would cause him to rasp, but that wasn't the only reason he felt ill. His last visit had been so different, watching men plot and strategize in an academic manner. They had raged on for hours about loyalty and honor, duty and righteousness. Dek had admired their dedication. Now, his mind reeled at what he was witnessing; men, so many men of the same land, marching shoulder to shoul-der into near certain death.

Alana had said it was honor, a strange, ancient human sense of duty, especially noted in earlier Americans. What else had she said? Yes, red-blooded brother against brother. There was no doubt in Dek's mind that human blood ran red.

Another scream tore through the battle noise, and Dek glanced down at the gathered observers to see a tiny woman with a baby clutched to her shoulder trying to reach the field. Again, the older man acted as guardian and held her back, wrapping his arms around her and keeping her close. So she wouldn't see? Whom had she lost out there in the clash of men and fire?

The fighting sounds lessened, and Dek heard the squall of her baby from below. The woman paced, soothing child, cooing, stroking its fuzzy head. As she moved, Dek saw her face clearly before she turned away, and he felt a small shock, as if he knew her. Her features were delicate, and pale, her hair pulled back in a tight clump that tugged her eyes squinty. Although her lips were full, they were stretched downward in grief, and her face was blotchy from crying. And yet she still seemed familiar.

Dek sighed. If only he could go to her, comfort her, offer to take her to a place far and away from here, light years from the waste and stupidity of war. Show her his world.

Men shouted orders, and the remaining soldiers moved in different directions, their talk buzzing over the sobs of the women, who now rolled their blankets, moving slowly, as if in a time warp. The groups dispersed, and Dek wondered if anyone stayed behind to tend to the dead.

He turned a dial on his wrist band and waited, his gaze still on the blonde woman, who paced with her crying baby. If he could stay and help her, he would. He'd risk being seen, he'd endure the wet air now saturated with the metallic smell of blood, miss reporting on his assignment, if he could spend time with the fair creature and soothe her. The urge was strong, and he couldn't explain it to himself, or to his crew. They'd want to know why he'd stayed on.

But it wasn't to be.

Dek touched his dial and it glowed in response. He peered through the branches to take one last look at her, where she'd paused just beneath him as her child quieted. It was time to go.

She looked up.

He froze.

Her mouth formed an 'O,' but she didn't break the line of sight. Didn't break the lock of their gazes.

He wasn't supposed to be seen yet. Dek's pulse raced, adrenaline pumping through him, a new feeling in this human form— he felt as if it flowed through his veins and into his gut. But he simply stared at her, and thought how beautiful she was. Familiar. Touchable.

And then he was gone.

The next instant he was at the other end of the earth, in a familiar vessel, his traveling workplace, rubbing the back of his neck. "It was primitive. Barbaric. Men killing, men dying."

"And what did you expect? You wanted to understand honor." Alana tapped the work counter with her nails. "I like the sounds the human body can make." She tapped a rhythm, moving her hips back and forth where she stood. "Anyway, there are many types of honor. We understand most of them, we live most of them. They are inherent in us. But without violence in our world—"

"I know!" Dek interrupted, having heard the speech before. "But perhaps I've learned more than I needed to know." He pushed away from his console, his chair gliding easily across the smooth floor. He took a full breath of the piped-in oxygen, still adjusting to the Earth's atmosphere. In drier air, his lungs seemed to work better.

Alana smiled, watching him. She began to pace the narrow lab. "I think you crossed that line when you decided to become one of them." She paused and admired her painted fingernails. "Although I am enjoying this female form, much more than I liked being a cat on Antrair."

Dek figured she'd like any form that allowed her to have claws but kept that to himself. "I am male in any form. This was a good decision." He also didn't mention the woman he'd felt drawn to, even as he'd struggled to balance in a tree. She had been decidedly feminine.

Alana moved in front of him, hands on her shapely hips, eyeing him as if she could read his thoughts. "You aren't considering making this permanent, are you? You know the risks."

Dek shook his head. He knew the chemicals that allowed his kind to meld into another form were toxic, and stayed in their systems until they reverted. "I haven't forgotten. But I barely remember the other days." He turned back to his computer screen. The round surface lit as he touched the elemental key, and his name and original face flashed across it. "I'd better start my report, then go back for the next observation period."

Not a human, but definitely a male face, he thought, and touched the image.

Alana moved behind him, placing one hand on his shoulder. She squeezed lightly. "Interesting muscles. Too bad they're not yours to keep. But I'll leave you to get ready now, and I have to help Jantzen get ready to transport. Get some work done."

Voices drifted through the closed metal door, and Alana straightened, then moved toward it. She paused as the door swished open. "Dek?"

"Hm?" He waited for her typical good wishes before departures.

"I like you in this form. I like me in it, too. When you return, I'd like to show you."

His jaw dropped, and Dek stared after her. What had she meant by that? Alana had never shown interest in him before, in any form. But he didn't have time to dwell on it now. Standing, he straightened the sash he wore over his wool coat. The leather of his worn boots squeaked as he moved, aligning his arm band dial with the screen. It was time for another trip back to the American Civil War.

Traveling there as a human had been more enlightening than as his own, true, rubbery self. This time he was going as a soldier, as part of the action. These short trips didn't present much risk to his health, and even if he stayed longer, he could meld back as needed. Dek grinned—each time was better than the last. With any luck, he'd get to see *her* again. And later, he'd complete the last section of his report.

If the war allowed.

Like before, Dek heard no birds chirping and began to doubt that they ever provided a common sound here. At least he recognized the roar of the evening's insects, the crickets. Dek checked his garments to make sure they'd traveled properly, and brushed lint from his wool coat. It was hot here, even without the glare of the sun.

Everything had arrived intact.

He hadn't meant to arrive at night, and wondered if there was a glitch with the elemental key. The small house in the distance glowed with light from within, pouring out from two small windows and a wide open door. Dek started toward the structure, unsure of when and where he'd landed this time. The grass he crossed was wet and his boots slipped if he turned his feet certain ways. This time, he could be seen without ramifications.

A figure appeared in the doorway, a petite one, swishing a hand in front of her face. Long skirts swept the threshold as he neared and Dek saw it was her. The blonde. She carried her infant in the crook of one arm, and he saw small insects hovering in the doorway, which she waved away from the baby. When she gently stroked the child's head, Dek had a brief moment of wondering what his own life would have been like had he had offspring to protect. He wouldn't be traveling these missions, of that he was certain.

Shaking off the solemn feeling, he moved forward. "Hello," he called, waving a hand over his head to greet her. "Madam!" Cooking smells came from the house, and Dek wondered if she was perhaps serving eggs with her meal. Ever since he attended the human study programs, he'd been fond of the white ovals laid by hens. "Is your husband at home?

She looked at him, tilted her head, then took two steps back toward the door frame.

Was she afraid of him? Dek slowed his pace, not wanting to scare her. It was logical, in this place of violence, and since he wore the suit of a fighter. Did she not know her wooden box of a house was not much protection had he meant her harm? He felt a surge of tenderness for her, this woman he didn't know. She reminded him of a baby faumpy he'd had as a youth. He'd protected it, and it was almost if——

Several soldiers approached from the surrounding woods, coughing, talking in low voices, spitting. Dek watched in fascination before the potential for danger struck him. His own version of adrenalin flowed through his veins once again, a sensation Dek was growing used to. Could he interfere with whatever happened next? Could he dare changing history? How could he not, if she was in danger?

The group quieted, staring from Dek to the woman. For moments no one moved, and Dek swore he could feel the hairs on his neck moving. As he planned a defense of the lady and her child, based solely on research, not experience, she surprised him by moving to stand by the men.

She shifted her bundle gently and addressed Dek, obviously buoyed by their presence. "Now, sir, how can my brothers and I help you?"

"Your family?" Dek let out his breath. They were not a threat. "Is your baby safe then?"

The tallest man, the one with a hole torn from his coat sleeve and stains of red decorating his side, spoke up. "What do you know of Corinne's son?"

Corinne, Dek thought. A very nice name. As he watched Corinne, he saw the flash of recognition when she realized where she had seen him before. Would she expose him? The men would surely brand him a deserter if she said he'd been up a tree, he knew enough of their history to worry. He'd be in just as much trouble if they merely assumed he meant to dishonor their sister. Men were devoted to the sisters, mothers and children here. Honorable, most of them.

Instead, she merely watched while he struggled for a response. Finally he scratched his chin, as he'd seen others do. "I know nothing about her child." He shrugged. "I'd ask the same about any tyke, I like them."

Corinne chimed in. "It's okay, Jeb, he means no harm. I saw him after the fighting and he didn't try anything then." As she spoke, the baby woke and began to cry. "Shh, Jonathan," she murmured to the infant."Come in, everyone, for something to eat. I don't have much but I'm willing to share." She shivered.

It was cool here now, without the sun, and Dek was glad for his outer coat as he watched the men file through the door. The end of Earth's mini-ice-age had certainly altered the temperature, though no one now living realized that. Corinne followed the men and beckoned for Dek to follow. Her smile was soft, speaking of the secret they now shared, but Dek suspected she'd want more information later, without the soldier's curious ears.

His stomach growled as another kind of hunger began, one he hoped to feed with Corinne's company. The sun had nearly set as he stepped through her door, glancing at the meager furnishings within. He recognized the smell of meat cooking, and opened his mouth to comment when his wrist dial began to glow.

No! He wasn't ready to return yet, but he backed away, out the door, turning his arm to hide the light which would be so obviously out of place here. He hadn't learned anything new, and he hadn't had a chance to taste Corinne's cooking. Or her lips.

"Are you leaving?" she asked, poking her head outside. "Are you not hungry?"

Dek turned to her and offered a smile, willing to memory her light hair and dainty nose. "I'm sorry, I have an obligation." And he was truly sorry. The hunger pangs turned to something deeper, something beyond nourishment or companionship.

"Will I see you again? I didn't catch your name." She seemed to hope that she would. Her gaze softened, her expression turned hopeful.

Unless that was Dek's imagination. He shook his head. "I'm Dek. And probably not. Take care of yourself and your little one. I assume your husband is gone?"

"In a manner of speaking. He was wounded in battle, wounded very personally, and he left me. Left the state. My brothers take care of us now."

"I am sorry for your loss, though I don't understand how any man could abandon you."

"Forgive me for speaking so plainly, Mr. Dek. I just get frustrated, with a husband who's alive but won't stay with his family because he doesn't feel like a man anymore. And I can't complain to my brothers, they'd set off trying to fix things for me. But thank you for listening. Since I saw you in that tree— and I won't even ask what you were doing there-"

"Thank you. You're an honorable woman. I wish you well." His dial glowed again, and he moved to cover it, but her gaze flickered over it in silence.

She nodded, her dark eyes wide in the evening shade. "Safe journey, then, Mr. Dek."

"Good bye." He waited for her to close the door and heard the men begin speaking with a bark of laughter thrown in before he touched his dial. It was time to return to his world, even though some miscalculation had rendered this trip unproductive —at least in any manner he could report on. This had been his third and final trip to Earth. With one final glance at the little house, Dek traveled. *Goodbye.*

"Get up! What do you think this is, friggin' Gettysburg?" The man's voice oozed with sarcasm, and something nudged Dek's side, none too gently. His head rested on something hard, a wall of stone, his neck crimped so that tiny spasms lined his spine. The shoulder he'd tucked under his head tingled with the feel of pins and needles, as they called the sensation. For a few seconds Dek felt disoriented. Lost, in time and place.

He sprang to his feet, ignoring the pain, eyes wide open now, his nose assaulted with the smell of unwashed humans in unwashed, tattered clothing. More of the adrenalin coursed through his veins. A quick look at his wrist dial told him nothing— it appeared inactive. The bright sun told him he'd slept at least eight hours, on the ground, the filth around him now well-lit. His gaze went back to their clothing.

Clothing that looked nothing like his own, Dek noted, and he stopped his perusal on the men's clutched fists. One stepped closer. Noise came from nearby, bouncing over the buildings that formed the maze he stood in. The sound of heavy machinery.

"Whatsamatter? Can't ya talk?" The man's beefy hand reached out.

Dek straightened. The strange apparel and sounds told him he wasn't in 1863 any longer. If he reached for the sword he carried, would they jump him quicker, or back off? He'd been through exercises like this, in which he traveled to the wrong place. Still, tension tightened his gut and sent his human pulse racing. Fight-or-flight response, he remembered now, as he tried to decide his next move. He'd been trained for emergencies like this. He must keep calm.

"Mornin,'" another man said, coming around the corner. He was younger and taller than the first two and looked cleaner. "Is there a problem?"

"Naw, ain't no problem, Mike, we just found this derelict sleeping it off in your alley." The man who had kicked Dek spoke rapidly, and Dek sensed he was afraid of the younger man.

"Well, no harm done. Just get going, all of you. The diner's opening up and you can't be hanging around." Mike tilted his head to indicate they should move on.

Dek didn't follow the men immediately, he wanted to thank the diner owner, who now turned a puzzled gaze on him.

"Do you need an invitation, Yankee?"

The obvious reference to his coat made Dek smile. "I wanted to thank you for preventing an altercation."

"Yeah, whatever," Mike said. He looked Dek up and down, apparently making some sort of judgement. "You won't be needing that coat today, it's gonna be a scorcher." Reaching out, Mike fingered the heavy wool of Dek's sleeve. "You one of those re-enactors? If you are, I reckon you're looking for Mrs. White." He chuckled. "Also reckon you're a little late."

Uncertain, Dek figured that was his best story. "Yes."

Mike scratched his head. "Why were you sleeping in my alley? You get lost, or intoxicated? Or are ya' hiding from someone?"

"You wouldn't believe me if I told you," Dek said, feeling the man warming to him. "Would there be any eggs in your diner?" Eggs and bacon were his favorite human breakfast. And did he have one long fast to break this day. Reaching into his pocket, Dek pulled out colorful paper currency he knew was worthless now, and held it up to Mike's inspection.

Mike stared for a few seconds, then took the bills and held them up to the light, turning the flimsy paper in different directions. Dek held his breath, unsure if the money would offend his new acquaintance, or if it would provide the rations he sorely needed. Already he could taste the bacon's grease, feel it warm and salty on his tongue.

Mike laughed then. "You're a riot. C'mon, bud, let's get you some grub."

They walked around the building, onto a street that was paved. Automobiles whizzed by, and the air smelled of motor dirt. More buildings, shops and offices, lined the two-lane street. Mike held the door open, a glass door under a striped awning that read "Mike's Place," and Dek followed him into the dim interior. What he recognized as rock music rolled over him in waves, and Dek saw a flashing neon light above a long counter.

No matter what he had intended, he was no longer in the nineteenth century.

Listening to the conversations around him, Dek decided he might not even be on the same planet. Far from the genteel conversations of the 1800s, the things he overhead here in the diner painted horrible pictures of the time and place.

"So," one young girl began, glaring at a man in the booth with her, "are you going to help me or do I have to pay for this abortion myself?"

Dek studied the coffee cup in front of him, his grip on the handle turning his knuckles white. As a waitress set a plate of eggs in front of him, a man two stools away told another about his being attacked at gunpoint the week before. Along with a side order of toast, Dek was presented with a poorly folded newspaper which he scanned quickly.

His mouth went dry at the number of violent episodes, the waste he saw documented. Even more troublesome was the date on the masthead— July 23, 2000. How had he ended up 130 years in the future? Why hadn't he taken the time to better study this time period? Why hadn't he been returned to his ship? They had never experienced mistakes in time travel before, why now? Had he done something wrong? Had the elemental key actually been damaged, not just out of alignment? With fingers dark from the cheap ink, Dek reached for a paper napkin and wiped his brow. His appetite gone, he waved to the waitress. He needed to go outside and try to figure out what had happened. Tapping his wrist dial, which rewarded him by remaining unlit, Dek wondered what he was going to do. All back-up plans relied on the wrist dial, which had never before failed.

"You all done, sugar? That'll be five seventy-five, please."

Dek looked around for Mike, the owner, but didn't see him. "I have an understanding with Mike," he said, his voice quiet. He watched the expression on the woman's face go from sweet to sour in an eye-blink. "Mike said you might try this, after palming off that funny-money." She let out a loud whistle that made Dek wince. "Yo, Mike, we've got you someone to wash dishes this morning." Then she turned back to Dek. "Shuck that coat and roll up your sleeves, soldier. Welcome to my world."

CHAPTER TWO

Karen White sighed as she closed the double front doors, then leaned her forehead on the warm wood. The last thing she had needed today was a visit from the broker who wanted to list her house, a greasy little man with dollar signs for eyeballs. She did not want to sell the place, and had the money to cover at least six more months of mortgage payments. It worried her to think that this time next year, someone else would probably own her home, and that there would be no more barbecues or re-enactments on her grounds.

Another part of Virginia's past would disappear.

A part that ran way back into her family's history.

With a quick, apologetic glance at the painting of her great-

great grandmother, Karen strolled through the hall and kitchen to the mud room in the rear of the house. It really wasn't such a large place, just old and stately, and Karen took care of most of the chores herself. Tucking cloth gloves under her chin, Karen reached up to tie her long hair into a ponytail. Her neck already felt sticky in the near hundred percent humidity, and it would be worse out back in her tomato patch. Jon had hated when she wore her hair up, and though he'd ended their marriage long before his death, she still recalled the way he'd teasingly hidden her hair bands.

But that was a long time ago. Now all she had was a money-draining property and heartburn every time she found something new to repair. Was it worth it? Should she sell?

The plants didn't seem to mind the sweltering weather. In fact, they actually seemed to thrive on the damp air. With a sigh, Karen plopped beside them, ready to do battle with the only other thing that seemed to love the heat—weeds. Before she could pull her gloves over her moist hands, a flash of movement caught her eye. She looked up and saw a man sauntering up the lane, his long coat a suit of armor in the July sun. His blondish, scraggly hair drooped across his forehead as he waved a hand in greeting.

Did he realize the battle re-enactment was last weekend? The history-loving soldiers and ladies had all departed, wilted after three days in heavy costumes and even heavier humidity. Karen didn't know how they did it without passing out. The approaching man moved well under the bulk of his coat, apparently comfortable, his posture nearly regal.

Brushing dirt from her bare knees, Karen stood and faced him, her head inclined. Had she seen him somewhere before? The flicker of recognition died as quickly as it sparked. "Can I help you?" she asked, reaching up to push her bangs from her forehead, aware she'd once again neglected to have them cut or let them grow out.

"Good afternoon," he began, smiling briefly before blanking his expression.

Without the smile, he looked nervous. Too bad, because he certainly had straight, white teeth, she thought, and nodded. "Hello.

Can I help you?"

"Mike, of Mike's Diner, sent me here to see you. The name's Dek." With that he moved closer and extended one hand.

Having no choice without looking rude, Karen brushed hers against her shorts and shook it. She met his gaze as their fingers touched, and thought again that she knew this man. His eyes were deep blue ponds that seemed to look right into her soul. Karen shivered and tugged her hand free. "Well, Mr. Dek, I'm afraid Mike's timing was off. The re-enactment was last weekend." She looked at him again, and his face showed his dismay."Have you come far?"

He nodded, reached up and undid his top button. Karen didn't know how he could have stood the heat of that get-up this long. The afternoon sun beat down with no mercy.

"Where are you staying?" she asked, hoping he lived close enough to just walk on back home.

Dek met her gaze but said nothing.

She sighed, for his eyes told her all. This was a man down on his luck. Common sense told her to be leery, to take it slower, but she felt like she knew him. Perhaps he just reminded her of one of the other re-enactors. "Do you have any bags?"

He looked down then and shook his head.

She knew she would regret this, but something about him caught her softer side. "You want to earn some loose change?"

"Cash?" His head rose, indicating his interest.

Karen laughed. "Yes, cash. I need some help in the yard here." She sighed again. "I'm either going to be showing the place to tourists or to real estate agents. I like doing some of the work my-self, but," she spread her arms wide, "as you can see, I could use another pair of hands." She held up one finger. "I'll be right back. I've got some old clothes of my husband's that you can change into. Please stay right here."

<hr>

The sun was setting when she returned to check on her new em-ployee, the shadows forming over the landscape. How long had he been working? Her mouth went dry when she caught sight of him trimming the hedges, in silhouette almost, the blue tee shirt she'd given him plastered to his chest. What a chest, she noticed. Down-on-his-luck or not, the man was built.

He also wore a ridiculously large wrist watch, reminding her of one of those trendy, plastic things teenagers liked to wear. Every few moments he glanced at it.

He was probably hungry! Karen felt a pang of guilt as she realized she hadn't even offered the man so much as a glass of water—she'd just gone on her merry way, finishing her indoor chores, grateful that someone else was taking charge of the yard. Every time she'd looked out an upper floor window, he'd been out there, working, sweating, muscles rippling.

Get a grip! She had to knock it off. She wasn't an emotionally charged teenager anymore. This was a laborer, probably homeless, and she had to maintain her distance. She'd go down there with a pitcher of iced tea and a bottle of water, then offer him supper, and send him on his way. Yes, that's what she would do.

⟶⊰⊱⟵

Karen woke with a start, her breath catching as her eyes tried to focus. She'd had a dream, a very real dream in which her great-great grandmother had been fighting for her life. Puling herself to a sitting position, Karen rubbed her eyes, then stared into the dark room for proof she was awake.

Corinne had been very young and holding off three roughnecks with her rifle. A baby had cried in the background, which may have been a wood house, but Karen could only be sure of a blurry brown haze. Although the scene had been very real, very distinct—she hadn't been able to focus on anything but Corinne and the men. Corinne had shouted, not to the intruders, but over her shoulder, almost as if she'd been addressing Karen.

"Don't turn away help. Don't turn him away."

Then the dream baby had shrieked and Karen's eyes flew open, her heart thudding.

She didn't believe in supernatural communications, but it seemed she had just received a message. Shivering, Karen scooted down and yanked the covers to her neck, then watched the night pass with open eyes.

Dek kept picturing the soldiers at Bull Run, moving at each other on the field, backs ramrod straight, facial muscles taut, weapons pointed. The scenes were just as the chronicles had described, but Dek's final report was going to be late. His committee leaders would have to wait to learn what Dek had seen, what his interpretation entailed. With the face of his dial remaining unlit, he had no way to communicate. He'd tried repeatedly to reach Alana anyway, with no success. Every contingency plan he'd trained for depended on his dial working. If that was not an option, he had to wait to be located and retrieved. If Alana still thought he was in 1863...

"Is the food okay?" Karen's question came from across the table, where she watched him with a shy smile.

"Wonderful, thank you." He'd been rude, not paying attention to his hostess. And she'd been so good to him, letting him use the shower in her outbuilding and providing yet another change of clothing.

"Are you worried about getting home tonight?"

A piece of chicken lodged in Dek's throat, and he coughed twice trying to remove it. How did she know he was thinking about that? No. Humans were generally not psychic.

"Drink some tea," she said, indicating his glass.

Dek followed her direction and regained his composure while Karen watched.

"I can call you a cab, or if you like, call my uncle to find you a ride. Depends on how far you have to go."

Oh, if she only knew the truth. Dek shook his head, staring at his plate while he pushed around chopped potatoes and meat, dragging the food through some sort of brown sauce.

She sipped her tea, watching him.

Dek could feel her gaze on him, trying to figure out his secrets.

"Dek. Is that short for Dexter?

He shook his head.

"Well, anyway, Dek, I've been thinking. I need a whole lot more help outside, even inside, and I have an apartment out over the carriage house that's empty. It's very plain, barely furnished, you know, just the essentials. But you're welcome to sleep there for a few nights if you continue to help me."

Why would she trust him? After all he'd heard at Mike's Diner, he didn't think anyone in this time was trusting or trustworthy.

Except Karen.

Karen, with the blonde hair and gray eyes that reminded him of someone else, someone in another time. Someone in 1863. Karen, who must have read his mind.

"It's okay. But I will warn you, this house is alarmed. No one gets in or out at night without my knowing, plus the local police. And my uncle and cousin will be here in the morning, and trust me, you don't want to cross them."

He nodded, picked up a crust of thick bread and pushed it through the sauce as she had done. There was only one thing left to say. "Thank you."

"You're welcome." Karen began to gather the dishes, and Dek stood to help. "At least you have manners," she said, smiling. "And if you hang your uniform coat on the post of the back stairs, I'll send it to my cleaner tomorrow."

Dek thanked her, found his coat, and did as she asked. In this form he tended to perspire profusely at times, and a cleaning and pressing would be nice. On the fourth hardwood step, Dek noticed a stack of paper books, which looked like they were designed for children. He'd seen similar ones in class and wondered if Karen had a reading problem.

"Are these yours?" he asked, reaching for a book with the words "The Hobbit" printed in large letters on the front. Was a 'hobbit' an alien also?

Karen moved closer and gave him a strange expression. "They belong to my son."

Dek's chest tightened with an unexpected pang of disappointment. He hadn't considered that she might have children, or a family. Or a husband. Just because she hadn't mentioned them didn't mean they didn't exist.

She went on. "He's ten and just starting to read longer books." Karen took the book from Dek's hands. "This is one of his favorites. Have you read it?"

Dek shook his head. He didn't think it was a good idea to mention the books he'd read were all on portable electronic devices. They hadn't had paper books in centuries. "Have you?"

"Oh yes," she said, her smile growing. "Many times when I was younger. When I was into that sort of thing."

"And what do you read now?" Dek found he was genuinely interested, and not from a strictly observe-the-human way.

"Oh, I like romance novels." Karen turned away and went to the sink as she spoke, turning on the faucet and letting the water crash over her words.

"Romance novels?" He was not familiar with these.

"You know, the story of how boy meets girl, boy loses girl, they overcome all odds and live happily ever after?"

"I haven't read about, I mean, I haven't read any of those. Do they portray how men and women typically meet and marry?"

She snorted, pouring a trickle of yellow soap onto a sponge. "Hardly. In fact, they're fantasy. The characters especially." She waved the sponge. "The heros are larger than life. They're honorable and loyal. Brave. Not like the men I know." With a flip of her hand, a plastic tumbler tossed into a dish rack where it bounced around quietly.

Dek watched the back of her head. "So you don't have honorable men here?"

She shrugged. "I'm sure there are a few, somewhere."

"What about in the past?"

"Oh, you mean like in historical novels? Well, you know, the characters in those stories make you believe that men were more honorable in real life back then. But that's probably just the good writing. And readers wanting to believe the fantasy." She rinsed a plate and placed it gently in the rack.

Dek took the last items from the table to where she stood, her head barely reaching to his shoulders. Her hair smelled good, and he bent a bit to take another sniff. "Tell me about your son. Does he live here with you?"

"Yes, during the school year. Summers he spends with his father's parents in Florida." Karen squeezed the soap bottle and a slew of tiny bubbles drifted into the air. "I'm sure he would have liked to meet you." She turned and started at how close he stood.

Dek backed away. He felt a mild burning sensation in his chest but knew it wasn't from Karen's cooking. After knowing her only one day he didn't want to think about leaving. He gave his head a shake, trying to clear his mind. Instead of picturing Alana's face at the control desk, he kept seeing Karen's.

She stepped toward him. "Jon didn't live here before his death, at least not for quite a while. The things he didn't take are upstairs, just a few old pieces of clothing and shoes. I've never felt like clearing them out-didn't want to even touch them—they're in a guest room—and you're more than welcome to anything you can use."

She was generous. He could imagine her being a mother. Would her son look just like her? He could ask to see a photo, but it wouldn't be the same. And even if he were welcome, there was no way he could stay. No way he could even tell her who and what he really was. Finally he reached out to touch her cheek. It was so soft, far smoother than his own. She flinched but didn't pull away, and Dek felt his heart sigh. Not quite remembering which thing he was already regretting, whether he'd miss her or meeting her son, he spoke. "Yes, I am sorry about that too." Did either of them remember what he was responding to?

"That I won't meet your son," he amended, and smiled.

Dek waited patiently while Karen went upstairs for more of her former husband's things, searching for a new toothbrush as well. She trusted him to wait below, not to follow her, not to harm her, or take any of her belongings without permission. The concept made his human heart beat faster and flooded his veins with warmth.

245

It was a nice feeling.

He examined several paintings in the entrance hall, one of a horse farm, one of a battle scene, and finally he turned to a portrait opposite the main door. A painting he hadn't seen yet.

His heart stopped beating as he froze, gaze imprisoned by the subject. It couldn't be. How could Karen, in the year 2000, have a likeness of Corinne hanging in her hallway?

Corrine, from 1863. Corrine, whose husband had felt less than a man because of a wound. Moving closer, Dek touched Corrine's faintly smiling lips with his finger, gently tracing the curves.

"That's my great-great grandmother," Karen said, joining him in front of the portrait. "Beautiful, wasn't she?" A tall clock ticked off long seconds.

Dek swallowed. "Yes." And she looked just like Karen, providing the reason he found his hostess so familiar. So lovely. He'd traveled in time, perhaps, but followed the same family. "She looks like you."

Her cheeks pinkened, but Karen continued as if he hadn't spoke. "Actually, I look like her. She survived the Civil War. They say she was even present at the First Battle of Bull Run."

She was. Dek knew, but of course, he couldn't confirm that.

"And see that painting?" Karen indicated the battle scene he'd noted earlier. "That is Bull Run. Well, at least some artist's rendition. But it's an original. Been in my family since it was done." Pride emanated from her voice. "Awesome, huh?"

Dek didn't know the word but grasped her meaning. "Yes. Awesum." He looked closely at each painted soldier, finding none familiar. Not that he'd expected to. The scene was done at sunrise, with a pink sky and orange tones, darker at the edges. The uniforms were clean and crisply portrayed, most certainly the artist's own improvement.

Karen straightened the frame, touching it with an almost loving caress, and drew his attention to the upper edge.

"What's that?" he asked, noticing smudges of paint in tiny dots in one corner.

"The moon fading away into day?" She sighed. "Or just an error? Who knows?"

Dek stared harder, stepped closer. No one here might know what it was. But he did.

Someone had been very observant that day, back when the war between the states had begun.

Someone had noticed Dek's arrival.

CHAPTER THREE

Dek didn't have to worry about the intricacies of modern gadgets in the apartment on Karen's grounds—there weren't any. Just a bed, table and chairs, a brown plaid sofa and a clean but well-worn counter. The cupboards held an assortment of chipped china and mismatched mugs. One lamp lit the room with a yellowed, almost hazy glow. It was fine for him.

He'd barely slept the night before after seeing the paintings in Karen's foyer. There were too many similarities to be coincidental. Was it part of someone else's plan? Was he meant to be trapped in this year with Corinne's lovely descendant? Could it even be some plan of Alana's to communicate with him without the wrist dial?

Washing his face with warm water, Dek opened his eyes to take a long look in the small, round mirror. His human bone structure was like the other men he'd seen. His eyes, just as evenly spaced. He winced now as soap splashed into them, burning slightly in the corners. After melding into his natural state for several hours while the humans slept, Dek felt a strange sense of relaxation being in this shape again. He felt good.

Clothed in another worn tee shirt and jeans too large for his form, Dek locked the small apartment and went down the narrow staircase. At last he was adjusting to the climate and could breathe easier, and he felt good. He had the few dollars Karen had given him for his labor, and he intended to return to Mike's Diner and pay for his breakfast this time. Then he'd go back into the alley and try to recreate his arrival. Dek sighed, kicking a rock in his path. It bounced a few times and skidded to a halt under a tree. He didn't have much hope that the alley would help him find a solution, but he hadn't come up with any other ideas, despite the time he had to think while working the day before. And though he hated to admit it, he had found the time with Karen, and the work, pleasurable.

Unfortunately, much as he enjoyed being with Karen, he had to figure out a way to get back—either in time, or in space.

⋯

From her kitchen window, Karen watched him go, admiring the way the soft cotton clung to his shoulders. The pants were too loose, but she couldn't help that. Dek didn't have the gut that her husband had had. Why didn't Dek have his own clothing? Where was he from? What had happened to make him lose everything and not want to admit it? How could he afford that quality of replicated Union uniform? And where was he in such a hurry to get to this morning? He'd not said goodbye, but since he hadn't taken his coat, she knew he'd be back.

That knowledge warmed her inside. Silly girl! He was a complete stranger, apparently a jobless, homeless, stranger. And here she was acting like a teenager with a crush. Well, she'd long since passed her teen years, in fact, had just responded negatively to an invitation to her fifteenth high school reunion. She poured herself a second cup of coffee and sighed. A tiny part of her wished she could go to that reunion, with Dek on her arm. In better fitting pants, of course. With a blink she put that thought away and took her coffee out to the front porch.

It would be another warm one, and Karen would need to work outside early in the day before the humidity sapped all of her strength. She needed to keep busy so she wouldn't dwell on her problems. As soon as Jamie went back to school in September, she had some tough decisions to make.

She set her mug on the top step and pulled the wrapped rubber band from her wrist, reached up and piled her hair on top her head. The band secured it, keeping the locks off her already damp neck. She had a fleeting thought of Dek watching her do that, and felt her cheeks warm. For Pete's sake, she didn't even know the man's last name!

She missed Jamie. Her son would have been a distraction. Actually, he would have kept her down-to-earth. Who would have time to drool over a man when a chattering child was around? Who could moon over a sexy stranger while playing tent or reading aloud from J.R.R. Tolkien?

Karen finished the last of her coffee and rose to take the cup inside when a rumbling came from the driveway. Squinting into the morning sun, Karen could just make out the white car approaching. *Damn.* She began to perspire, felt beads of moisture on her forehead. Tugging her shorts down to make sure she was decent, Karen felt an acidic pang in her stomach. Probably too much caffeine. The car's horn sounded loudly, making her jump.

She really did not feel like dealing with *him* today.

Dek let himself fall heavily onto the padded seat near Mike's front window. Resting his hands on the built-in table, he watched with a detached sense of curiosity as blood seeped from several tiny breaks in his skin. They had burned when he washed them with the diner's pink 'anti-bacterial' soap.

Mild pain and frustration from being no closer to resolving his situation didn't diminish his appetite for fried eggs and sausages, and he inhaled deeply over his meal. The first bite was the best, as Dek had first learned while visiting another planet, similar to Earth. For two worlds separated by millions of light years, their taste in foods was remarkably alike. He broke the yolk and watched the deep yellow flow across the plate.

Mike approached, a towel crumpled over one shoulder. "So, Yankee, are you planning to do K.P. for us again this morning?"

Dek snorted. He didn't know what K.P. was, but he could guess. "Not today. I have cash."

"Good for you." Mike smiled, tilted his head and seemed to study his customer. "Did you find what you lost out back yesterday?"

"No. I did not." Dek watched a man at a nearby table use his toasted bread to sop up the egg yolk, and decided to do the same. "I will have to rebuild it. When I've earned more cash, I'll need to locate some electronic components. Do you know where I could secure them?"

Mike waved with a limp hand to a couple coming in the front door, then turned back to Dek. "Can you believe them? That guy left his wife of twenty years and is prancing all over town with that child on his arm. Anyway, there's an electronics store about twenty minutes from here." He placed both hands on the edge of Dek's table. "But that stuff ain't cheap. Doing yard work for Mrs. White isn't going to be enough, unless you've got lots of time. What do you have to make, anyway?"

Dek shifted on the bench. He couldn't reveal too much. Mike was still a stranger, and hadn't proved trustworthy yet. "Well," he began, using his last crust of bread to circle the plate. "I'm not from around here."

"No kidding."

"And, I need to be able to communicate with my co-workers."

"Ever heard of a telephone?"

"Yes. They won't work. Neither will telegraphs, citizen band radios or computer modems. It must be something more. . . sophisticated." He knew that much from his own technical education. Humans had not yet created a communication or transport system like his own. If and when they did, it would certainly not be small enough to fit into a wrist band. More likely the units would fill entire rooms, like their early computers. But perhaps he could create something portable enough to use to signal Alana.

Mike slid into the seat across from Dek, both hands on the table, his restaurant forgotten. "Are you a spy?"

Dek shook his head.

"A secret agent?"

"No." Dek looked around, to make sure no one was within whispering range. "I can't tell you what I do exactly, but I can say I'm here to observe. And report." That was the truth, and Mike could make what he would of it.

Mike's eyes widened, and he whistled softly. "I knew there was something you weren't saying, Yankee." The bells over the door chimed again when more customers flowed inside. Mike suddenly sat up and looked toward the counter, saw that his staff was taking care of things, and turned back to Dek.

Dek fished some bills from his pocket and laid them on the table. Mike made no move to take them. "Are you on our side?"

"What do you mean?"

"Are you a good guy or a bad guy? You know, CIA or KGB? Black or white knight? You don't have to tell me anything else, but I need to know whose side you're on. My lips are sealed."

Dek looked directly into Mike's eyes, seeing the sincerity there. "I'd never harm anyone. Where I come from, we don't harm anyone. Ever."

That seemed to satisfy him, and Mike nodded. "Then if you need anything while you're here, just ask. If you need more money, I have a brother who owns a landscaping service. You could work there part-time without raising any eyebrows. I'll call him today if you want." He gazed at Dek with admiration now, as if he were a hero.

"Thank you. I would appreciate that." He knew he couldn't take much cash from Karen, who despite her large house, didn't seem to be overloaded with it. If Alana couldn't reach him, he'd need to prepare a system to contact her. And for that he would need funds.

Dek left Mike's Diner and headed back to Karen's, his tension slightly eased by having a plan of action decided. And because of the fact that he'd finally seen a better side of a male human in this century, finally seen a little honor, in Mike.

"What do you want, Frank?" She'd told Dek last night that she was expecting her uncle and cousin today, just in case he had any funny ideas. Telling that fib must have jinxed herself, because lo and behold, dearest Cousin Frank had just climbed her porch steps. Uninvited.

"Is that any way to greet your only cousin?" Frank pasted a phoney hurt look on his face as he sat on the top step. He patted the wood. "Sit beside me."

Karen sighed. It was too hot to have this argument again. Still, she knew the only way to get rid of Frank was to humor him. She sat.

Frank spread his hands toward the front yard. "Look around, Karen. This place is going to the dogs. Now I admit, you've gotten some of the yard taken care of, and that's to your credit. But look at everything— the house needs painting, the drive needs to be repaved, the fence has holes, the—"

"Knock it off, Franky." Karen's pulse thumped and she felt her cheeks warming. "It's not that bad, and it's none of your business. This house is Jamie's legacy, it—"

"Yeah, yeah. I know. Heard it before. Grandma wanted you to have it. But that was before she knew you and Jon were splitting up, and before it started falling apart. How're you going to pay for all the repairs?" Frank stood and started to pace. "Jon didn't leave you all so much money when he died, did he?" He paused and stared at her.

She could feel his gaze on the back of her head.

"What had he been doing with all your money, Karen?" Frank lowered his voice, throwing in some fake concern for effect. As if he cared about her and not the money.

But Karen didn't buy it. "Again, none of your business. I am close to having this place deemed a historical landmark, and when I do—"

"Yeah. I know, you'll open your bed and breakfast and overcharge the tourists. I've heard it all before." He knelt behind her, putting a hand on her shoulder. "You still need to fix the place up first."

Karen shivered and shrugged him off. "It's just a matter of time."

"Time is money, sweetheart."

That was it! Karen stood and whirled on her cousin. "Don't," she said, hands on hips, "call me sweetheart. And don't pretend you care about me and Jamie. There's one reason you're here and we both know it."

They stood face to face, shoulders squared, neither willing to give an inch.

Until Frank changed tactics. "You know you want a family again, someday. More kids. Don't you want to start getting ready for that?"

She simply stared. The man's gall was overwhelming.

"If you sell now, Uncle Dick and I will give you a nice share of the profit, and you can put that away for your nest egg. Buy a smaller place for you and Jamie." He waved a hand around again. "Let it go, Karen. You don't have to do this by yourself. Get a nice little place for you and your son. You'll have some money to put away for his future."

"But most of the money will go in your pockets, right where you want it. I'm well aware of what Grandpa put in his will." She pushed her bangs from her forehead. "Even if I wasn't, you would have clued me in months ago. And stop," she said, raising her voice as her thought processes worked, "sending that slimy little real estate broker over here!"

Frank tried again, putting his hands on her shoulders, looking into her eyes. "Okay, I promise. Just say you'll consider what I'm saying?" With a long finger, he mimicked Karen's earlier action and pushed her bangs out of her eyes.

Karen snapped. With as much force as she could muster, she lifted his arms and threw them far from her body. "Consider this. Leave and don't touch me again, or I'll go for a restraining order on Monday. You're not the man I thought you were." This was her home, and she was keeping it, and she was through listening to dear Cousin Frank. She was through being wishy-washy. It was her home, and Jamie's, and she was going to find a way to keep it.

Frank hesitated, looking over her shoulder out into the yard.

Another male voice spoke. "I believe the lady has asked you to leave, sir."

Dek! Karen felt her heart lighten and her pulse race. What timing. She turned to smile at him, wondering at the same time how much he had overheard.

"Who are you?" Frank turned, his shoulders raised and fists clenched.

Karen wondered if her cousin realized how much he resembled a cartoon character. "Frank, this is Dek, and I really think it would be best if you left now."

"Yeah? Why's that? Is he gonna make me?" Frank jerked his thumb at Dek. "Who is he, anyway? Looks like a bum to me."

"Frank!" Karen stood straighter. "*He* is my guest. *You* are not. Please go."

She watched Frank's expression change several times, as he obviously tried to decide what to do. Common sense must have prevailed, as Frank relaxed his stance, shrugged, and mumbled something unmentionable. He stalked away, staring down Dek as he went.

They watched Frank get in his car and pull around the circular drive, leaving them alone in the silence of the warm day. Karen wrapped her arms around herself, fending off a shiver which would give away how shaken she felt.

Finally Dek moved nearer, not touching, but watching her closely. "Can we go inside, please? You need some water and we need to talk."

She nodded, arms still crossed, and led the way back into her hallway. When she reached the kitchen, she noticed Dek hadn't followed, and wondered if he was staring at the foyer artwork again. Her sneakers made no noise as she retraced her steps, and found him by the front door, tapping his big plastic watch.

The face of it looked lit.

Dek looked up, and for a second she thought he looked guilty. But why? Then the expression changed and he was once again solemn. "I have to go back to my apartment for a few minutes. I will return and then you can tell me about that man."

Karen watched him leave, his wide shoulders barely clearing the door frame. Where his watch sat, he cradled his wrist as if it had been sprained.

CHAPTER FOUR

———◆◇◆———

Covering his dial, Dek hurried back to his own rooms, tapping the face as he went. At the landing that topped his stairs, the glow brightened. He pushed a button on the side of the casing.

"Alana! Are you there? Do you read?"

Static answered.

"Alana!"

"Dek. Adjust your frequency."

He turned a rimmed wheel. "What's going on? Do you know where I am?"

Static cracked again, then cleared. "We know where you are. Do you know when you are? What year is it?"

"Two thousand."

Alana swore, in her own language. "We're having problems here. Can't transport you until we get them resolved."

"How long?" Dek didn't spare time for pleasantries, in case contact was lost again.

"Two to three days, your time. Do you have a place to wait?"

"Yes. With a woman who thinks I'm here as some sort of war actor."

"Good. Is it private?"

"Yes. I have my own rooms."

"Then don't forget to meld back, every day. I mean it, Dek."

"Of course. Is there anything I can do from here? I was planning on building another communicator."

"I don't think you'll find an Elemental Key on Earth, Dek," Alana said, chuckling. "Just blend in, and we'll retrieve you as soon as possible. I notified headquarters that your final report would be late." Static interrupted for a few seconds. "And Dek? I mean it—don't take any risks. I want you back, and I want you back fertile." The dial went dim as Alana signed off.

Dek stood staring at the darkened dial face, briefly wishing it had been Karen who was doing the propositioning. But once she knew what she really was, Karen wouldn't want anything to do with him. Much like the man she'd seen earlier, Dek wasn't *who* she thought he was. He wasn't even *what* she thought he was.

Still, he felt relieved that he wouldn't have to try and assemble his own wrist dial. Dek went inside to take a shower, then bundled his laundry up to take to her basement. That's where she said the dirty garments were taken care of, and Dek assumed the machines would be easy for him to manipulate.

He liked the way humans showered with water, warm and comforting as it drizzled over the body. There were so many more comfort features here than he had at home, or had seen in other time periods. With his bundle under one arm, Dek walked across the yard, stopping once to look up at the cloud cover. Every sky was so unique, and now that he knew Alana was aware of the problem and working on a solution, he could relax a bit and observe again.

He found Karen in her kitchen, standing at the counter peeling potatoes.

"Hi," she said, "come on in. I'm just making potato salad for supper."

Was she trying to force a cheerful tone? Perhaps she didn't want to tell him about the man. Well, he'd insist on it, it was his duty as a guest to help if he could, and then he had to tell her about his job offer and obtain her permission to stay with her for a few more days. Or longer. He moved behind her and could smell a sweet scent on her skin.

"Would you like a drink?"

"I like your iced tea. Is it in the refrigerator?"

"Yes, help yourself. Make me some, too, please."

The glass pitcher was on the top shelf, and Dek poured the tea into two shiny metal tumblers he'd filled with ice. He set hers on the counter where she was working, neatly cleaning the vegetables. On the stove top, a large pot of water bubbled. "Can I help?"

"You've already helped."

"What do you mean? I just got here."

She shot him a shy smile. "I've made a decision. I'm going to keep this place if at all possible."

"You were not planning to stay here?"

"I was hedging. My grandmother wanted me to keep this place, well, for my husband and me to keep it. For Jamie, you know, to keep the family home in the family. But when she and my grandfather passed away together last year, their will said something quite different."

"How so?"

She shrugged, and began to plop the potatoes into the boiling water. "They specified that if I sold the place within the first five years after their death, I had to split the proceeds with both my uncle and my cousin. They really wanted Jon and me to live here. They didn't know we'd..."

"Parted ways?"

"Exactly."

"And you do want to stay."

"True. But they didn't know I would be a single parent without funds to make repairs or renovations. I can't keep the place up by myself, at least without a whole lot of work and stress, and of course what little family I have left is no help because they want me to sell. They want me to fail." She shrugged again as if it didn't matter.

Dek knew that wasn't the case. "What if you had someone else living here, to help you all the time? Would that help?" Dek sat at her wood table, staring down into his tea.

"Of course. But I couldn't pay anyone, even when I'm teaching part-time this fall I could only offer a residence in trade. Besides, it would have to be someone I could really trust."

"You've trusted me," he said, whispering the words.

She stirred the contents of the pot before looking at Dek. "Yes, I have. More easily than I've ever trusted anyone. And I'm not sure why that is. Maybe because Mike liked you. But, as you said, you're just passing through." Karen pulled the chair out across from him and sat down then leaned forward on her elbows.

He thought she looked very attractive with a few curls of hair, damp from the steaming pot, hanging around her face. "Yes, I am just passing through." He almost wished it wasn't so.

"It's okay. I understand." Her face lit into smile. "And I'm actually glad Frank showed up today and made me mad, because I've made a decision I've been procrastinating making. I'm going to do everything I can to keep this place." Tapping her nails on the table, Karen appeared deep in thought. "I can do it myself."

"I'm glad. But how did I help you decide?" He knew he'd helped with the yard work, and helped drive away her nasty cousin, but he hadn't even known she was having this dilemma.

"By being here, by not having your own home, I've seen how that made you feel. In the back of my mind, I kept seeing your face when you first walked up my driveway." She reached across the table and moved his tumbler aside, then put her hand in his.

Dek felt a rush of something, something that must be so human he couldn't identify it. He squeezed her hand gently.

"I know that sounded terrible, like your misfortune has helped me, but I didn't mean it that way. Please don't be offended." Her brows knit together over her eyes.

He closed his free hand over their joined ones. He liked the way her skin felt, the way their fingers wrapped together. "I'm not offended. I'm honored. But I really haven't been unfortunate—just had a temporary set-back. That's all."

Karen nodded, a sympathetic expression on her face.

"But don't feel bad for me, please. In fact I may have a job arranged, for a few days, if you don't mind me staying on here. I'll keep working in your yard, also." He hated lying to her, hated hiding the truth. He wasn't a homeless vagrant. He had a highly respected position in his society.

Karen had moved on and went back to the stove. "Of course you can stay. Perhaps you can even help me find your replacement before you go."

Oh. Dek felt punched in the gut, as Mike would say. He reached for his tea and tipped it so that several cubes of ice fell into his mouth. His tongue numbed quickly. It was called stalling, so he wouldn't have to respond. Karen's innocent comment had made him feel sad, lonely, by reminding him he would be leaving. It hurt even contemplating finding a different male for her. It didn't matter if she meant a man to work for her. He didn't like the thought of other men around her, for any reason. It was a strange feeling, one he hadn't experienced before, and Dek wondered if there was an equivalent of ice to numb his emotions.

Karen stirred the potatoes once more, then turned off the burner. "Come with me, please? I want to show you something."

He followed her out the back door and into her yard, noticing how much nicer her grass looked than the lawn around Mike's Diner. The afternoon sun was to their backs, and he watched Karen's hips sway as she moved.

Purposely, he caught up with her and matched her pace. Before them, in the horizon, was the start of a forest. "Is that your property also?"

"A bit of it. The line is just inside the trees." She pointed to a small, neglected patch of weed strewn earth. "That used to be my mother's garden, years ago. Over there is where the well was, before the county put in water and sewer about ten years ago."

He nodded as they passed her landmarks, then moved into higher grass. It looked like half of an acre still stood between them and the tree line, and they walked at a leisurely pace. Being with Karen here, Dek felt no need for conversation. It felt good to just be there, as if they'd done this before, many times.

When the tallest oaks loomed over head, Karen grabbed Deks's arm to stop him. She pointed into the forest, at a small semi-cleared area. "There."

He saw nothing. "What is it?"

"That's where the original house was. My great-great grandmother's house."

"Corinne?" He whispered the word.

Karen whirled on him. "How did you know her name?"

"I . . . you must have mentioned it that night when we were looking at her painting."

"Oh, I guess so. Doesn't matter. I've just been thinking about her a lot lately, since you've been here." She shrugged. "It seemed like a good idea to bring you here."

"Are we close to the battle field, then?"

"Bull Run? No, not really. Why?"

Dek shrugged this time. "No particular reason." So, he thought, my last trip to 1863 wasn't to the same place I had been before. Something had been wrong with the dial even then.

They returned to the house, and Dek held the kitchen door open for Karen before heading back to the woods. Alone.

Comfortable near the small clearing, he knelt on the dry ground and crossed his arms. Eyes closed, he concentrated on his inner being, his cells, his molecules. And they began to change.

"So, where's your new handyman?"

Karen eyed Stacy, who had let herself in and had obviously finished off the pitcher of iced tea in her absence. Normally she loved her friend's spur-of-the-moment visits, but today she wondered what would happen when Dek returned. The red head now lay sprawled across the family room love seat, her sandals on the floor beside it. "Outside, I presume. When did you get here?"

"Long enough ago to see your backside disappearing into the woods with a broad-shouldered Viking of a man."

Karen laughed. "Oh, please, he is not. He's just. . . tall. And does physical labor."

"Nothing at all like your ex, huh?" Stacy held up one hand. "And I know, I shouldn't speak ill of the dead, but you know it, and I know it, Karen. Jon got soft. Mean and soft."

"He was Jamie's father," Karen said, stiffening. He hadn't had more going for him than that, at the end, but without Jon she wouldn't have had her son.

"You're right." She sighed. "And I'm sorry." Stacy stood and moved to Karen's side to take her arm conspiratorially. "So tell me about the hunky handyman. Your cousin Frank called me and said you'd hired some homeless guy and that he was worried about you."

"Franks's worried all right, about not getting any money off this place. You know that. But he's right in a way—I don't know anything to tell about Dek. He's very nice. Polite."

Stacy's eyebrow arched. "Uh-huh. What else?"

"I thought at first he was a battle re-enactor, you know, like I get here every year. And then I thought he was a drifter."

"And now?" Stacy seemed to hang on every word, like a boy-crazy teenager. "Has he kissed you yet?"

"Geez! You need to get a life. I'm sure Frank wouldn't have called you if he'd thought you would be enjoying this so much." She put a hand to her forehead, which felt sticky from the heat. If she kept this up she'd need a tube of Clearasil, like a teenager. "And now, I don't know. I feel like I've known him forever without knowing anything at all about him. I feel good when he's around. Sounds crazy."

Stacy clucked her tongue. "Sounds like love. You know, love at first sight." Leaving Karen speechless, she went into the kitchen and yanked open the refrigerator door, sticking her head in to examine the contents. "What's for dinner? I'm staying."

Together they prepared a simple meal of thinly sliced pork chops, potato salad and freshly shucked corn on the cob. Dek joined them for dinner around the kitchen table, which suddenly felt smaller to Karen as he bumped her knee.

"So, Dek, where are you from?" Stacy asked, scooping salad onto her plate. "Originally, I mean?"

Karen glanced at Dek, wondering herself. She hadn't asked so directly. Would he answer?

He examined an ear of corn in mid-air. "Washington."

"What do you do, when you're not doing home repairs?"

"Travel." He bit into the corn, made a pleased expression. "Tell me, Stacy, have you met Karen's son?"

"Of course," she said, warming to the subject. She sat up straighter, raised her glass and swirled the cubes and liquid. "I'm his godmother." Stacy proceeded with several stories about Jamie, making Karen smile with motherly pride.

Dek's knee touched Karen's again. Through the thick cotton of a pair of Jon's old work trousers and the khaki of Karen's capri pants, she still felt the tingle. Knowing a blush gave her away to her friend, she rose and took her dishes to the sink.

Stacy followed. "You were certainly quiet in there," she said, as if it were an accusation. "Mr. Handyman didn't talk at all. I'll load the dishwasher."

"Thanks." Karen filled a frying pan with warm, soapy water.

"Were you playing footsie under the table the whole time?"

"Don't you need to head home now?" Karen reached for the coffee maker.

"And miss your gourmet brew? Nah."

Dek brought the last of the plates in and set them gently in the stainless steel sink. Karen watched Stacy watching him and couldn't resist a smile. There was truly nothing subtle about her friend.

"Can I help with this?" he asked, glancing from Karen to Stacy.

"Oh, no thank you. But if you could set the garbage cans out front before you go up?"

He nodded. "I'll leave you ladies to finish your visit. Thank you for dinner. Good night." He left through the kitchen door, almost sauntering, Karen noticed, as did Stacy.

"Are you finished drooling?" she asked, filling the filtered basket with coffee that smelled wonderful.

Stacy chuckled. "Nah. I'll come back another day to drool some more. He's gorgeous, girlfriend. And he hasn't tried anything yet, has he?

"Stacy! He just got here. And he's a gentleman, if nothing else. Of course he hasn't."

"Yeah, Frank told me how conveniently he was shooed away by your gentleman the other day. That's to Dek's credit, of course." Stacy reached to an overhead cupboard for two tall mugs. "Fill me up to go, please. I have to be at the office at an ungodly hour tomorrow."

"Why? Another audit?"

"No." She winked. "There's a new guy I want to run into in the elevator. What a stud."

⭑━⭑

Dek walked, his mind full of the things he'd talked with Karen about the night before, and the things he'd heard her discuss with Stacy. Karen loved her child even more than his parents had loved him, and that was something he hadn't found on many other worlds. She wanted more children, making him wonder if there wasn't something to the experience. Perhaps that was why Alana hinted at wanting a child.

She most likely wasn't as interested in Dek as a man, but in having a child. He felt a little pang in his gut— though he'd already had breakfast at the diner. He could imagine having a child with Karen, but that could never happen. He couldn't let that happen because he'd be leaving. If he chose not to leave, he'd become sterile. There was no choice.

Crossing the street of the quiet neighborhood, Dek smiled at the group of children who were nearly naked as they ran through sprinkling showers of water in the grass. The girls squealed as if frightened, but looked to be having fun. Ahead on the right, two small boys were firing at each other with obviously artificial laser guns, and Dek smiled wider at the simple structures. Human toy makers had no idea what real laser weapons looked like.

"Hey Mister, hands up!" A boy aimed his toy at Dek's head.

Dek complied, a warm feeling sprout in his chest. He hadn't played in such a long time.

"Shoot him!" the second boy cried, "He's an alien! An awful big one."

A jolt ran through Dek. An alien? Could they tell? He glanced around, but no one else was near. That was ridiculous, he told himself, these were merely children at play.

"Yeah-he's from Melmac, like Alf."

"No way—he's Klingon. Very strong."

"Nuh uh, he's Borg. He wants to 'similate us." The child turned to Dek. "What's your designation?"

Not knowing the references, Dek remained still, kept his smile

263

pasted on. He couldn't draw the children into a game. He didn't have the time and it would scare them. "I must be going."

As he dropped his hands and turned away, he heard, "I know. He's like Odo on Deep Space Nine. He can change shapes whenever he wants." The fine hairs on the back of his neck stood straight up, and Dek began to walk. The boys continued their debate behind him, punctuating their claims with pretend gun fire.

He followed the directions Mike had given him earlier that morning and finally saw the faded wood sign that marked the landscape company who needed a helper. Plain old labor, Mike had said. But Dek could use the exercise and the currency, and since he could only wait for Alana and the crew to repair the transporter, he could make himself useful for the next few days.

The dirt and gravel shifted under his feet as Dek followed the lane curving toward the small, wood building labeled 'office.' On either side, swarms of small rounded bushes grew. He reached out to touch one and felt the foliage prick at his skin. Behind the main building was a glass enclosed hot house, which Dek knew was used to grow special flora. A sign marked 'nursery' was to the left of the drive, and he wondered briefly if the workers kept their children there during the day.

The door clicked open and a wide man with no hair appeared. A red bandana was tied to the baldest part of his head, and jewelry sparkled in his ears. He wore blue denim pants and a tee shirt smudged with dirt.

"You Mike's friend?" he asked, looking Dek over. "I'm Pete."

Dek was pleased to be taller than the man who looked like a pirate from a history book. As it was on his homeland, height seemed to connotate authority. At least, physically. "Yes." He looked around. "Where should I start?"

Pete turned his head and spat. "Need to load the pick-up with peat. You got a weight belt?"

Not understanding, Dek shook his head. Did the man want him to lift him onto something? The smell of fertilizer drifted toward them, despite the lack of breeze, and Dek closed his mouth. He could almost taste the foul material. "Please show me what you need me to do."

"Oh, great. A rookie." Pete shook his head and then spat again. "This is going to be a long-ass day."

CHAPTER FIVE

Dek could not out walk the smell of peat moss that afternoon, but he tried. It clung relentlessly to his borrowed clothes and damp skin as he made his way back toward Karen's home and the woods beyond. At least he now knew what the stuff was.

He drew his tee shirt over his head and rubbed one corner of soft cotton around the back of his neck. The insects surely wouldn't bother him while he smelled like this. Heading for the same clearing where he had melded back yesterday, Dek considered what he'd seen working for Pete. Crude men on the job, leering at women. A lunchtime news report showing a gang fight in the city nearby as well as a local man who had killed his brother. Before he'd left for the day, he'd seen one of Pete's employees pocket cash from the register.

Was there no honor here, in the year 2000, among human men? Dek considered filing a new report for his superiors, one detailing his observations in this time. Of course, he'd leave out mention of Karen, because her behavior was the opposite. She was holding onto her home to keep her late grandmother's wishes, and for the sake of her child. It would be so much easier for her to give it all up and sell the property, but she didn't. And then, she took him in when what humans called 'common sense' would have directed her not to. She was amazing.

Near a lumbering tree, Dek knelt and crossed his arms, preparing, when he heard voices raised in the distance. A male and a female, arguing, and then a shriek from the woman. Dek rose and followed the sound, staying in the cover of trees, his feet making little sound in the flexible grass. He quickly found the source of the commotion and watched for just seconds before deciding he needed to assist the female.

The young man with her had her pinned to the ground and was fondling her in an obscene manner. She shrieked again, assuring Dek that she did not want this to happen, despite what the man kept telling her. As he stepped toward them, another man, really a boy, emerged from the woods. Breathing hard, his face was red and the brows drawn into a furious arch. Dek pulled back, wondering the intent of the new man. Would he now have two men to fight off?

"Get off her!" the boy yelled, and yanked the arm and shirt of the assailant. They began to hit each other as the woman shrieked more. Dek heard the sickening thud of fists meeting soft human flesh, heard garments ripping. When the boy stood up to the attacker, Dek saw how much smaller he was than the other man, and moved toward the pair to give him an advantage.

He surprised them, obviously, for they paused and looked at him.

"Who the hell are you?" the older man demanded, rubbing his chin.

Dek crossed his arms, pleased again to have the advantage of height. With peripheral vision he saw the girl rise and back away, straightening her clothes.

A silence ensued, while the men contemplated each other and their situation. The boy sported a trickle of blood from his nose and a rapidly darkening eye, but he maintained his stance. A bee buzzed near Dek's ear, and he brushed it away. Finally the man grunted, uttered more curses and fled before Dek could suggest he make an apology.

The boy turned toward Dek, extending one hand. "Hey, thanks man. I owe you."

Dek shook his hand. "You're welcome. But you were doing just fine before I arrived."

He snorted. "Yeah, right. My name's Tom, and this is my neighbor, Katie." Tom moved to her side and asked her if she was okay.

She nodded. Dek watched as Tom touched her cheek tenderly.

Very gently.

"Tom," Dek asked, feeling the flow of adrenalin wean from his muscles. "How could you do that? Face that man all alone?" It went against all he'd seen so far about human nature.

Tom met his gaze. "Did what I had to do." He wiped his mouth with the back of his hand.

"The honorable thing?"

"Yeah, I guess you could say that." He shifted his eyes, clearly uncomfortable with the concept. "Thanks again, Man." Tom took Katie's hand and led her out of the woods, leaving Dek standing there, pleased to know on some counts, he'd been wrong.

His dial began to glow.

Dek made contact with Alana again, a sense of relief filling him.

Her voice dismissed that feeling. "Dek, I'm afraid there's another delay. We had to send to another ship for the part, and there's been a problem."

"What? They told you we've used our quota for this mission?"

Alana sighed. Had Dek ever heard her do that before? "No, Jantzen's dead. He didn't make it back from his last transport."

Stunned, Dek looked around, then sat heavily on the forest floor. Jantzen had been a decent friend, a better team member. Dek's face felt strange, heavy, as if the sinus cavities now held hot water behind his eyes. His nose itched.

"Dek? Are you there? Report."

"Yes." He folded his hands beneath his chin, his elbows on his knees. Petals of a flower stuck to his ankle, and another bee buzzed around his ear. "When was he returning from?"

"1941."

"Did he have a chance to report?"

"The data's been lost. But that's not crucial. I don't think we'll be sending any crew members back for a while. We'll get you out of there in a few days. Are you still secure?"

"Yes," he repeated, not thinking of his own predicament, or even of the security of his own job. "Alana, there is no urgency for me to leave. Do what you and the others must for Jantzen's dependents. I will be here when you're done."

Alana signed off, making none of her usual light-hearted comments. Dek sat silently for many minutes, mentally sending his last words to Jantzen. A light breeze kicked up, tossing white, fluffy weeds of some kind around Dek's head. He reached for a piece and caught the delicate fiber between his fingertips. He watched a squirrel move in front of him and studied the animal, who didn't seem to be afraid. Bobbing his tiny head, the animal made soft clicking noises before turning toward a tree. For a moment, he wished that he was more like the squirrel. Then he crossed his arms for the meld.

Karen unlocked her front door then shuffled three large shopping bags into the foyer with her knees. Although she'd protested, Stacy had insisted on buying back-to-school things for Jamie; clothes, a backpack and an assortment of brightly colored folders and pencils. The kid would be going back in style this year.

The thought made Karen a little wistful—her baby was going into the fifth grade in a few short weeks. Time was passing too fast, and it seemed to knock her aside as it went, leaving her spinning in one place. She picked up the mail from her box and took it to the kitchen table, allowing the catalogs and department store flyers to slip through her fingers. White envelopes were what she wanted.

And there were two. A utility bill, and a letter from the local private school office. Fingers shaking, she picked it up, ripped it along the seal and took out the crisply folded letter. It would either say yes, she was now a full time teacher with her own class, or that she was still part-time, substituting as needed. Since deciding to apply for full time status last month, she'd waited on pins and needles for the decision. The money would further help her reach her goal of keeping the house. Karen closed her eyes and took a long, deep breath.

Then she looked. It was a contract! She could work close to home, with children, and be home with Jamie in the afternoons. Relief pored over her and she felt tears form in her eyes. This was so good!

She'd have summers to work in the yard. She'd just need one person to assist her, to be here for all the routine maintenance required of a working bed and breakfast. But she'd worry about that later. With a sniff she brushed a drop from one eye.

"Are you all right?"

Karen turned, her heart racing. "Dek! I didn't hear you come in. I just got the best news." She told him as he approached, went to the sink and drew two glasses of water. His hair was wet and slicked back, as if he'd just come from the shower. He handed her a glass and raised his own to his lips.

His face looked pale, and he drank the entire glass at once.

"I should ask if you're all right." She took a sip. "What's wrong, Dek?" When he didn't answer, she set her glass aside and stood in front of him. "Can I help?"

He shook his head. "No, but thank you. I just found out. . ."

"What?"

"I just read in the newspaper that one of my former co-workers had been killed."

"I'm so sorry." She touched his arm. "What happened?"

"Industrial accident, of sorts." Dek took a step forward and looked down at her, his eyes a bit misty.

Before Karen could respond, he had pulled her to him, crushing her to his chest, and lowered his mouth to hers. His lips were hot, and when they opened, she allowed hers to as well. One of his hands cupped her head, cradling it gently, and Karen slid her arms around his neck.

She felt drawn inside of him, cared-for, even loved. No man had ever held her so tenderly in such a tight grip. He smelled so good, fresh like soap, but underneath, he smelled like Dek. Strong. Mysterious. Honorable. A bit like the outdoors and a bit like something otherwordly.

"Karen," he said, whispering into her ear. Then he turned his head to one side and merely held her tight to him.

She felt a loss when his lips left hers, as if she'd just been the first woman he'd ever kissed, and she wanted more. But he was grieving for a friend, not celebrating, as she was. He would have to take the lead.

He released her and stepped back, looking into her eyes. "Did I hurt you?"

She shook her head. "Not at all. I liked being that close to you. I wouldn't mind getting closer." She wasn't sure, but she thought he looked guilty for an instant before turning away. Oh, God, was he married?

"You don't know anything about me. You should be more cautious." Dek refilled his glass at the sink, staring down into the basin.

"Then tell me. Are you wanted by anyone—like the police?"

"No."

She tapped her nails on her glass. "Married?"

"No." His head stayed down.

"Seriously ill?"

He shook his head. "Just leaving, Karen. In a few days, maybe a week, I will have to leave."

"Have to? Or want to?" A terrible thought snagged her attention. "You're not working for my cousin Frank are you? Or my uncle?" He hadn't given her any reason to think that, but what other reason could he have? Unless he was some kind of undercover agent, which was ridiculous.

"Of course not. I wish I could. . ."

"What, Dek? What do you wish?"

He reached up and ran both hands through his hair, the water long forgotten. "I wish that I could stay here and help you. I feel like I belong here, in your home. In this time. I'd like to meet your son. I'd like to plant more trees out near the road, and make an elegant sign for your front gate."

Dek slipped from the room without meeting her gaze, and Karen just stood and watched him go. What did he mean, 'In this time?' Was he for real? Probably was, she thought, because he wasn't staying. The joy of her new job melted away. Anything that good was only real if it wasn't to be hers.

"I really have liked you being here this week," Karen said, squeezing Dek's hand as he held it. She'd taken it impulsively. "Are you sure you have to go?" It took all of her courage to ask. The answer was that important. Over the past few days she'd realized Dek wouldn't want to stay if she acted depressed and gloomy. Besides, she had plenty to be happy about, but having him stay would make things even better. She squeezed his hand again, then tapped his palm. Outside, the crickets began their nightly chorus, unaware of the tension inside the big white house.

Dek pushed his glass to the center of the table, not breaking contact with her hand. "I've liked being here." He looked up at her. "The time has passed quickly, and I've almost forgotten. . . other things. It's been more like a home than anywhere else."

"Dek," Karen began, pulling free of him, pushing so that her chair scraped backward along the wood floor. "I hate that you're leaving! It seems like you don't have a place to go. You like it here. We could work well here together." She paused and looked at him, her eyes threatening to water. "Does it have anything to do with the way you keep disappearing for hours at a time? I have noticed."

What could he say? Should he just blurt out that he was born on another planet and had to shift into another form every eighteen to twenty-four hours or he'd neutralize his reproductive organs? Was there an Earth-made Hallmark card to say all that?

"Can you tell me anything?" Her eyes lit. "Are you an undercover cop? Oh, I know, you're undercover for the Historical Society and you want to be convinced this place deserves a designation." She leaned closer, placing an arm on Dek's shoulders. "Or did my uncle hire you to convince me to sell?"

He raised an eyebrow, as he'd seen her do. That seemed to suffice as an answer.

"Okay, well, I didn't think so. And I'm sorry that I keep asking. It's just making me... nuts. If that were the case, if you wanted to talk me into selling, you didn't do a very good job." She offered him a smile, a weak one, not even showing her pretty white teeth.

"What happened in the hallway. . . Did you mean to. . ."

"Kiss you?"

She answered with a blush.

"Yes, I meant to. Do you think I took advantage of you?" He hoped not, though he'd had a similar thought himself. It wouldn't have bothered Alana at all.

"No! I didn't mean that." She twisted her hands in a knot in front of her.

Dek slid around the table and stood behind her. 'It meant a lot to me, Karen. I've never met anyone like you. Anywhere. And if things were different. . ."

"Yeah," she said and sniffed. "I know. I just don't know why."

Behind her, Dek rubbed her bare shoulders lightly. He'd never forget the tiny shirts she wore. If only he could rub away her mood. Better she think he was a bad human man, leaving her, than a freak she'd never understand. Better she find herself a human man who can give her more children, better than settling for a humanized, sterile Dek.

He kissed her neck, touched the warm, soft skin with his tongue, then traced the cord of muscles up to her hair line.

Karen shivered and pushed back toward him, wanting more. She didn't need words to tell him.

Forgetting any sense of honor, Dek grasped her shoulders and turned her to face him, then dropped his hands to her waist and lifted her onto the counter. She was small, and they were eye to eye as he pushed her legs apart and stood between them. He could feel the tension between them pulsing, as palpable as if they had an Elemental Key shorting out in the room.

Karen surprised him, taking his face in her hands and putting her mouth to his. Sensations of warmth and sweetness flowed over him, and he wished he had found this, this thing with Karen, on his world. With their lips joined he reached between them and found a plastic button, slid it through its hole and then found the next. She wore nothing beneath her blouse, and Dek found the skin of her breasts softer than anything he'd ever touched. Or imagined.

He had no idea human skin could feel this way—nothing on his body did.

She leaned toward him, pressing closer with her body and her lips. "Dek, I think we should go—"

The back door slammed. "Mom! I'm home," a boy's voice called from the mud room.

Karen stiffened, and Dek felt her retreat as she reached for her blouse and jumped from the counter. Quickly redoing her buttons, she gave Dek one final kiss, on his cheek. "It's Jamie."

CHAPTER SIX

A boy bounced into the room, as if the breeze blew him in. He moved toward his mother until he spied Dek, which stopped him cold.

"Who's that?" he asked, tilting his head up to check out the strange man. An overstuffed backpack slid from his shoulder to the floor with a thud.

Karen hugged Jamie, ruffled his hair, beaming at him in a manner Dek felt most endearing. He couldn't picture Alana smiling at anyone, even a child, with such warmth.

"This is Mr. Dek." She nodded toward Dek. "This is my son, Jamie." With his mother's nudge, Jamie offered a hand to Dek.

He shook it. Firm grip for someone so small, he thought.

"What are you doing home and how did you get here?" Karen recovered from the surprise and held her son at arm's length, looking him over. "Are you all right? Are you sick? Hurt? Have you been skateboarding again?" She put her palm on his forehead. "Do you feel hot?"

The boy twisted free but grinned. "Naw, I'm okay. Uncle Cole brought me home—said you were missing me so bad I should come home early."

"Your Uncle Cole?" Karen's lips pressed together tightly.

"Yeah. He and Frank came to Grandma's for a while. Check this out." Jamie bent to his backpack and unzipped it, then pulled out a dirty white ball.

"Look what they left me— a baseball signed by Cal Ripken. Cool, huh?"

Dek smiled since he seemed so enthused. "Very cool. May I see it?" Jamie tossed it underhanded, and Dek caught Karen's grimace.

"Sorry, Mom. I won't throw it in the house again."

Dek rolled the ball around in his fingers. It was strongly made, but with a soft, outer coating and stitchery. Indeed, someone had signed it. Having not studied American baseball history, he didn't recognize the name. "Should we go outside and play with it?" He felt pleased with himself for thinking of the right thing to ask.

But Jamie didn't return the pleasure. "No way!" He grabbed the ball away from Dek, and looked at it carefully. "This is a collector's item. It's valuable."

Karen laughed and grabbed Jamie again, pulling him to her for an embrace. "That's right, sweetie. Why don't you take your stuff up to your room and wash your hands? Then we can have some ice cream."

"Cool!" Jamie gathered his belongings and took off, his small feet pounding the wood floors through the hall and up the stairs, leaving an echo in their wake.

"So that is Jamie?" Dek asked, still staring at where the boy had disappeared.

"Mm-hm. Adorable, isn't he?" Karen sighed. "He's everything to me."

"Everything?" Dek caught her hand and held it between his own. The skin on her knuckles felt a hundred times rougher than that on her breasts, but Dek decided that was something he should keep to himself.

"Well," she said, looking up at him from under her fringe of lashes. "Maybe not quite everything. But Dek," She lowered her voice. "Since Jamie is here, we can't—"

"I understand." He met her gaze evenly and lifted her hand again.

As he knew men did in the Civil War era, he lifted it to his lips and kissed the back of it, brushing his lips back and forth several times before releasing her. "What should we do now?"

"Well, if you wouldn't mind having ice cream with Jamie, I have a phone call to make to my dear Uncle Cole."

Dek's mouth watered as he considered the tempting dessert he'd recently discovered. "Do you have chocolate?"

"Yes, do you mind scooping it into bowls for both of you?"

Pretending to seriously consider the request, Dek stroked his chin. "Perhaps."

Karen tried to look stern but didn't succeed. Dek was already reaching into a cupboard for two ceramic bowls. Large ones. With the carton of ice cream in one hand and the bowls in the other, he snuck a glance at Karen, who had picked up a cordless telephone. The sound of Jamie's sneakers approached.

"You are such a man. Have fun. I'll make this call in the other room."

"Do you have whipped cream, like they do at Mike's Diner?"

Jamie came in, looking at Dek with respect. "Yeah, whipped cream and chocolate chips."

Dek nodded stoically. "Yes, they are essential."

"Go ahead. Top shelf of the pantry." When they moved in unison, Karen snorted. "I take it back, Dek. You are such a boy."

Dek set the bowls on the table and flipped the carton open. As he scooped, a trickle of slightly melted cream found his hand, and he slurped it up, much to Jamie's delight. But Dek was deep in thought, replaying Karen's words. It seemed such a compliment. 'You are such a man.' Man or boy, he liked being a human male, and he liked Karen and her son.

Perhaps too much.

To remind himself of who and what he was, Dek left the kitchen and once outside on the porch, touched his wrist dial until it glowed in response. When Alana responded, he asked how long it would be before they could transport him. He had to leave before he grew further connected to the White family. There was no way he could stay without cutting off part of his self, in a manner of speaking. Soon, she had said. The part had arrived and she could transport him very soon.

"Mom?" Jamie asked that night when Karen went to tuck him into bed. She was glad he was old enough now to shower and change by himself, then wait for her to come upstairs. Although sometimes she missed the baby bathing, the night time stories, the rocking and even the diaper changing. What she needed was to have another child, and she couldn't help but daydream over what Dek's babies would look like. A shiver racked her as she considered how large his children would be.

"Mom?"

"Yes, sweetie?"

"Is Mr. Dek your boyfriend? Are you going to marry him?" His face was stony but his voice wavered a bit. Downstairs the mantle clock chimed nine.

Karen pulled his sheet up, covering his knees. "No, he's doing some work for me, and we have become friends. But he has to leave soon."

"Oh. Well, I like him. He's a little weird, and doesn't seem to know some stuff that's pretty easy, but he's alright, you know? He must work out at the gym a lot, 'cause he said he'd teach me some self-defense moves tomorrow night. And I said I'd teach him about baseball, but I can't believe he doesn't already know. I mean, geez, where's he been, under a rock? Oh! Maybe he's just pretending not to know so he can beat me real bad— you know, like they do in pool?

"You mean is he a hustler? Jamie, I don't think that's the case. He seems too, um. . ."

"Honest?" He nodded with a sincerity Karen found beyond the boy's years. "I think he's very honest. I can tell." Jamie reached for a young-adult mystery book from his night stand, the conversation finished as far as he was concerned. "Can I read for a while?"

"Not past nine-thirty, okay?" Karen kissed his cheek and started to leave, taking one last look at her baby from the doorway. She blew him a kiss and pulled his door closed behind her.

Downstairs, she found Dek on the sun porch, staring out at the stars. With his arms crossed in front of him he looked rigid and unapproachable. "Dek? Are you okay?" She decided to approach anyway and laid a hand on his arm. Was he thinking of leaving? "You want to talk?"

He turned then and looked at her with such a sense of longing in his eyes that Karen sucked in her breath. "I want something I can't have."

"Why not?"

"Wasn't meant to be." His arms dropped. "But let's not ruin our evening with such talk."

"Can you tell me where you'll be heading when you leave?" Karen held her breath, hoping for the answer she'd been contemplating for days. When would he open up and tell her? When he didn't answer, she rushed on. "Jamie likes you. You have his seal of approval."

Dek smiled. His shoulders relaxed, and he reached up to brace himself against the metal window frame. "I like him too."

"About these self-defense lessons—"

"I will be very careful. I realize he is young."

"Thank you."

"Karen? If something happens and I have to leave very quickly, would you please say goodbye to Jamie for me?"

"Are you planning on just running off?"

"No, but I may not have a choice."

Karen nodded, slowly. He must be an agent, she thought. Nothing else could explain his extreme secrecy. Unless he was a criminal on the run, but that didn't fit with the man she'd gotten to know. "Then of course I'd tell him you said goodbye." She began to pace the glass enclosed room, catching her own reflection at times from the corner of her eye. Dek remained as she found him, staring up at the night sky. It was a clear summer night and hundreds of stars were visible.

Stars. Planets. Galaxies. A crazy thought flashed through Karen's mind, and she shuddered.

That was ridiculous. The man was as much an Earthling as she was. Jamie had her watching too many movies on the Sci-Fi channel.

Finally he spoke. "You still plan to remain living here?"

"Yes. I have a full time job starting next month, the one I requested last month when I found some repairs needed around the house. I will have to hire someone to help, because I'm opening the first floor rooms to guests by Thanksgiving." Karen felt a grin emerging as she made the decisions just now, while pacing. Lifting her hair from her neck to cool her skin, she went on, her pulse racing as she planned. "There are four rooms that are ready, perfect, to rent out. I'll advertise, and offer a big turkey dinner here that weekend. If it works out, I can keep those rooms open through Christmas, and then I'll have a few weeks off from school to work around here. I've been waiting for the whole place to be ready, but I don't have to!" She glanced at Dek, who was watching her now instead of the sky. "Maybe next spring I could give tours of the house and grounds, well, if everything's in order. And keep up the battle re-enactments. As soon as my historical property designation comes through—"

"Sounds very ambitious. You will definitely need help."

"You're right. The job's yours, if you want it." She raised her hands in mock defense. "I know, I know, you have to go, just wanted to offer again." She resumed pacing, faster now. "If I can rent enough rooms by the end of the year, I can accumulate the funds I need for next year's taxes, and then keep up with the mortgage once my prepaid-payments run out."

"Couldn't you have done this before?"

"Wasn't sure I wanted to, and then wasn't sure I could, especially on a part-time salary."

"Mom, we can use the money I earn mowing lawns and raking leaves." Jamie's voice came from the entrance way, where he stood in his sleep tee and shorts. "I don't want to move, either."

Karen went stark still, exchanged looks with Dek, then went to her son. How much had he heard that he already didn't know? She took his shoulders and hugged him to her. "That's sweet, Jamie, but you've just started those jobs. I want that to be money for you to spend on stuff like comics and baseball gloves, and to save for college. And why are you up again?"

Jamie shrugged away from her and looked at Dek. "Couldn't sleep. And I think Dad would have wanted me to be a man since he's not around. School starts soon, and I can work after school and still do my homework at night. What do you think?"

Dek considered the question for several moments. "I think college is very important. But, I think it's very honorable of you to want to contribute to the family finances. Very mature. Your father would have been proud."

The answer puffed up Jamie's chest, though he tried to remain serious.

Warmth flooded Karen's face. She hadn't thought about Jamie sensing her distress, and wanting to contribute. But Dek had. With a grateful glance thrown his way, she escorted Jamie back to his room, leaving Dek alone with the stars.

He walked out beneath them, enjoying the first night of dry, humid-free air he'd sampled here. It felt almost crisp, and Dek knew it was an early harbinger of the coming autumn season.

He thought of the night when he'd seen Corinne and her baby for the last time, remembered her sweet face and thought how much it resembled Karen's. Even Jamie had the family bone structure and eyes.

Crickets chirped as a background to Dek's thoughts, and he realized he would miss the comforting noise when he got home. The ship had its own set of sounds, the motors hummed constantly like its own insect choir. He'd also miss the claps of thunder he'd heard in the summer storms, restlessly tossing in his bed over Karen's garage. Who would she hire to replace him? Would she come to care for that man like she had for him? Would it happen as fast as it had with him? He could only hope not.

But that was a selfish thought. She deserved to find a good, trustworthy male, one to keep her company and to help raise her son. One who would work to make the estate into everything she wanted. One to father more children for her.

Dek's gut clenched. He looked up at the sky, seeing the same patterns he'd seen from his ship, feeling that same sense of oneness with the universe. But it was all hogwash. He didn't want to travel anymore, he wanted to stay here. Wanted to make this his universe. Alana would laugh at him, call him the equivalent of an Earth 'wussy.' She had hinted she wanted him, as a human, so perhaps she too had considered changing permanently.

No, that would never happen. Alana always sought the adventure.

As if on cue, a fading star shot across the black velvet sky, and Dek bowed his head to say a word for its passing. His own journey would continue on very soon. Tomorrow, he'd tell Karen the truth. Ease her mind about what he was not, and probably increase her anxiety over his sanity when he revealed what he was. He walked to the edge of the wood, looking toward the spot where Corinne had lived. He could almost hear her saying to him, "Safe journey then, Mr. Dek."

CHAPTER SEVEN

Karen let the last of her tomatoes hang on the vine, still too green for picking. Two weeks from today, she'd be in her classroom, welcoming two dozen or so second graders to their first day of elementary school. She'd already planned the first week of lessons. She couldn't wait.

"Hey Mom!" Jamie's voice called from across the yard, "Can I go over to Bobby's for a while? I haven't seen him all summer."

Karen looked up to find him neatly rolling up the garden hose, exaggerating each motion to score maximum brownie points. Not even trying to control her grin, Karen waved him on. "Sure. Be back before lunch."

"What if Mrs. Jenson invites me for lunch?"

"Then you call me." She patted her pocket, which bulged with the cordless phone. Jamie agreed and dashed to the house next door. Karen turned her face up to the morning sun, enjoying the warmth on her sunscreen protected skin. She was so glad to have him home.

The next sound sapped the joy from her moment. Karen stood and shielded her eyes, and as she suspected, Frank's car roared up the drive. At least Jamie was gone and wouldn't hear this, she thought, peeling off her floral garden gloves. She brushed dirt from her clam diggers and moved toward the front porch, frowning as she saw both Frank and Cole get out of the car.

Closing her eyes, she mentally counted to ten.

It didn't help.

When she opened them, the two men stood before her in business suits. Cheap Polyester blend suits, but suits nonetheless. Karen groaned. What were they up to?

"Hello, Karen. How are you?" The older man asked, straightening his toad-green tie.

"Cole. Frank." Karen bit off the names, wishing to spit them out. This was like something from a bad movie, she thought, with me as the lonely widow trying to raise the mortgage money to beat back twirly-mustached Simon Legree. "What brings you both here again?" She pushed her bangs from her forehead. She was definitely getting a haircut.

Frank stuffed his hands in his pockets. "Cole said you told him the other night you weren't going to sell the place. For sure this time."

She nodded, crossing her arms. "That's right."

"And we can't change your mind?"

"Not unless you plan on trying something underhanded."

Frank help up both hands, pulling them so fast a pocket lining flapped out. "Whoa. We are family."

"Uh-huh." Karen wondered what they were up to. Hearing whistling, she looked to see Dek start up the drive, not trying to hide his smile. It was as if he'd just discovered whistling and couldn't get enough of the sound.

The men looked from Dek to her, then began to grin knowingly.

"Looks like our handyman sure lights up her day, doesn't it, Cole?"

"Knock if off," Karen snapped, unamused. "There's nothing going on."

They lapsed into silence, watching Dek approach.

He was obviously aware of them now, having stopped whistling and stiffening his spine, as if on guard. Karen admired the stretch of cotton across his chest and the way his thighs moved under the cheap navy work pants.

"Hi, Dek," Karen called, straightening her own short pants and brushing off dirt specks. She caught a smug look on Frank's face and stopped primping.

"Karen." He stopped in front of the group and studied the men. "Are you all right?"

"I'm fine. Frank and Cole just stopped by on their way. . somewhere. . . and are leaving now."

"Now, wait a minute—"

"We need to talk to you about—"

'Please stop!" Karen raised her voice. "I'm sorry you'll lose some money, but this is my home. And Jamie's. He's your nephew for heaven's sake!"

"And his home?" Frank jerked a thumb at Dek. "Are you shacking up?"

"No. He's moving on soon."

Dek spoke up. "I need to talk to you about that, privately."

"Get in line, handyman," Cole said, hands on hips.

"We have an offer," Frank said, trying again for Karen's attention.

She pretended not to hear them but wondered what Dek wanted to say. That he would stay after all? Dare she hope? Either way, she wanted to get rid of her relatives.

"Okay, Uncle Cole, you have five minutes to speel me with the latest scheme." She turned toward Cole, but kept Dek in her side vision. He didn't fidget, just crossed his arms and spread his legs into a waiting stance.

"Karen," Cole began, "we understand you want to stay here."

She looked at Dek, full on, thinking her side vision must be failing. He looked—less focused. Or the heat was causing a mirage. Was she getting heat-stroke?

"And you know we get nothing if you don't sell in sometime soon."

Dek was adjusting his Swatch watch, tapping it. "No, not now," he said into the watch. He had all of them attentive now. "I need thirty minutes," he said again, his head turned partially away. But he still had his mouth near the watch. "Please!"

Karen's mouth dried and she gulped, staring, as Dek began to shimmer. He appeared translucent, and he looked at her with a guilty grimace.

"Holy shit."

"What the hell?"

Dek appeared normal again for a split second, and Karen took a step forward.

And then he was gone.

Her knees gave out, and Karen sank to the ground.

───※───

Dek swore, in several languages, as he materialized in front of Alana.

"Well, I'm glad to see you, too."

Dek spun to find Alana watching him, an amused smile on her human woman's face. Without replying, he went to his own station and flicked on his monitor.

"Dek." Alana's tone was sharp. "Just hours ago you pleaded with me to quickly retrieve you. What's with this attitude?"

He sighed. She was right. It wasn't her fault her timing was painful. After bringing up his mission file on the computer, he looked at her. She still just stood there, watching him. Waiting.

"My apologies. I just needed more time. I was ready to tell Karen everything, and instead she watched me disappear before her eyes. Oh, and in front of her family, too."

"Karen? The lady who gave you shelter?"

He nodded. "More than that. She trusted me. She liked me." A tiny pang of guilt racked him as he recalled Alana's expression of interest in him earlier. He should have set her straight then.

"And you liked that, didn't you?" Alana tapped her nails on the engineering panel. "You know she liked what she thought was a human man."

Dek nodded again, laced his fingertips behind his head and rocked back in his chair.

"She has a dependent, correct?"

"Yes. A male."

"And she wants to have more."

Little spasms shook Dek's gut. He knew exactly what Alana was trying to say.

"It's natural for humans, Dek," she went on, her voice softer. "Just as it's natural for us." She moved behind him and began to knead his shoulders. "I still like these muscles."

Since she'd wasn't trying to look at him, he clicked his keys and scanned his report to date. "Do we know what went wrong with the Elemental Key?"

"Barlx said the key was out of alignment, loosened by an unnatural vibration." he leaned closer and whispered in his ear. "He hinted that perhaps you were seen before you were ready on one of your trips. I told him you would have reported it so we could make the proper adjustments." She started to massage his neck, then gave it a good squeeze, making Dek gulp.

"Don't contradict me in front of him."

He felt his Adams-apple bob again as Alana left the bridge. He'd contributed to his own stranding in the year 2000, and Alana had covered for him. When Corrine had first spotted him in the tree—it must have been then. He'd thrown it all out of alignment and not reported it. Closing his eyes, he recalled the incident, then refused to replay it anymore. If he hadn't failed to notify his crew of a potential problem, he never would have met Karen.

He pulled up his history archive, typed in Karen's name and address, then her family information. And began to scan.

When his neck began to protest, Dek shut off his machine, having no idea how long he'd been searching. Frustration pounded at his temples. There was nothing in Earth's records of Karen or her family. Or Corinne. But what had he expected? She wasn't well-known or overly important. Except to him.

"Hi Dek," Barlx called, startling him. In his human form, Barlx moved to the open floor centered on the bridge. "I'm on duty next. Want to meld now?"

Dek joined him and they knelt on the carpeted floor, preparing to revert back for a much-needed session.

Barlx crossed his arms. "I have to keep this up for a while so I can stay human for Alana."

"Why? A new mission?"

Barlx slid him a sly look, and sat straighter. "Of sorts. She said she wants to get to know me better as a human. Yeah. . . in *that* way. Says she likes my muscles."

Dek burst out laughing.

———

He wanted to see Karen again. Slowly stretching, Dek tested his natural ligaments, enjoying the stretch he just couldn't get while in human form. His vision heightened, he could see the true colors sparkling from the stars and the dark tones of Alana's aura. Feeling lighter, he moved around the bridge, touched a keyboard and enjoyed the sensation of his digits bouncing in rhythm. He could think differently in this form, on the ship the hum of the engines blended with his thoughts and made him focus inward. On Karen.

He could visit her again, but that would only delay the inevitable and hurt them both. If he made a commitment to stay on Earth, if she even wanted him to, he'd never see home again. Never shift again. Have a finite number of years to live. Be rendered sterile.

Dek watched the trail left by a shooting star, its tail a twist of colors humans couldn't see. If he became human, he'd never see the vibrant hues again. But did any of this matter as much as being with her? His world would have less color either way.

As far as he knew, it remained a mystery if aliens and humans could produce offspring, human or otherwise, despite Earth tales of aliens snatching innocent humans to mate with. There was not even a hint of a chance if he were sterilized. But she had asked him not to leave. The question— Was he man enough to give up the option? Which was the honorable thing to do: go back and be with Karen, or give her up so she might someday find a human mate? That thought made him shudder, and Dek decided. It was time to go back.

CHAPTER EIGHT

The mealy smell of garbage woke Dek, and he found himself once again in the alley behind Mike's Diner. Jumping to his feet, he brushed off the work pants and tee shirt he'd been wearing when he'd last seen Karen. What he wouldn't give for a trip to her laundry room right now.

It was dusk, and no one stirred in the alley. Dek made his way to the front of the building and headed in the door directly toward the wash room. A waitress he didn't know nodded, her gaze following him down the narrow hall. The cooking smells gave way to the disinfectant ones of the men's room, and Dek didn't linger after washing his hands.

When he got back to the dining room, Mike waved to him with one hand from behind the counter, while he rung up a customer's tab with the other.

"Mike," Dek said, choosing a stool. "I need a favor, please."

"Yeah, buddy? Thanks Mrs. Grubbs, see you next time." The woman smiled at Dek and pocketed her change.

"I just got back into. . . town, and I'd like to eat before I see Karen."

"What'll you have?"

Dek swallowed. He'd never been in this type of situation at home.

Mike made an understanding grunt and scratched his chin. "Guess you missed payday again. Well, I could let Leta go home early if you want to help me close up?"

"In that case, I will have the special."

Mike turned and yelled toward the kitchen. "One blue plate." Then he leaned on his elbows in front of Dek. "Why so glum? Lose all your friends or all your money?"

"A few days ago—both." Dek sipped the water Leta had brought. "Have you seen Karen or her relatives?" What if she had told people what she'd seen? His pulse quickened as he waited for the answer.

"Nah. Not lately. You have a fight?" Mike pulled a toothpick from behind his ear and stuck it into his mouth.

"Not exactly." Dek scanned the room, seeing only a few diners, scattered, not paying him any attention. "Tell me something. In your experience, how much importance do women put on having children?"

Mike shrugged. "Depends on the woman. Some are more maternal than others. Why?"

This time Dek shrugged, picked up his fork and tapped it against his knife.

"Oohhh, I get it."

"What?"

"One of the two of you's shooting blanks, am I right?"

Not having felt such acute embarrassment in this form before, Dek placed his palms against his fiery cheeks. How had Mike figured it out so quickly? At least, come so close?

Dek looked away as Mike rang up more customers, then answered a phone call. Leta brought his Eggs Benedict and a basket of toast, which Dek tore right into, savoring the rich white sauce and crunchy bread. When Mike finally got back to him, Dek was sopping up the end of the sauce with a piece of crust.

"Tell you what. You clear those last few tables and we'll call it even. And about the other thing— if you love each other, don't matter none whether you can make your own babies." Mike coughed into his hand and muttered, "Adopt. Or try some of those fancy doctors that do miracles in labs. But don't give up something good, the right person don't come along that often." Mike winked at Dek, a feat Dek had not yet mastered with just one eye.

He slung a towel over his shoulder and gathered Dek's plate and cup. "Now get outta here, and take this to Karen." He slapped a white take-out box on the counter.

"Thank you."

"Don't worry about it. Sometimes you have to give 'em chocolate, you know, to soften 'em up? And I know you'll be back to spend more money. You haven't tried my eggs au gratin."

The stars twinkled by the time Dek reached Karen's front door, and he looked up several times, just to remind himself how they appeared to human eyes. He rapped three times on the glass insert, peering in and down the main hallway, holding the small box from Mike in his other hand. The sound of Jamie's feet pounded on the hardwood

Dek watched as Karen caught up to her son and shooed him away from the door. Practicing good parenting, he supposed, he watched her point him back toward the kitchen. When she came to the door and peeked through the stained glass side panel, their eyes met and gazes locked. He couldn't miss the flash of fear there, the uncertainty.

He didn't speak, just stood there, trying to convey his feelings through his eyes. Feelings. Who would have thought he'd have them for a human female? One who was now looking at him like she'd never seen him before. Or maybe like she knew him too well. He wasn't sure.

Long moments passed before Karen slid the dead bolt over and opened the door. Dek let out a breath he hadn't known he was holding, fearful she'd never open to him again. And he couldn't have blamed her for it. He stepped into her dim foyer and closed the door behind him, as she had backed away after unlocking it. He put both hands behind him and leaned against the door, supporting his body against the cool wood. She would not want him to reach out and touch her cheek, or her hair, so he kept his fingers out of sight.

"I'm letting you in only because you could have hurt me or Jamie already, if that's what you intended." She crossed her arms, the loose, curly cuffs of her white blouse fluttering as she moved. Several feet of air and Asian carpet remained between them.

"Okay, Mr. Dek," she said, glancing over one shoulder, probably to check if Jamie was listening. "Just who, and what, are you?"

Karen waited, having wondered for days now about the questions she asked. And then he just walks up to her door, looking so studly and strong in the old clothes. It wasn't fair. She'd considered and dismissed many theories since she'd seen him vaporize; that he was an illusionist, that he was undercover military testing new defense procedures, that he'd only been a hologram like on Star Trek. Even worse, that he was an alien like on Star Trek.

She shivered.

"Thank you for letting me in." He didn't move.

"I'm listening." She glanced over her shoulder again, called to Jamie to go up and get ready for bed, then pierced Dek, she hoped, with a glare.

He looked at the painting of her great-great grandmother, closed his eyes briefly and then turn a sincere gaze back at her. The standing clock chimed eight, and continued to tick while she and Dek held their standoff.

Finally he cleared his throat. "I don't know how to say this with what you call finesse, so I'll just say it." He sighed, then continued in a quiet voice. "I'm not from here. I'm not like you."

She waited. That was not an explanation. She'd figured out that much herself.

"I'm from a galaxy humans haven't discovered yet. I don't look like this at home." He took both hands from behind him and gestured over his body. "I can look like this only if I revert back to my own form for a few hours every Earth day. Otherwise, permanent changes would take place in my system. Unless I decide to remain human, or any other form I choose, and make it permanent.

Karen's stomach flipped as if she had just gone airborne in her car flying over the big bump on the old country lane. Was she relieved to hear what she feared confirmed, or horrified?

"Karen, I'd like to stay. With you."

Her heart pounding now, Karen hugged herself, resting her chin on the back of one hand.

"But only if you want me to. If you can accept what I am. If you think Jamie would accept me."

Her mind raced with images of Dek playing ball with Jamie, of Dek holding her hand as they walked through the woods. Of Dek patting her pregnant tummy.

Of Dek sprouting antenna and green skin. Karen groaned.

"What are you really?"

"Not that different from you. Really. Our bodies are similarly shaped, but my skin is more like your rubber. We can see better, we see things humans miss. We see colors you can't even imagine." When she didn't respond, he went on. "Do you want me to show you?"

"No!" That she didn't want. She wasn't sure she wanted to see him in human form anymore. If she hadn't seen him vanish, she'd think he was nuts right about now.

"Mom! I can't find my pajamas so I'm wearing shorts to bed," Jamie called from the second floor, shattering some of the tension below.

"Okay, sweetie. I'll be right up. Brush your teeth." She needed to be alone to think. "Dek, I don't think there can be anything between us, but I need some time." With one hand on her forehead, she pushed her bangs back to cool her. Perspiration trickled down the inside of her blouse.

Was she actually breaking up with an alien?

His eyes expressed his disappointment, and Karen realized she wasn't quite ready to let him go. "You can stay in the apartment tonight. I'll call and let you know when Jamie's asleep."

He nodded, glanced at the portrait again, and turned to go.

"Hey, Dek. No funny stuff over there— no beaming anyone up or down or spaceship landings, okay?"

Karen watched him go, for he hadn't even looked up at her last crack. She felt a bit of loss watching him walk away, but had to admit, for an alien, he had great buns.

She'd known there was something unusual about Dek all along. Of course, she'd not imagined anything like this. But it explained a lot— why he had no money, change of clothing, or home. The silly looking-Swatch watch. The bit more formal speech. What it didn't explain was why she still wanted him.

Jamie snored lightly when Karen looked in on him. She'd been sitting in the hall on the top step for an hour, digesting Dek's announcement while her son tried to fall asleep. Oh, to be that innocent again. But then, children were much more accepting of things like ghosts and aliens than adults.

Her stomach clenched each time she recalled Dek's face while he explained. He'd had that longing look again. The look that made her want to melt in his arms. Sheesh. She had to get a grip. This was an alien, for god's sake.

Following a path of moonlight from the foyer, Karen made her way to the front porch. Her favorite thinking place. The moon, half full, threw light across her lawn. She stared at it, tried to drink it in for a few minutes, smiling as she always did at the cratered face she saw on the big cheese head in the sky.

Her smile faded when she lowered her gaze and found Dek there, standing in a beam of light. His hair looked lighter that way, but his expression was dark. What could he be thinking?

Dek didn't know if he should try to talk to her now or wait. He didn't have enough experience in human matters. So he just stood there, watching her watch him. Leaning against the porch rail, she crossed her arms and looked up at the sky.

"Why didn't you tell me sooner?" Her voice broke the silence of the dark, sounding young and lost to Dek's ears.

"Would you have believed me?"

She sighed. "Probably not."

"I didn't want you to fear me."

"I wouldn't have. Ever. I had been hoping you'd stay."

He nodded, took a few steps closer and stopped. "I had been hoping you'd never find out the truth."

"Why, Dek?" She stood then, reaching for the painted white post, as if she needed support.

He liked the way the white light played on her hair, making it shimmer, and wondered what colors would be there if he were to suddenly meld back.

"Never mind. I know why."

you. Sorry that I can't stay. I had to come back to say all these things."

"Why?" she asked again, stepping forward to lean against the post with her entire body. "You said you could stay if some changes became permanent. Are they that terrible?"

Pain sliced through him. Would it truly be that terrible? To lose his visual abilities? His opportunity to travel through space and investigate other worlds? To lose his ability to reproduce? Wouldn't that be what Karen called losing his manhood? Alana had implied he'd be less of an individual if he wasn't fertile. Would Karen feel that way?

Would he?

"What are you thinking about so hard? I can see smoke coming out of your ears."

Dek started to reach for his ears before realizing she was teasing him.

"Come here." She sat on the top porch step and patted the wood beside her. When his thigh was pressed firmly against hers, she went on. "I know it's a major decision to stay. Don't know if I could do it in your shoes. You'd become human, right? Mortal?

That's the biggie, am I right? And you wouldn't be out gallivanting through the universe anymore. I'm sure living here seems pretty boring in comparison. So it's up to you— you have to decide. If you want me and Jamie and making a life here, in the almost-suburbs of historical Virginia, USA. You have to decide if you could be one of us. People would talk, you know, unless we got married. Hell, they'd talk even if we got married. And I don't think I could tell Jamie about you until he was an adult." She put a hand on his thigh, and Dek felt a tingle. "But for what it's worth, I'd like you to stay and make a go of it. With us."

When he didn't speak, she gave him another light squeeze, then patted his knee. "That's a selfish request, I know." She looked away, up, toward the moon again. "And I know there may be a different woman for you out there. I realize you may have someone back home waiting for you. Even if you stay, I may not be the one."

Dek touched her chin, drawing her face back to his. "You're the one."

"But?"

This was it. He had to tell her. "But you want more children. Brothers and sisters for Jamie. If I stay, I can't give you that. If I stay, I couldn't stand to watch some other man give you that."

Her mouth had opened, but no words came out.

He smiled a little, feeling his facial muscles pull taut. "Now, I see smoke coming from your ears."

Karen's smile was dimmer than his own. She swatted a mosquito, slapped her knee. "We could come with you instead."

Warmth flowed through Dek. She had to love him to offer such a sacrifice, one he couldn't let her make. She had no idea what she asked. Taking her shoulders, he turned her to him, slowly, then slanted his mouth across hers, brushing her lips gently. They were soft and hot and opened in response.

He could have this every day.

"Dek?" She pulled back to see his face. "I don't mind if you can't have kids. I like you just the way you are. I like you more than I like the idea of a bigger family. If I increase the head count around here, I would like your head there. Stay here. Help me run this place. Come inside and be with me."

A groan came from his throat, surprising both of them, and he kissed her more deeply, trying to show her how he felt with his lips, fingers lightly tracing the sides of her breasts.

"I think you're family now," she whispered, her hands pushing his hair back from his face. She touched his chest with one finger, teasing his nipple through the cotton until it was hard.

An icy chill racked Dek's spine as his mind taunted him. Nipples. Nursing. Infants. He couldn't stay and be less than a human man. He untangled his arms from Karen and stood. "I'm sorry. I love you." He left her on the porch, crossed the speckled lawn and retreated to his silent apartment without looking back.

Safely inside her bedroom, Karen curled into a ball and hugged her knees. She knew the tears would start soon, she'd always been a bawler, but at least she could control the onset until she was hidden away, where Jamie wouldn't hear. Or Dek.

Even snuggled under her fabric-softened spring fresh comforter, Karen shivered. What had she been thinking—asking a man from another planet to live with her? Was she out of her mind? What did she have to offer him that he couldn't find on a more exciting world? The tears didn't come.

Karen sat up, stretched her arms above her head. She should be wailing by now, like she had when Frank first threatened to get his share of the money out of this place. Like she had when Jonathan had first announced he was moving out. Like she had when Dad died.

But now, she felt restless. Still shivering on a night meant for sweating, Karen pulled a shaw from the back of her desk chair and left the room. After checking on a still peacefully sleeping Jamie, she made her way downstairs, stopping in the foyer. The moonlight streaming through the sidelights bathed great-great grandmother Corinne's portrait in a ghostly beam, and Karen got the creepy sensation she was being watched.

Her neck prickled, and she raised her shoulders in response. She stood in front of the portrait, reached up and touched the corner sprinkling of paint, the dots that looked like shooting stars to her. Family legend said Corinne had been abandoned, and had been strong and carried on for her child.

Karen smiled at the painting, which of course, did not smile in return. If her great-great grandmother could live through the Civil War, surely Karen could live through falling in love with, and losing, an alien.

CHAPTER NINE

Dek found little comfort in the knowledge he was doing the right thing, the honorable thing, by allowing Karen to find a man who could give her children. A normal, human man who could love her and raise a family with her, not someone who shifted back to a natural state that would send her screaming into the night should she witness it. Not someone who really had no idea as to what would happen after a long time period in a human form.

He avoided the little apartment and instead headed for the woods, glad for the cover of darkness. Crickets chirped and an owl hooted from somewhere nearby, providing all the company he needed. Kneeling in the now damp grass carpet, Dek crossed his arms, closed his eyes, and concentrated on shifting. The familiar rush of warmth began, but instead of blanking his thoughts, his mind lit on Corinne in these very woods, that night so long ago. They'd stood very near where he now waited, and she'd confessed her husband had felt less than a man. At the time, he'd been amazed that she felt comfortable telling such intimate details to a stranger. Now, he could only compare her plight to Karen's.

Dek knew what Corinne had implied—that her husband could no longer be with her.

And wasn't that exactly why he had left Karen? Because by staying he'd feel less than other men? Other human men? Barlx and his other crew mates were the same way, obsessed with being male, no matter what form they took.

Evening dew began to seep through Dek's pant knees, and he stood, needing to pace the tiny clearing in the trees. Hadn't he thought Corinne's husband a fool a hundred and thirty years ago?

That was it, then, he decided. The only way to become a man, a human man, was to accept what that meant and carry on.

Something large buzzed by Dek's ear, and he swatted at it, a grin stretching his face. He suddenly noticed the fireflies lighting in scattered places and smelled the pine as he strode across fallen needles.

He touched his dial, watched it glow like a trapped firefly, and tapped the face. He needed to talk to Alana. With any luck she'd be on duty instead of off spending time with Barlx.

Strains of music filtered from Karen's house the next afternoon. Dek walked up the curving drive, hopeful it would be the last time he approached alone, unexpected, uninvited.

Several cars were parked out front, cars Dek didn't recognize. An American flag, at least six feet wide, waved with the breeze from the front porch. Across the yard, he saw Jamie playing with several other children, chasing a ball. He wondered idly if it was signed by some famous football player.

Since the wood doors stood open, Dek entered, nodding at a couple studying the hall paintings. Voices came from the kitchen which smelled of fresh coffee, and he followed them to find Karen, three men and two women deep in conversation at the kitchen table. Their volume rose and fell with some excitement, coming to a crashing halt as they spied him.

The men looked at him with open hostility, reminding Dek of Corinne's brothers gathering around her in the woods. The women looked at him with. . . interest.

"Dek! What are you doing here?" Karen sounded puzzled as she rose, scraping the floor with her chair.

"Well, I have been working here." He knew that sounded inappropriate, but it was the truth. Did she think he would have returned to his ship forever without saying goodbye? Even after the few moments he'd had with Corinne, in a war zone, he'd managed to say goodbye.

"He probably wants his final paycheck," one of the men said, and the others nodded.

Karen stood in front of him, blocking his view into the room. "Is that it, Dek? Did you come to get paid?" She looked him up and down. "Guess you're not ready to return the clothes, huh?"

He winced. He deserved anything she could throw at him. "Can I speak with you alone, please?"

Her eyes narrowed, she studied him for a few seconds. Behind them, the guests had resumed their lively conversation, throwing around phrases like walking tours, continental breakfast and room rates. "Okay, let's go into the parlor."

They passed through the foyer and Dek glanced at Corinne's portrait, silently thanking her for that meeting long ago, and for whatever role she played in leaving descendants for this century.

Karen plopped on to a beige velvet settee where she could look out the bowed window with criss-crossed panes. She picked up a square pillow and rolled the tassels on its edge through her fingers. "Are you going to tell me or am I supposed to guess?" Dek knew she was trying to sound cross but thought she was failing.

He took that as a good sign.

Clearing his throat, he settled on one knee in front of her. He would have reached for her hand if she hadn't hidden them under the pillow. This had to be perfect, it had to work. He'd told Alana to break orbit and head on without him, listened to her final warnings, and taken off his wrist dial. For the last time.

"I'm staying."

She looked at him then, eyebrows raised. "Oh really? Where are you staying?"

He'd hurt her, and she wasn't taking him back easily. Still, he almost grinned. He loved her when she tried to look tough. "I'd like to stay here, but if you've changed your mind, I understand. I'm sure Mike would help me find a place, and a permanent job."

"Permanent?" One hand reappeared and twisted the tassel mercilessly.

He nodded, staring into her eyes. They had widened as he spoke. "I was wrong, Karen. I don't need. . . I only need to be here with you and Jamie. It's what you do with what you have that makes you a man. It's marching into any battle with the weapons you already have that makes you. . . "

"Makes you honorable," she said, softly. The pillow tumbled to the floor, forgotten as Karen sat forward and slid her arms around his neck.

"Yes."

"Speaking of battle," she said, her mouth against his cheek. "Can you tell me now why you first arrived here in a Yankee uniform?"

"It's a long story, my love. But it was all part of my long journey to find you."

The End

Like anthologies? We'd love to hear about it.

What is your favorite kind of anthology?
a)romance, b)horror, c)paranormal, d)fantasy, e)thriller, f)other_____

Do you like sexy reads? yes_____ no_____
      Erotica? yes_____ no_____

Anything else you'd like to tell us? _____

_____

_____

We want to bring you the stories you're looking for!

Send your thoughts to us at:

New Concepts Publishing
Dept. M.
4729 Humphreys Rd.
Lake Park, GA 31636